Chapter 1

'*Daring raid liberates British prisoners . . .*' The newsboy's strident tones caught my attention and I went to buy a paper. 'That's right, love, read all about it . . . rescued from the *Altmark* . . . British prisoners in daring escape.'

I smiled and walked on, scanning the headlines in the paper. It was February 1940 and at last there was some good news. Something to cheer us up after weeks of gloom in the papers. Though London itself was still far from gloomy despite the official black-out, and I had just come from a lunch-time chamber concert. They were drawing crowds. People were determined to make the best of things, to enjoy themselves where they could, and most of the theatres were opening up again after closing down when the lights first went out all over the city.

'Watch out, sweetheart!'

'Oh, I'm so sorry!'

Absorbed in my paper, I had walked straight into a man. He caught my arm, steadying me, a huge grin on his face. I noticed that he had very dark, almost black hair, and that his eyes were a dark, bitter chocolate brown. He was also very good-looking!

'If you're not careful, you'll hurt yourself,' he said, seeming concerned for my welfare.

'I'm fine – but did I hurt you?'

'Not so as you'd notice. I guess I'm pretty tough.'

His smile was infectious, making me respond with one of my own. 'Perhaps that's as well, seeing as I must have trodden on your foot. It was clumsy of me. I wasn't looking where I was going, because I was just so pleased to read about those prisoners being rescued . . . it's marvellous news, isn't it?'

He seemed to know what I meant, nodding agreement. 'Yes. It's always good when something like that happens.'

'Especially at the moment.'

'Yes.' He looked serious now. 'It can't be easy for you British at the moment, and I'm afraid it's going to get a hell of a lot rougher before this is all over.'

'Yes, I'm sure you're right . . .' I smiled at him again. 'Forgive me, but I must go. I have to get back to work.'

'I guess so . . .'

'Bye then.'

He caught my arm as I tried to pass him. 'I'm Jack Harvey. American, single, free, here on business, and feeling lonely. You wouldn't have time for a drink one night? Maybe tonight even? I promise I don't bite . . .'

'I'm sorry,' I said, shaking my head at him but smiling because he was looking so eager. 'I'm engaged to someone, a man I love. It was nice meeting you, Mr Harvey – but I must go.'

'OK. It was worth a try.'

He let me go with a rueful grin. I walked on, smiling

Rosie Clarke

Emma's War

EBURY
PRESS

5 7 9 10 8 6 4

Ebury Press, an imprint of Ebury Publishing
20 Vauxhall Bridge Road,
London SW1V 2SA

Penguin
Random House
UK

Ebury Press is part of the Penguin Random House group companies whose
addresses can be found at global.penguinrandomhouse.com

First published as *The Bonds That Break* in 2000 by Severn House Publishers
This edition published in 2015 by Ebury Press

www.eburypublishing.co.uk

A CIP catalogue record for this book is available from the British Library

ISBN 9780091956110

Typeset in Times LT Std by Palimpsest Book Production Limited,
Falkirk, Stirlingshire

Penguin Random House is committed to a sustainable future for
our business, our readers and our planet. This book is made from
Forest Stewardship Council® certified paper.

MIX
Paper from
responsible sources
FSC® C018179

Printed and bound in Great Britain by Clays Ltd, St Ives plc

to myself. It wasn't the first time I'd been asked out by a stranger. There were a lot of young men at a loose end in London at the moment. Young servicemen on leave from their units. Many of them were alone in a strange city and feeling a bit lost . . . or frightened. Mr Harvey wasn't one of them, of course. His country wasn't officially at war, though Sol believed the Americans were helping us more behind the scenes than anyone yet knew.

Thinking of Sol made me remember I was going to be late for work, and I began to run. That afternoon was an important one for me and I didn't want to start out on the wrong foot.

I was in the workshop when the telephone rang that afternoon, but didn't take much notice. This was the first time Sol had trusted me with the good cloth, and I wanted to get it exactly right.

I was concentrating very hard as I cut carefully round the edge of the dress pattern. We couldn't afford to waste cloth, even though clothes rationing had not yet begun. Sol said the government was only waiting for the right moment before they imposed it. Besides, it was a matter of pride that I should be able to cut well. The cutting was the most important part of tailoring. Sol had impressed that on me from the very beginning.

'A good cutter is worth his weight in gold,' Sol had told me that first morning. 'Never forget it, Emma. In this trade you can cut corners in a score of ways, but never economise on your skilled labour. They *are* your business.'

Sol should know. He had started out as a cutter himself, the son of impoverished immigrants, and now he was an extremely wealthy man – also a very wise and a very kind man.

I glanced behind me. Mr Jackson, Sol's top cutter, was watching me from his corner of the workshop, though trying not to let me see it. He gave me an encouraging smile, but let me get on with it. Sol had given strict instructions that I was to be given no help, and I wasn't going to ask.

'Emma!' One of the girls from the showroom came to fetch me. 'Telephone – for you!'

My heart stopped then raced on wildly. It wasn't very often that anyone telephoned me at work, and my mind was starting to invent worrying images. Had something happened to my son, to my mother . . . or Jon?

'Who is it?' I asked when I reached the office and saw the receiver lying by the side of the phone. The girl shrugged, and my heart jerked with fright as I put the receiver to my ear. 'Yes . . . Emma Robinson here. Who is it please?'

'It's me, Emma . . .' Relief flooded through me as I heard Jonathan's voice. 'Didn't that girl tell you?'

'No . . . just that I was wanted on the phone.'

'No wonder you sounded breathless. It's good news, Emma. I'm getting a two-week leave. I'll be home on Sunday. We can arrange the wedding at last . . .'

'Oh, Jon,' I said, a catch in my throat. 'That's wonderful . . . really good news. I'm so pleased.'

'I can't wait to see you, to be with you, my darling.'

'Me too . . .' I laughed with relief. 'Have you told your mother yet? She will want to get started with all the arrangements.'

'I'll ring her now, but I wanted to tell you first, Emma.'

'I'm so glad you did.'

'Look, there's someone waiting to use the phone. I'd better go. I'll see you on Sunday.'

'Yes. I'll be watching for you. Take care, Jon.'

'I love you . . .'

'I love you, too . . .'

I was smiling as I left the office. Sol had been showing a regular customer the new stock when I answered the telephone call, but he came to me now, brows raised.

'Good news, Emma?'

'The best. Jon is coming home for a two-week leave on Sunday. It means we can arrange the wedding at last.'

'That is good news,' Sol said, his thoughtful, grey eyes narrowing as he looked at me. 'Got that dress cut yet?'

'No, not quite,' I replied. 'You can come through and look in another five minutes.'

I went back to my task, determined that I was going to make this dress myself without anyone's advice or help: it had to be good enough to go out on the rails with the others, or I would have failed the test. Only when Sol declared himself satisfied that I understood the basics of the trade; could I move on to the showroom, which was out front of the cramped workshop.

I had been surprised when I saw the workshop the morning I started to work for Solomon Gould. Somehow I had expected it to be larger because of all the racks of dresses in the showroom, but I now knew that as soon as something was finished a girl took it out to the front. Nothing was allowed to linger in this place!

The working conditions for the two cutters and three tailors had seemed cramped and airless in the beginning, but I had soon become used to it, and now, when I visited the main factory with Sol, I found it noisy and somehow impersonal.

Sol's new factory – which he had set up just before the start of the war to manufacture uniforms for the armed forces – was outside of London.

'Safe from the bombs,' Sol had told me when we were discussing our joint venture. 'The East End will catch it once they start. And the dock area. We don't want all our money to go up in smoke. Some of the women grumbled about the move. They don't like living in the country, and I can't blame them, but once the government started to evacuate the children . . . well, they saw the advantages.'

'You mean like eggs?' I'd asked with a smile. Fresh produce was becoming harder to find in London.

For the first few weeks after war was declared, I had wondered if it would be better to send my own son out of town for his own sake. My mother had offered to have James with her, but I was reluctant to be parted from him, and he was so happy at home with Margaret. When the expected bombs had failed to arrive, I was glad I hadn't lost my nerve and sent James away.

It was some months now since I'd moved in with the Goulds. They had a Georgian terraced house in a pleasant garden square. Although narrow, the house was built on four separate floors. Sol had had the attics converted into a nursery and playroom for James.

'Plenty of room for you and the boy, Emma,' Sol had said to me over and over again. 'There's no need for you to move out when you and Jon marry. You know we love having you with us. And Margaret is so fond of James . . .'

It was a convenient arrangement. I could take the underground or a tram to the Portobello Road on the days when Sol didn't drive me to the workshop. Despite being Sol's partner in the new factory, I preferred to make my own way to work, and I had made it clear to Sol from the start that I wanted to be treated like any other worker during business hours.

Sol had been scrupulous about keeping to our agreement. He was teaching me the trade, and if I made a mistake I was put right very firmly – which was exactly the way I wanted it. However, on the days when Sol drove down to the new factory, he treated me and James as if we were his daughter and grandson.

He and Margaret would have loved children of their

own, but unfortunately Margaret hadn't been able to have a child. She was very close to being an invalid, though she refused to give into her illness and tried very hard to hide her suffering from us all. I had noticed it was getting more difficult for her to walk up and down stairs, but when I'd suggested she see her doctor, she had sworn me to secrecy. Sol must not know she was feeling worse. He had enough problems with the war restrictions and red tape.

Because of Margaret and Sol's kindness, I wanted to be an asset to the business. I was in the fortunate position of not having to work unless I chose, because I had some money of my own. However, I wanted to work. I had asked Sol to teach me the trade, and I wanted to learn and understand it all properly.

My pattern was cut. I glanced towards the showroom door just as it opened and Sol came in. He was frowning as he approached the table where I was working, and I felt a shiver of apprehension trickle down my spine. If I hadn't done my work properly, it would be as big a disappointment to Sol as it would to me.

He took his time looking at what I'd done, checking the run of the cloth and whether I'd made the best use I could of the length I'd chosen to cut, then he looked at me. He was trying very hard not to grin, and I knew he was pleased.

'Not bad,' he murmured. 'Not bad for an apprentice . . .'

'Oh, Sol!' I cried impatiently. 'Is it good enough? Will you put it on the rails with the others?'

'We'll see when you've finished it,' he said, nodding at me. 'I was thinking of taking a run up to the factory tomorrow, Emma. If you want to come with me, you'd best get on. I haven't got time to stand about all day if you have.'

If he hadn't been satisfied with the cut he would have said as much. He was just teasing me as he so often did these days. Sol was only in his early forties, twenty years or so older than me, but I loved him as dearly as if he were my father. He had shown me more love than my own father ever had, and I was so grateful.

'Of course I want to come,' I said. 'Go and serve some customers, Sol, and let me get on with my work.'

Our factory was in Chatteris, a small market town in Cambridgeshire. Sol had chosen to set up there, because I'd mentioned the availability of suitable premises – or that was his excuse. I suspected a part of it was because it was close to my home.

I had lived in March for most of my life. March itself was a railway town with one of the largest marshalling yards in Europe, and Sol thought it might be vulnerable to attack from the air because of all the trains. Chatteris was tucked away in the heart of the fenland, and he had hoped to avoid some of the risk when the bombing finally started . . . but the Air Ministry had opened an airfield at a village just down the road, so the factory was now between two likely targets.

Not that we had seen any sign of the air raids starting yet. After all the talk and preparation it almost seemed as if it was a phoney war, but Sol told me not to become too complacent.

'Hitler has been busy elsewhere,' he warned, 'but he hasn't forgotten us, Emma. It's going to be bad when it starts. When it does, you ought to think of going somewhere safer.'

I hadn't argued with Sol, but I had no intention of leaving London. Coming here in the first place had been a big step for me, but I had never regretted it despite sometimes missing my mother. She still worried about me and wrote often, giving me all the local news and asking me when Jon and I were going to get married.

We had planned to marry sooner than this, but Jon's training as an air force navigator had been intensive, and though he'd had one or two short spells of leave, he hadn't been able to fit in the wedding. At least, not the kind of wedding Mrs Reece wanted.

It was of course the second time for me. My first unhappy marriage was behind me now, and the grief of losing my beloved Gran was becoming easier to bear – except when I remembered how she had died, and then sometimes I woke from a bad dream with tears on my cheeks.

My husband – Richard Gillows – had murdered Gran. Of that there was not the slightest shadow of a doubt, though his other wicked deeds could not be proved. He had met a violent and sudden death by running in front of a fast train, and I believed that act had been quite deliberate. Richard had known it was only a matter of time before he was caught and tried for Mother Jacob's murder.

After his death and my decision to live in London, I had decided to use my maiden name. I preferred to be called Emma Robinson rather than Mrs Gillows, and not just because my husband's name had been in all the papers at the time when the police were hunting for him.

James was not my husband's child. He was the son of a man called Paul Greenslade. Paul was Jon's cousin, and we had first met through him. Jon had helped me after I became pregnant and had no one else to turn to. Although my son had been registered as my husband's child at birth, I had since had his name changed to Reece by a legal deed. Jon had arranged that for me so that James would not grow up to believe himself the son of a murderer.

Neither Jon nor I saw anything of Paul these days, and I believed he might have gone back to America, where he had been working for some years. I never thought of him. Paul and all that his brief presence in my life had meant belonged to the past – as did my first marriage.

The events leading up to the murder of Gran and Richard's death were something I did not wish to remember. I had a new life ahead of me now, and I was determined not to let the shadows of the past spoil my new-found happiness.

Sometimes it surprised me when I found myself singing and realized that I was truly happy for perhaps the first time in my life. As a young girl, I had suffered from my father's strictness and this was my first taste of freedom. And I was looking forward to becoming Jon's wife . . . once the wedding reception was over.

Mrs Reece wanted to invite so many people. I had tried to tell her all we needed was a quiet ceremony and a small reception for family and friends afterwards, but she had been so upset that I had somehow found myself agreeing to her hiring a hall and giving us the kind of wedding she thought we deserved.

'Jonathan is my only son, Emma,' she'd said, looking at me anxiously. 'You won't deny me the pleasure of giving you a special day – a day you will always remember?'

It would have been ungracious of me to refuse her, especially as Pops was nodding at me from behind her back. Jonathan's grandfather was a dear man, and it would have been beyond me to have refused his request when he asked so little.

I decided to telephone Mrs Reece that evening. We could discuss anything she wanted to know over the phone, and I would see her with Jonathan at the weekend.

'You look very nice this morning, my dear,' Margaret said to me when I came downstairs carrying James the next day. She kissed the child, then me. 'Have a lovely time – and give my love to your mother, Emma. Tell her that she and her husband must come and stay with us for your wedding. I wouldn't dream of them going to a hotel.'

'It's very kind of you,' I said, gazing at her anxiously. She was still an attractive woman despite her illness, but she looked very tired and I was worried about her. 'Are you sure you wouldn't like to come with us? You could stop with my mother while we visit the factory?'

'The drive would be too much for me,' Margaret admitted with a sigh. 'I am going to have a nice lazy day here alone. Perhaps sit in the garden if the sun comes out later . . . or read a book . . .'

'As long as you rest,' I replied, kissing her again. 'We shall be back by supper.'

I glanced at myself in the mirror. I was wearing a smart grey dress and a coat with a black fur collar, black shoes and a matching leather bag. My long brown hair was swept up and back from my face in a rolled style that I'd copied from one of Bette Davis's films, and I was wearing a hat with a cheeky feather at the front. I had never thought of myself as being pretty, but I did have a certain style these days – very different from the Emma who had worked in her father's shop!

'Are you ready, Emma?'

Sol was getting impatient. He was always slightly on edge when we visited the factory. It wasn't easy complying with all the new rules and regulations the government kept throwing at us, though being an official supplier to the armed forces did have its compensations.

I went out to the car. Sol had the door open for me.

He held James while I settled myself in the front seat, then placed the child in my arms.

'I swear he gets heavier every day,' he said. 'What do you feed him on, Emma, lead puddings?'

I laughed and shook my head at him. My son was thriving, and Sol was as proud of him as if he had been his own flesh and blood.

'I telephoned Mum,' I said. 'She says she has some eggs for us, and a few extra goodies she managed to buy somewhere or other.'

'Your mother will get herself locked up for trading on the black market one of these days.'

'Sol! It isn't the black market. It's just that in the country people grow their own food, and Mum happens to know someone who makes farm butter and has just slaughtered a pig they kept in the back yard.'

'Yes, of course,' Sol agreed, amused by my mother's excuses. 'I'll drop you off with your mother, Emma, and go to the factory alone. It's all rather boring stuff these days, nothing for you to worry about. You'll be much happier enjoying a chat with Greta.'

'If you're sure there's nothing I can do to help?'

'I'm going to check on quality, and look at the stock control,' Sol said. 'It would be a waste of your time to come with me. No, you treat it as a little holiday, and visit all your friends.'

'You spoil me, Sol,' I said, and smiled at him. 'But I would like a little time to visit my friends.'

'That's what I thought,' he said. 'You'll want to talk, with the wedding coming up.'

'Oh, you do look lovely, Emma!' Sheila exclaimed as I went into the shop. 'Really smart. And your son is just gorgeous!'

'Thank you.' I glanced round the shelves. So far the rationing of sugar hadn't affected Sheila's sweet stock, though I supposed she had bought in as much as she could before the shortages started to bite. 'How are you managing?'

'Not too bad so far,' she replied and pulled a face. 'Some things are slow coming in, but others don't seem to have suffered yet. Our suppliers say we shall get our share same as everyone else – but once the government makes us have coupons for sweets I shall go potty.'

'Is it getting too much for you, working here?' Sheila was in the middle stages of her pregnancy. 'If you wanted to give the shop up, I would understand.'

'You don't want it back, do you?'

She looked so anxious that I laughed and shook my head. 'No, of course not. I was just concerned for you, and Eric, of course. I wouldn't want you to feel tied just because you've signed a lease.'

'What would you do if we packed up?'

'I'm not sure. Things are going to be difficult for a while. I might just leave it empty and try to sell after the war is over . . . whenever that is.'

Sheila looked thoughtful. 'Would you sell to us, Emma? If we could raise enough money to buy?'

'Are you sure you want it?'

'Eric was talking about selling other things – maybe

groceries or alcohol, if we could get a licence. Make it an off licence . . . He thought about packing in his job and running the shop himself.'

'Won't he be called up?'

'He's got a weak chest.' Sheila frowned. 'Eric failed his medical last month. It threw him a bit I can tell you. That's why he's thinking of expanding the shop . . .'

'I'm sorry he isn't well. I didn't know, Sheila.'

'Nor did we. He gets a bit chesty in the winter, but . . .' She shrugged but I could see she was concerned. 'He would be better off working indoors.'

'You can do what you want with the shop,' I said. 'You don't have to buy it. Apply for the licence. If I can help in any way, just telephone me.'

Sheila's face lit up. 'You're a real friend, Emma.'

'Let me know how things go,' I said. 'I'm going to see Madge Henty now.'

Sheila nodded. 'I buy all my things there now. No one else in town has such pretty dresses. I hope the government isn't going to stop us buying clothes next?'

'Sol is sure it will come. He has a lot of contacts, Sheila, and he knows things – so if you want something new buy it now while you can.'

I left the shop as a customer entered. At first it had seemed a little strange to see Sheila standing behind the counter of Father's old shop. He would have hated it, of course: he had never approved of her, but the property belonged to me now, and I had always liked Sheila. She paid her rent regularly, and that was all that counted as far as I was concerned. Besides, she was married and perfectly respectable. Whatever people had said of her once, they had to admire her these days. She worked hard, and it was quite something for her and her husband to own and run their own business.

A few doors further along the High Street was the dress shop run by Mrs Henty. She was another close friend, and my partner in the dress shop. Trade had been brisk these past few months. I chose most of the stock myself in London and had it sent down to her by rail.

Sol didn't make costumes or knitwear, but he had been able to advise me on the best places to buy at the keenest prices, and my own instinct for what would sell in a country town had proved reliable.

Mrs Henty was serving a customer with a pretty blouse when I went in. I amused myself by rocking James in his pushchair and glancing through the rails. Judging by how thin the stock was, my friend had been rushed off her feet.

'I could do with a cup of tea,' she exclaimed as the door shut behind her last customer. 'I was going to telephone you, Emma. Everyone has been going crazy these past two weeks. I am sure they are all terrified the government is going to ration clothes!'

'They will before long. I'll sort some more stock out for you, Madge.'

'Yes, please do,' she said. 'We could probably double or treble our usual orders at the moment . . . for as long as the panic lasts anyway.'

I liked to keep the stock fresh, sending Madge a

few of the most attractive new dresses from Sol's rails at a time, but now I saw that it might be wise to build up our stock a little.

'I'll send whatever I think you can sell,' I promised as I followed her through to the back room and watched her put the kettle on. 'Sol won't mind if we owe him for a few weeks. So, how are you? Other than being busy?'

Madge laughed. 'Very well, Emma. I'm comfortable here in my own little way – but tell me what you've been up to, my dear.'

'I'm getting married next week.'

'To that nice Mr Reece?' I nodded and she looked pleased. 'Well, I think that's lovely. I like Mr Reece – he's a real gentleman. So kind and gentle, and polite too. You will be settled at last, Emma.'

'Yes, I'm sure I shall,' I said. Jon was kind and gentle, and I loved him. 'Do you think you could come up for the wedding? Or is it too difficult?'

'I can get a girl to look after things here.' Madge beamed at me. 'Lily is a nice little thing, helps out sometimes on a Saturday when I'm busy. I can leave her in charge for once. I wouldn't miss your wedding for the world!'

I stayed for nearly half an hour talking to Madge, then made my way back to my mother's house. Sol would return in a little while, and I wanted a few minutes alone with Mum.

She had been baking when I went into the kitchen, her face flushed and smeared with flour.

'I had some sugar put by,' she told me as she brought a sponge cake from the oven. 'You take this back with you, love.'

I went to kiss her cheek. 'You needn't worry about us, Mum. Honestly, we're fine.'

'London food isn't worth the eating,' she said. 'I've got a box of fresh stuff for you to take back, so you won't starve for a while.'

'No, we shan't starve.' I smiled. She was convinced I had lost weight since I'd been living in London, which might have been true, but was due more to the fact that I was always busy than any shortage of decent food. We were still managing despite the recent rationing of butter, sugar, ham and bacon. 'Thank you, Mum. We shall enjoy that sponge.'

'I do worry about you, Emma, but you'll be all right when you're married to Jon. I trust him – he will look after you.'

'I'm fine now. I don't need looking after. Besides, Margaret and Sol are so good to me.'

'Yes, I know.' She sighed and reached out to touch my cheek. 'It's just that . . . well, I can't forget how it was for you. I want you to be happy, love.'

'I am happy, Mum. Very happy.'

She nodded, then reached into her apron pocket and brought out a letter. 'This came for you last week,' she said. 'I opened it, Emma. I thought it might be important. It's from a solicitor down in the west country . . . I wasn't sure whether to give it to you. If I were you, I should just tear it up.'

'Mum?' I stared at her, seeing the unease in her eyes. 'Why? What does this solicitor want? Why are you frightened?'

'I'm not exactly frightened, Emma. I just feel it might be best to let things stay as they are.'

I took the letter out, made curious by her attitude. It was from a firm of solicitors that I had never heard of before. They had been contacted by a relative of the late Harold Robinson . . . someone wished to know if he had an heir. Apparently, they had seen a notice of his death and now wished to trace any family.'

'They've heard he left money,' my mother said. 'Depend on it, Emma. They're scroungers, out for what they can get.'

'You don't know that,' I said, laughing at her expression. 'Aren't you curious about them?' I turned the page, looking for more information. 'The solicitor says he believes I may be the person he is looking for, and will I reply at my earliest convenience.'

'Tell him you don't want to see them, whoever they are,' my mother said. 'Your father didn't want to know his family. In all the years we were married, they never tried to contact us. Why should you bother with them now?'

'I don't know. Perhaps I shan't.' I slipped the letter into my pocket. 'I'll send this to our lawyers, Mum, let them find out what it's all about. Don't worry, I shan't get taken in by someone who wants money.'

'Well, just be careful, Emma.'

'How is Bert?' I asked, changing the subject. 'You said he had a nasty cold when you last wrote.'

'He's better now. We're both fine, Emma. Happy . . .' She bent down and took James from his push-chair as he held out his arms to her, kissing his cheeks. 'I miss you and this little fellow – but I wouldn't change my life. Bert is the man I should have married years ago. If I had how different our lives might have been . . .'

'Don't look back, Mum,' I said, squeezing her waist with gentle affection. 'I've made up my mind I won't, not ever. I'm not going to waste time in regrets. Life is what you make it, and I intend to make the most of mine.'

'Yes, you must,' she said. 'But you will, I know that. We all underestimated you when you were a girl, all tried to take care of you – but you're in charge now, aren't you? You look so different, Emma – such a smart woman, a townie . . . not a country mouse any more. Sometimes I hardly recognize you in your posh frock!'

'But I'm still me underneath,' I said, and reached out to take James from her as he started to grizzle. 'I think that's Sol coming back now. We shall have to go in a few minutes, Mum. We don't want to be too late back. Sol never says anything, but I know he worries about Margaret.'

'It was good of him to bring you down,' she said. 'A man like that . . . I can't help wondering why he's taken to you the way he has . . .' She frowned. 'I mean, what does he get out of it?'

'Mum! Why should he want anything?' I said. 'I've told you. I trust Sol. He and Margaret are good people. Now, please, stop worrying about me and let him in . . .'

Chapter 2

I had been eagerly anticipating Jon's arrival, but it was a bitterly cold day, the mist freezing so that it was impossible to see more than a short distance. Jon had telephoned to say he was on his way, but that had been ages ago and I was beginning to fret.

'Don't worry, my dear,' Margaret said as I went to the front windows yet again. 'Jon will . . .'

The front door bell pealed at that moment, and then we heard Jon's voice answering the housekeeper's anxious inquiry.

'I'm fine, thank you, Mrs Rowan. The mist is pretty bad, but I managed to . . .'

I flew into the hall. Jon opened his arms, catching me and crushing me to him. We kissed passionately in front of a slightly startled Mrs Rowan and an approving Margaret, who had followed me into the hall and was smiling benevolently as she watched us.

'I've missed you so much,' Jon said. 'You smell gorgeous, Emma, like a wood after a shower of rain.'

I laughed with pleasure. Jon always said nice things to me. Sometimes, I thought he ought to have been a poet. He had been a solicitor before the war, though it was not a job he particularly enjoyed. Once, he had confessed to me that he would have liked to be a farmer. I had teased him then, but the slow, gentle life, caring for the land would have suited this man who had come to mean so much to me. Perhaps after the war was over we would think about making a new life together in the country.

Jon always said of himself that he was a plain, ordinary chap, the kind of man you might pass in the street without giving him a second glance. Perhaps his sandy-coloured hair and rather square features were not remarkable, but inside he was beautiful. There was something fine, almost noble about Jon at times. Of course I would never dream of telling him that – he would cringe with embarrassment.

'I'm so glad you're home,' I said now, clinging to his arm as I drew him into the warm, comfortable room where we had been sitting round the fire. 'I can't believe we've got two whole weeks together!'

'It's good, isn't it?' Jon smiled at Margaret. 'How are you, Mrs Gould?'

'Quite well, thank you,' she replied. 'Your uniform looks rather smart. I believe congratulations are in order, lieutenant?'

I realized Jon had various new stripes and badges sewn to his uniform jacket. 'Does this mean you've passed everything?' A tiny shiver went down my spine as he nodded. 'So the training is finally over . . . that means . . .'

'Yes.' Jon touched a finger to my lips. 'We don't need to talk about any of this, Emma. We have a wedding to plan, and two glorious weeks to spend together.'

'Lovely,' I said and smiled up at him. 'Your mother has the wedding planned for next Wednesday . . .'

'She wanted to wait until Saturday, but I said no.' A gleam of determination showed in Jon's eyes. 'Anyone who can't make it by then can send their apologies. I want to spend my leave with my wife. I'm not prepared to waste time . . .'

'Well said, Jon!' Sol came in at that moment carrying a tray of fine crystal glasses. Behind him was Mrs Rowan with an ice bucket and a magnum of champagne. 'This is vintage,' Sol announced triumphantly. 'I've been saving it for the right moment . . . and I think this must be it, don't you?'

'That's rather splendid of you, sir,' Jon said and grinned. 'Much appreciated.'

Sol opened the champagne. It popped beautifully and we all toasted one another, Mrs Rowan staying to wish us health before taking her glass away with her.

'To a long and happy life for you both,' Sol said. 'May all your troubles be little ones.'

We all laughed, sipped our champagne and talked about the wedding. No one mentioned the war, or the fact that Jon would be flying combat missions once his leave was over. I knew he didn't want to discuss or even think about war when he was with me. He said our time together was special, and must not be wasted.

'It's always there,' he'd told me on one of his flying visits home. 'I live, breathe and sleep war when I'm in camp, Emma. I don't want to think about it when we're together.'

I wondered if Jon was afraid. Surely any man would be? But somehow I sensed Jon's feelings went deeper. In his heart he probably felt that war itself was wrong: killing and death were something so foreign to his nature that he must hate the very idea. Perhaps that was why he had chosen the air force instead of the army? To keep the death and killing at a distance . . .

'What are you thinking about?' he asked suddenly. 'Why the frown?'

'I was wondering if we ought to leave. We don't want to keep your mother waiting, Jon.'

'No, of course not.' He laughed. 'I was told not to be late for lunch.'

'We mustn't keep you,' Margaret said, and waved us away with a smile. 'Now don't worry about James, Emma. Nanny will see he eats his lunch, and I shall sit with him while he has his nap afterwards, as I always do.'

'Don't let him tire you then.' I kissed her cheek. 'I expect we shall be back by teatime.'

'You look very well, Emma.' Dorothy Reece smiled at me in her sad, wistful way. 'It seems ages since I saw you, my dear.'

Immediately, I felt guilty. It was almost a month since I had last brought James to see her and Pops – known to the rest of the world as Sir Roy Armstrong.

'Yes, I know,' I apologized. 'I've been so busy. Sol wanted me to produce a dress from start to finish, just to prove that I really understand what goes into the production of a finished garment. It was just a classic cut with a gored skirt and fitted waist, but I had to practise and study Mr Jackson's work for several weeks . . .'

It was a weak excuse and we both knew it. The workshop was closed on both Saturdays and Sundays. I could visit every week if I chose, but the truth was I found Mrs Reece difficult to please. It wasn't that she criticized me openly, but I was always aware of something . . . a look of disapproval or a lift of those fine brows.

She was a small, fragile woman who dressed in pretty, flowing gowns that made her look rather like a doll. However, I had soon discovered that beneath that wistful air was a very determined woman, a woman who usually knew how to get her own way.

'Well, you are here now,' she said with another of those smiles. 'I've drawn up a list of guests I've invited. Most of them by telephone, Jonathan, since you insisted on such short notice . . .' She frowned as she handed me the list. 'You haven't invited many friends, Emma. Are you sure you remembered everyone?'

'I don't have much family,' I replied. 'Just three uncles on my mother's side, but they are scattered all over the place and Mum says not to bother inviting them. Sheila couldn't leave the shop – but Mrs Henty is coming. I invited Mary and her husband, but she says it's too far to come for a day and she can't leave her father because he isn't well. Mum and Bert are coming, of course, and Sol and Margaret. They are the only ones who really matter. I can send a piece of cake to the girls at work and a few other friends . . .'

'Oh yes, the cake.' Mrs Reece looked pleased with herself. 'As you may imagine, wedding cakes are going to be in short supply, but I had made arrangements weeks ago. Your cake was already made and stored, Emma, and the icing sugar was bought and saved.'

'She's a clever girl,' Pops said, beaming at us. 'You should see the tinned food Dorothy has in the cellar. Fruit, salmon, ham . . . enough to feed an army, let alone a few wedding guests.'

'I thought about it in advance,' she said. 'I didn't need to rush out and spend all my sugar rations in one go. Not like that silly woman in the newspaper!'

'You mean the one who was fined for being greedy and unpatriotic?'

'Yes. So foolish. One only had to think, Emma. It was obvious months ago what was coming. I bought a little more than I needed every time I went shopping, and it has mounted up, that's all.'

'Don't you believe her,' Pops said, chuckling. 'She has been like a general in the field preparing for a siege.'

I smiled and thanked Mrs Reece. She had been so determined to give us a splendid wedding. All I wanted was to marry Jon. If I were honest, I would have preferred a quiet ceremony and a small reception, but I didn't want to spoil her pleasure.

'You've been so kind,' I said now. 'I really will try to visit more often in future.'

'But surely . . .' She looked shocked. 'You will be living here once you and Jonathan are married.'

'No.' I glanced at Jon. 'Didn't Jon tell you? We've decided to stay with Sol and Margaret for the time being. It's easy for me to get to work from there, and James is settled. I don't want to move him until Jon and I can find a home of our own.'

'I did tell you, Mama,' Jon said. 'You might not have been listening, but I did tell you Emma wants to stay where she is for the moment.'

'But surely Emma doesn't need to work,' she said. 'Not when you are married. I had expected her to come here, to live with us. I was looking forward to it so much.'

'Jon understands that I want to work,' I said. 'It is important to me. I've always been honest about this, Mrs Reece. I'm learning a trade. One day I hope to be in business for myself. I'm not sure whether I want to make clothes or sell them to the public, but working with Sol is teaching me so much . . .'

'In business . . .' She looked horrified. 'But is that quite nice, Emma? In my day ladies didn't . . . well, it wasn't done. Respectable women just didn't dabble in trade.'

Pops laughed. 'Nor would you have wanted to work, Dorothy. But that doesn't mean Emma shouldn't. She is a very intelligent young woman. I think it's a splendid idea. Why shouldn't women run their own businesses if they choose?'

Mrs Reece frowned but made no further comments. She was forced to accept defeat this time, but I had a feeling that she was not going to give up the battle. She was used to having her own way.

'Luncheon is ready, madam.'

The housekeeper's announcement put an end to the discussion. After lunch we talked of other things. Pops gave us a beautiful silver tea and coffee service complete with its own tray, and Mrs Reece presented me with two sets of wonderful embroidered linen sheets and pillowcases, much nicer than anything I had been able to buy recently.

I thanked them both. Jon said we had to leave because of the fog, which was as bad as ever and didn't look as if it would clear all day. He gave me a meaningful look as we went out to the car.

'Thank goodness you didn't cave in over living there, darling. I couldn't put up with it. We'll have to look for somewhere of our own when things calm down, but for the moment I think it best if you stay where you are. After all, I shan't be around that often . . .'

'No . . .' I smiled at him. 'Only two days and nights, then we'll be together. Where are we going for our honeymoon?'

'It ought to be Paris. That's where I would like to take you, darling. One day I shall, I promise.' He gave me a regretful look. 'But it can't be . . . but we'll go somewhere.'

'You're not going to tell me?'

His eyes were bright with mischief. 'It's a surprise, darling.'

I nodded, my lips parting in anticipation as he leaned towards me. We kissed, a slow, lingering kiss that made me tingle with pleasure.

'I can't wait. Oh, Jon . . .'

'We've waited this long,' he said. 'We'll wait a bit longer . . .'

I found it difficult to sleep the night before my wedding. My dress was hanging in the wardrobe. Not white this time, but a simple plain ivory satin with long sleeves and a high neck.

Once before I had lain wakeful, thinking about marriage. I had been desperately unhappy then, carrying the child of the lover who had deserted me and forced by my father to marry a man I did not love.

What terrible results had come from that marriage! A man's love – if Richard had ever truly loved me! – had turned to hatred. Greed and jealousy had played their part, and I had been caught between them.

How different were my feelings now. I wanted this marriage with all my heart. I was looking forward to being Jon's wife. I loved him, but I also trusted him: he was my friend.

It was all going to be so wonderful! I could hardly wait for the moment we were alone at last.

The wedding itself was beautiful. I carried a small bouquet of snowdrops and lily of the valley, which Pops had grown specially in pots under glass for me. The perfume of their delicate flowers was sweet, and the thought that had gone into Sir Roy's loving gift to me was even sweeter.

Tears gathered in my eyes as I took my vows that

morning. I was so lucky to have such good friends . . . people who loved and cared for me. I could hardly believe it was all happening. Life had been so hard, so bitter for a time, and now I had so much.

We were showered with confetti as bells rang out joyously, and then the wedding car was speeding through the damp streets to the reception.

So many of the guests were strangers to me. The thought occurred to me that this wedding was more for Mrs Reece than either Jon or I – that the people I met for the first time were her friends, not ours.

It did not matter. They were pleasant, kindly people and the gifts they had given us were generous: linen, silver, good china and expensive glass, quite different to the gifts I'd received on my first marriage. None of it was important. All that mattered was the look in Jon's eyes when he smiled at me, and the certainty that I was loved.

At last, at long last, the taxi arrived to take us to the station. Jon had decided to travel by train rather than drive all the way up to Scotland. He had told me our destination the night before, warning me to pack plenty of warm clothes.

'It's going to be cold, darling,' he'd whispered, 'but not for us. I promise I shall keep you warm . . .'

We said goodbye to all our friends, kissing and hugging, thanking them for coming and for their good wishes and gifts.

'Be happy, Emma,' my mother said as she held me close. 'You deserve happiness, my darling.'

'I am happy, Mum. Jon loves me and I love him. I couldn't ask for more.'

'Be happy, Emma,' Margaret said, 'and don't worry about James. He will be safe with us, and as loved as if he were our own.'

'He loves you,' I said. 'Kiss him for me every night.'

'Of course I will,' she promised.

'Be happy, Emma,' Sol said, his eyes twinkling. 'Take care of that man of yours. He is about as good as they come.'

Sol and Margaret had refurbished our bedroom for us, giving us the choice of whatever we wanted: a truly magnificent gift we would be able to treasure throughout our married life. But more than that, they had both given me so much support and love.

'I know that, Sol,' I said. 'I'm so lucky in my friends . . .'

At the station, Jon bought magazines and chocolates for the journey. It would take several hours and he had booked a sleeper cabin for us. Now we were truly alone. The cabin door was closed and locked. We were man and wife, and as Jon reached for me I knew true happiness – and it was as if the past had never been.

The narrow beds in a sleeper cabin are perhaps not the most comfortable place to make love, but for me it was all we needed: with a few bumps of arms and legs and elbows, and some laughter, we managed. Jon was so sweet, and tender, so careful to give me pleasure.

I had never known a man to be so unselfish in his

loving, but Jon was always the same in everything he did: he would not have known how to be any different.

'You are so lovely, Emma,' he whispered as he caressed my breasts, kissing me, teasing me with his tongue, setting me on fire. 'I've dreamed of you like this, wanted you so much . . .'

'And I want you, Jon,' I said, kissing him back. I was no shy virgin to be afraid of love, but a woman who wanted to give her man the love he needed. 'I do love you, Jon. So much . . . so very much.'

We came together, gently at first, a soft blending of hearts, minds and bodies, passionate but not desperate, not frantic. This was a new experience for me. It was as if we were somehow comfortable together, almost as though we had been married for some years, had always known each other's thoughts and needs.

Afterwards, I felt warm, safe, loved. There had been no crashing of drums, no wild, tempestuous crescendo of feeling, just contentment.

I knew that it was possible to feel more excitement, but I was not disappointed as I nestled in my husband's arms. Sexual desire was only a small part of what I felt for Jon. He had been so good to me, was so loving, so generous in all he gave of himself. I loved him and I wanted to make him happy. I wanted to be happy. I wanted quiet and contentment, the ordinary things of life . . . the respect decent people gave to each other every day.

I was ready to settle for what I had. It was so much more than I had ever had before.

*

Our days in the Scottish highlands were very precious: days of mists and bright clear mornings when the sun broke through, of dark nights and wood fires, and beauty that touched the soul.

Jon had rented a wonderful cottage where we could be alone. It was part of a large estate and set in huge grounds, with a lake, a mountain in the distance, purple and grand, smudged against the skyline, and gentle hills where deer roamed amongst the heather.

A gigantic hamper of food was waiting for us when we arrived. It was packed with all kinds of luxuries, from venison to pots of pates and peaches in jars of brandy syrup. Each day we were there, a man came down from the house with baskets of fresh provisions. Some of it was ready prepared, needing only to be reheated in the wood-burning oven, but there was also bacon, which I cooked for our breakfast, and fresh trout or salmon. Jon showed me how to poach these in a special fish kettle, and I discovered he was good at preparing these kinds of dishes. Yet another surprising aspect of this man who was so dear to me.

'Where do you think all this food comes from?' I asked Jon once. 'Do they know there's a war on?'

'What war?' Jon laughed. 'Look around you, Emma. How can there be a war in such a perfect place?'

'It is perfect,' I said, leaning my head back against him as his arms surrounded me. 'You were so clever to find it for us, Jon.'

'I've been here before,' he said, his breath warm

against my ear. 'For the fishing. It's wonderful here in September, Emma. We'll come again one day.'

'Yes, please. I should love that.'

'It would be wonderful to live in a place like this,' Jon went on dreamily. 'Don't you think so, Emma? You said you wondered where the food comes from, but this estate must be almost self-sufficient, wouldn't you think? They have so much game in their woods . . . deer, grouse at the right time of year, fish in the lake. I'm sure they live as people used to in the old days, make their own bread, milk their own cows . . .'

I turned to look up at him, gazing into his eyes as I heard the wistful note in his voice. 'Is that how you would like to live, Jon? Away from all the noise and turmoil of the city?'

'Sometimes I think it would be paradise,' he replied and then laughed. 'I'm a dreamer, Emma. Life isn't that simple, is it? Even here they must have their serpent.'

I sensed something in him then . . . a kind of fear. What was Jon afraid of? I knew he hated the idea of war, of the wanton waste of life and destruction of all that made living good. Was he afraid of death – or that life would become too ugly?

'Now what are you thinking?' He lifted my chin with his finger. 'Are you bored here, Emma? Would you rather I had chosen a city? Do you miss the noise of your beloved London?'

'I think I might if I lived here all the time,' I admitted. 'I was born in a country town, Jon. I love the bustle of London. I love being able to go to a theatre when I want, and I love shopping – but this time here with you has been wonderful. Being together, walking, talking, listening to music on the radio when the fire is warm . . . I wouldn't have changed it for anything.'

'But we'll spend the last two nights of my leave in London,' Jon said. 'I mustn't be selfish. I want to please you, my darling. We'll go to the theatre, and we'll go shopping . . .'

'Oh, Jon,' I whispered as I turned in his arms to kiss him. 'You could never be selfish . . .'

'Don't be too sure of that,' he murmured as he bent his head to mine. 'I want you so much, Emma. When a man loves a woman as much as I love you . . . pleasing her *is* selfish. I want to see your eyes light up, to see you smile and hear your laughter.'

I laughed then as he kissed me. Jon's idea of being selfish seemed funny to me. I was beginning to realize there was so much more to this man I had married than I had yet guessed. He went so deep, his thoughts so complex, way beyond my understanding. I could not hope to follow all the secret, twisting trails of his mind. I knew only that he was a sensitive, loving, gentle man, and that I loved him.

When I thought about it, I realized we had met only a few times before our wedding. Jon had been there at a difficult period of my life. He had helped me when I needed a friend, but our meetings had been brief – apart from one holiday by the sea.

It took more than that to know a man like Jon. But

we had a lifetime before us, and I was sure deep inside of me that he would be worth the knowing.

And so our lovely, special time drifted away, the days passing with a dreamlike quality as we walked the hills, the wind blowing fine, powdery snow into our faces when the weather turned colder, then racing back to the warmth of our cottage – to our bed. Was any woman ever as loved as I? Had lovers ever been so content as we were then?

All too soon, we were back in London. James wept as he saw me for the first time, and held out his arms to Margaret. I felt guilty as I saw the accusation in my son's eyes. For several days I had almost forgotten him.

However, when he saw the teddy bear I had bought for him, he decided to forgive me. His arms closed about my neck, his tears drying as I held him to me and kissed his soft, baby curls and his face. He smelled so good, and I felt a wave of love for him.

'Mummy is sorry,' I whispered. 'She won't go away again, darling.'

'We should have taken him with us,' Jon said, a note of regret in his voice. 'It was selfish of me, Emma. He loves you, too.'

We both knew it had not been possible. James could not have shared our idyll. It would not have been the same. Besides, we had needed that special time alone together. Jon had needed it, and for this once at least his needs had necessarily come before my son's.

Now that we were back in London, Jon was more like the man I had known before we were married. Whatever part of him I had glimpsed during our time in the highlands was now safely hidden. He was his usual polite, smiling self.

True to his word, Jon took me to the theatre two nights running. He also took me and my son to the park. We watched the horses parading past the palace, and Jon helped my son to sail a boat on the lake, then bought us all cream cakes and tea, most of which James managed to get all over his clean sailor suit. We were just like any other family on a day out.

This was how I had always thought family life should be. It was what I had longed for, and it made me so happy.

The night before Jon was due to return to camp, I clung to him after we had made love. I was crying, but trying not to let him see it.

'Don't, Emma,' he whispered against my hair. 'Please don't cry. I can't bear it. I can't bear it that I may never see you again . . .'

I leaned over him, my hair brushing his naked shoulder. For one terrible moment his soul was as naked as his flesh. I could see his fear, almost touch it. He was afraid of losing all that we had, all that we meant to each other.

'It isn't that I might die,' he said, his throat caught with emotion. 'We all have to die one day . . .'

'What then, my darling?'

'If something should happen . . . if you have reason

to believe I am dead . . . don't waste the rest of your life, Emma. I want you to be happy. More than anything else, that is what matters to me. I think I could face death if I knew that you would go on . . . that you would live for me.'

'Oh, Jon . . .' I could not hold back my tears now. 'I can't bear the thought that . . .'

He kissed me. 'Forgive me, darling. I just want you to be happy.'

'I am happy, here with you.' I bent to kiss his face. I touched my lips to his eyelids, his forehead, his cheeks, the tip of his nose, and then his mouth. 'I never want to be with anyone else,' I vowed. 'I love you, Jon. You've given me so much – and I don't mean material things.'

Jon smiled, reaching up to stroke my cheek. 'I'm a fool, Emma. Take no notice. I have dark thoughts sometimes, but they are just bad dreams. I love you. I can't die. I have too much to live for, my darling.'

'Of course you do,' I said. Then I began to kiss his body, tiny, teasing kisses that made him moan and throb with desire. I laughed as I moved lower, knowing what I was doing to him. 'Just so as you remember exactly why you have to come home to me . . .'

I didn't go to see Jon off at the station the next morning. He wouldn't let me.

'Stay with James,' he told me, kissing me goodbye. 'He needs you, Emma. He needs you as much as I do. You mustn't forget that, my darling. I know you enjoy your work, but make time for James. Think about me, my darling, and about the way it will be for us when all this is over. We shall be a family then. You, me and James . . .'

'Yes, of course. I always do think of both of you.'

I was a little hurt that Jon should think I would neglect my son. I spent as much time as I could with him, but perhaps it wasn't enough.

Watching him with Margaret later that day, I realized he went as easily to her as to me. For a moment I felt a pang of regret. James was very precious to me. I had never intended to neglect him, but perhaps I had without realizing it.

Jon was so observant, so thoughtful. Damn this wretched war! I wished so much that we could be together as a family, that we could have our own home, live as we pleased . . . but I was not alone. All over the country women were wishing for the same thing, hiding their tears as their men went off to war, perhaps never to return.

I held James on my lap after I had bathed him that evening, rocking him in my arms before putting him in his cot, my cheeks wet with tears.

For a little while, a precious fragment of time, I had forgotten reality. I had believed in Jon's paradise, but now the shadow of war loomed large. Until this moment, I had not really seen it as more than a nuisance, as an excuse for the government's petty restrictions – but quite suddenly I realized how terrifying it was.

The dangers of training seemed puny against those Jon would face once he began flying missions for real.

'Come back to me, Jon,' I prayed. 'Please come back – for both of us. We both need you.'

I smiled as I touched my son's head, stroking the soft downy hair. He had fallen asleep almost as soon as I laid him down.

I would spend more time with my son, even if it meant cutting down my hours a little at the workshop. And I would go to visit Mrs Reece when I could. I owed Jon that much.

As I went downstairs, the telephone rang. I answered it.

'Emma . . .' Jon's voice came to me sure and strong. 'I just wanted to tell you . . . I'm all right. Last night, it was silly . . . all the chaps feel the same when they've been home. But I'm back now and it's all right. Do you know what I mean?'

'Yes, of course, darling. I felt the same. It's just the thought of saying goodbye.'

'I'll be home when I can,' Jon said. 'Just a few hours next time, but this damned war can't go on forever, can it?'

'No, of course it can't,' I replied, knowing that this was what he wanted me to say. 'Don't worry about us, we're all fine. I've just put James to bed. I read him a story, and he's fast asleep. He looked so sweet, Jon, all warm and pink and soft . . .'

'Good – that's how I shall think of you,' Jon promised. 'Sitting by his bed, your hair glinting with gold in the lamplight . . .'

'My hair is a mousy brown,' I said, laughing. 'You ought to write poetry, Jon. You see everything with a rosy glow.'

'You don't see yourself the way I do,' he replied. 'Sometimes your hair looks like silk . . . and you *are* beautiful, whatever you say.'

'Flatterer!'

'Take care, Emma. I'll telephone you again soon, my love.'

'Yes, please do. I love you, Jon.'

'Bye . . .'

I replaced the receiver. My hand was shaking. Jon had not told me, but I knew he was going on his first mission that night . . .

Chapter 3

'I think that film will be interesting,' Margaret said and handed me a newspaper with a report of the record-breaking box office takings in America. 'Three hours and forty-five minutes – and Vivien Leigh won an award for it. After everyone said the role should have gone to an American actress.'

'*Gone With The Wind*,' I said. 'Yes, I'm looking forward to it – that's if we can get tickets. Everyone is going mad for them.'

Margaret nodded. 'Now, Emma dear, about the reception this evening . . .' She sighed, brushing a hand over her eyes. 'I honestly don't think I can go.'

'Sol will be so disappointed . . .'

'Not if you go with him,' Margaret said. 'He has to attend, Emma. It is expected of him. You know he's worried about all these new laws. An official reception is where he makes his contacts, finds out how everything is going to work – if he knows what's in the wind, he can make contingency plans . . .'

'Yes, I know.' I bit my lip. 'It's just that I've never mixed with that sort of people . . . important people. I'm afraid of letting Sol down. Supposing I don't know what to say to them?'

Margaret laughed. She looked so much younger at

that moment. I'd thought she had been feeling better recently, but her tiredness was worrying.

'You will think of something, my dear. Please – to save me?'

'Yes, of course.' I could not refuse her such a small request. 'What shall I wear?' I reviewed my dresses anxiously in my mind.

'I have something you might like,' Margaret said. 'I bought it for a similar reception years ago and never wore it. It's French, made in Paris, dark blue velvet and a classic style that doesn't date. Would you like to try it on, Emma?'

'Yes, please. I'm not sure I have anything of my own that would be suitable.'

'Come with me . . .'

I followed her up to her bedroom; it was a pretty room furnished with beautiful antique pieces and decorated in muted shades of green and gold. I knew that she and Sol had separate rooms. That had bothered me at first, but Margaret had told me she was a restless sleeper. Sol would be kept awake most of the night if he shared her bed, and he needed his rest. I did not doubt the love between them, even though the intimate side of their marriage might be over.

The dress Margaret showed me was quite simply stunning. It was long and had a rather medieval look, the skirt slender over the hips yet flowing out to a little train at the hem. The neckline was scooped and plain, the sleeves long and cut to a V over the wrists.

'You wear it with this girdle,' Margaret explained,

showing me a narrow rope of metallic gold threads. 'Do you like it, Emma?'

'It's wonderful,' I said. 'It looks like something a thirteenth-century lady might have worn to court.'

'Yes, I suppose it does,' she said, smiling at my description. 'I hadn't noticed that particularly. I just felt it was simple and classical.'

'May I try it on?'

'Of course. If you like it, it is yours.'

'I'm only going to borrow it; it is your dress, Margaret.'

'I shall never wear it. This gown was meant for a young and beautiful woman – like you.'

I took the dress to my own room and put it on. The soft material draped over my body with a simple elegance that made me feel wonderful . . . like a princess! I had never worn anything like this before. It was something quite unique, made by an artist for a special woman. Even if I had been able to afford it, I could never have found anything to compare with this dress these days.

Margaret smiled approvingly when I went back to show her. 'I knew it would fit you,' she said. 'It becomes you well, my dear. It might have been made for you.'

'Why did you never wear it?' I looked at her curiously.

'I bought that dress to celebrate something,' Margaret said, and her eyes glistened with unshed tears. 'I believed I was to have Sol's child – but the night I should have worn it, I miscarried. After that, I put it away and forgot it.'

'Oh, Margaret . . .' I stared at her in dismay, feeling the depth of her pain, pain she had hidden so cleverly from me until this moment. 'I am so very sorry . . .'

'No, don't be,' she said, and the tears were gone as though they had never been. 'I've been so lucky, Emma. Sol has always adored me, never reproached me for . . . besides, now we have you and James.' She smiled at me lovingly. 'You are the daughter I lost that night, and James is my grandson, the gift you brought to this house. I don't think the dress will be unlucky for you, my dear.'

'No, I'm sure it won't,' I said and went to kiss her. 'I love it. It is beautiful and it will give me confidence this evening.'

'You look lovely. Sol will be very proud of you. He – we are both very fond of you, Emma.'

I accepted the gift of the dress. How could I refuse her? I knew it must have been expensive, far more than I would dream of paying for a dress. When I looked at myself in the mirror, I did not know the woman who stared back at me.

I was someone different. Perhaps the Emma of the future?

I was so thankful for Margaret's dress amongst the wealthy, powerful and sophisticated people at the reception that night. Without it, I truly might have wanted to run away.

It wasn't so bad during the early part of the evening. We all had dinner, and there were speeches by important men from both government and business. Because I had listened to Sol, I understood more of what was being said than I would otherwise have done. The war was costing so much, becoming so much worse than anyone had imagined, that the government was on the point of taking drastic measures.

'Does he mean that they are going to take everyone's property away from them?' I whispered to Sol as one of the speakers sat down. 'Surely they can't do that, can they?'

'Almost,' Sol replied grimly. 'It seems as if they are going to take over the banks, business . . . everything will be under strict government control. They are not actually taking our businesses away from us, but they will tell us what we can do and how much profit we can make for doing it.'

'That sounds serious.'

'It could ruin anyone who wasn't prepared for this . . .'

I heard the harsh note in Sol's voice and knew he was angry about what was happening. Like many others, he had been making considerable profits from his factory, and he was concerned about the future.

After dinner, the men huddled into groups, their faces reflecting anxiety, anger and fear. The ladies were talking amongst themselves, most of them obviously friends or at least on nodding acquaintance. I felt lost, out of my depth, though one or two smiled a friendly greeting in passing.

I held my head high as I went to the powder room, a pink and perfumed haven, where I touched a tiny puff to my shiny nose and applied a smear of lipstick. When I returned to the main reception room, there was no sign of Sol. I hesitated, wondering what to do next. Should I go in search of him, or wait for him to find me?

'Hi there,' a deep voice said from behind me. 'Do you by chance feel as lost as I do in this company of worthy men and their rather dull ladies? You wouldn't be American, I suppose?'

I swung round, feeling a jolt of surprise as I gazed up into a pair of dark eyes. Surely I had seen this man somewhere before?

'Sorry, I'm English,' I said. 'What made you think I might be American?'

'It was more a hope,' he said, giving me a rueful grin. 'And the dress, of course. It is fabulous. Where did you buy it?'

'It belongs to a friend,' I replied. 'I believe she bought it in Paris several years ago.'

'When it was all right to flaunt your wealth and style, before you all had to become patriotic. It looks wonderful on you,' he said. His eyes narrowed thoughtfully. 'By the way, I'm Jack Harvey . . . Have we met somewhere before?'

I took the hand he offered and laughed as I suddenly realized why he looked familiar. 'Well, sort of,' I said. 'I bumped into you one day in the street. I was reading a newspaper . . .'

'Of course!' He was still holding my hand, a look of amusement on his face. 'Yes, I remember you. I asked you out for a drink but you turned me down. It was the dress that threw me for a start – but I never forget a face. Especially such a lovely face as yours, Miss . . .?'

'*Mrs* Jonathan Reece,' I said and laughed as he looked disappointed. 'Emma to my friends. I'm pleased to meet you, Mr Harvey.'

'Jack to everyone,' he replied. 'Unless it's official business, of course. So how does one become your friend, Mrs Reece? How do I qualify?'

'I'm not sure,' I said, feeling that I had been hit by a whirlwind, and rather bemused. 'I suppose if we were introduced by someone we both knew . . . Why do you ask?'

'Who brought you tonight?'

'Sol . . . Solomon Gould,' I replied. 'As a matter of fact he has just come in. He is looking for me. Perhaps I should go . . .' I saw that he was smiling as if very amused about something. 'Why are you smiling like that – is something funny?'

'It just so happens I know Mr Gould,' he replied. 'We were talking a moment ago. I think we have business together . . .'

Sol came up to us then. His gaze narrowed as he looked at Jack Harvey. 'So . . .' he said. 'You've met Emma . . .'

'I introduced myself,' Jack replied. 'Mrs Reece is the most attractive lady in the room. I couldn't pass up the chance to say hi . . . besides, we have met before. Just briefly, haven't we, Mrs Reece?'

'Briefly, yes.'

Sol nodded. He seemed a little on edge about something. 'Have you thought any more about what I asked you?'

'I think we need to discuss it some more,' Jack replied. 'Perhaps we could meet somewhere . . . more private?'

'Come for dinner tomorrow?' Sol invited. 'My wife would be pleased to entertain you, Harvey.'

'Jack, please,' he said. 'I don't think we need to stand on ceremony with each other. It seems likely we'll do business, Sol . . .'

Sol looked surprised but pleased. 'That's what I like to hear, Jack. You know where I live, of course. We'll see you tomorrow then, at seven-thirty.' He glanced at me. 'Would you like to go now, Emma?'

'Yes please, if you're ready.' I turned to Jack Harvey. 'It was nice meeting you, Mr Harvey.'

'And you, Mrs Reece.'

I tucked my arm through Sol's as we left the hotel together.

'Who is he? What kind of business is he in?'

'Mr Harvey is the business of making money,' Sol replied. 'His family owns a chain of fashion stores in America, but he's more what you would call an entrepreneur . . . has his fingers in a lot of pies: he knows a great many influential people. I've been trying to establish an outlet with his family's firm for my stock for years, but they've always turned me down flat. I offered Jack a deal this evening, but I thought he was going to turn me down again . . . something must have changed his mind. I wonder . . . ?'

'What kind of a deal, Sol?'

He shook his head. 'Just something that might protect our profits a little, Emma.'

'I'm not sure what you mean?'

'I want to invest some money with their firm,' Sol said as he took me out to the car. 'I have quite a bit of spare cash, Emma, money that I've been keeping out of the way. I knew things were going to get difficult in this country, and I didn't want to put all my eggs in one basket. If the war goes badly here, we could lose everything – but America will survive. I just need someone who is willing to take my cash out of the country and invest it in a business there.'

'Is that legal, Sol?'

'No . . . not now that the government is taking over the movement of funds and controlling all trading.'

'Would you be in trouble if this came out?'

'Yes . . .' Sol met my eyes. 'I'm taking a risk, but I trust Jack Harvey. I knew his father well years ago. He was reluctant to accept my money, but if he does . . . he will be fair with me.'

I nodded, but made no comment. What Sol was doing was wrong. The government needed to control the flow of money because the country needed all its resources. I suspected that some of Sol's money might have been made without the payment of taxes, and it worried me a little that he should take such risks, but it was not for me to comment.

Sol had taken me into his home and taught me a trade. He had invested my money in one of his businesses, and although I had not yet received any profits from the factory, I knew the money was being used wisely. When I wanted money it would be there for me. Sol would be scrupulous in his dealings with me, if not with the government.

I was silent as we drove home. Sol glanced at me once or twice, then frowned.

'Are you shocked, Emma? Think I'm a bit of a rogue?'

'No, I don't think that, Sol. You know I care for you too much to ever think that – but I'm a little worried, for your sake.'

'Don't be,' he said. 'In business you have to take risks, if you want to get somewhere that is. My money is earned honestly. Maybe I haven't paid all the taxes I should, but that's the game . . . most businessmen get away with what they can. I dare say I'm no worse and no better than most.'

'You're better than most men,' I replied and smiled at him. 'I know what you're doing is to protect Margaret and me too . . .'

'I like being rich,' Sol admitted. 'We're living in uneasy times, Emma. I don't intend to come out of this war without a penny to my name. I'm too old to start again.'

'Then do what you have to,' I said. I smiled at him, a wicked lift to the corners of my mouth. 'Just don't get caught, will you? I don't want anything bad to happen to you, Sol.'

'Bless you for that, my dear,' he said. 'Believe me, I know what I'm doing. If anyone can get money out, it's Jack Harvey . . .'

Margaret didn't know about the money Sol wanted to send out of the country. He had asked me not to tell her, and I gave him my word. I wouldn't have dreamed of telling her. I knew she would worry too much, and that wouldn't be good for her. The doctor had made it clear she ought not to be upset more than necessary.

She was pleased that we were to have a guest for dinner that evening, and remembered Mr Harvey's father.

'Yes, I do remember him. We met once in New York,' she said when we spoke the next morning. 'A charming gentleman, but quite ruthless, I think.' She smiled at me. 'I would tell you to be careful of Mr Harvey's son, Emma – except that I know you are quite safe from him or any other flirt. Your love for Jonathan will protect you.'

'Yes, of course,' I replied. 'Mr Harvey is very good-looking, no one could deny that – and he has such a direct manner. When you talk to him it feels as if you're caught up in whirlwind, but he could never be more than a friend. I love Jon and I always shall.'

Margaret nodded. 'I know that, dearest,' she said
and touched my cheek. 'So – did you enjoy yourself
last evening?'

'It was all right,' I replied. 'I was glad I was wearing
your dress. Mr Harvey thought it was rather special,
and I noticed several of the ladies looking at it when
they thought I wasn't aware of their interest.'

'Good. Would you like to borrow something else of
mine for this evening?'

'No, thank you,' I said. 'It is very kind of you, but
I have plenty of dresses I can wear for dinner at home.'

'Yes, I'm sure you have,' she said. 'But if ever you
do need something, for a special occasion . . . I have
several dresses that might fit you. A few adjustments
perhaps . . .'

I thanked her, but I couldn't imagine wanting to
borrow clothes on my own account. The dress I had
worn the previous evening was lovely, but it had made
me look like someone else. I wanted to look like myself
when Mr Harvey came to dinner.

He had asked me how he could become my friend,
but it was the girl in the blue velvet dress he had
wanted to know. When he saw me as I truly was,
perhaps he would lose interest – and that might be the
best for all of us.

I wore one of my plainest dresses that evening. It was
grey with a gored skirt and a buttoned-up bodice. The
collar was white, and very demure. I saw Mr Harvey
smile as he saw me, a smile that seemed to mock and

challenge me, as if he were trying to tell me that I could not deceive him by wearing a dress that I knew did nothing for me.

Before dinner we had drinks, and Mr Harvey sat beside me on the sofa nursing his glass of sherry.

'So, Mrs Reece,' he murmured, a hint of mischief in his voice. 'What do you do with yourself all day? Have you given up your work? I seem to remember you saying that you went to work . . .'

'I work for Sol,' I replied, frowning at him. He knew I was married. He had no right to look at me in that way, as if he thought I might be prepared to flirt with him. 'I have been learning the trade. And when I come home at night, I play with my son.'

That made him pause for thought, but after a moment he nodded.

'So you have been married twice,' he said, assessing me with his eyes. 'You were a widow – and now you work in the Portobello Road. At Sol's showroom or the workshop?'

'I've been working at the back, learning to cut and make up the dresses.'

'And are you any good?' he asked, brows rising. 'Do you enjoy your work, Mrs Reece?'

'Emma is more than an employee,' Sol said, coming to my rescue at that moment. 'She is a partner in the factory. She had some money left to her, and I invested it on her behalf. It is Emma's interests I need to protect, as well as my own.'

'Is that true?' Mr Harvey raised his brows.

'I leave the business side of things to Sol,' I replied. 'One day I may go into business for myself, but not just yet. At the moment I have too much to learn.'

He nodded, his gaze narrowed, eyes intent on my face. 'And what sort of business would that be, Mrs Reece?'

'Perhaps the same as your family,' I replied. 'Retailing rather than manufacturing.'

'You haven't mentioned that to me,' Sol said, looking interested. 'Set your mind on a chain of fashion shops, have you? I rather like the sound of that, Emma. Shall you make me your partner?'

'Perhaps – one day,' I said. 'It may depend on what Jon thinks when the time comes.'

'And Jon is your husband?' Jack Harvey asked.

'Yes.' I raised my head slightly. 'He is in the air force at the moment, but I'm not sure what he will want to do when the war is over. He may want to live in the country.'

'But you will do whatever he thinks right?'

'Of course . . . isn't that what wives do?'

'Yes, of course it is,' Margaret said. 'Mr Harvey, I forbid you to tease Emma. You are making her blush.'

'But she blushes so delightfully,' Jack Harvey said, then grinned. 'Forgive me, Mrs Reece. I confess I was teasing you a little. It is my nature. I like to push people, to see how far they will go . . .'

'In what way, Mr Harvey?'

'In whatever way they choose, of course.'

The housekeeper came in at that moment and announced that dinner was served. Mr Harvey got to his feet immediately, and offered his arm to Margaret. Sol escorted me, speaking to me softly as we followed on behind.

'Humour him, Emma, for my sake. I want this deal if I can get it – but don't let him upset you. I would rather throw him out now – if you can't put up with him?'

'I am not in the least disturbed,' I replied. 'Mr Harvey means nothing to me one way or the other.'

'Good, that's what I wanted to hear.' Sol smiled at me. 'He means no harm, Emma. It's just his way.'

'Yes, of course,' I said. 'Don't worry, Sol. I shan't say anything to upset him.'

It seemed however that Mr Harvey had decided enough was enough. Throughout the rest of that evening, he behaved with perfect propriety, and at the end of it he smiled as he said goodbye to me.

'I am returning to New York the day after tomorrow,' he said. 'It was a pleasure to meet you, Mrs Reece. Perhaps we shall meet again when I return?'

'Are you intending to return, Mr Harvey?'

'Oh yes,' he replied, a faint twist to his mouth. 'I have unfinished business here, and I never give up once I have set my mind to something. Believe me, Mrs Reece. I am very determined.'

'I imagine that is a quality much needed in business,' I said. 'I think it is one I shall strive to acquire.'

'I would think you are already quite a determined young woman,' he murmured. 'But that is something I may yet discover.'

'Perhaps when you return?'

'Yes, quite possibly.' I offered my hand but instead of shaking it, he lifted it to his lips and kissed it, just briefly. 'I shall look forward to our next meeting, Mrs Reece.'

'Then I can only wish you a safe journey.'

He nodded, and turned to Sol. As the two men went out into the hall together, Margaret looked at me and smiled.

'I believe you may have made a conquest, Emma.'

'Please do not say so,' I begged. 'I have no desire to draw Mr Harvey's attentions on myself.'

'There is really no harm in his admiring you,' Margaret said. 'Providing you are aware of the dangers involved.'

'What dangers?' I tossed back my hair, smiling at her confidently. 'I love my husband, Margaret. Mr Harvey means nothing to me and never will.'

Sol came back to us at that moment. He walked over to kiss Margaret on the cheek, then glanced at me, a look of triumph in his eyes.

'Thanks to you, Emma, I think we are all going to be rather more wealthy than we are at the moment.'

'What do you mean?' Margaret asked, eyeing him curiously.

'You know I've always wanted to do business with the Harveys, well, now it seems that they are interested at last.' He smiled at me. 'When the war is over, big things are going to happen, Emma.'

'When the war is over,' Margaret said. 'I only wish it were, Sol!'

'It will be one day,' Sol told her. 'We have only to be patient. Things may be difficult for a while, but I have every confidence in the future.'

I took that to mean that Sol had managed to persuade Mr Harvey to do what he wanted, and I wondered how much of a part I had played in that decision. I hoped it was very small. I did not wish to think myself obligated to the American, charming though he was – nor did I wish him to become involved in something illegal for my sake.

But perhaps it was only a small crime. The loss of Sol's unpaid taxes would not bring the country to its knees. Nor should it cause harm to Mr Harvey himself. After all, what could it matter if Sol transferred some money to America? I did not suppose Mr Harvey would have agreed to take the cash out of the country if he thought there was any danger of his being caught.

The telephone rang in the hall at that moment. It was answered by Mrs Rowan, and then she came into the sitting room to fetch me.

'It's your husband, Mrs Reece.'

'Jon – on the telephone?' I ran into the hall, my heart racing. 'Jon – is that you? Are you all right?'

'I'm fine, Emma. I just wanted to tell you that I have a thirty-six-hour pass for this weekend. I'll be home about twelve on Saturday.'

'Oh, Jon,' I cried. 'That's wonderful! I'm so pleased, darling.'

'I have to go,' he said. 'Don't forget I shall be thinking of you, darling. I'll see you on Saturday.'

'Yes, please. Bye . . .'

I was smiling as I went to say goodnight to Sol and Margaret. Jon was coming home for the weekend, and everything was just as it ought to be. Already I was forgetting the man who had come to dinner . . .

Jon took me dancing that weekend. He seemed happy, relaxed, free of the shadows that had haunted him on the last night we had been together. Yet there was still that reluctance to talk about the war.

'What have you been doing, darling?' he asked as we lay side by side later that night. 'Keeping busy, I expect?'

'Oh yes, we're always busy at the workshop. Sol seems to be able to get hold of the materials we need, though things may change over the next few months.'

'Have you been anywhere nice?'

'I went to a civic reception with Sol one evening. Margaret lent me a special dress – but it was boring really. I only went because Margaret didn't feel well enough.'

'Yes, I noticed she seemed tired . . .'

The subject was turned and we talked of other things. I wasn't sure why I hadn't told him about Jack Harvey. There was no reason why I should not have mentioned him, but somehow I didn't and the opportunity passed.

Jon made love to me that night, and as usual it left me feeling warm and contented inside. My only regret was that my husband's leave was over far too soon.

Again, he asked me not to go to the station with

him. I let him go alone. Parting was no easier than it
had been the first time, but I did not feel quite so
frightened as I had then. I knew that Jon had flown
several missions now and come back safely. I prayed
that he would continue to do so, but I had realized it
was best not to dwell on such thoughts.

Instead, I put most of my energy into learning everything I could about Sol's business. I was spending much
of my time in the showroom now, getting to know the
customers and their likes and dislikes. I could greet
them by name now as Sol did, and I enjoyed talking
to those who came regularly to buy from us, making
sure that I always asked about their families. They came
from all walks of life, and different parts of the country,
some with shops in London, others with small country
businesses. They always had time for a chat and a cup
of coffee, and I counted many of them as friends.

It was a busy life, a full life, but I made time for
my son and Mrs Reece, telephoning at least once a
week and taking James to visit every other Sunday.

I had offered to help Sol with the accounts, but as
yet he had not taken me up on my offer. I suspected
there might be a reason for his reluctance. I believed
Sol kept two sets of books, one for his accountant's
benefit and one for his own.

He would not involve me in anything not quite legal,
of course. I had heard nothing more of his business
arrangements with Jack Harvey. I believed they had
come to some agreement between them, but I could
not know for certain. Nor did I truly wish to.

I was happy the way things were, working, learning and playing with my son. Jon's visits were the highlights of my life. I looked forward to them, but did not let them become my whole existence.

The war continued and the papers seemed to be full of bad news, of ships sunk and battles won or lost.

When I read that our soldiers had been encircled on the French coast, I feared the worst, but when I learned of the heroic rescue of our brave men, much of it by little ships and ordinary people, who had taken their boats across the Channel to do what they could, I wept tears of joy and pride.

I was proud to be British then, and I began to think that perhaps it was time I did something to help in the war effort. Many women were beginning to work in munitions factories and all kinds of jobs they would never have considered before the war. I discussed it with Jon when he came home on leave, and with Sol. Neither of them thought it was necessary for me to work anywhere else, but I felt that I wanted to do something.

Surprisingly, it was Mrs Reece who came up with the suggestion that satisfied all of us.

'Some of us are getting together to entertain the troops,' she told me when I visited one Sunday. We are going to have concerts, dances, and provide tea and hot meals for the men. We shall need teams of volunteers for the catering side, Emma. I wondered if you would like to help us? You could spare us a few hours in the evenings, or at weekends – couldn't you?'

'Yes, of course,' I agreed at once. 'I should like to help.'

It was not quite the vital war work I had envisaged, but it was useful. We had quite a few men from the Canadian Air Force in Britain, and men from other countries – men who had been driven out of their homes by the German invaders, and had come to join us in our struggle. London must seem an unfriendly place to them sometimes, and anything we could do for them and our own men who were on leave was surely worthwhile.

The news continued to be bad. The Germans had marched into Paris, and invaded the Channel Islands, and now they were turning their attention to us as the bombs began to fall on London.

We had grown used to reading of men killed at sea and in battle, but now, quite suddenly, it was our own city at risk.

Night after night, the flames reached high into the sky as the docks were attacked and wave after wave of enemy planes came over. The destruction in London was terrible to see, rows of houses disappearing in a few hours, heart-rending and very frightening.

My mother telephoned, begging me to go home and take James to her, but I refused to leave Sol and Margaret. Some people *had* left for the country, but most Londoners were sticking it out, their cheerful voices chattering away as they huddled in the underground when the sirens went, emerging into a grey dawn to find their homes destroyed and all their possessions gone.

Sol had built an Anderson shelter in the garden, and we all ran for it as soon as the first siren went, gathering up books, knitting and something to munch while we waited. At first it was terrifying, but after a while we began to make jokes, and take the bombing in our stride.

The battle for Britain was being won in the skies above us by our brave airmen, who were flying non-stop missions to try and protect us. I worried for Jon during those tense weeks, my heart in my mouth every time the telephone rang or the postman came to the door, but the weeks passed and there was no official telegram, no sympathetic message from a friend. Jon was too busy or too tired to telephone often himself, but now and then he managed a brief call.

'I love you, Emma. I think of you all the time, my darling.'

'I love you, Jon . . . so very much.'

'With luck I'll get a pass soon . . . but we can't get away just yet.'

'No, of course not, darling.'

Nothing about the missions he was flying day after day, hour after hour. Just a few words to say he loved me and was missing me.

And then, all at once, we knew that the battle was won. Thirteen thousand civillians had been killed during the raids on London alone, but we had come through. The threat of invasion was seemingly over, and the bombing raids were suddenly less severe. It seemed that Hitler had decided he was wasting his time trying to flatten our cities. Now he had begun to turn his attention to the convoys in the Atlantic. If he couldn't bomb us into submission, he was going to try and starve us of all essential supplies.

It meant that there was endless queuing at the shops, and some things were becoming harder and harder to find, but somehow we all managed. Life went on much as it always had. We were all determined that Hitler was not going to beat us.

And so the months passed away, and it was almost Christmas. It was then that I received a letter from a Miss Gwendoline Robinson.

'*Forgive me for taking the liberty of writing to you,*' she began.

I did try to contact you through our solicitor some months ago, but I have heard nothing and I wondered if you ever received the letter? It is my belief that you are my brother's daughter. My brother was Harold Robinson. I know that he lived in a town called March in Cambridgeshire for many years and ran a newsagent and tobacconist shop there. I thought perhaps you might wish to know that my mother is still alive, though an invalid. We have recently moved nearer to London, and I wondered if you would consider visiting us one day . . .

I remembered the letter my mother had given me months ago, and felt guilty. It was still in the pocket of the coat I had worn that day. I had intended to send it to my own lawyers and ask them to find out what they could, but somehow it had been forgotten in the excitement of my wedding and everything that had happened since.

Somehow Miss Robinson had discovered where I was living and had decided to write to me personally.

I glanced at the address, which was in Hertfordshire, a village called Aldbury. I was not sure how I would be able to get to such a place, which might be miles from anywhere, nor was I certain I wished to visit these relatives of my father. If Miss Robinson had known where my father lived all those years, why had she never tried to contact us before his death?

And yet perhaps she had, perhaps it was my father who had wished to keep his secrets to himself. Yes, that was very much more likely. Harold Robinson had been a man who liked to keep his own counsel.

I thought about her letter for a week or two, turning it over in my mind. In the end I decided to write to Miss Gwendoline Robinson and tell her that I did not think I could visit at the moment, but that if she would care to come to London I would find the time to see her . . .

Chapter 4

'I told you,' my mother said when Sol took me to visit her the next week. 'This Gwendoline . . . she wants something, Emma. She wouldn't have written unless she had good reason.'

'You can't know that, Mum,' I said, breaking a piece of her special fatless sponge and feeding it to James. 'She might just want to know me. She is Father's sister – and her mother is my grandmother. I think I might like to know more about them.'

'You're not thinking of visiting them, Emma?'

'I've told her I can't, not for the moment. I just haven't got time – and nor has Sol. We've only come today because there was a small fire at the factory. Sol was worried. He wanted to assess the damage for himself. I think some bales of material may have been spoiled. He has to account for every little thing these days. The government inspectors are so strict. It makes lots more paperwork for Sol.'

'Well, why don't you help him out, Emma? You kept the accounts for your father for years.'

'I would if Sol would let me,' I said. 'But I don't have much time to spare myself, Mum.'

I had never told her anything about the financial side of Sol's business. She might have frowned over some of his methods, though to be honest she wasn't above a little trading on the black market herself. We never visited without taking back bacon, eggs and a slab of fresh farm butter, none of which had ever seen a Food Ministry stamp! So although she could not exactly hold the moral high ground, I kept my silence. Whatever Sol chose to do was not my business.

I knew that he would never rob or harm anyone. His behaviour could be called unpatriotic, and was perhaps a little shady at times, but he was not a bad man. I was very fond of him, and still grateful for all the kindness he had shown me.

Sol was my friend. Those weeks of dreadful bombing, when we had all sheltered together, never knowing if that night would be our last, had formed a special bond between us. I would stand by him no matter what.

'Have you heard about Sheila's husband?' Mother asked, bringing me abruptly from my reverie. 'He was rushed into hospital the night before last.'

'Oh, no!' I cried, looking at her in alarm. 'I haven't heard from Sheila for a few weeks. I was going to ask if I could leave James with you and pop along to see her?'

'Of course I'll have James. I don't see enough of him.'

'You could come and stay for a few days, Mum. Margaret would be pleased to see you.'

'Perhaps I shall one day,' she said, surprising me. 'Bert wouldn't mind. He has suggested it more than once.'

'Then come,' I said. 'I would love you to. And now, I shall go to see Sheila. She must be worried to death, with the shop to see to and a young baby . . .'

Sheila was serving a customer when I arrived. She looked as if she hadn't slept all night, her eyes shadowed and her nose red from crying.

'Oh, Emma,' she said as soon as her customer had left. 'I'm so glad to see you. Eric is in hospital. They've told me . . . he may have consumption.'

'Sheila, I'm so sorry,' I said. 'That's terrible. You must be so worried about him, and you were getting on so nicely. Is there anything I can do? How will you manage?'

'My cousin Alice has offered to come and stay, so she will look after the baby. I can just about manage the shop alone if I have to.' She gave me an anxious look. 'I don't want to give it up, Emma. This shop was a chance for us to make something of our lives.'

'Why should you give up? If your cousin helps you, you can manage. It's going to be hard work, but there must be a young boy or girl who could come in on a Saturday – and perhaps after school. You could ask around or put a card in the window.'

'Yes, that's what I thought.' She bit her lip. 'I had to pay some bills this week, Emma. Eric hadn't been well and he had let them mount up. It means I'm short in the rent . . . I can make it up next week, though.'

'How much are you short?'

'Ten shillings . . .'

I opened my bag and gave her a pound note. 'Give the rent to Mr Smythe as usual. You can pay Mum the ten shillings when you've got it to spare, the other is a present for the baby. And you don't have to pay Mum the money next week. You might need money for visiting the hospital. If you need anything, Sheila, let me know. I'll do whatever I can to help.'

Her eyes were moist with tears. 'You've always been a good friend to me, Emma.' She caught back a sob. 'I don't know what I shall do if anything happens to Eric.'

'Nothing will happen,' I said. 'He may have to go away to a sanatorium, though. It might mean you won't be able to see him very often.'

'Yes . . .' She nodded, looking thoughtful. 'The doctor said they might send him to a special place near the sea. The air would be better for him there.'

'Let's hope it's just his bronchitis,' I said. 'I'll say a prayer for all of you, Sheila.'

She smiled and thanked me. Another customer came in then, and I left her after promising to write.

I visited Madge Henty next. Madge had heard about Sheila's husband and promised to keep an eye out for her. We talked about the business, which was ticking over nicely. We were too small to be bothered much by all the new regulations, though of course we had to adhere to them.

'They won't bother me much,' Madge said. 'I reckon they've got bigger fish to fry. I've heard it said there's been some terrible rackets going on. Some folk should be ashamed of themselves!'

'You mean some firms were making excessive profits out of government contracts? And overcharging for goods, yes, I know. It does go on. I've seen it in London shops.' She nodded, making a tutting noise. 'I think that's part of the reason for the clampdown, Madge. We all have to account for every penny now.'

'There's ways and means,' Madge said. 'I read about a load of meat that was supposed to have been contaminated by a flood in a basement store. It was all nonsense. They were selling it out the back door the next morning.'

'Well, I'm sure they will be caught,' I said. 'Some people will get away with things for a while, but in the end they will find themselves in trouble.'

'They deserve it,' Madge said, looking cross. 'I've always been honest, Emma. I don't hold with racketeering.'

'It isn't right,' I agreed. 'Not when everyone is having to cut down – but people do things, Madge. It's human nature to get away with a bit here and there if you can.'

She nodded, then laughed. 'Well, I must admit I wouldn't say no to a packet of sugar under the counter! And I wouldn't mind if it did cost me a bit extra. I can't do without my sugar.'

'There you are then.'

We laughed, had a cup of tea, and then I walked back to my mother's house. I was a little anxious as I thought about the fire at the factory. Surely it *was* genuine? Sol wouldn't try to make extra profit by pretending material had been ruined . . . would he?

No, of course he wouldn't! I dismissed the idea as unworthy and forgot about it.

It was the following Saturday evening. A dance was in progress in the next room, and I was busy preparing the Spam sandwiches and jugs of orange squash we were offering as refreshments that evening. We were also fortunate in having tinned fruit salad, which had been donated to us by an American benefactor.

'Two cases of it arrived this morning,' Pamela Marsh told me. 'They came off an American ship so I've been told – and our name was on the label. Fancy that, Emma. All the way from America, and specially for us.'

I looked at the woman who was sharing the evening shift with me.

'That can't be right,' I said. 'The consignment must have come from America, and then someone in authority here decided we should be given a share.'

'Yes, I expect you're right,' she said. 'I don't suppose anyone in America even knows our little organisation exists.'

'Why should they?'

She nodded in agreement, and we carried on spreading the mixture of margarine and butter very thinly on the bread.

'Do you think we've done enough?' she asked after a while. 'Only, I've run out of Spam. It means opening another tin.'

'We'll take these through and see what happens. We

can make some more if they get eaten. But once we put the tinned fruit out, everyone will leave the Spam – at least, they will if they are as bored with it as we are.'

Pamela laughed and agreed. 'It does get you down a bit, but it beats the whale meat I had at Lyons the other day. I've never tasted anything so awful, Emma. It was like eating old boots. I think I would rather go hungry!'

We picked up our trays of sandwiches. Some were with mustard or brown sauce to make them more interesting. Others had a slice of pickled onion on top of the meat. We did our best with the supplies we were given, much of it donated by friends, people who had managed to scrounge a little extra food from somewhere and wanted to share it with the brave men who were doing so much for us.

The music had stopped for a while when we carried in the refreshments. The quartet had gone off for a welcome cup of tea, and the various soldiers, sailors and airmen were talking to the girls they had met that evening. Most of the men came alone. It was to help newcomers find friends that our social club had been set up, and it was proving popular.

We held dances each Saturday. In the week there were concerts or social evenings. We had dart boards, table tennis and a pool table in the adjoining room. It was somewhere for the men to come, and there were always a few single girls to keep them company.

'Hi . . .' The deep voice behind me made me jump.

I gave a cry of surprise as I turned to see Jack Harvey. He was dressed in a smart grey business suit, which looked somehow out of place in the dance hall. 'Sol told me I might find you here this evening. I see you got the tinned fruit all right.'

'Did you send us that?' He nodded. 'That was thoughtful of you, Mr Harvey.'

'Sol thought it might come in useful.'

'Is that what you've been doing all these months? Arranging to send us things we need?'

'Something like that,' he replied with a grin. 'We can't have our British cousins starving, can we?'

'At least your ship got through,' I said. 'A lot of ours are being attacked and sunk now.'

'Unfortunate, but I shouldn't worry too much. They can't get them all, and my ships sail under the American flag. This is a private venture, nothing to do with government. Besides, we aren't at war with Germany yet.'

'No, you aren't, are you?'

He frowned, a glint of annoyance in his eyes. 'Does that mean you think we ought to be?'

'Perhaps . . .' I shook my head. 'No, I won't get into an argument with you over it, Jack. I'm grateful for what you sent us – and it's nice to see you again.'

His eyes were suddenly bright with laughter. 'Does this mean I can call you Emma now? Have I been promoted to the rank of friend?'

'Well, I think you might be,' I said. 'Especially if I can scrounge some more food for our men when your next ship comes in, Jack – or even now if there's any going spare.'

'I like the way you do business,' he said. 'Sol told me you were more than just a pretty face.'

'Oh did he,' I said, frowning at him. 'I'm not sure I like that. Why were you discussing me at all?'

'Now don't get touchy,' Jack said, and grinned in a way that disarmed me. 'I just happened to ask Sol how he came to know you, that's all. I was curious about you.'

'You could have asked me what you wanted to know.'

'Could I?' His brows rose. 'I wasn't sure you would welcome my interest.'

'I didn't know you,' I said. 'I am only just beginning to know you now.'

'But you would like to know me better?'

'I didn't say that . . .' I laughed as I saw his expression. 'Don't look at me like that, Jack. You know I'm married . . . happily married.'

'But I can be your friend?' He was serious now. 'I would like that, Emma. I do have some influence in this country. I've been useful to your government in various ways, and there are people who owe me a few favours. If there's anything I can do . . . pull a few strings or wangle something for you . . .'

'Get thee behind me Satan!' I said, shaking my head at him. 'Thank you for the offer, Jack, but I don't need that kind of a favour, at least not for myself – any donations of food to the club are always welcome, of course.'

'Got you,' Jack said. He arched his brows as the musicians began to play again. 'Any chance of you dancing with me?'

'Well . . . I don't see why not . . .'

I was on the verge of saying yes when Pamela came hurrying towards me. Something in her manner told me that she had bad news and I felt a shiver go down my spine.

'What's wrong, Pam?'

'Mr Gould telephoned,' she said. 'You have to go home, Emma. He wouldn't tell me what was wrong, but he said to send you home immediately.'

I felt the room spin round me, and I must have gone white because Jack caught my arm as I swayed. I blinked, then took a deep breath as my vision cleared.

'I'll get my coat . . .' I turned and looked at the man still gripping my arm. 'Jack . . . will you take me home?'

'Of course,' he said. 'I have my car outside. Don't worry, Emma. It's probably nothing.'

'No . . .' I took a deep breath. 'Sol wouldn't have rung me if it wasn't urgent.'

My heart was racing as I fetched my coat. I tried to apologize to Pamela for leaving her with all the washing up, but she told me not to worry.

'What I can't manage, I'll leave for the morning shift,' she assured me. 'I hope it isn't too bad, Emma.'

I nodded but couldn't bring myself to speak. I knew instinctively that it was something that would change my life . . .

*

'I'm so sorry, Emma,' Margaret said as she handed me the telegram. 'It came an hour ago. I waited until Sol got home . . .' Jon's plane was shot down over France last night. They don't know whether he got out in time or not . . .'

'Jon . . .' I gasped, feeling as if I had been punched in the stomach. 'Jon's plane . . . went down over France . . .'

I swayed and might have fallen if Jack Harvey had not been there to catch my arm. He steadied me, then led me to a chair and made me sit down. I sat forward, my face in my hands as I tried to take in what Margaret was saying. My husband's plane had been shot down. It was my worst nightmare, the one thing I had never allowed myself to think about.

'Breathe deeply,' a voice was saying. 'You'll be better in a minute.'

'How can I be better?' I cried, lifting my head to glare at Jack Harvey accusingly. 'I shall never be better – my husband . . .' I choked on the words as the sob broke from me and then the tears coursed down my cheeks. 'Jon . . . my darling Jon . . .'

I couldn't believe that I would never see him again, never feel his touch or have him hold me close. He had given me so much love, and our time together had been so brief. He was a kind, gentle man who hated this war, and he didn't deserve to die this way. The pain was unbearable, overwhelming. I wanted to die, because life without Jon would be so empty.

'He's missing, Emma,' Sol's voice came to me

through the pain. 'You don't know that he was killed. He may have got out . . . I rang a friend of mine at the War Office and asked for more details. He told me one parachute was seen after the plane was hit . . . it could have been Jon . . . he may be alive.'

'Only one . . .' I choked. 'That means the rest of the crew . . .'

'Stop it, Emma!' Jack Harvey said sharply. 'Stop that right now. Your husband is missing. You can't change that, but it doesn't mean you have to stop hoping.'

'No . . . it doesn't mean I have to stop hoping.' He had got through to me somehow. I looked at him eagerly, then at Sol and Margaret. 'Jon is missing in action – that doesn't mean he is dead, does it? He could have got out, even if no one saw him . . .'

'I shouldn't let yourself hope too much, dearest,' Margaret warned softly. Her eyes were sad, filled with love. 'But you don't have to give up just yet.'

'What will happen?' I asked. 'If he is alive and in France . . .'

'Someone may be able to get him out, or at least hide him,' Sol said. 'It is happening all the time, Emma. Just because the Germans have taken over the country, it doesn't mean all the French have surrendered. I happen to know that there is a strong resistance going on there.'

'Then Jon could come home?'

I looked at their faces, and I knew that not one of them really believed it. But I was going to cling to that hope. I couldn't give up on Jon. Only if I carried that hope in my breast would he have a chance of coming back to me. It was a foolish superstition, but I had to hold on to it. I had to believe that one day Jon would return to claim me.

I stood up, lifting my head, facing them proudly. The shock had made me weak, but I was strong now. I had been hurt before. I had faced despair and grief and come through it, and I would this time. I refused to believe that Jon was dead. He couldn't be, mustn't be, because I needed him so much.

'I'm sorry,' I said. 'I'm going upstairs. I need to be alone.'

No one spoke. I was conscious of them all watching me as I went out of the room. They all believed Jon was dead, but I couldn't. To accept that he was gone for ever would be unbearable.

I didn't cry as I lay on my bed staring at the ceiling. I just thought about Jon, about the wonderful times we had spent together, so few of them I could almost count them on my fingers.

'Come back to me, Jon,' I whispered into the darkness. 'Please come back to me, my darling. I love you . . . need you . . . so much.'

I tried not to think of what might be happening in France. What did German patrols do if they found an airman who had been shot down? Would they arrest him . . . put him in a camp for prisoners of war? Or would they shoot him down where he stood? No, surely not – not if he surrendered without a fight.

Jon wouldn't try to fight. I believed that he would

surrender and wait out the war in . . . wherever they sent him. Perhaps to a camp in Germany. I felt chilled as I thought of my beloved husband being shut away for months or even years. Who knew how long this wretched war would go on?

Perhaps he would be found by the French resistance. Perhaps someone would hide him, and he might be able to get home somehow. Was it possible? Sol said it had happened, was happening . . . but he might have said that to comfort me, because he had known I couldn't bear my loss.

Jon might be dead . . . or injured. I curled up in a ball as the pain struck inside me. It was almost worse to think of him badly injured than dead. The misery was like a tight, hard stone in my guts. I felt as if I were dying of some dreadful disease, as if my body were being stuck with hot needles.

Jon must feel so lost, so alone. If he was alive . . . but I had to believe it had been his parachute another pilot had reported having seen. I had to believe it!

Would the War Ministry know if the Germans had taken him prisoner? Did they get lists of men held in camps? Could someone find out for me?

Jack Harvey had hinted that he could pull all kinds of strings. Perhaps in time . . . weeks or months . . . he might be able to find out something for me.

'Oh, Jon my darling,' I whispered over and over again as a prayer. 'Live! Live for me, my love. Come home to me. I want you to come home.'

*

'I can't believe it,' Mrs Reece sobbed into her handkerchief. 'I can't believe our Jon is dead . . . it isn't fair. He never wanted this war. Why him? Why my son?'

'Now then, Dorothy, stop that, my dear.' Pops laid a hand on her shoulder. 'You know what Emma said just now. We don't know for certain that Jon is dead. They think at least one man parachuted out; it could have been Jon.'

She shook her head, looking at me with her sad eyes. 'Emma wanted to give us hope,' she said, dabbing a lace handkerchief to her cheeks. 'But I know Jon is dead. I've felt something bad was going to happen for weeks now. I know . . .'

'You can't know,' I said. I was irritated by her weeping. She was giving up too soon. I wanted to shout at her, but I would never forgive myself if I did. 'I shan't give up hoping. I'm going to ask a friend of mine to make inquiries. If Jon has been arrested by the Germans . . .' I paused as she gave a shriek of alarm. 'Yes, I know. I know – but it's better than him being dead. If he is a prisoner he will survive. I know Jon. He will keep his head down and do whatever he has to . . .'

'Yes, you're right,' Pops said, looking at me keenly. 'If Jon were to be taken prisoner, he would survive. He would accept what had happened and do what he had to until the war ends.'

'And when will that be?' Mrs Reece asked bitterly. 'From what I can see of things we'll be at war for years . . . until they finally grind us to our knees and we have to surrender. Why they had to start this terrible war in the first place I don't know. I don't understand what it is all about. I don't know why we have to suffer like this . . .'

'The government didn't have a choice,' Pops said, shaking his head at me from behind his daughter's back. 'You mustn't be a defeatist, Dorothy. I know things look black just now, and it may take us years – but we're going to win.'

'Yes, we'll win,' I said, lifting my head to look at him, smiling in spite of the pain in my heart. 'We'll win and Jon will come home. I know it – I feel it . . .'

'You are so calm,' Mrs Reece said, a flash of anger in her eyes as she looked at me. 'I don't know how you can take this so calmly, Emma. But of course, you have so much more in your life. Jon was all I had . . .'

'Now that's not fair,' Pops said, and he gave her a stern look. 'Emma is doing what she has to do, just as we shall. I think you should apologize to her, Dorothy.'

For a moment I thought she would refuse, then she went pink and dropped her gaze, looking at her hands as she twisted them in her lap.

'I'm sorry, Emma. I shouldn't have said that. I know you are upset – of course you are.'

'It's breaking my heart,' I said. 'But I'm not going to give up on Jon, Mrs Reece. If I do that he won't come home . . .'

She lifted her head and looked me in the eyes, then nodded. 'You are right,' she said. 'We have to keep him alive in our hearts . . . whether he comes back or not.'

I got up and went to kiss her.

'He will come back,' I said. 'I promise you, Mother – he will come back to us.'

'I had to come up,' my mother said, as she embraced me. She was crying, trembling as she held me close. 'I couldn't bear to think of you facing this alone . . . my poor Emma. You've had so little time with him. And you were so happy. It just isn't fair . . .'

'What we had was worth fifty years of the kind of marriage I would have had with Richard,' I said. 'Jon was special, Mum. No, he *is* special. I'm not going to give up on him. I know he's alive, and he's going to come back to me one day.'

'Oh, Emma . . .' My mother looked at me sadly. 'I wish you would accept the truth, dearest. Jon's plane was shot down. It is most unlikely that he survived the crash.'

'They believe someone got out . . . a parachute was seen . . .'

'They think someone *might* have got out,' Mum said. 'It hasn't been confirmed officially, has it? You only have Sol's word that one man might have bailed out.'

'Sol wouldn't lie . . . not about something like that.' I raised my head. 'Besides, he doesn't believe it was

Jon. He is just like you, Mum. He thinks I should accept that Jon has . . . gone. But I can't. I don't want to. I love him and he has to come back to me.'

'Supposing he doesn't, Emma?' Her eyes met mine, forcing me to acknowledge what she was saying. 'I'm not saying you should give up all hope yet – just don't bank on it, dearest. Jon wouldn't want you to live alone all your life . . .'

'Don't!' I held my hand up, warning her to be silent. 'I don't want to hear this, Mum. I refuse to even think about it.'

'No, of course not. It's much too soon. Forgive me. I just don't like to see you this way . . .'

'I'm all right. Honestly. I'm still going to work, and I'm going to start back at the social club next week. I know life has to go on, Mum. Jon would expect me to carry on as usual . . .'

'Yes, you carry on,' my mother said, nodding to herself. 'Maybe that's best. Just carry on the way you always do. You'll get through this, Emma.'

'Yes, of course I shall. It's just a case of waiting . . .'

But the waiting was so hard, and the nights were filled with fear and pain. It wouldn't be so bad if I could just hear something . . . a confirmation that Jon had been taken prisoner perhaps.

'Emma, I think . . .'

Our conversation was interrupted at that moment by Mrs Rowan. She came into the room, hesitating before speaking.

'I am sorry to disturb you, Mrs Reece, but Mr Harvey

is here. He would like to speak with you . . . Shall I tell him you are busy?'

'No . . .' I said. 'Please ask him to come in.'

My mother looked at me as the housekeeper departed. 'Who is Mr Harvey?'

'A friend of Sol's,' I replied. 'I asked him to call, Mum.'

'Why, Emma?' She turned as Jack entered, the question unanswered.

'I'm sorry I couldn't come before,' Jack said. 'I've been rather tied up, Emma . . .' He glanced at my mother. 'I'm sorry. I didn't realize you had company.'

'This is my mother,' I said. 'Mrs Fitch . . . Mum, this is Mr Harvey. I asked him to call because I'm going to ask him if he will help me.'

'Emma . . .' she said. 'Oh, Emma . . .'

'You know I will do whatever I can,' Jack said, his eyes meeting mine across the room. 'But I think I can guess, Emma. You want me to find out what I can . . . about Jon. That's it, isn't it?'

'Yes, please,' I said. 'I know it's early days yet, Jack – but Sol can't find out anything more. He has tried, but they just keep telling him they don't know. I thought . . . perhaps there might be some way to cut through red tape . . .'

'Your government probably doesn't know anything,' Jack said, 'but there are people who can find out these things. It may take months. If Jon is in a camp . . . even a year or longer . . .'

'Yes, I know that,' I said. 'But if there is any way to find out for certain . . .'

'It can be done,' Jack said. 'I know people. I'll set things in motion. But you will have to be patient, Emma.'

'Yes, of course. Just as long as I know someone is trying . . .'

Jack's eyes met mine. 'It gives you hope, and that helps.'

'Thank you for understanding,' I said and he smiled at me.

'That's what friends are for,' he said; then he came to take my hand in his. 'I'll do what I can, Emma. I promise you. If Jon is in a camp, I'll find out somehow . . .'

'It's all I ask,' I said. I raised my head, gazing into his eyes. 'I know I have no right to ask anything, but I should be so grateful . . .'

'You can ask me for anything you want,' Jack said, and grinned at me. 'I'm leaving for America tomorrow, Emma. I may be away for months. If you don't hear anything, don't think I've given up. I shan't forget you. Remember that always.'

'Yes . . .' I felt my cheeks go pink and took my hand from his. The expression in his eyes and the warmth in his voice was too revealing. 'Thank you, Jack. Thank you for being my friend . . .'

'I'll be seeing you,' he said. 'Keep your chin up, Emma. If life kicks you in the guts, kick it back – that's what I do.' He was grinning as he gave me a swift kiss on the lips; then he turned to my mother. 'Look after her, Mrs Fitch. Just until I come back . . .'

I stood where I was as Jack walked from the room, feeling stunned. I had known Jack was interested from the moment we met at that reception, but I hadn't realized it went so deep with him. I'd thought he was the kind of man who enjoyed playing games, that he was merely flirting with me to pass the time.

'He's in love with you, Emma,' my mother said after a few moments in which neither of us had spoken.

'No, of course he isn't,' I said. 'We've only met a couple of times – and I hardly noticed him the first time.'

'All it takes is one look in some cases,' she said, and there was a hint of satisfaction in her eyes. I knew what she was thinking and I was angry.

'I love Jon,' I said. 'I shall always love him, Mum.'

'Always is a long time, Emma.'

'Please don't! I can't bear this. I asked Jack for his help, because he has all sorts of powerful friends. He is a rich man, Mum – a man from a wealthy, important family in America. They own a chain of fashion stores, and Jack has his fingers in all kinds of pies. Just remember who and what I am . . . even if I was interested, which I'm not.'

'Not now, of course not,' she said. 'Forgive me, Emma. I shouldn't have spoken my thoughts aloud – but that man does love you. And I doubt very much if he cares who or what your father was.'

'Which reminds me,' I said, changing the subject. She meant well, of course, but I didn't want to think about a future which did not include my darling Jon.

'I had another letter from Gwendoline. She says her mother has been ill, and she hasn't been able to leave her – but now Mrs Robinson is better again and she wants to come and see me. Gwendoline, that is, not her mother.'

'She wants something,' Mum warned. 'Believe me, Emma. I suppose you can't stop her coming if she wants – but don't give her money.'

'At the moment I don't have much to give her,' I said. 'Everything I have is tied up in some way. I only have what I earn and and a few pounds for emergencies. The profits from Madge's shop are a little extra now and then, but we've been putting most of it back into stock while we can.'

'Good.' Mum looked pleased. 'You can't give away what you haven't got. And she's coming to beg, Emma. I'd bet my last shilling on it.'

Chapter 5

Having my mother with me in London for the next few days helped me a lot. I think her being there reminded me of a time when I had been miserable once before. Somehow I had managed to get through that period of my life, and I was managing now. It hurt. It hurt desperately whenever I allowed myself to think about Jon, to wonder where he was and how he felt about what was happening to him.

My husband was a sensitive man who felt things keenly. I tried to think about his situation calmly. Would he find it humiliating to be taken prisoner – or would he be able to retreat inside that world in his head?

There was nothing I could do to change things, but the fact that Jon was missing made me more aware of how precious the people in my life really were. I began to spend more time at home with James, and as Christmas drew nearer, I took him to the big department stores to see the toys and decorations. There were no festive street lights, of course, but the shops had brought out the glitter and baubles in an effort to help their customers forget the shortages on their shelves.

Margaret came shopping with us sometimes. She

seemed a little better again, or she was pretending to be for Sol's sake. For James's present she bought a very grand wooden rocking horse with a red leather saddle and bridle studded with brass.

'It's bigger than he is,' I said, laughing as I saw the flush of excitement in her eyes and knew how much pleasure buying the horse had given her. 'You spoil him, Margaret – we all spoil him.'

'What harm can a little spoiling do? I'm just glad we were able to get the rocking horse. We were lucky to get such a nice one. I thought it might be impossible to buy anything of quality, but this must have been in stock for a while.' She smiled at me. 'Now – what can I give you, Emma? What would you like for yourself?'

'I don't mind – anything,' I said. 'Make it a surprise.'

'Yes, that would be more exciting.' She looked thoughtful. 'Shall we have a traditional Christmas, Emma? I wondered if you might prefer just a quiet day on our own?'

'That wouldn't be fair to James. This is the first time for him. Last year he didn't understand. This time he will know what presents are.'

'Then we'll just carry on as if . . .' She saw the flash of pain I could not quite conceal in my eyes. 'I'm sure it is what Jon would want, Emma.'

I blinked hard, refusing to let the tears fall. 'It is exactly what he would want. He told me once that I wasn't to waste my life if . . . anything happened.'

Margaret nodded but said nothing more. She believed

Jon was dead, but she never tried to impose her beliefs on me. Instead, she was gentle, supportive, there if I needed her. I understood now why Sol loved her so much, because I did too.

When we returned to the house that afternoon, Mrs Rowan told me that a woman had called to see me earlier.

'She said her name was Miss Robinson. She is staying in London for one night, and will call again in the morning.'

'What a pity we were out,' Margaret said. 'Had your aunt let us know, we could have been here to greet her. Did she say where she was staying, Mrs Rowan?'

'No, madam,' the housekeeper said. She looked at me. 'There is a parcel in your room, Mrs Reece. It was delivered by special messenger while you were out.'

'Thank you.'

I took James up to the nursery, kissed him, and delivered him into Nanny's hands. She was a woman of perhaps fifty, a little reserved, but devoted to her charge.

'I think we'll have some juice now, Master James.'

I smiled as she led him by the hand into the nursery. James was a very pampered and much-loved little boy. He had four women to fuss over him, and Sol was almost as bad. I hoped we were not guilty of spoiling him, but I was very much afraid we might be doing just that.

After leaving my son, I went down the short flight

of stairs to my own room, noticing that the carpet was beginning to fray in one place. I would mention it to Sol. It might be possible to have it repaired, because I was sure a carpet like this could not be replaced at the moment.

The parcel sitting on my bed was quite large. It was a stout cardboard box wrapped in brown paper and tied with string and red wax; it had several kinds of official stamps all over it – one of them American.

My heart jerked oddly. I knew at once who had sent it to me, and I cut the strings with haste. Would there be a letter inside? Had Jack Harvey discovered something important?

Inside the parcel was a box containing two dozen pairs of silk stockings. Also some tins of red salmon . . . and a small velvet box. When I opened it, I saw there was a string of tiny pearls inside. The beads glistened so beautifully that I was sure they must be real, and the gold clasp was set with diamonds.

There was also a brief letter.

'*I'm hoping you will get this,*' Jon had written.

I'm sending it through diplomatic channels with a friend, so it should arrive in time for Christmas. I'm afraid I shan't be able to make it for a while, Emma, though I shall be thinking about you. There's no news of Jon yet, but I've told my people to keep trying. If he's alive, we'll find him. Take care of yourself. I'll send something useful when I can. Love, Jack.

I was aware of an overwhelming disappointment. I had hoped so much that Jack's letter would tell me my husband was alive, but at least he was trying. I was grateful for that, and the stockings, which I would share with my friends. Most of the tinned salmon would go to the social club, but I would have to return the pearls when I next saw Jack.

I could not possibly accept such an expensive gift from a man I hardly knew, even though they were beautiful and I knew he had meant to please me.

I closed the lid of the velvet box, then put it away carefully in a drawer.

I dreamed of Jon that night, waking from a nightmare, shaking, my body drenched with sweat. My husband had been calling for me, and he was in terrible pain. I had felt the pain in my dream and it was still with me as I lay shivering in the darkness.

Where was Jon? What was happening to him? I felt his presence near me as though he were hovering between life and death, and his soul had come seeking me for comfort.

'Oh, Jon,' I whispered, tears trickling down my cheeks. 'If I could help you I would. Whatever it is, accept it, Jon, be strong for my sake. I love you, my darling. I want you to come home to me.'

For a while the feeling of dread continued to hold me, and then all at once it had gone and there was nothing left . . . nothing but the certainty that Jon was alive.

I got up and wandered over to the window, gazing out at the wet streets. London was just beginning to wake up. I could hear the rumbling of traffic somewhere and a sparrow was chirping just beneath my window.

Jon was alive, I felt it, sensed it, believed it. Something bad had happened to him that night, but I was sure he had come through it.

'We're trying to find you, my darling,' I whispered. 'You are not forgotten. I shall never give up. I promise, Jon. However long it takes, I shall never give up hoping . . .'

Margaret and I were sitting together in the front parlour when Mrs Rowan announced the visitor.

'Miss Gwendoline Robinson to see you, Mrs Reece.'

'Please show her in,' I said, shaking my head as Margaret made to rise. 'No, please don't go. I would like you to stay.'

Margaret nodded. 'I will stay for a while, but if you want to be alone with Miss Robinson, you have only to say, Emma.'

'I don't suppose I shall . . .'

I got to my feet as a woman came in. She was tall, thin, rather mannish in her dress, her hat shaped like a gentleman's trilby and pulled down tight over straight hair rolled into a bun at the nape. I could see something of my father's features in her face, which made her look a little harsh and unappealing.

'Miss Robinson?' I said, getting up and offering her my hand. 'I am so sorry we were out yesterday. May

I introduce Mrs Gould to you? This is her home and I live with Mr and Mrs Gould as their guest.'

'Emma . . .' she said, looking at me uncertainly. 'May I call you that? I'm always called Gwen by my friends.' She nodded in Margaret's direction. 'Forgive me for calling unannounced like this, but I had to come to London on business, and I thought it would be the ideal opportunity to visit my brother's daughter.'

'You are very welcome,' Margaret said. 'Shall I send for tea – or would you prefer a sherry? And do please sit down . . .'

'Oh, don't put yourself to the trouble,' Gwen said and chose a seat opposite me on a rather hard sofa. Her back was very straight, and she looked slightly uncomfortable. 'I don't want to be a bother. It was just a few words with Emma . . .'

'I can assure you it is no bother,' Margaret said. 'I thought we might persuade you to stay to lunch, Miss Robinson?'

'That is very kind of you.' Gwen looked even more awkward. 'But I want to catch the next train home. If I might speak to Emma alone? Just for a moment or two . . .'

Margaret glanced at me, and I nodded. 'I'll take Gwen into the study,' I said, and got up to lead the way. It would have been unkind to deny my aunt the privacy she so clearly wanted after her trouble.

'What can I do for you?' I asked as we sat down in the study. It was a room furnished in leather and oak, rather dark and much less comfortable than the

parlour, but my aunt seemed to relax in these surround-
ings as she could not in Margaret's pretty parlour. 'I
am sorry I couldn't come to see you as you asked, but
things . . . well, they have been difficult.'

'Yes, I know you're busy,' she said. 'I knew you
worked for Mr Gould. You may wonder why I should
be so interested in you, Emma, but it is for my mother's
sake that I've come here today. Harold was her
favourite child. She had three of us. My youngest
brother died when he was still a baby . . . and I was
a disappointment to my mother. She wanted another
boy, you see.'

I stared at her, not quite sure what to say. 'I see . . .'

She laughed, and the sound was pleasant, her harsh
features softened a little by her amusement. 'No, I'm
sure you don't. I never minded that Harold was
Mother's favourite. I was always fond of him, which
is why I understood what Mother did . . .'

'What did your mother do? I'm sorry. I don't understand. My father never spoke of his family. We didn't
even know you existed until your letter arrived.'

'No, I gathered that much from your reply,' she said.
'I don't know why Harold should have wanted to keep
us a secret from you – unless he was ashamed. He
wrote of his wife and daughter in his letters to Mother
several times I believe . . .'

'Ashamed of what? Did he do something wrong?'
I had sometimes wondered why Father had never talked
about his past.

'He quarrelled with our father,' Gwen said, pulling

a face. 'That wasn't hard. Father was a difficult man. Quite frankly, he made our lives a misery, and it was a relief to my mother when he died some years ago . . . or it would have been if he hadn't managed to spend all my mother's money without telling her. It *was* her money, you see. She came from a wealthy family. My father was no one until she married him, the son of a blacksmith. Mother was the daughter of gentry. She married beneath her and regretted it within a month of her wedding.'

'The wrong marriage can lead to unhappiness. I know that.'

'Yes, I believe you have been unfortunate in that area yourself.'

'How do you know that?'

'I made inquiries, and I saw things in the newspaper. It is always possible to find out things if one is determined enough, Emma.'

'Yes, I suppose so.' I waited for her to go on, but she was silent until I prompted her. 'You were saying my father quarrelled with his own father?'

'Yes . . .' She grimaced. 'They had always argued, ever since Harold was quite small, of course. This time Harold hit him . . . knocked him down with his fists. Father told him they were finished, disowned him, cut off his allowance. We were still quite wealthy in those days, you see. Harold shouted a bit, then went to pack his things. Mother gave him what money she had, a hundred pounds I think – and some jewellery. My father was furious when he discovered what she had done, but I understood. Harold said he would sell the jewels, but pay her back one day.'

'But he didn't, and now you've come to ask me for what he owes you mother?'

Gwen shook her head. 'No, that's not quite how it is, Emma. Harold did repay her, in small amounts over the years. He sent a few pounds every month. I suppose he has repaid all she gave him, but . . .' Gwen paused, looking awkward. 'We had grown accustomed to receiving that money. Mother would never ask for anything, she is much too proud, but I am more practical. I know Harold had a business, Emma, and I've come to ask if there is any possibility that you might be able to help us . . . even a little.'

'I'm not sure . . .' I stared at her uncertainly. It was clear that my father had used his mother's jewels to set up his business, so in a way we did owe her something, even though he had repaid the original loan. 'I think perhaps your mother is entitled to something, Gwen – but it isn't easy. All the money he left me is tied up in various businesses. I have my wages and some rent from Father's shop but . . .'

'I'm not asking for a huge amount,' Gwen said quickly. 'Mother would never accept it. She has no idea I'm here asking you. She would be angry with me if she found out I had approached you. But Harold sent us ten pounds a month and that made a lot of difference to our lives. After he died things became difficult. We've already moved out of the house we were living in. A cousin of Mother's has rented us a cottage at three shillings a week, which is just about affordable on Mother's income, but it's still very hard to manage. I would work if I could, but Mother is an invalid. I have to look after her. Someone stayed with her while I came to London, but I can't ask very often.'

'I do understand,' I said. 'But you see, I give my mother most of the rent from the shop. Father was very tight with his money for years, always telling us that the shop wasn't making much of a profit. I wondered what he did with his money, because I knew the shop was profitable, but now I see that if he was sending your mother money . . . well, it must have made a difference all those years. I don't feel I can deprive my mother of the rent from the shop. She is entitled to something.'

'Well . . .' Gwen gathered her gloves and bag, clearly ready to leave. 'I hope you didn't mind my asking, Emma? I don't want to make things difficult for you. It was just the chance that Harold might have left you well off . . .'

'He did leave me some money besides the shop,' I told her. 'I invested it, but as yet I have not seen any profits. I'm not sure what I can do, Gwen. Give me time to discuss it with my mother and my business partner. I need to think about what I can afford to do.'

'As I said, I don't want to make things difficult,' she said. 'I didn't come here to demand or to beg, just to ask if you could manage to help. I'm well aware that Mother would not approve, and I know Harold repaid her . . . but we are finding things hard.'

'I'm sure I can do something,' I said, making up my mind. 'I'm just not sure what at the moment.'

'Well, I shan't bother you again,' she said and smiled at me. 'And I shan't hold it against you if you decide not to help us. Mother would love to see you if you can spare the time one day.'

'Thank you for coming to see me,' I said. 'You have cleared up a lot of things that had bothered me about Father's past. It always seemed so strange that he wouldn't speak of his family . . . and I understand now why he was so careful with his money.'

'Well, I dare say he got that from Mother,' Gwen said. 'She was always trying to restrain my father. He drank too much and he gambled, you see. He didn't see why he should work once he was married to a lady of property – but eventually he spent every penny she had. Except for a small trust fund that my grandfather had set up for her. That dies with her, of course – but I shall manage when she has gone. I wouldn't ask for myself, Emma.'

I could see the pride in her face, and I suddenly knew how much this must have cost her. Impulsively, I went to kiss her cheek.

'Don't worry, Gwen,' I said. 'I'll do something to help, I promise. I shan't tell your mother you came to me – and perhaps one day I can come to visit you both.'

For a moment her eyes sheened with tears, but she

blinked them away. 'You're a nice person, Emma. Thank you for being so understanding. Most people would have shown me the door.'

'I've been short of money myself,' I said. 'I know what it's like to want things you can't have . . . and I'm very lucky. I live with kind friends who share their wonderful home with me, and I lack nothing. It would be very selfish of me not to respond to a request for help from my own family, wouldn't it?'

'Thank you,' she said. 'I'll wait to hear from you then – and don't worry. If you change your mind, I shan't come knocking at your door.'

'I shan't change my mind,' I said. 'You will hear something very soon. I'm just not sure what I can do . . .'

'You're a fool if you give them anything,' my mother said when I telephoned and told her about Gwen's visit. 'When I think your father was giving them ten pounds a month all those years . . . it's more than he ever gave either of us, Emma!'

'Yes, I know,' I agreed, 'but don't you see, Mum? He thought he owed it to his mother. It explains why he was careful with his money. He wasn't really so very mean when you think about it. We never went short of anything, did we – not really? We may not have had much freedom, or money to spend as we chose, but there was always food in the house and coal for the fire. We had good clothes and . . .'

'I made most of our clothes, Emma, yours and

mine. I think Mrs Robinson had back what she lent Harold. What you've got now belongs to you. I've told you I don't need the rent from the shop. Bert gives me money for myself – but I might as well keep it as give it away to them. Besides, you don't know for sure that they are Harold's family. She could be anyone . . .'

'If you'd seen her, Mum, you wouldn't say that. She looks like Father – and she's obviously had a hard life, taking care of her mother. Mrs Robinson is an invalid. Gwen can't leave her very often. That can't be much of a life for her, can it?'

'No . . .' Mum hesitated. 'I'm not saying I don't feel sorry for her, Emma – but I don't see why you should give her your money.'

'Well, I want to do something. I'm going to ask Sol for advice.'

'Just be careful,' my mother said. 'Once you start something like that she will expect you to keep it up.'

'That's why I didn't promise anything straight away,' I said. 'I don't want to give her hope if I can't manage to do anything to help.'

'Well, it's up to you – but I should think long and hard before you commit yourself, Emma.'

'I shall,' I promised. 'Anyway, have you and Bert decided – are you coming up to stay over Christmas? Margaret would love to have you both.'

'It's very kind of her to invite us,' my mother said. 'But I don't think we shall. I might pop up on the train the week before to see you and James.'

'That's lovely,' I said. 'Bye then. Take care of yourselves. Give my love to Bert.'

After I had talked to my mother, I spoke to Sol about my aunt's request. He listened, frowning and nodding as I explained the situation.

'So what do you want, Emma?' he asked. 'A lump sum – or a regular payment?'

'Which would be best?' I said. 'More importantly, would it be possible for me to withdraw some of my investment from the factory?'

'It wouldn't be easy at the moment,' Sol said. 'I don't have much spare capital lying around, Emma. What with the war and various investments, I've left myself a bit tight – but you could certainly draw a few pounds each month from the business. You've never asked for a penny, so I've credited your share to your account – but if you need some money you can have it.'

'Ten pounds a month . . .' I said hesitantly. 'Would that be too much to ask, Sol?'

'Good grief, no,' he said. 'You can treble that if you like – have more money for yourself?'

'No, I don't need more,' I replied. 'Neither you or Margaret will take a penny for my keep. What I get from Mrs Henty and my wages are as much as I need, but I would like to draw that ten pounds a month if I may. It won't make things difficult for you, will it?'

'If it would, I should tell you, Emma.' Sol's brows narrowed. 'You'll be a wealthy young woman one day. I've invested for you as well as myself, that's why there's no capital to spare at the moment – but the ten pounds a month is no trouble, as long as it's what you really want to do?'

'Yes. Yes, it is,' I said. 'I think it's what my father would have wanted. He obviously cared for his mother. He continued to send her money regularly all his life. If I had known about them at the time of his death, I would have given them something. I think Gwen must have been quite desperate to come to me the way she did. It can't have been easy for her. My father was a proud man, very harsh at times, even cruel – and I think his sister would be proud, too.'

'You're a generous woman, Emma,' Sol said. 'You didn't have to do this, but it shows character. I like it in you.'

'I've been so lucky,' I said. 'You and Margaret . . . all my friends. But I know what it is like to be trapped by lack of money. I know what it's like to feel that there is never going to be anything better, that your life will always be the same. If the money helps my aunt a little, I'm glad to give it.'

'I'll arrange to have it paid to her through my bank,' Sol said. 'It will be easier that way, and saves sending money or postal orders through the mailbox. She won't want her mother to know about the ten pounds.'

'I'll write to Gwen and tell her,' I said. 'You will need details of her own bank I expect.'

'You do that,' Sol said. 'But if she comes back for more – you leave her to me, Emma.'

'She won't do that,' I said. 'I'm sure of it, Sol. I

quite liked Gwen. I think she is a very honest, straight-forward person. I shall try to get down to visit her and my grandmother one day.'

'I'll take you when I get time, Emma.'

'Thank you.' I looked at him thoughtfully. 'I've been thinking, Sol. Perhaps it would be a good thing if I learned to drive . . .'

'Would you want to?'

'Yes, I think I might.'

He grinned at me. 'It would come in useful, Emma. I could send you off to your mother's for a few days, and you could go to the factory and see how things were going. Save me a lot of time and trouble.'

'How do I learn?' I asked. 'Should I book lessons – or what?'

'Professional lessons are best,' he said. 'Leave it to me, Emma. I would have suggested it ages ago, but Margaret never wanted to drive.'

'Well, I do,' I said. 'It will give me some independ-ence, Sol – and I can use Jon's car. He left it at his mother's house. It will mean I can visit Mrs Reece more often, too.'

'That's if you can get the petrol,' Sol said, grimacing. 'But we'll manage something. You just leave it all to me . . .'

Christmas arrived. I received so many cards and small gifts, many of them from the customers at the show-room. I still went in for several hours every day, and it was surprising how many of them came in when they knew I was there so that I would serve them myself.

'We like it when you're here, Emma,' they told me. 'You always know just what we want – and you always have a smile to cheer us up. It makes things look brighter no matter how hard the damned government tries to knock us down!'

'I could retire now,' Sol joked sometimes. 'I believe you could run the business single-handed, Emma.'

'No, I don't think so,' I said. 'You still deal with all our suppliers, Sol. I'm not sure I could get such a bargain on some of the materials as you do – and how you manage to get hold of things like elastic is beyond me . . .'

He tapped the side of his nose and grinned at me. 'Ways and means, Emma. It's not what you know these days, it's who you know – and how well you know them. I twist a few arms when I need to.'

The workshop was still doing surprisingly well despite everything. The government had not yet dared to bring in clothes rationing, but like Sol I believed it was getting closer with each month that passed.

Christmas Eve brought a card from Gwen Robinson and her mother. Gwen had already written to thank me for my help, and she did so again now. I was pleased to have made life better for her and the woman who was after all my own grandmother.

So despite the war, the festive season was happy enough for me, my friends and my family. We were able to buy a turkey and confectionery, though the government had asked us to make what sacrifices we could, but in Sol's house there was not much evidence of austerity. His cellars were still stocked with wines and spirits laid up before the war, and we had saved two of Jack Harvey's tins of red salmon for Christmas tea.

As the carols were sung and the celebrations went on all around me, I thought of Jon, longed for him, prayed for him, but I tried not to let anyone else see that only half my heart was in the celebrations.

It was just after Christmas that I received the sad news that Sheila's husband had died in the sanatorium.

'I can hardly believe he has gone,' Sheila had written.

> *I went to see him just before Christmas, and he seemed better. We were talking about him being home by the summer, but then he deteriorated almost overnight and they sent for me. He died soon after I arrived. I'm not sure what to do, Emma. I would like to try to keep the shop on, but I shall have to think about it over the next few months. I thought I should tell you . . .*

I felt so sorry for my friend. I wasn't sure that it had been a great love affair, but I knew she had been fond of Eric. And when they had first taken over the shop, she had been so full of plans for the future. I wrote back and told her to take her time about making her decision. She was welcome to stay there in the accommodation even if she couldn't manage the shop.

You might be able to sell the stock, and then we could let the shop to someone else . . . but I'm in no hurry, Sheila. Think about it for a while, and then let me know . . .

Life went on as usual. I looked every day for a letter from Jack Harvey, but though the occasional parcel reached me from time to time, there was no news of my husband. So far no one had heard anything about a British airman taken prisoner in France who might be my husband, or if they had they were not prepared to disclose details.

It would have been very easy during the next months to have given up hope, but I refused to let go of my belief that Jon was alive . . . that he would come back to us one day despite his suffering.

For I knew that he *had* suffered in some way. I had shared his pain that night, and I believed that Jon had almost died then. My family and friends were all convinced that he must have been killed in the crash when his plane was shot down, but I did not believe that.

In my heart, I felt that Jon was alive. I could not know where he was, but I was sure he was somewhere . . . still living, perhaps a prisoner, perhaps in hiding. I was anxious for him, and I often felt close to tears. How could Jon bear what was happening to him? It was hard enough for me, how much worse must it be for my sensitive husband?

I believed now that this was what had been in his mind when he spoke of what might happen to him. It was not so much that he might die, but that he might not be able to contact me, that we might be apart for years. He would be so alone, without friends or hope . . . knowing that I would have been told he was dead.

Yet as long as I believed he still lived, there *was* hope. And I would cling to that hope for as long as I could . . .

Chapter 6

'This damned government,' Sol muttered, throwing down his letter in disgust. 'The way things are going, we shall soon need a licence to go to the bathroom.'

'Sol dearest,' Margaret reproved gently. 'Please don't upset yourself. Surely it can't be that terrible?'

I wondered what had upset him. The clothes rationing we had expected had arrived in June 1941. It was now the beginning of December. At first we had needed margarine coupons to purchase our clothes, but the new coupons had been in circulation for a while and people were getting used to the idea. The rationing had made little difference to families on low incomes, but for women who could afford to dress smartly it meant cutting down considerably.

Sol frowned as he handed me his letter to read. It was an official notice to employers, about the call-up of unmarried women between the ages of twenty and thirty.

'That means we shall lose Janice from the show-room,' Sol said, clearly annoyed. 'I've had difficulty in holding on to her as it is. She wanted to volunteer before this, but I persuaded her to stay. Now she will be off like a shot.'

'We'll lose some of our best girls from the factory, too.'

I understood how Sol felt. It was already difficult

to find the labour we needed, and this was going to make things harder.

'They are going to register women up to forty, Emma, married and single – but I'll make sure you're exempted. I can't afford to lose you.'

'Mrs Reece . . .' Mrs Rowan hesitated in the doorway. 'There's a telephone call for you.'

I excused myself and went out to the hall.

'Emma . . . it's Gwen. I hope you didn't mind my ringing? I just wanted to make sure you were coming today. Mother was asking and she hasn't been too well . . .'

'I'm sorry to hear that, Gwen. Yes, I'm coming. Sol has managed to wangle me some extra petrol this month. I'm driving down later this morning, bringing James, and we'll stay for two days – if that's all right with you?'

'You know it is. Mother looks forward to your visits so much. She knows you've been giving us money now. I had to tell her, but not that I came to you. She doesn't know I asked, Emma. She would hate that . . .'

'I shan't tell her. Besides, it's so little, Gwen. I've asked Sol for extra money this Christmas, and I've managed to get a few bits and pieces to bring down. James is excited. He knows he is coming to see Grandma today.'

'I shan't hold you up then. We'll see you later.'

I went back to the breakfast parlour. Sol had already left. Margaret was lingering over her tea. She seemed tired, her skin a little grey, her eyes heavy.

'Are you feeling unwell today?'

She sighed and shook her head. 'Don't worry, Emma dearest. I'm no worse than usual. It's just the war and what it is doing to us all. Sol seems so agitated these days. He isn't like himself. I'm worried about him. He never tells me anything.'

I went to sit on the chair next to her. 'Please don't fret over Sol, Margaret. If he has been a bit short-tempered of late it's not his fault. He's just frustrated. It has been difficult for him recently. We've got the government breathing over our shoulders the whole time, and I think it can only get worse. Sol knows that profits are down, but it's more than that. The factory has had problems. Our best machinists keep leaving to join up or work elsewhere. Sol can't afford to offer them inducements to stay. And we had another fire. There was so much fuss and bother over spoiled material, it would drive anyone crazy.'

'Thank you for taking the time to explain.' She smiled. 'Sol refuses to answer my questions. He won't talk to me about his work, but I've sensed something was wrong.'

'He only refuses to tell you because he thinks you would worry and make yourself ill.'

'I worry when I don't know what's going on, Emma. Sol always has taken risks, but things were different before the war. Life was easier, more gentle somehow. I don't like what's happening to us now. Everything seems ugly, harsh . . .' She sighed, looking unhappy.

'It's a struggle to keep things going. At the start,

the factory made a lot of money very quickly. I think Sol invested some of that abroad. These days, we're only just managing to keep our heads above water. We might have to think about closing the factory. It depends on how things go this next year.'

'You invested your money in the factory, Emma.' She looked at me in concern.

'So did Sol. Don't worry. I'm sure Sol will turn things round – but he has a lot on his mind just now.' I kissed her cheek. 'I'm going to fetch James down. I want to get started. You know what my son is like in the car. He never sits still for five minutes together, and he wants the toilet every few miles.'

Margaret laughed, the shadows banished from her eyes. 'I think you are brave to take him with you, Emma. But you are always so good with him, and you have so much energy.'

It made me sad to think of Margaret always being so tired. She had missed so much in life through her illness. Her heart was not strong. The doctors never seemed to explain exactly what was wrong with her; they spoke of her heartbeat being irregular, of a weakness in the valve, but did not offer any solutions. She was just delicate and must take care not to overtire herself.

I was thoughtful as I carried all my baskets and parcels out to the car. In my grandmother's case, it was easy to see what ailed her. She was a tiny, frail lady of seventy-odd years and crippled with a painful arthritis. It was difficult for her to walk even with assistance, and her fingers were so twisted that she could not dress herself. She was often in pain, but remained good-tempered despite it, her smile so sweet and gentle that it was impossible to do anything but love her.

The first time I'd seen her, a few months ago now, I had been pleasantly surprised. Her eyes were bright, still youthful despite her wrinkled skin and thin white hair, but she had obviously been pretty once and was not at all like her daughter or my father.

'So you're Harold's girl,' she'd said, nodding at me. 'You must be like your mother. You are far too pretty for a Robinson.' She smiled at me. 'So, child – come and kiss me and tell me all about yourself. We've been strangers for too long.'

We had taken to each other at once. She was very different to my beloved Gran. Grandmother Robinson was very much a lady. She might have been reduced to poverty by her husband's careless spending, but she refused to let her standards drop. She had kept her dignity and Gwen was never allowed to set the table with anything other than the best linen, what silver she had left, and the finest bone china I had ever seen.

I was looking forward to my visit with Gwen and Grandmother Robinson. Their village was rather old, its name Saxon in origin, and attractive. About the triangular green, duck pond and beautiful old elm tree, were grouped timber-framed, brick and tiled cottages, many of them dating from the sixteenth century. Also a whipping post and stocks, reminders of a harsher age. Beyond were the rising beechwoods, a Doric column crowning their summit.

In the summer the village had seemed to slumber in the sun, a tranquil haven away from the noise and hustle of the city. I had thought then how much Jon would have liked it. We would go there together one day, when the war was over.

There had been no news of Jon. It was more than a year now. I had hoped to hear something from Jack long before this, but his last letter had not been hopeful. My husband's name was not on any of the lists compiled by the Red Cross or other international agencies who were able to make contact with prisoners of war.

It seemed likely that Jon had died in the crash, but I was not willing to accept his death as fact. Sometimes I almost gave in to my despair, but then I would feel him close to me again. I would feel that inner certainty again, and something inside me refused to let go.

I still wanted to believe that Jon would come home.

My visit to Gwen and Grandmother Robinson was pleasant, but I was a little concerned about my grandmother's health.

'She hasn't been at all well,' Gwen told me when we were preparing supper together. I had brought some tinned food with me – courtesy of Jack's last visit in the summer – and we were making corned beef hash. 'I've been a bit worried, Emma. I'm not sure she will get through this winter.'

'I'm so sorry, Gwen. I must admit I have noticed a difference in her this time.'

'Well, she is seventy-seven,' Gwen said, sighing. 'I suppose it's a good age, but . . .' Her face crumpled as she gulped back her emotion. 'I shall miss her. To be honest, I'm not sure what I shall do. I've never been alone.'

'Well, you won't need to be,' I said. 'We're so short of help, Gwen. I know Sol could find you work.'

Gwen laughed and shook her head. 'I'm not clever with my hands, Emma. I can't set a stitch straight. I wouldn't be much use to you.'

'I'm sure we can find you something,' I said. 'Promise me you will come to me if . . .'

'It's a case of when not if,' Gwen said sadly. 'I know it can't be long, Emma.'

I shook my head, but in my heart I knew she was right. It made me feel sad. I wished I had known Grandmother Robinson sooner, and I regretted all the years we had lost.

'Go and sit with her now,' Gwen said, as if she could read my thoughts. 'She has talked of nothing but your visit for weeks.'

I went through to the tiny parlour. There were a few nice pieces of furniture which Grandmother Robinson had managed to cling on to despite having seen most of her precious possessions sold to pay her husband's debts. However, the room still had an air of shabbiness despite some bright new curtains I had sent Gwen.

Grandmother smiled as I entered the room, lifting her crooked fingers to beckon me closer.

'You are such a lovely girl, Emma. I can hardly believe you're my Harold's child, but I know you are. He told me about you in his letter when you were first born. I remember particularly how excited he was, how proud of his daughter . . .'

'Was he? Are you sure?'

My father had always accused my mother of cheating him, but if he had told his mother about me he must have thought of me as his own child.

'Oh yes. I think I might still have the letter somewhere. I'll ask Gwen to look one day.' She smiled at me. 'And now, my dear, I have a little present for you.' She pointed at a small, faded box on the table next to her. 'That was my mother's, Emma. It has always been special to me, and I want you to have it.'

I opened the box. Inside was a gold brooch that must have been new when Queen Victoria was a young bride. It was set with tiny turquoises and pearls.

'It is beautiful,' I said. 'But are you sure you want to give this to me? Should it not go to Gwen?'

'Gwen has other trinkets. It is not very valuable, Emma, but I have enjoyed wearing it. I would like you to keep it . . . to remember me by. We have not known each other long, but I have become fond of you.'

'And I of you,' I assured her. My eyes stung but I blinked away my tears. 'I shall never forget you. I don't need the brooch to remind me of you, Grandmother – but I shall always treasure it.'

She nodded. 'Give me a kiss then, child – and now it's time for our supper. I am ready for my bed.'

My visit was over all too soon. I was thoughtful as I drove home. It was likely that I would not see Grandmother Robinson again. I would have to consider what best to do for Gwen. She was determined to find work. She had told me that she would not accept the ten pounds a month after her mother was dead.

'You have been more than generous to us, Emma. I shall manage when I don't have Mother to worry about. I'll find work of some kind.'

But what kind of work could Gwen do? She was not trained for anything other than looking after an elderly relative.

I knew she wanted to be independent. She would not accept an offer to come and live with us and help out at the showroom, but I believed she would find it difficult to support herself without help.

Something must be done to enable her to earn her living – but what? It was quite a puzzle, but one I was determined to solve. I liked Gwen and I believed her life had been hard. I would find a way of helping her somehow, a way that did not rob her of her pride.

It was 7 December 1941 and the news had shocked us. Sol handed me his paper and I stared at it in stunned silence. We had heard the announcement on the radio but could hardly believe it, now here it was in print. The Japanese had bombed the American Navy in Pearl

Harbour, destroying nineteen ships and over two hundred planes.

'What does this mean?' I asked at last. 'What is going to happen now, Sol?'

'It means that the bloody Japs are idiots and Britain has just got lucky,' Sol said, a huge grin replacing the shock on his face. 'The American isolationists have been pulling most of the strings up until now, Emma, keeping Roosevelt from doing as much as he wanted to help us – but they won't be able to stop him now. America will be in the war and that is good for us. It's what we've been praying for.'

'Yes . . .' I looked at him thoughtfully. 'Does this mean that Jack Harvey will be called up?'

'I doubt it very much, Emma.' Sol's eyebrows gathered as he looked at me. 'Worried about him? You needn't be. He's too important. His government won't want him getting his head shot off . . . money and power, Emma, that's Jack's middle name.'

'I see . . .' I smiled at him. 'I suppose I always knew that. He has never said very much . . .'

Jack had been here again in the summer, just after that terrible night in May when London had been devastated by one of the worst bombing raids ever. It had been a night that almost took the heart out of the city, shocking even the most hardened Londoners.

Like many others, I had wept to see the wanton destruction of our beautiful city. Westminster and the Chamber of Commons was hit, as was St. Paul's, but they were only a few of the many areas destroyed by the five-hundred-odd German planes that had rained fire and vengeance on us – vengeance for the raids our bombers had made on their towns.

'Don't cry, Emma,' Jack had said to me then. 'The bastards will pay for this, I promise you. One of these days they will get such a kick up their rears they won't know what's hit them.'

Jack and I had become real friends on his last visit. I had tried to give him back his pearls, but he wouldn't let me.

'They were a gift,' he said. 'No strings attached, Emma. If you're really my friend, you won't insult me by trying to give them back.'

How could I refuse after that? Jack was a good friend. He had shown me a sheaf of reports relating to the search for Jon, and I knew it had cost him a lot of time and money to set all this in motion.

If he wanted me to keep the pearls, then it was the least I could do. Now, despite Sol's reassurances, I was worried that Jack would be drawn into this terrible war, a war that was robbing so many women of their loved ones.

I had not heard from him for some weeks, and I wondered where he was and what he was doing . . .

I was in the showroom two days later, going through the rails to check on our stock levels when the front door opened. I did not immediately turn my head, because Janice was dressing the window and would call me if I was needed.

'Busy, Emma?'

My heart jerked and I spun round in surprise as I heard Jack's voice.

'Jack!' I cried, feeling pleased to see him. 'When did you get back? We weren't expecting you for months. We weren't even sure you would come back . . . I'm so sorry about what happened, Jack.'

He nodded, his mouth tight and grim. 'We were caught with our pants down, Emma. It's a lesson learned the hard way.'

'Yes . . . I'm sorry.' He shook his head. I sensed he did not want to talk about it. 'So what brings you here then?'

'I decided to spend Christmas in England. Do you think Margaret will invite me for dinner on the big day?'

'I'm sure she will,' I said. 'Oh, this *is* nice, Jack. It's so good to see you!' I leaned towards him impulsively, kissing his cheek.

'That alone was worth crossing the Atlantic,' Jack said, grinning at me. 'I've no need to ask how you are, Emma. You look beautiful, as always.'

'And you talk nonsense!' I retorted. 'I'm not beautiful, Jack. You must need to get your eyes tested.'

'Same old sweet tongue,' he murmured, a wicked glint in his eyes. 'So, with spectacles I'd see that you're just a plain, ugly old woman – but I like my eyesight the way it is, thanks all the same.'

'Are you ever serious, Jack?'

'Not unless I'm forced.'

I shook my head at him, but I had to admit I was pleased to see him. Far more pleased than I would have expected.

'How long are you here for this time?'

'A few weeks . . . it depends.'

'Things to do, people to see? Lots of big deals on the cards?'

Jack nodded, amused. 'Something like that. There was a time when some Americans didn't really want to know about this war, Emma. Roosevelt has always been on your side, of course, but certain business people simply didn't want to risk being involved. I'm glad to say the tide was turning even before Pearl Harbour, now of course we are in for the duration.'

'But even before that it was people like you who were keeping hope alive for us . . . helping us in all sorts of ways we didn't even guess . . . selling us weapons that were supposed to be surplus to American requirements – and perhaps a few that weren't?'

'Who told you that?' Jack's gaze narrowed. 'Has Sol been telling tales out of school?'

'He didn't have to, Jack. You gave yourself away with those parcels you sent. You have to be someone important to send silk stockings by way of diplomatic channels!'

Jack threw back his head and roared with laughter. 'That appealed to you, did it? I knew I would get to you one day, Emma.'

'You have the devil's own cheek, Jack. I dare not think what else you get up to.'

'You don't want to know, Emma.'

'No, I certainly don't!'

I had no doubt that Jack was making a profit out of this war. He was not a man to fail. When he set out to achieve something, he did not do it by half measures. So he was certainly making a great deal of money somewhere along the line, but he was also helping our poor, beleaguered country. Some people would have condemned him for the profiteering, but I was enough Harold Robinson's daughter to know that people expected to be rewarded for their work. Business was one thing, generosity on a personal level was quite another.

Jack had been generous to me. I hadn't asked him if he had news of Jon. I'd known the answer from the moment I looked at him. He would have been full of himself if he'd had something good to tell me.

'Would you come out with me this evening, Emma? I've got tickets for a play . . . *Blithe Spirit*. You may have seen it?'

'No, I haven't been to the theatre for ages. We usually stay home and listen to the radio these days, Jack. I suppose with the bombs . . . but yes, I would like to go. It would be really nice to go out again . . .'

I wore a new dress to go out with Jack that evening. I had bought it just before rationing came in and put it away at the back of my wardrobe, saving it for a special occasion. It was a deep midnight blue, made of a soft wool and very flattering to the figure.

'I like you in blue,' Jack said as we walked home from the theatre. 'I shall never forget the dress you were wearing the night we met . . . you looked so lovely, standing there on your own. Like a medieval lady . . .'

'A damsel in distress?' I asked, teasing him. 'So you rode in to the rescue – my knight in shining armour.'

Jack smiled. 'Something like that. Unfortunately for me, someone else had got there first . . .'

'Don't Jack . . . please. You know I love Jon. You've always known.'

'Jon is dead, Emma. You're going to have to face that one of these days. I'm sorry, my darling, but it's true.'

'You don't know that. I accept that it seems that way, but we can't be sure.'

'No, we can't be certain,' he said, and stopped walking. He took my arm, turning me to face him. 'How long are you going to wait, Emma? You know I care for you . . . want you . . .'

'Please don't,' I whispered, my throat tight with emotion. When he looked at me like that it made me feel weak inside and I needed to be strong. 'Don't ask me to choose, Jack. If you do, I shall have to choose Jon. I can't give up. I can't just abandon him, forget him. Not yet. I have to go on believing, waiting . . .'

'Yes, I see that. I thought perhaps . . . but you're not ready to forget him. He's a lucky guy, Emma. A lot of women stray five minutes after their husbands leave home.'

'I'm sure that's not true.'

'You want to bet on it?'

I shook my head. I supposed there were women who were so lonely they went with other men while their husbands were away fighting, but that seemed so cruel to me.

'I love him, Jack. Don't you believe in loyalty?'

'Yes, I do.' He smiled ruefully. 'I think that may be one of the reasons I fell for you, Emma. I respect you. I know you love Jon – but I think you feel something for me, too. Or am I kidding myself?'

His eyes seemed to bore into mine, seeking the secret places of my mind.

'No . . .' I couldn't look at him. It was true that a part of me found Jack very attractive. He made me laugh, and I was beginning to look forward to his letters and visits. I was aware of an attraction between us, had been aware of it from the first. 'No, you're not mistaken, Jack. I am becoming fond of you . . .'

'Fond, Emma?'

Before I knew what he intended, Jack reached for me, gathering me into his arms and kissing me in a way that left me breathless and shaken. I stood still within the circle of his arms, refusing to let myself cling to him, but when he let me go at last, I put my fingers to my mouth, staring at him in bewilderment. How could I feel this racing excitement inside me? How could I experience such wild, pulsating desire? I loved my husband. I loved Jon so much . . . and yet I had never once felt like this when he kissed me. This was something new . . . something I feared while it thrilled me.

'Fond, Emma?' Jack said again. His eyes were leaping with a mixture of excitement and triumph. He had felt my response, try as I might to conceal it. 'I would say your feelings were a little stronger. I think you want me . . . almost as much as I want you.'

It was true. A wave of horror swept over me as I realized everything he claimed was true. I did want him. His kiss had aroused a huge, aching need in me, a need I had suppressed without knowing it through months of lonely nights.

'No! I can't . . . I won't!'

I broke away from Jack and began to run along the pavement. I was angry, with myself and with Jack for making me face the truth. Yes, I wanted to make love with him. I wanted, needed the physical comfort I knew he could give me, but I did not want this to happen. It would be a betrayal of my husband. It would be like abandoning Jon, as if I had thrown dirt into his open grave.

Jack came after me. He caught my arm, swinging me round to face him.

'No, Emma. I won't let you run away from this . . . I refuse to let you go on hiding behind your grief.'

My desperate reply was lost as the sirens wailed.

'Damn!' Jack looked about him. 'What do we do now?'

'We head for the nearest underground,' I said, grabbing his hand and pulling him with me. 'It may be just a false alarm, but I'm not going to risk it.'

We joined hands and followed the general rush towards the nearest entrance to an underground station.

'We're going to have to talk about this, Emma. I'm not prepared to give you up.'

'Yes, I know we have to talk,' I said. 'But not tonight, Jack. Please? Give me time. Let me think about this . . . please?'

There was a terrific roar somewhere close by, then a flash as fire shot into the night sky. Jack pulled me against the wall, sheltering me with his body as the ground shook and a building across the road came tumbling down. We had been standing in that very spot only a few minutes earlier, and the knowledge that we could have been killed was sobering. I buried my face against Jack's shoulder as the shudders ran through me.

'Jack . . .'

'It's all right, darling.'

'But we . . .'

'I love you, Emma,' he whispered against my hair. 'I'm not going to lose you. I'll wait for as long as it takes – but one day you'll come to me. You won't be able to help yourself. You will come to me, because we were meant to be together . . .'

'Come on, Jack,' I urged as I heard the whistling sound that struck terror into the hearts of Londoners. 'Let's get inside before another one falls . . .'

'You were so late in last night,' Margaret said to me the next morning at breakfast. 'I had begun to think something must have happened to you.'

On the radio they were playing one of the popular songs of the year – *Blues in the Night*. I turned the sound down slightly.

'I'm sorry if you were worried, Margaret. The sirens went as we were walking home after the play. We had to take shelter until the all clear went. I hope I didn't wake you when we came in? I asked Jack in and gave him a brandy. I hope you don't mind?'

'Of course not. This is your home, Emma. You can always bring your friends here.'

'Thank you.' I poured myself a cup of tea. 'Jack has business elsewhere for a few days, but when he comes back . . . I thought we might ask him to dinner one evening?'

'Yes, of course. Surely you know you don't have to ask?' Margaret looked directly at me. I felt myself blushing, because I sensed what was in her mind. 'You know that Jack is very much in love with you?' I nodded. She paused, then, 'Did you know that when he returns to America he is planning to join the army?'

'No, of course he won't. Why should he? Sol said his government wouldn't want Jack to fight – that he was too important . . .' The thought of Jack risking his life was somehow too terrible to contemplate.

'Jack is his own man,' Margaret said gently. 'He will do whatever he thinks is right. While his own country stayed out of the war he was content to make money and help us in whatever way he could – now he feels he should be prepared to do more.'

'That's silly,' I said as the fear began to crawl down

my spine. 'He can't . . . why should he? Anyone can shoot guns and get themselves killed. Jack can do so much others can't. He is needed in other ways . . . I don't see why he has to fight.'

'I suppose he needs to fight,' Margaret said, her brow wrinkling. 'Some men do. Forgive me if I'm wrong, Emma – but I thought you should know. I understand that you still love Jon, and you haven't given up hope of his return – but don't lose this chance to be happy. We none of us know how long we have. So far we have all been lucky. It sounds wicked of me to say this, my dear, but people were killed last night. It could have been you. Does it make sense to be faithful to a memory when you could be killed on the streets any day? Is it sensible to deny your own heart?'

'Margaret – please don't!'

'Think about it, Emma. For your own sake, that's all I ask – and for Jack's. We all have just a few chances for happiness in our lives. They go by so quickly. If we miss them, they may not come again. Take what you can, my dear. You are too young, too alive, to waste your life in regret. I'm sure Jon would not blame you.'

'No, he wouldn't,' I said. 'He would want me to be happy. You are right, Margaret. I know that. It's just that it feels like a betrayal . . . that I'm abandoning him . . .'

'I know,' she said and smiled at me in understanding. 'But Jon loved you, really loved you. He would hate to think of you alone. He wouldn't want you to go on grieving for ever. You must know that, Emma. Face the truth, my dearest – or you may regret it for the rest of your life.'

Tears welled up inside me. I turned away, my shoulders shaking. I had filled the past months with working, suppressing my grief, suppressing my loneliness, never letting myself think about my situation – about what I would do if Jon never came back to me.

My love for Jon had not diminished. I would never stop loving him, never forget him, but I was young. I was alive. I needed to live and to love – and I did love Jack. I loved him in a way I had loved no other man.

I thought of nothing else for the next three days. My conscience told me that I must not betray my husband. I had promised to love him, forsaking all others for the rest of our lives, and I had fully intended to keep those vows. Until the moment when Jack kissed me, I had not even thought of seeking comfort in another man's arms. I had accepted my loneliness as a part of the price we all had to pay for this dreadful war, and I had consoled myself with the hope that at the end of it all Jon might somehow come back to me.

A part of me still clung to that hope. Sometimes, I dreamed that he came to me, that he opened his arms and held me close, and I could almost taste the salt of his tears . . . but when I woke it was my own tears that I felt on my cheeks.

Yet it was an accepted fact that Jon was dead. I had received notification from the War Office that my husband was officially dead and I was classified as a war widow. I had torn up the letter angrily, furious that they had just given Jon up, and I had gone on hoping, praying for someone to find news of him, but it had not happened. Despite myself, I was beginning to think now that it never would.

How long was I prepared to live alone? I was a woman who enjoyed the physical side of marriage, and I knew I could not bear to live alone all my life. Besides, Jon had told me he wanted me to find a new life for myself if something like this happened.

'Don't waste your life, Emma,' he'd told me. 'Live for me . . . I want you to be happy, my darling.'

He had wanted to think that I would go on, that I would find happiness again.

Yet supposing I went to Jack and then Jon did come home . . . what would he think then? Would he understand, or would he feel I had betrayed him?

The thoughts went round and round endlessly in my mind during three sleepless nights, and I was no nearer to making my decision.

Chapter 7

'Is something the matter?' Margaret asked. I had been frowning over my letter for several minutes when she spoke. 'Not bad news I hope?'

I looked up, still frowning. 'It's from my friend Sheila. She says she can't manage to keep the shop running for much longer. It hasn't been very profitable for a while now. She wants to sell her stock if she can and find work . . .'

'Will that make things difficult for you?' Margaret looked anxious for my sake. 'What will you do, Emma – let to someone else or sell the property?'

'I'm not sure. I shall have to think about it. The rent is really my mother's income. I may have to discuss it with her.'

'You wouldn't want to run the shop as a business again? Pay someone else to manage it for you?'

'I suppose I could . . . but I would have to find the money to buy Sheila's stock. I do have some money in the bank, but probably not enough.'

'Sol would lend you some, Emma – or give you some of your own money back.'

'Yes, perhaps.'

I didn't tell Margaret that Sol had enough problems of his own. The factory had run into trouble again. I knew Sol had had a hefty fine to pay recently. Apparently, he had been breaking the rules too often, and had been punished in a way that really hurt. I knew that there was a possibility we might be losing one of our government contracts when it came up for renewal.

We heard the telephone ringing in the hall, then Mrs Rowan came to fetch me.

'It's Miss Robinson for you, Mrs Reece.'

Her tone alerted me and I was expecting the worst as I went to pick up the receiver.

'Gwen – is something wrong?'

'Mother died last night, Emma. She went in her sleep, very peacefully. She was quite happy last night, and she kissed me when I put her to bed. I found her this morning . . .'

'I'm so sorry, Gwen. I'll try to come down . . .'

'No, don't do that, Emma. I can manage. I really can. I'm glad you visited when you did. Mother did so enjoy seeing you again. She was quite happy. It is a welcome release for her in some ways.'

'I suppose so. Are you sure you don't want me to come?'

'It's too far and too difficult for you.' She hesitated, then, 'I would like to come to you afterwards. Mother wanted you to have a few of her bits and pieces. Nothing valuable, just letters, keepsakes. I would like to bring them to you – and ask your advice. I shall be needing a job. You might have some idea of what I'm best fitted for.' Gwen laughed. 'Not very much is the plain answer.'

'You put yourself down too much, Gwen. Come to us when you're ready – for Christmas if you like. Yes, come and stay over Christmas. We would love to have you with us.'

'Mother's cousin has asked me there. Philip has been good to us, and I have to settle about the cottage. I can't stay here, even if he would let me. I'll probably come to you in the New Year, Emma – if that's all right?'

'Just let me know,' I said. 'Whatever you decide, we're not going to lose touch, Gwen. I want us to be friends. Don't worry. I'm sure we can work something out between us.'

I was thoughtful as I replaced the receiver. I might be able to arrange something, but first I would need to talk to my mother.

'I'm not sure how Gwen would feel about it,' I said to Mum. 'She might not want to live in March, even if I could arrange to buy Sheila's stock.'

Mum looked at me thoughtfully. She had come up to London on the train to spend a few days with us before Christmas.

'I never did see why you let Sheila rent the place from you, Emma. That business kept us and your father's family for years by the sound of it. I don't see why your aunt shouldn't live there and run it for us. I've kept the money you gave me when Sheila bought your father's stock, and the rent. I didn't need it, so I put it by in case you ever wanted it. You can have that and welcome.'

I was surprised by her generous offer. She hadn't wanted me to have anything to do with Father's family at first, but now she was making it possible for me to provide Gwen with a home and a living.

'Are you sure, Mum? That money was for you – you are entitled to it. I wanted you to have something of your own, just in case.'

'Bert gives me all I need,' she said. 'He's got a bit of money by him, Emma, and he's generous with it. Not like your father. I never have to ask, it's always there for me every week. I'm giving the money to you, mind, not Gwen. It will be your business. She'll work there for a wage and live rent free. If she's satisfied with that, then so am I.'

'You're an angel, Mum.' I hugged her. 'Sheila wants to leave the shop after Christmas. She's moving away from March, going to stay with a friend in London.'

'Her little girl is a beauty,' Mum said. 'I think Sheila is right to make the break. People never did take to her being in that shop. It wasn't so bad when Eric was there, but you know how folk are: give a dog a bad name . . .' She stopped and shook her head. 'I wonder if . . . no, I'm sure that was just a tale.'

'What is it, Mum? What aren't you telling me?'

She looked hesitant, then seemed to make up her mind. 'I've heard people say she drinks . . .'

'Oh, Mum! Surely you can't mean that – not Sheila? I've never seen any sign of it.'

'You don't see her that often, Emma.'

'No, that's true, but . . . it just doesn't sound right,

not like the Sheila I know.' I frowned. Sheila had never been the sort to drink too much. She had always been so bright and full of life. 'She must have changed a lot, that's all I can say.'

'People do change, Emma. I think it shocked her when Eric was ill. She had high hopes of that shop, and somehow it all went wrong for her. Some people can't cope with setbacks. Not the way you have. I suppose she was lonely, and with the drink being there . . .'

'Yes, I suppose it must be a temptation, if one is miserable.'

I knew how it felt to be lonely. And Sheila was not as lucky as I had been. She didn't have good friends to help her conquer her grief and bewilderment. I was her best friend, but I'd been too busy to see her often. Yes, I could understand her loneliness, but drinking wouldn't help.

I decided to go down and see my friend as soon as I could after Christmas. In the meantime, I would write to her and tell her to contact Mr Smythe. At least I could make things easier for her by buying her stock.

And if Gwen agreed to move into Father's old shop, I would have no further need to worry about her future.

All I had to think about now was my own.

'You look lovely, Emma.' Jack's eyes were warm with approval as they went over me. 'That dress is still something special.'

I was wearing the dress Margaret had given me the night I'd accompanied Sol to that reception – the night I'd met Jack. Our first meeting in the street had been too brief to count. It was at the reception that Jack had fallen in love with me, or so he had told me.

'One look at you in that dress was all it took, Emma,' he'd said, and the look in his eyes was so positive that I had to believe him.

Now it was Christmas Eve and he was taking me to a special party. He'd asked if I would wear *the* dress, and I had put it on to please him. I was also wearing the string of pearls he had given me.

'Who is going to be at this party?' I asked as we went out to his car.

It was a black Bentley this time. Jack used what he vaguely termed *official* cars when he was in the country, and he never seemed to have trouble obtaining fuel. Another proof of his status, had I needed it.

'Oh, friends . . . people,' he replied to my question. 'It's part pleasure, part business, Emma. But there's dancing and supper, and I shan't desert you. It won't be like that damned dull reception Sol took you to, I promise.'

I nodded but made no reply. I sensed it was going to be what my mother would call a *posh do*, and I felt a little nervous.

However, when we arrived at the large private house in Mayfair, where the party was being held, my apprehension soon melted away. From the moment Jack introduced me to our hosts, I felt at home.

'This is Robert Melcher – a fellow American, Emma. And this is Jane. Robert's superior half.'

'And if that doesn't put you off, nothing will!' Jane Melcher cried wagging her finger at Jack in mock reproach. 'Oh, my dear, you look gorgeous! Where did you get that dress? Don't tell me. I know it came from Paris before the war. It's impossible to buy anything half as good these days. I adore it. I'm so envious!'

Jane had soft brown hair which she wore swept back in an elegant chignon. Her fine brows were pencilled and her make up was immaculate. She was dressed in a very striking crimson gown, which was obviously expensive.

'Jane has more clothes than any woman I know,' her husband said before I could think of a reply to her remarks about my dress. 'Never let her into your wardrobe, Emma. She will want to borrow everything she likes.'

'Robert simply has no idea,' Jane said, her eyes brimming with laughter. 'It's fun to swop clothes with friends sometimes. It must drive you mad being rationed, Emma. How can you bear it? I couldn't. Thank goodness I brought loads with me.'

Jane tucked her arm through mine. She took me through the crowded reception rooms, introducing me to all her friends, many of whom were also American.

'Has Jack told you anything about us?' she asked, pulling a wry face as I shook my head. 'Isn't that just like a man! Robert is attached to the embassy. They also have business together . . . lots of lovely money, darling! Jack is such a wizard at fixing things.' She squeezed my arm. 'Now tell me about yourself, Emma. I know Jack adores you – and I can see why. I believe you have been married?'

'Yes. Twice. My first husband was killed in a train accident, and Jon . . . he was in the air force. He was reported missing in action over a year ago.'

'How awful for you,' Jane said, looking at me with sympathy. 'You've had rotten luck. Poor you. I don't know how you can stand it. Jack told me you were awfully brave. He admires you so much.'

'Jack has been a good friend.'

'And now he has brought you to us,' Jane said. 'And we're going to be friends, Emma. I always know I either like someone or hate them immediately – and I like you. Now do say you like me or I shall just die of mortification!'

It would have been impossible not to like Jane. She was irrepressible. Full of life and confidence. I felt as if I had been swept up by an irresistible force.

I had never been to a party like this before. There was no shortage of food here, of course. Jane had prepared a sumptuous buffet of all kinds of delicious canapés, smoked salmon, salads, cold meats and gateaux, some I had never seen or tasted before. The champagne was the finest I'd ever had, and the bubbles went up my nose, making me giggle.

Or perhaps it was just sheer relief? After all the gloom of the past months, this was like stepping into a fairytale. It was the glamorous world I had dreamed of when as a young girl I had smuggled magazines about filmstars up to my bedroom: a world that was new and exciting to me.

'Are you enjoying yourself, Emma?' Jack asked as we danced. 'You don't feel lonely or bored here, do you?'

'No, of course not.' I glanced up at him, knowing my eyes must be reflecting my excitement. 'It's fun, Jack. I'm loving it. I don't think I've ever had this much fun in my life.'

'Good.' He grinned at me. 'I thought you would like Jane. She's one of the best people I know.'

'Who could help liking her? Robert seems pleasant as well.'

'He's OK. Mad about Jane, of course. They are my closest friends over here. At home there are lots more – life is better there, Emma. You would like it.'

'Would I?' He nodded. 'Perhaps one day . . .'

'When the war is over, Emma.'

His eyes seemed to demand a commitment from me. I knew what he was asking me, the promise he wanted me to make.

I smiled at him. 'I think I might like to see America. When the war is over . . .'

When the war was over, and *if* Jon didn't come back. I believed Jack understood the words that remained unspoken.

'I'll remind you of that one day.'

'One day . . . if you still want me to come.' I gave

him a teasing look. 'You may have forgotten me by then. You may have found someone a lot more exciting than me . . .'

'You want to bet?' His eyes challenged me. I shook my head and he smiled. 'Just as well. You would have lost your money, Emma.'

I leaned my head against his shoulder. The music was soft and dreamy, and I had drunk perhaps three glasses of that delicious champagne. I was feeling relaxed and it was good to be close to Jack. He smelled of something that reminded me of heather – the scents of Scotland.

My throat caught with emotion. I was filled with a sense of longing, of need. I could not bear to go on being alone, without hope. I wanted to be loved.

'What's wrong, Emma?'

The note of concern in Jack's voice brought tears to my eyes. I blinked them away as I looked up at him.

'Could we go somewhere, Jack? Could we be alone?'

I saw the swift gleam in his eyes and knew he understood what I was asking.

'Yes, of course,' he said. 'Come on, I'll show you.'

Jack took my arm, steering me through the crowded room. We went out into the gardens through a conservatory.

'I stay here when I'm in London,' Jack said. 'There's a kind of apartment over what was once the stable or something. It's just through here. You will like it . . .'

He took my hand, leading me through the shrubbery. There wasn't much light, just a sprinkling of stars in an otherwise black sky. We went down some steps and through a courtyard, then arrived at a rather odd-looking door that was split in the middle and studded with black iron bolts.

'It still looks like a stable,' I whispered, feeling the need to keep this escape of ours secret though there was no one around to overhear us.

'You'll see . . .'

He switched on a light once the door was shut. The room we were in was like a continuation of the garden, with plants in pots, a tiled floor and basketwork chairs. The windows were long, right down to the floor, and had wooden shutters, which were tightly shut. In the summer they could be opened up, enabling the room to be used as a summer house.

Stairs led up to the living accommodation. There was a self-contained apartment with a kitchen, sitting-room, bedroom and bathroom. The furniture was oak, well polished and ancient, the curtains a soft rose damask.

'It was done over originally for the son of the owner,' Jack told me as I looked around with interest. 'He was an artist and he used the room downstairs as his studio.'

'Yes, it would be good for that . . . when the shutters are open.'

'Plenty of light,' Jack agreed. His voice sounded husky, a little breathless. He was staring at me, watchful, waiting. 'Emma . . . you know I love you . . .'

'I think I'm in love with you, Jack,' I said. 'I'm not sure. I just know I haven't felt like this about anyone else.' I moved towards him, my eyes meeting his in silent appeal. I wanted him to understand that I wasn't giving up Jon. My love for Jon wasn't affected. This was different. It wasn't Jon's wife who stood here. It was a different Emma. A woman I had only half suspected was there inside me.

'I know how I feel about you,' Jack said, moving to take me in his arms. 'I've wanted you since the first moment I saw you at that reception. You looked so beautiful standing there, and yet slightly vulnerable. I wanted to sweep you up in my arms, to run off with you there and then, to keep you safe and love you.'

I laughed. Being with Jack always made me feel like laughing. Suddenly it all seemed so right. It was as if the past had faded away, taking with it all the pain and hurt. I didn't want to think about the things that caused me grief. Jack was here. He was alive, strong, vibrant – and the excitement was coursing through my veins.

'Love me, Jack,' I whispered, moving closer to him. 'Make love to me now. Make me believe there is a place for us, a world where people are happy as a right. I want all the good things of life. I want to be like Jane and . . .'

I wanted to feel alive again. As Jack drew me to him, I felt it begin to happen. It was like a rebirth, a new beginning. The old Emma was throwing off the shadows that had claimed her as a bird might moult its feathers, to emerge wearing a shiny and new coat.

Our lips met in a passionate kiss. It was a lightning bolt from the sky. Not for us sweet content. We were tearing off each other's clothes in our urgency, panting, gasping as the shudders of delight ran through us.

Jack's body was lean, hard, honed to a masculine beauty I had not seen before. He was a young pagan god, and I his goddess. We had no religion but love, the love we shared that night in Jack's bed. There in my lover's arms I discovered all the pleasures I had never experienced with any man before him.

He had all Richard's virility and strength but without the brutality. He was tender, patient, inventive and yet arrogantly male. He claimed me, possessed me, made me his, and I adored him for it. I wanted nothing more than to lie in his arms my whole life long.

For those sweet stolen hours we spent together there was only Jack. I knew then that the feeling I had for him was very special. There are many kinds of love: the love of a mother for her child is also special, but that night I discovered something I knew I would never find again. I might love again, but this . . . completeness . . . would never come with anyone else.

I had known content with Jon, and a kind of slow, gentle happiness, but my love for him had been a pale shadow of what I felt now. Jon had been good to me. He was there when I needed a friend . . . he *was* my friend.

Suddenly I saw how true that was. Jon had always been my loving friend. I had married him because I was afraid of losing his friendship. I had never been *in love* with him.

The threat of war looming over us had made me rush my decision. I had meant to wait. After Richard's death and the realization that what I had felt for my first lover, Paul Greenslade, was merely a naive young girl's infatuation, I had meant to wait until I was certain, but the fear that Jon might die had made me promise to marry him.

Yet it had not been a mistake, no never that. We *had* been happy together, and had it not been for this cruel war might be still. Many women married for less reason. Jon had loved me desperately and I loved him. Had he not been killed . . .

I did not believe I would have betrayed my husband if he had lived. I would never have allowed myself to think of Jack. Perhaps he would never have entered my world. Had there been no war, Jon and I might have lived in the country, content and safe in our own home.

Would I have been content to live that way for ever?

So many doubts to torture me!

Yet I did not feel them as I lay in Jack's arms that night. No, they would return to haunt me one day, but not that night. For a time I thought only of him and the pleasure we both shared.

'You are so lovely, Emma. I've thought of you this

way. So many times. I hoped, *knew* we would be together one day. I'll never let you go, my darling. You are mine now.'

I did not answer him, except to press myself against the warmth of his body. There was nothing to say. I had learned never to take too much for granted. Life had a habit of knocking down your dreams. Jack was here at this moment. Neither of us knew where he would be the next week or month.

'Don't make promises, Jack,' I whispered. 'We won't promise each other anything; we won't ask too much. The gods punish us if we are too greedy. Let's take what we can tonight and forget tomorrow . . .'

'Foolish, Emma,' Jack murmured against my throat. The touch of his mouth sent the trickles of desire running through me once more. 'You need have no fear for me. I'm indestructible. Like a bad penny. I always turn up whether you want me to or not . . .'

'Oh, Jack . . .' The emotion caught my throat as I clung to him. I wanted so much all the things he had promised would be ours. 'Jack hold me . . . hold me for ever . . .'

He laughed, confident, arrogant, sure of himself and his ability to win no matter what. Yet I felt his own urgent need as he took me once more. Even Jack could not be sure he would return from the war that was so soon to swallow him up.

And so we made love again and again, as if our hunger for each other could never be slaked.

*

Jack spent Christmas Day with us. He brought extravagant presents for all of us, but especially for me. Fine, delicate stockings, good perfume, make up, confectionery, all the things it was becoming impossible to find in England – and a beautiful diamond pendant set in a white gold mount that was shaped like a heart.

'Jack,' I said when we were private for a moment. 'This is far too expensive, too much for me to accept.'

'It's a trinket,' he said. 'One day I'll give you real diamonds.' He smiled as I looked doubtful. 'Don't frown, Emma. You look guilty, as if you thought you were doing something wrong. You do have the right to happiness, you know.'

'Yes, of course I do. I'm sorry. I'm just not used to . . . it's beautiful and I'm a fool. I love it, Jack. And I love you, more than you know.'

'We are going to have so much fun together,' he said as he drew me close. 'There's a big wide world out there, Emma. I want to share it with you. I want to show you what life is all about.'

All I thought of as he kissed me was how good it felt to be in his arms. Jack's world did sound exciting, and I longed to be a part of it, but being held like this meant so much more. I clung to him, knowing I had to make the most of every moment we had together.

Yet there were others to claim our attention. James was really enjoying his toys this year. Sol and Margaret had given him so many lovely things: soft animals he could cuddle, a spinning top, building bricks, a music box and a kaleidoscope were just a few of the toys he was given that day to add to the growing collection in the nursery.

Jack had bought him a bright red pedal car. It was the sort of toy only the very rich gave to their children, and as I watched my son playing with his things I felt oddly afraid. James was in danger of having too much too soon.

Yet how could I think that? All my friends loved both James and me. They gave freely out of their love for us – so how could that be a bad thing?

It couldn't of course, and I was a fool to let even the smallest cloud spoil our perfect day.

My mother telephoned just after three that afternoon.

'Are you having a nice day, Emma?'

'Yes, thank you, Mum. Are you?'

'Oh yes. There's just me and Bert, but we had a good dinner. Bert is having forty winks in the chair now. Thank you for that lovely cardigan, Emma, and all the other things. I don't know how you manage to get hold of stuff the way you do.'

'I've got friends in high places,' I joked. 'Most of it comes through Jack, Mum. I'm not sure how he does it, but he seems to be able to get hold of almost anything.'

'Is Jack with you today?'

'Yes . . . Yes, he's here.'

She was silent for a moment, then, 'You sound different, Emma. Is there something I should know?'

'There might be . . . one day. I don't want to talk

about it yet, Mum. Jack will be going away soon. America is in the war now. I can't think about the future, not until this is all over.'

'But you're happier than you were. I can hear it in your voice.'

'Yes. At the moment I am very happy.'

'That's good,' she said. 'I had better go or Bert will tell me I am costing him a fortune.'

'You know he doesn't care,' I said and laughed. 'James loved the clown you sent him, Mum, and the blouse you made for me is exactly what I need to go with my best costume. Give my love to Bert, won't you?'

'You'll be down to sort out the shop soon,' she said. 'We'll talk properly then.'

I smiled as I replaced the receiver and went back to join the others. They were nodding over a glass of sherry and listening to music on the radio.

James went to bed at seven that evening. Afterwards, Jack and I slipped away. We spent the night in his apartment, holding each other, whispering words of love . . . making love.

Jack cooked bacon and mushrooms the next morning. It was only when we had eaten and it was time for me to leave that he told me was going away that afternoon.

I felt the dread strike into my heart. Was I going to lose him so soon? I had hoped for a few more days, a few more weeks, before he had to go.

'Do you have to leave so soon?'

'If I don't take this opportunity it may be weeks before I can get back,' Jack said. He brushed a wisp of hair away that had stuck to my cheek. 'You know I don't want to leave you here, my darling, but you wouldn't come with me if I asked, would you?'

'No . . . I couldn't, Jack. Not yet. Not until the war is over and things are more settled. It would feel wrong . . . as if I had abandoned everyone.'

'That's what I expected you to say.' Jack smiled and kissed my forehead. 'It's the way I feel too. My country is in this war now, Emma. Americans are going to be killed – and I have to do what I can. I've been offered a commission, and I intend to take it.'

'But what difference will one man make? Surely you can do so much more in other ways, Jack?'

'I doubt if I'll see much combat,' he said, but I knew he was lying to comfort me. 'I expect they will make use of my talents in other ways. I'm very good at planning and moving things. I dare say I'll be at head-quarters most of the time, looking after the logistics of the thing.'

'Honestly?' I gazed up at him, wanting to be convinced. 'Is that a promise, Jack?'

'If you're asking me to promise I'll come back, the answer is I'll do my damnedest, Emma.'

'When?' I demanded, knowing I was being unfair to ask such questions but not caring. 'Tell me, Jack – is there any chance of you coming back to London before the war is over?'

'I don't know. I would be lying if I pretended

otherwise.' He looked rueful. 'I'm sorry. I shan't be a free agent any more, Emma. If there's a chance, I'll take it, believe me, but I can't promise.'

'I just wondered . . .' I took a deep breath. 'We'll just have to hope it doesn't go on too long . . .'

'The tide will turn in our favour before long,' Jack said, and put his arms around me. You'll see, my darling. Things will start to get better soon. I promise . . .'

Chapter 8

'I've talked to Sol,' I said to Sheila. It was three days after Jack's departure, three nights of holding back the tears, of suppressing my fear and my loneliness. I had come down to March on the train, to help my friend sort out the details of giving up her lease. 'Sol will be very pleased to have you working in the showroom. If you want to come, he can probably find you accommodation near Portobello Road.'

'I've got somewhere to live,' she said, turning away to move something on the shelf. 'My cousin lives in London, not far off the Portobello, somewhere around Kensington. Annie will look after my little Lizzy while I'm at work. She has got three children of her own so she can't work and the rent I pay her will help her.'

'That sounds a sensible arrangement,' I said, a little surprised but pleased that her cousin should live in one of the nicer parts of London. 'It seems as if things will work out for the best, Sheila.'

'Yes, I suppose so.' She looked doubtful, slightly resentful as she turned to me. 'I wanted to make a go of it here, Emma. I feel I've let myself down – and you.'

'I've told you it won't affect me. My aunt will

probably come and live here. I haven't spoken to Gwen yet, but I think she will agree. If she doesn't, then I shall have to find someone else to run the place – but I'll cross that bridge when I come to it.'

'You won't sell then?'

'No, I don't think so. When I went to London, I just wanted to close the door on the past. I couldn't wait to get away, but things look different now. I've learned to live with my memories. Besides, after the war life will get back to normal, Sheila. My father had a good business here, and I think it could be made to work again.'

'Yes, you will make a better job of it than I could.'

Sheila sounded bitter. I knew she was disappointed, and I felt unable to help. What could I say or do that would make up for the loss of both her husband and her dreams?

'I know it's hard,' I said at last. 'I know how difficult it has been for you. If you want to try again, Sheila, I might be able to lend you some money . . .'

'No!' She was quite determined. 'No, I've made up my mind. I've had enough of being stuck here. I want to be where there's a bit of life going on. Besides, people hate me here. You don't know what they're like, Emma. Your father was always respected. People looked up to him – they resented my being here. They wouldn't give me a chance. It wasn't so bad while Eric was here, but after he . . . well, everything went wrong. People stopped coming in, and they insinuated things. They were just waiting for me to fall flat on

my face – and now they've got their way. I hope they're
satisfied!'

'Oh, Sheila . . .'

I looked at her sadly. I wasn't sure how much of
what she was saying was true and how much was in
her mind. Surely people hadn't been that unkind? Yet
my mother had suggested something similar. And it
was true that Harold Robinson had always been
respected. It had meant a great deal to him – so much
that he had forced me into an unhappy marriage to
save his good name.

That was all over! I hardly ever thought about
Richard or my childhood now. All those things had
happened to a different Emma. The Emma who had
lived and worked in this shop.

It looked very much changed these days. Eric had
put up a lot of extra shelves and racks to hold his wine
stock. Even though there wasn't much of that left. I
wondered if Gwen had an objection to strong drink.
If she did, we might get rid of what there was and go
back to what we had always sold.

'It isn't your fault,' Sheila said, coming out of her
mood suddenly. her eyes gleamed and she was more
like the girl I had known before I went to London. 'I
shall be glad to get away and start again. Who knows?
In London I might meet a rich man who will keep me
in comfort for the rest of my life.'

'Yes, you might,' I said. 'It happens sometimes,
and if it doesn't, you can keep working for us. One
day I would like to have a dress shop in London,

Sheila. There will always be a job for you if I'm around.'

'Thanks.' She lit a cigarette, drawing the smoke in and exhaling it through her nostrils. 'I needed that. I smoke far more than I ever did. Being here amongst all this stuff has led me into bad ways, Emma. It's a good thing I'm getting out, making a fresh start somewhere else.'

'So when are you leaving exactly?'

'In the morning. I'll drop the keys off with your mother. You can pick them up from her – or your aunt can.' Sheila's red mouth screwed up with resentment. 'She's welcome to all this. I can't wait to leave.'

I was sorry that she was so bitter, but there was nothing more I could do for the moment. When she was living in London we would be able to see more of each other, then perhaps I could help her to find a new life for herself and her child.

'Mother wanted you to have these,' Gwen said, setting down the cardboard box on the desk in the study. 'It's just letters she kept from your father, some photographs and a couple of her personal things – a silver compact and an ivory fan. I'm not sure you would really want them, but she made me promise to give them to you, Emma.'

'I'm very grateful to you for bringing them all this way. What are you going to do with all the rest of her things?'

'Pack them into trunks and have them stored for the

time being I suppose. I'm not sure yet where I shall settle . . . or what kind of work I can manage. I suppose they want women in the factories – or am I too old? I thought you might know . . .'

She was trying not to look anxious, but I knew how worried she must be. It was hard to start working for a living after so many years of being at home.

'Would you consider living in Father's old shop, Gwen? Or rather in the rooms above . . .' I smiled as she stared at me. 'My tenant has just moved out. I was rather hoping you might consider running the shop for me . . .'

'You mean serve behind the counter?'

'Yes. You would have to reorder the stock when we run out, and keep the accounts – I could show you, Gwen. It's quite simple. I can go through them with you when I come down and explain anything that worries you.' She hadn't spoken and I thought perhaps she disliked the idea. 'If you would rather not, you could still use the rooms and look for work in March . . .'

She looked at me then, and I saw the sudden leap of excitement in her eyes. 'You mean you would really trust me to look after things for you, Emma? I would be in charge . . . of everything?'

'Yes, of course. I'll take you down and go through it all with you, of course, but afterwards – it would be up to you.'

'I could do just what I liked – arrange things the way I want? Choose what we sell?' She started to laugh as I nodded. 'And you're going to pay me for doing that?'

'Yes, of course. I thought three pounds a week to start, and your accommodation. Once things are up and running, perhaps a share of the profits at the end of the year.'

'My wage will be enough,' she said decisively. 'I've never had so much freedom in my life, Emma. After I've settled everything, I'll have a few pounds over, and with my wage and no rent to pay . . . all I can say is thank you. For your help – and for believing in me. That means more than all the rest.'

'I'm just glad you're going to take the shop over,' I said. 'I might have had to sell if you hadn't agreed, and I doubt I would have got anything like its worth at the moment.' I looked at her anxiously. 'You aren't doing it just to please me?'

'Good gracious, no! I would tell you if I didn't think it would suit me, Emma. Believe me, this is exactly what I want. I've always thought it would be nice to work in a little shop.'

'Sheila's husband had a licence to sell alcohol, but we can give that up, Gwen. I should need to apply for a new licence anyway. How do you feel about selling wines and spirits?'

'Mother and I always enjoyed a glass of sherry in the evenings,' Gwen said. 'You apply for the licence if you want, Emma. It won't affect me either way.' She looked at me eagerly. 'When can I move in?'

'I could take you down tomorrow if you like?'

'The sooner the better,' she said. 'Mother's cousin is dealing with the cottage. He will send on the things I want and sell the rest. There's a market for second-hand furniture at the moment, and clothes. Of course I shan't sell her clothes, though she had some nice things.'

I stared at Gwen thoughtfully. I hadn't thought much about what it must be like to lose everything until now. But people who were bombed out would have only the clothes they were wearing. All of a sudden, something Jane Melcher had said to me was adding up with my aunt's casual remarks.

'If you do decide to sell your mother's clothes, would you let me see them first?'

'Of course.' Gwen looked surprised. 'I doubt you would want them, Emma, though the material is good. Years ago, Mother bought only the best. I know some people might think they were worth a few shillings – to cut up and make into rugs or quilts, but as you know, I'm not a needlewoman.'

'I think they might be suitable to be remade into something wearable,' I said. 'The government is always telling is to use our imagination and save materials. You've given me an idea. I'm not sure it will come to anything, but save her personal things for the moment, please. Anything at all you think is attractive or useful.'

'You can have them and welcome,' Gwen said. 'I packed the best things in a trunk by themselves. I'll ask Philip to have it sent direct to you.'

'Thank you. I'll look through them, then I'll be in touch before I do anything.'

I looked through the box that Gwen had given me that evening. The silver compact and fan were pretty, and things that I would always keep to remind me of Grandmother Robinson, but it was the letters that interested me most. Letters from my father to his mother.

I had always been curious about my father's life before he came to March, and getting to know my grandmother had only partially satisfied that interest. Now I discovered that she had kept letters from before the time I was born, when Harold Robinson first met my mother . . .

Tears stung my eyes as I read of his excitement at opening up his own shop and his hopes for the future . . . then his feelings when he was getting married.

'*Greta is the prettiest woman I've ever seen*,' he had written.

> I didn't think she would have me, but I've managed to persuade her. I think it best you don't come for the wedding. He might make things awkward for you, and there's no point in causing more rows than you need. I am enclosing ten pounds, and I shall send more when I can.

There were letters telling of his marriage, of my birth, and then a gap of several months. When he wrote again, his letter was very brief and made no mention of either me or my mother. He did not mention either of us for three years, then he began to write about me, telling his mother how bright I was for my age – but never any word about my mother.

I closed the last of the letters, written just a month before he died. Not once had he mentioned the true reason for my marriage, or that it had been a mistake. Obviously, he had not wanted his mother to know of the part he had played, perhaps out of a sense of shame.

I felt sad as I put the letters away in a drawer. How different all our lives might have been if my father had not been so bitter.

Margaret was right to say that we must all make the most of our chances to be happy. Once gone, that chance did not always come again.

I took Gwen down to March the next day. My mother had been in and cleaned the rooms for her and she was waiting to welcome us with a cup of tea and one of her fatless sponges.

'You are very welcome,' she told Gwen. 'Emma has spoken well of you, and I'm glad we've finally met after all these years. Harold never mentioned his family to me. I was angry when you first wrote – but I'm over it now. I hope we shall be friends.'

My aunt nodded her agreement. 'I see no reason why we shouldn't be, Greta. I've had nothing but kindness from Emma, and I mean to do my best to repay her.'

'If you're fair with us, I'll be fair with you.'

I watched them sizing each other up and was a little amused, since I knew they would both be trying to win my good opinion. They were much the same age. Both had been restricted by circumstance and duty for years, now they were both free to live as they pleased. I hoped they would come to appreciate each other, and I sensed a certain rivalry.

I stayed with my mother that night, leaving Gwen to settle into her new home alone. In the morning she and I opened the shop together. We checked the stock list, finding that a few items were missing. Sheila must have miscounted the bottles of spirits. We were short of two bottles of gin and a hundred cigarettes.

'You should speak to your lawyer, Emma. She owes you money,' Gwen said.

'It doesn't matter. We both know where we are, Gwen. We'll start from here.'

By lunch time we had gone through everything Gwen needed to know. Watching her serve the few customers who came in, I was convinced that she would cope easily. For years she had cared for her invalid mother and balanced their meagre income. By comparison, the shop would be simple for her to manage.

Satisfied that she was settling in, I left her to it and went to visit Mrs Henty. Half an hour later I was on my way home.

'This came for you,' Margaret said as I went into the sitting room the next morning. She smiled and my heart missed a beat as I looked at the handwriting. It was a letter from Jack. 'Run away and read it, my dear. We can talk later, when you're ready.'

'No, I'll read it later,' I said, sitting opposite her. 'There has been so much to do recently that we've hardly had time to talk. How are you?'

'I'm just the same,' she said. 'Tired but no worse than usual. Please don't worry, Emma. I dare say I shall go on this way for ever.'

'I do hope so – oh, not that you should feel tired, of course.'

'I know exactly what you meant.' She smiled in understanding. 'You are like a daughter to me, Emma.'

'You've been like a second mother to me.'

'I'm glad you are happy here with us.'

'Yes, I am. Very . . .' I paused, then as I suddenly thought of something, 'Oh, I wanted to talk to you, Margaret. Do you remember telling me once that you had some dresses you would never wear again?'

'Yes, of course. I said you could have them – would you like to have them now?'

'I was thinking I might buy them from you,' I said. 'I'm not sure how much they would sell for . . .'

'Are you thinking of having a stall in Petticoat Lane?' She looked intrigued, amused.

'Not a stall – a shop.' I laughed. My thoughts were still forming, still tentative. 'It's just an idea at the moment. Something Jane Melcher said about women liking to exchange clothes. Gwen was talking about her mother's things. Apparently, my grandmother had some good clothes years ago. Second-hand clothes are not subject to rationing. I wondered if some women had clothes they could no longer wear because they simply don't fit . . . they might like to sell or exchange them. We would give them a value for theirs and make a charge for our service or simply buy and sell . . .'

Margaret looked interested. 'I think that's a good idea, Emma. If you could make sure everything was good quality. You wouldn't want the kind of thing they sell in the flea market.'

'Oh no,' I said, warming to my theme as we talked. 'If it is to work, the idea must appeal to women like Jane Melcher. But I don't see why it shouldn't work. There must be lots of women who are bored with their own clothes at the moment, don't you think so? Some of them are good at sewing; they would probably buy just for the material . . .'

Margaret's eyes sparkled with interest. 'How clever you are, Emma. I think this is very exciting.' She stood up. 'Shall we go upstairs and see what we can find?'

'Are you sure you are not too tired?'

'Do you know,' she said. 'I suddenly feel much better. Let's go now, Emma – unless you want to read your letter first?'

'Oh no,' I said. 'It will keep. I would like to look through your wardrobes, Margaret. Jane was right, looking at other women's clothes is fascinating. And I love clothes, don't you? Even things that have been put away and not worn for years.'

Margaret agreed. 'Oh yes. When I was young I spent a fortune on them! I haven't bothered to open some of my wardrobes for ages. Everything is wrapped and will probably smell of mothballs, but they can be aired. At least everything is clean. I always had my special gowns cleaned before I put them away.'

The next hour was so exciting, rather like opening up an Aladdin's cave. Before her illness, Margaret had loved to go out, and to entertain. She had one large wardrobe devoted to her evening clothes.

'But these are wonderful!' I exclaimed as I went through them, discovering expensive gowns she had bought in Paris years ago and worn perhaps once or twice at most. They had been kept so beautifully that the material looked new. 'You can't possibly bear to part with them, Margaret?'

'Most of them would be too tight for me now, even if I had any use for them. I prefer something simpler these days, and I have gained almost a stone in weight since I was a young woman. Besides, they are old-fashioned. Some are still wearable, but others would be of use only to someone who was clever with her needle.'

'That is exactly what I had in mind.' My thoughts were racing ahead as I handled the rich velvets, silks and satins. 'It is almost impossible to buy material this good at the moment. Even the trimmings – handmade buttons like these would thrill someone like Jane.'

She smiled at my enthusiasm. 'If you want them, they are yours, Emma.'

'Thank you.' I did a rapid calculation in my head. 'I saw a shop to let in Kensington High Street the other day. It was just a tiny place, but I know it would be big enough to start with, and the rent won't be much. I'll need to have it refurbished . . . buy rails, hangers, mirrors . . .'

'Sol can help with those, but you'll want one or two nice chairs and little tables to stand about,' Margaret said. 'Give the place a pleasant atmosphere, Emma. If you want people like Jane Melcher to feel comfortable, you must make them think it is fun to shop with you. It should be more like visiting friends than shopping. Go for something out of the ordinary . . . I know!' She opened another large wardrobe, which contained costumes and day dresses. 'Up there . . . on the shelf. I'm sure I kept it. A large fan made of ostrich feathers . . .'

I reached it down for her. It had been carefully wrapped in silk and looked as fresh as if it were new.

'It was always far too big to use,' Margaret said. 'But it would be amusing to have on your wall – or as window dressing.'

'Yes . . .' I was beginning to see what she meant, and I knew it would appeal to Jane, and therefore her friends. 'I see what you're getting at. Something outrageous and fun . . . like the twenties. A time when everyone did what they liked and no one cared about the rules. It is a start, Margaret, and I could see what else Gwen has kept of her mother's. There might be all kinds of things we could use to create the right mood, things she would only throw away.'

'It will be like a breath of fresh air,' Margaret said and laughed. 'Everyone is so sick of the war, Emma. All we are told is that we must be prepared to make sacrifices. Of course we all do, every day, but there must be a lot of woman with money to spend who would enjoy buying from you – a little madness is sometimes a good thing. I am sure I have lots more things you could use. It doesn't have to be just clothes. I have several beaded evening bags and shoes I've hardly worn.'

'Oh, you are an angel,' I cried and hugged her. 'I shall never be able to repay you.'

'I don't want money, but I would like to share in the fun, Emma. Perhaps I could help in the shop. Just three afternoons a week. I get so bored sitting here day after day.'

I looked at her uncertainly. 'Would Sol mind? He worries about you, Margaret.'

'Too much sometimes,' she said with a wistful air. 'He would never have consented to my working – but this is different. I shan't really be working. You won't need to pay me, and we could have a regular woman to keep things tidy. I would just be there to talk to the customers and keep an eye on the staff for you.'

'It might even make you feel better, being with other people.'

I looked at Margaret thoughtfully. Her air of weariness had lifted. She seemed brighter, more alive than usual.

'Of course you can share the fun,' I said. 'I would love to share it all with you, Margaret. We shall have to reassure Sol that you won't do too much, but if he agrees . . .'

'He will have to,' Margaret said, a gleam of determination in her eyes. 'Why don't you go out this morning and see if that shop is still to let?'

'I will,' I said. 'I'll take James with me. The fresh air will do him good.'

I did not read Jack's letter until I was alone in my room that night. In a few short hours, I had signed the lease of my little shop, arranged for it to be painted inside and out, and spoken to Jane about my plans.

'How marvellous,' she exclaimed. 'Darling Emma! How clever of you to think of it. I have several things I would love to exchange or sell, and I know my friends would be amused by the idea – especially if you will let me help out sometimes. They will all think it is so funny! I am sure we can make it a success.'

'Margaret wants to help, too. She has thought of some unusual things for us to sell. How would it be if the three of us became partners? I'm not expecting to make lots of money, Jane. I just thought it would be exciting. Something to make us all forget about the war and the shortages.'

'And you were right,' Jane said. 'But I see no reason why we shouldn't make some money, too. Robert will be amazed. He won't believe I am actually going to work! Oh, darling, you can't imagine how thrilled I am.' She went into a peal of delighted laughter. 'Now tell me, Emma. What do you need? I can help with money or things – whichever you need most.'

'We want it to look rather like a lady's parlour,' I explained. 'We'll have rails for the clothes, of course, but we wanted a couple of elbow chairs and a pretty settee – and some gilt-framed mirrors. Perhaps a glass-fronted cabinet to put small items in. You know the kind of thing, Jane. Do you have any spare curtains put away that we could use for the dressing rooms?'

'I'm sure there are loads of things packed away in the attics, and I know there are a few pretty pieces of Edwardian furniture there. Robert doesn't care for anything like that. He likes good solid oak or mahogany, so he wouldn't mind us having them.'

'That's wonderful,' I said. 'And any clothes you don't want, of course. We will put a value on them, and credit them to your share.'

'You are so businesslike,' Jane said, laughing again. 'I'm sure we shall all make our fortunes.'

'I very much doubt it,' I replied. 'But I think we shall all enjoy ourselves trying – and just think! We don't have to worry about rules and regulations because everything is second-hand. It is going to be a bit like a church bazaar but in a London street.'

'Oh, glorious,' Jane said. 'You must come and have lunch with me one day soon, Emma. We will raid the attics together. I know there are several trunks up there. Who knows what treasures we shall find!'

Margaret was enthusiastic when I told her of Jane's reaction.

'That will help make the shop a success,' she said. 'Jane knows all the right people, and she is popular. If she is seen to approve, others will follow her lead. It will give everyone an uplift to believe they are actually entering into the spirit of make do and mend, while having lots of fun. We could give our customers tea, and possibly biscuits – home-made, of course.'

'In a way the original idea was Jane's,' I said. 'It all came from a chance remark at a party, and Gwen talking about her mother's things – but you have made it all seem so much more exciting.'

Margaret shook her head. 'No one else thought of the shop,' she said. 'That was your idea, Emma.'

I spoke to Sol about our plans that evening, stressing the lighter side of it and playing down the fact that we actually intended it to be a business.

'Well, if it amuses you both,' he said, smiling indulgently. 'It may give Margaret an interest. As long as she doesn't tire herself – and you don't desert me. I shall still need you at the showroom, Emma.'

'No, of course I shan't desert you,' I said. 'I enjoy working with you, Sol. And I know you have enough problems. I promise I shall never leave you in the lurch, whatever happens.'

He nodded, an odd expression in his eyes. 'I may be about to solve one of my problems. No, I shan't tell you just yet. It may come to nothing. I'll wait until I'm sure.'

'As you like.' I looked at him thoughtfully. 'How is Sheila doing in the showroom? Are you pleased with her?'

He considered for a moment. 'She's bright enough in her way, and attractive. We'll see how she shapes up. I dare say she will do. In any case, we are probably lucky to have her. We're not exactly priority these days. The government soaks up all the best labour. If it wasn't for Sheila's daughter, they would probably take her away from us. It's only because she claims to be needed at home for part of the day that we get away with it – much the same as you, Emma.'

'Yes, I know.'

Sometimes I felt guilty. Perhaps I ought to be doing more vital work. I was still helping at the social club, of course, but other women were doing so much more: working on the land or in the factories.

'I must get Sheila to do a few hours' voluntary work,' I said. 'It all helps. Just in case someone decides you don't need both of us.'

Sol agreed. We said goodnight and I went up to the nursery. It was my habit to look in at James before I went to bed. He was sleeping peacefully. I was glad that both Nanny and Mrs Rowan were over forty. Otherwise we might have lost them to the government's war work.

As I went back to my own room, I frowned over the worn carpet on the nursery stairs. It had been repaired once, but I could see that it was beginning to fray again in places. Something must be done about it or it might become dangerous in time.

Alone in my bedroom at last, I took out Jack's letter and slit the envelope with a silver paper knife Sol had once given me. There were three sheets covered in Jack's bold script.

He told me what was happening in America, of the changes in attitude towards the war, and how strange it was to see so many men in uniform on the streets.

'*In London it was not unusual, but here it seems odd*,' he wrote.

> *Yet it is a change I welcome, Emma. I have always felt it was a war that all right-minded men should want to fight. We cannot allow Hitler to get away with the terrible things he has done. We have to beat him, and do it in such a way that no one will ever dare to commit such atrocities again. But enough of war, my darling. My thoughts are always with you. I wonder every day what you are doing and hope that you are happy and well. If you write to me, Robert will see that your letters are sent on wherever I happen to be. He and Jane are good people, my darling. I trust them to look after you while I'm away. I'm sending you a parcel. It will arrive in the usual way . . .*

I laughed, then read his letter again twice before folding it and putting it away in the drawer next to the gifts he had given me.

How long would it be before I saw Jack again?

Tears stung my eyes. How I hated this war! It had robbed me of Jon. Would it take Jack, too?

I would not allow myself to dwell on such morbid thoughts! Jack had promised to come back, and somehow I believed he would. Jack was too confident, too full of life to be defeated by a little thing like war . . .

Chapter 9

'I wish you had let me know you were ill,' I said and bent to kiss Pops on the cheek. He was sitting in his chair in the front parlour, but he looked very frail and I thought he probably ought to be still in bed. 'I would have come over sooner if I had known.'

'If you visited us now and then, you would have known Pops hasn't been at all well for a while,' Mrs Reece said, giving me an angry look. 'But I suppose we are not really important to you now. You've forgotten us, just as you've forgotten Jon.'

Something in her eyes at that moment made me wonder what she had heard. I had never tried to hide my friendship with Jack, but she couldn't know that we had become lovers on his last visit. No one else knew that for certain, though both Sol and Margaret suspected it. Neither of them would have told Mrs Reece, however.

'That's not fair,' I said, controlling my urge to strike back. Losing my temper would not help anyone. 'I shall never forget Jon. Nor you and Pops. I know I haven't been to visit for a while, but it has been difficult. There is so much to do these days I've been opening a new shop with some friends, that's besides working in the showroom and helping out at the club.

I like to take James to the park on Sundays. It's the only day I have with him.'

'We understand,' Pops said and caught my hand. He gave me his sweet smile. 'I know you come when you can manage it, Emma. I wouldn't let Dorothy telephone you, because I know you have so much to do – but I am very glad to see you now. Sit down and talk to me, my dear. Tell me what you've been doing . . .'

I did as he asked, spending far longer than I had intended with him. I would be late for work, but that would have to take second place for once. Seeing him so poorly had made me feel guilty for neglecting him. To be perfectly honest, I would have been glad of an excuse not to visit Jon's mother, but I really loved Pops. If anything happened to him I would miss him – and it would make coming here to this house even more of a duty.

'I really will try to visit more often,' I promised as I kissed Pops goodbye later. 'Take care of yourself.'

'You take care of yourself, Emma.' He studied my face anxiously. 'You do look a little tired, my dear. You should take more time to relax yourself. You're not overdoing things, are you?'

'No . . .' I sighed. 'It's just that I can't sleep some-times . . .'

I lay awake often at night, thinking about Jack, about the war – and all the people who were no longer with us.

Pops squeezed my hand. 'It isn't much of a life for you, Emma. You should get out more, enjoy yourself.'

'At least I'm enjoying getting our new shop ready,'

I said, and smiled at him. 'It gives me something to think about . . . makes things a little brighter somehow.'

'The war will be over one of these days,' Pops promised. 'You are very young, Emma. There are a lot of good things out there waiting for you. You just have to be patient.'

I smiled and thanked him, but I was thoughtful as I caught a bus home. There were times, often when I was alone at night, when the waiting seemed unbearable, but there wasn't much else we could do. We just had to make the most of what we had, and at least I had good friends – and my shop.

We called our shop *Charm & Elegance*, and it was an instant success.

Our first customers were all Jane's friends, of course, but within hours we had women coming in off the street, more out of curiosity than anything else at first. However, when they saw the beautiful things we had on offer, many of them were keen to buy. Some purchased whatever took their fancy then came back the same day with a garment of their own to sell, then bought something else from the rails. They stopped for a cup of tea and a chat, and went away vowing to tell all their friends about us.

The idea of being able to part exchange their unwanted clothes seemed to amuse and intrigue everyone who came in, and the sales were even better than I had expected.

'One woman bought three dresses from me this

afternoon,' Margaret told me when we were talking at the end of our first week. 'Not one of them would fit her, but she has three granddaughters who are apparently very good at sewing and she was thrilled to be able to get such lovely material. The dresses all have very full skirts and I am sure her granddaughters will be able to make something rather nice with the material; she was pleased anyway.'

'So our idea is working?'

'Your idea, Emma.' She smiled at me. 'I was beginning to think we would sell out in a few weeks and have nothing left to offer, but two of Jane's friends brought a load of dresses and costumes in this morning. Most of them are perfectly wearable for anyone a size or two smaller. One of them changed hers for a pair of evening shoes that I had never worn because they pinched my toes after I'd bought them, and the matching bag. The other lady took that black velvet cape of your grandmother's. That was a lovely thing, Emma, and the fur trimming alone was worth the price we had put on it.'

'Yes, it was nice,' I agreed. 'Gwen's trunk turned out to be full of treasures, didn't it? And the money I gave her was useful, even though she didn't want to take it. Some of the dresses went back to Edwardian days. Grandmother must have bought them when she was a young woman, before she was married, and like you she hardly wore them. She had put them away so carefully that some of them could have been new. Jane wore a pretty apricot silk tea gown to a cocktail party.

She said everyone thought it was wonderful, and so of course they wanted to know all about the shop.'

Margaret nodded and smiled. She was enjoying herself, as both Jane and I were. Serving in the shop was like being amongst new friends.

Sol was intrigued by our success.

'I thought it would never work,' he told me some weeks later. 'But I suppose a man sees these things differently.'

'I don't suppose it would have caught on so well if it were not for the war,' I said truthfully. 'But women get very bored with wearing the same things all the time. And most of us have something that we bought before rationing came in and never wore because it just wasn't right. In my case, it was a silk blouse that didn't suit me. Usually, I would simply put the offending article right at the back of the wardrobe and forget it was there, but the chance to sell it and buy something else is tempting with the way things are just now.'

'Well, you might find something you can use in the storeroom,' Sol said looking thoughtful. 'There are some boxes of dresses that go back twenty years or more. I'm not sure exactly what's there – a few end of line oddments, or stock that didn't sell and was too outdated to keep on the rails. I wrote everything off years ago, so they're not on the books. I suppose someone might cut them up and make something out of them. You're welcome to take whatever is there, Emma. They are of no use to me.'

'Thank you. I'll see what I can find.'

By the end of six weeks, most of our original stock had gone, but the rails were bulging. The idea had certainly proved popular, and we soon had a thriving little business. Quite a few of our customers were women who had lost everything when their homes were bombed.

'We've been given extra coupons,' they told us as they searched the rails for bargains. 'But it's so hard to find anything nice these days. Some of your things are old-fashioned but good quality. All it takes is a little time and thought to make something really smart.'

Most of the women who came in found something they liked, and often they would come back a few days later to show us what they had made from whatever they had bought.

'You ought to advertise to buy things,' my mother said when she came up to visit me in the spring. She had been to the shop and bought several bits and pieces she intended to use for trimming a new dress for herself. 'If you put a little card in other shop windows, Emma, I'll bet you would get lots more replies. I'm sure there must be no end of women with things put away who have never heard of your shop.'

'At the moment we are buying as much as we can hold,' I told her. 'If I went round to people's houses, we would need to move into bigger premises!'

I did not particularly want to expand the business. It was already taking up more of my time than I had anticipated. Besides, I believed it was a novelty.

Already, some of Jane's friends had stopped bothering to come in, but now we were getting most of our trade from the ordinary woman off the street. Besides, I was sure that once the annoying restrictions on clothing were eased, everyone would naturally prefer to buy new clothes.

However, there was no sign of that happening just yet. The war was still claiming too many ships. Our little island was suffering from the need to concentrate on importing vital supplies, and instead of easing, the shortages were getting worse. We were constantly being told we must manage with less of everything. It was no longer just a case of drawing a line on the bath to make sure we didn't use too much water, now we were short of things like shaving soap and razor blades. Some women were using beetroot for lipstick and soot for eye make up.

Fashion was being dictated not by French designers, but by the Board of Trade in London. Hemlines were to be shorter in line with the new Utility label. We, as manufacturers, had been told to limit the number of styles we could have on offer in our showroom. However, we were still able to provide a service to customers who wished to purchase their own cloth and have it tailored to their own requirements.

The tailors of Savile Row were in demand by those wealthy clients who still required suits that might cost up to thirty guineas each, but our customers were the shopkeepers who sold to ordinary women who needed ready-made dresses, and we were bound by law to restrict our lines to very basic designs. The dresses were shorter than would have been worn a year or so earlier, the skirts usually straight without gores or flares. Sleeves were often short, and the collars were plain, the trimmings regulated to cut down on the amount of material needed. We were not allowed to produce one of our most popular dresses, which had a full, fine pleated skirt that swished as you walked.

'I'm sorry,' I found myself apologizing over and over again to our regular customers. 'We can't make that style for the time being. We're not even allowed to use extra braiding.'

'The government is bent on ruining us all,' Sol complained. 'It's hardly worth the effort keeping going at all these days.'

It was not surprising that many women were finding ways of getting round the restrictions in whatever way they could. Good for our little shop, but soul destroying for the millions of women forced to go without. Their men were away fighting; they were finding it more and more difficult to feed their families, and now they were expected to go out to work for at least a few hours every week.

England was in the grip of austerity, and as the months wore on and the papers continued to print almost nothing but bad news, it became harder and harder to find something to be cheerful about. And yet we managed it somehow.

Jane had become a special friend, and when she discovered our social club for servicemen, she went to some trouble to find supplies of tinned foods for us and insisted on taking her turn at making the refreshments and washing up.

'We should have a children's party,' Jane said when Christmas loomed on the horizon once more. 'I think we should get someone from our embassy to play Father Christmas.'

During the summer of 1942, Sol had surprised me with the news that he had sold the factory and what remained of our government contracts.

'We haven't come out of it too badly,' he told me. 'You will have five hundred pounds to come, Emma. The rest of your investment is safe and sound, but I thought you might like to have a bit of cash to play with?' His eyes were warm with amusement. 'Now that you're in business for yourself. You could open another of your shops. Have a chain of them perhaps?'

He was teasing me, of course. I had definite plans for the future, but for the moment I decided to put my money away safely. The government was urging us to buy War Bonds, but Sol refused to buy a single one himself.

'They've damned near ruined me as it is,' he said. 'I'll not trust them with a penny.'

I invested a few pounds out of a sense of duty, but most of the money went elsewhere.

Now that Sol no longer had the factory to worry about, he was able to spend more time in the showroom. That meant I was able to cut down my own hours, and I volunteered to do three afternoons a week answering phones for the Fire Service. Sometimes, I had to drive a control vehicle for them, and that often meant travelling through streets which had been attacked by enemy bombers. The raids were not as frequent or as heavy as during the blitz itself, but were perhaps even more devastating when they happened, not just in London but all over the country. Many of our cities were being relentlessly bombed with terrible consequences.

It seemed to me to be the worst year of the war. We had so little to look forward to and so much to fear.

Even Jack's letters did not always get through. There were months when I heard nothing from him; then in the spring of 1943 I had six all together. Some of them had obviously been delayed.

I read them eagerly. Jack had been in action. He did not say where or when, just that he was well and hoped he might see me quite soon.

'*I can't promise, Emma,*' he had written.

> *But I think I may be sent to London in a few weeks time. You never know, your bad penny might turn up one of these days . . .*

I hoped so much that he would come, but the days passed and I heard no more and my hopes of seeing him began to fade.

'Jane's Christmas party for the children was such a success,' I said to Sheila that morning. It was June and the weather was being kind to us. 'She is talking of having another when the schools close for the holidays. Why don't you bring Lizzy, and your cousin's children? Jane has managed to get some sugar and we are going to have sticky toffee – there will be jellies and cakes, and various other treats. We're going to have the party outdoors if the weather is fine, probably in the park, and then we'll have plenty of room to organize races and games with prizes for the children.'

'I don't know . . .' Sheila's eyes didn't quite meet mine. 'I'm busy most weekends. I shall have to see what I feel like. I might bring them if I haven't anything better to do.'

I couldn't argue with her, though I knew she spent several evenings a week at the social club – and not just helping out either.

Pamela had complained to me about her just a couple of days earlier.

'She doesn't pull her weight,' Pamela had said. 'I know she is a friend of yours, Emma – but it's not fair. If I'm on with her, I end up doing all the work while she's out there dancing with the men. Or drinking . . .'

'What do you mean, drinking?'

Pamela hesitated, then nodded, as if making up her mind. 'Some of the men bring alcohol in with them. We've tried to stop it, Emma, but it's impossible. Especially since the Americans have started coming. They always seem to have a bottle of bourbon, and they share it with the girls. Sheila has been very nearly drunk on a couple of occasions when she left here. I spoke to her about it once, but she told me to mind my own business. If she wasn't your friend . . . well, I would have told her we didn't need her kind here.'

I frowned. 'What do you mean, Pamela? Her kind?'

'Well, you *know*.' Pamela had been married six years before the war started. Since then her husband, Tom, had been given home leave only once, but she had never to my knowledge looked at another man. And it wasn't because she hadn't had offers. All of the woman who worked at the club were asked out regularly. 'She never goes home alone, Emma. Mostly she leaves with an American soldier these days, but if he isn't in that night she goes with someone else.'

'You believe she takes them home?' I thought about it, then shook my head. 'I'm sure she doesn't, Pamela. She lodges with her cousin, and there are four children in the house. She wouldn't take men there . . . her cousin wouldn't stand for it, surely?'

'Well, I've seen the way they look at her . . . and I've heard a couple of them laughing about her behind her back. You know the way it is, Emma. If a woman lets herself down . . . the men have no respect for her. Not the way they do for you.'

'And you,' I said, smiling at her. She was hard-working, and seldom complained. Sheila must have upset her. 'I hope you are wrong, Pamela. We can't stop the girls who come to the club going home with the men. We aren't responsible for what happens when they leave, but we should stop heavy drinking if we can. That wasn't the idea when this club was set up. It's a social club, a decent place to meet friends. If people want to drink they should go to the pub.'

She hesitated, then, 'Mrs Reece and a couple of the other ladies were saying we should ban any women who drink at the club. We can't stop the men, though we can ask them not to bring spirits with them . . .'

'Perhaps I should have a word with Sheila,' I offered, knowing that was what she had hoped for all along.

'Well, she might take it better coming from you.'

'I shan't say anyone told me,' I said. 'But I'll change shifts with you, Pamela – so that I'm here when Sheila is supposed to be helping. If I see her drinking, I can tell her about it then.'

Now, in the showroom, I looked at Sheila, observing the changes in her face, changes I had not taken too much notice of before this. She looked pale and unhealthy, her face a little puffy, dark shadows under her eyes.

'Are you feeling well?' I asked. 'You look a bit tired, Sheila. Haven't you been sleeping?'

'I'm all right,' she replied, her tone abrupt, harsh. 'As well as most people. You're lucky, Emma. Your friends see you don't go without, but it's harder for the rest of us. When I leave work, I have to queue for ages to get food, that's if there's anything left. Anything that comes in fresh during the day is usually gone by the time I get there.'

'You get your basic rations,' I said, feeling a little

hurt by her tone. 'We all do, Sheila. I know I'm lucky that Jane gives me some tinned food sometimes, but it isn't that often, and I always share it with everyone. Most of the time, we have to manage on what we can get from the shops the same as everyone else. I queue most days, too. Usually as soon as the shops open. It's best to go first thing, before you come to work.'

'I'm too tired to be out that early,' Sheila said. 'Lizzy cries half the night. She drives me crazy . . .'

Why didn't I believe her? I had the feeling that she was lying, that there was another reason entirely for her being too tired to go shopping early in the morning.

I found the idea that Sheila was letting herself drift into bad ways upsetting. It would have been easy for any woman to take that road these days. The Americans seemed to have so much money, far more than our own men, and they often had luxuries that we simply could not buy. Wonderful stockings that made anything on sale in our shops look dowdy, and chocolate, even perfume so I had been told.

Hardly surprising then that the girls liked to be with them. I knew there had been a few scuffles in the club between British soldiers and their American allies. It was usually over a girl and so far nothing terrible had happened, but that was because we had never served alcohol. If some of the men were bringing spirits in with them, it could make tempers flare out of control.

'You're on tonight at the club, aren't you?' I asked, looking at Sheila. She nodded, her mouth sulky, turned down at the corners. 'I shall see you there then. I've changed shifts with Pamela.'

'Why?' Her eyes narrowed suspiciously. 'I suppose she has been gossiping about me?'

'I'm not sure what you mean, Sheila? Why should she gossip about you?'

Sheila looked angry, but the doorbell went at that moment and two customers came into the shop together. For the next hour we were both busy serving, making out invoices and having the customers' purchases packed in the cardboard boxes they had brought with them.

In the past we had always provided new boxes, but these days our customers helped out by bringing back their old ones.

When at last they had gone, the opportunity to talk was over. It was time for me to leave for my fire duty.

'I'll see you this evening then,' I said to Sheila. 'Don't be late. We're cooking corned beef hash tonight. Jane sent me a box of tinned stuff and I've had a sack of potatoes delivered. It will take a while to peel the carrots and spuds. The men enjoy a cooked meal, and it's only a whist drive tonight.'

'I'm not sure I shall be able to come,' she said, her eyes evading mine. 'Lizzy wasn't well this morning. If she's no better I might have to stay home with her. Annie has to have some free time. She hasn't been out for ages. If I were you, Emma, I should telephone Pamela and ask her to come in.'

I stared at her, but there was nothing I could say to

compel her. All our efforts at the club were voluntary. No one could force Sheila to come and help us out.

'I'll come in on Saturday,' she said. 'It's a dance then. I like helping out on Saturdays.'

I went out and left her without a word. I did not believe for one moment that her daughter was unwell, but it was Sheila's choice. If she did not want to come to the club that night there was nothing I could do to persuade her.

Pamela agreed to come in and help, even though her sister was visiting and she had arranged to go to the pictures with her that evening.

'It's too much for you to do alone,' she said. 'Especially as it's the night for a cooked meal. Of course I'll come – though I don't believe Sheila's daughter is ill. She has used that particular excuse before, several times in fact.'

Pamela and I were kept busy with the cooking and serving for most of the evening. Afterwards, we left the dishes soaking in hot water while we went out to listen to one of the men singing sentimental songs. Some of them had really nice voices, and quite often they would find someone to play the piano and give us an impromptu concert.

That evening, the singer was an American. He had a strong voice and had been crooning *Thanks for that Lovely Weekend*, but now he had upped the tempo and was belting out, *Ma I love your Apple Pie*.

Everyone clapped enthusiastically. We liked nothing

better than when the men got together for a sing song round the piano. When he had finished, another man took his place and starting singing about the *White Cliffs of Dover*.

'Hi . . .' The American who had just left he piano tapped me on the shoulder. 'You're Emma . . . I've heard about you from a mutual friend.'

'Oh . . .' I raised my brows. 'Who was that? Jane Melcher?'

He shook his head. 'No, Miss Sheila Tomms. She says she knows you from way back . . .' He glanced round the room. 'I was expecting to see her here this evening. I'm sure she said she would be here. Any particular reason why she didn't come?'

I was about to tell him Sheila's daughter was ill, then checked myself. If Sheila was calling herself by her maiden name she might not want him to know she had been married – or that she had a child. It was not for me to tell him the truth.

'I'm not sure why she couldn't make it,' I said. 'But she said she would be here on Saturday.'

He frowned. 'I probably shan't be around by then. I guess it doesn't matter. It leaves me at a loose end this evening though . . . any chance of you coming out with me after you've finished here? I know a place where the drinks are good . . .'

'It's very nice of you to ask me,' I replied. 'But I don't go out with any of the men. I have someone special . . .'

'I'm glad to hear that, Emma.'

As I heard the teasing voice behind me, I spun round in surprise, hardly believing it as I saw him standing there in his uniform.

'Oh, Jack,' I cried. 'Jack my darling . . . you're back. You're back!'

I flung myself into his arms, and he caught me to him, kissing me passionately right there in front of everyone. There was a rousing cheer from the men watching, which made me blush as Jack let me go.

'Sorry, General,' the soldier who had asked me out said, looking awkward. 'I didn't know the lady belonged to you.' He saluted smartly, obviously shocked to find himself in such exalted company.

'At ease, soldier,' Jack said, smiling easily. 'If Emma had said yes, you might have found yourself on the way to the Pacific pronto, but as she said no I'll excuse you.'

The soldier grinned and moved away. I looked at Jack, my heart racing, still unable to believe that he was actually here at last.

'I've missed you so much,' I said. 'Your letters haven't been arriving as often or as promptly as they used to . . . I wasn't sure if you were really coming to London.'

'Nor was I,' he admitted ruefully. He touched my cheek with his fingertips. 'There have been delays and problems, Emma. However, I am here now and I'm staying for at least a month, maybe more. As it happens, I have the next ten days free. I arranged it that way so that we could be together. I hope that is OK by you?'

'Of course it is,' I said, thrilled at the prospect of being with him again. 'Have we really got ten whole days, Jack? No business deals, no important meetings?'

'None at all. I thought we might go away somewhere?'

'Yes, please!'

'How long before you're finished here?'

'I must help Pamela with the washing up,' I said. 'It wouldn't be fair to go off and leave it all to her. Talk to the men, Jack. Amuse yourself for twenty minutes . . . OK?'

'Fine,' he said, and smiled. 'I play the piano – is it all right if I have a go?'

'I'm sure it is,' I said. 'Go ahead. I can hear you while I'm working in the kitchen.'

I went though to the kitchen as Jack sat down at the piano and began to play, bright, cheerful tunes that the men could sing along with. Pamela looked at me as I began to wash the stacks of dirty plates and glasses.

'Why don't you go and leave this to me?' she asked. 'You always do your share, Emma. I wouldn't mind finishing off alone.'

'No, I shan't do that,' I replied, smiling at her. 'It wouldn't be fair on you, Pamela. Besides, Jack seems to be enjoying himself for the moment – and we've got ten days to be together.'

'Is that him playing now?' I nodded and Pamela went to the door to listen. 'He could be a professional. He's good . . .'

'I think Jack is good at anything he does,' I replied. I looked at her seriously. 'I was going to speak to Sheila this evening if she had come in, Pamela. I shan't be around now for a few days, but if you get any more trouble with her, let me know when I come back. I will speak to her then, see if I can sort things out.'

Pamela blushed. 'Maybe I was going on about it a bit too much,' she said. 'I suppose it's hard for her, living with her cousin and no husband. Maybe there's no harm in her having a boyfriend. I shouldn't judge everyone by my standards.'

'There's no harm in her having friends, but she still shouldn't drink here,' I said. 'She knows the rules, Pamela. If she does it again this weekend, I'll talk to her about it again.'

'All right.' Pamela smiled at me, relaxing now. 'Enjoy your holiday. Do you know where you're going?'

'I have no idea – but it would be lovely by the sea if the weather stays like this.'

'Yes. I was thinking I would like to get away this year. My sister is visiting me now, but has invited me to visit when she goes home to Hunstanton. I might go down there for a few days if I can manage it.'

'Yes, I should if I were you. It makes everyone feel better to get away for a while.'

I had finished washing the dishes. I dried my hands, picked up my coat and went into the other room. Jack saw me and stood up. There were cries of disappointment as he left the piano, but it was late and the club would be closing very soon now.

As I went outside with Jack, I glimpsed a woman standing in a shop doorway across the street. She turned away as she saw me, but I was sure it was Sheila. Obviously, after telling me that she needed to stay home, she had not dared to come into the club, but was waiting here in the hope of meeting her American soldier . . .

'Something wrong, Emma?'

I glanced up at Jack, then shook my head. 'No, nothing, nothing at all. Everything is wonderful now you are here.'

'We're going to have fun,' he promised, bending his head to kiss me briefly on the lips. 'I promise you, Emma. The next few days are going to be great.'

I smiled and hugged his arm as he opened his car door for me to get in, tucking my dress in carefully before shutting the door again. As we drove away, the lights flashed full on Sheila for a moment as she ran across the road to meet someone, and I knew it was definitely her.

I was sorry that she had thought it necessary to lie about her daughter being ill that night, but I could not blame her for wanting to meet the man she loved. It was really no different from my wanting to be with Jack – and there was no reason why Sheila should not go out with any man she wanted. She was a widow and perfectly free to love where she chose.

I was glad I had not said anything to her at the showroom. Pamela had already admitted that she might have made too much of things. Sheila ought not to get drunk at the club, of course. She knew our rules. Besides, she was only laying up trouble for herself – but that was really her own business.

It was not for me or Pamela to judge her. Pamela's husband might be away fighting, but she heard from him regularly. And I had Jack. Who were we to dictate what Sheila could do with her own life?

Chapter 10

Jack surprised me by saying that we would take my son and Nanny on our holiday.

'You won't want to be separated from the boy the whole ten days,' he said. 'It would spoil things for you. There's plenty of room where we're going to accommodate all of us. We shall have James with us for part of the day, and his nanny will be there to take care of him when we want to be alone.'

'You're so thoughtful, Jack.' I hugged his arm as I looked up at him. He was such an attractive man, so vital and alive.

He smiled and kissed me. 'I want you to be happy, Emma. I know you would worry if the boy was left with your friends. It's only natural. Besides, I want him to get to know me. We're all going to be living together one day. It's best he has good things to remember about me while I'm away.'

Jack was taking it for granted we would be together after the war. I didn't even think of arguing. After all, it was what I wanted, and I was convinced now that my husband had died in that plane crash. If he was alive some word would have reached us by now. So there was no reason for me to feel guilty when Jack spoke of our life together. I accepted that our marriage would happen one day, when all the fighting and killing was over, and the idea made me happy.

We drove down to East Sussex in easy stages, stopping for a delicious picnic of cold fried chicken, fresh bread and some exotic pickles that Jack had brought with him. There was also a tin of chocolate finger biscuits for my son, who managed to get the chocolate all over him and gave every sign of being in heaven.

Nanny scolded when he spilt orange juice over his white shirt, but Jack told her we were all on holiday and she wasn't to worry if the boy got himself dirty. His air of authority had impressed Nanny, who obeyed him without question. He also seemed to have the knack of controlling James's exuberance, and we stopped far fewer times than was usual when travelling with my son.

The cottage Jack took us to was really much too large to deserve that name, but it had belonged to his family for years and was always known as the *Cottage*.

'My great-grandfather left it to my grandmother,' he explained when we arrived to see the rambling old house, its grey stone walls half covered by climbing roses and honeysuckle. 'She lived here until she married and went to America with her husband, and when she died she left the property to me, because I was her favourite. I had never seen it until I came to England just before the war, but I believe my mother and father visited a couple of times when they were young.'

Inside, it was cool and smelled of lavender and

polish. The furniture was very old, quite beautiful and obviously well loved and cared for. Jack had a permanent housekeeper in residence, even though he seldom stayed there. He did allow friends to stay there from time to time, and there was a visitors' book in the hall, which, I discovered when I peeped one day, included a few famous names, both American and English.

The cottage itself was situated just outside the picturesque village of Sedlescombe, which slopes gently down a Wealden hillside. The road past the village was a main one leading to the resort of Hastings-on-Sea, and could be busy sometimes, but we were tucked away in our own private hollow, hidden by trees and near a pretty stream.

'We are near enough to the sea to take James on the beach sometimes,' Jack told me. 'But private and secluded enough for him to run around the gardens in safety.'

James had never known such freedom. Although there were periods when he was given into Nanny's charge, he was with us for much of the day. Jack did not believe in being over strict with young children, and he enjoyed playing with the boy. He had brought a small baseball bat with us, and it was funny to watch my son struggling valiantly to hit the balls Jack threw to him.

'He's going to be a proper American,' Jack said, lying on the dry grass at my feet after James had been taken off for his afternoon nap. 'I'll teach him everything, Emma. When he grows up, we'll send him to

Harvard and then I'll start him off in some kind of business.'

I was sitting in a canvas chair on the lawns outside the open French windows. It was a warm sunny day, peaceful, the silence broken only by the droning of insects and the occasional call of a meadow lark.

'You have it all worked out,' I said, smiling at him as he broke off a long stalk of grass and tickled my bare feet. 'What am I going to do, Jack? What have you decided for me?'

'You will do whatever you want, my darling.' Jack grinned at me. 'I don't see you as being the meek little wife sitting at home in the kitchen waiting for me to come back at the end of the day. So what do you want, Emma? What would make you happy?'

I closed my eyes, taking my time before I answered.

'To be with you,' I said at last. 'Have more children, perhaps a girl next and then another boy – but I would also like to own and run a chain of fashion shops one day. Not the sort that only rich women can afford to patronise. I think things will be different after the war. We are all going to be so fed up with wearing what we're told we ought to wear. I think ordinary women . . . women like me . . . will demand access to fashion. We want to choose for ourselves. To have the right to be different, to make a statement . . .'

'Whoever said you were an ordinary woman?' Jack asked, chuckling at his own thoughts. 'Somehow, I don't think there are too many around like you, my darling.'

'I was a very ordinary girl,' I said and smiled as he looked at me in disbelief. 'You didn't know me when I was younger, Jack. Until I came to London I seldom had a shop-bought dress. My mother made my clothes. I was very naive, very ignorant.'

'Well, you sure changed somewhere along the line, sweetheart.'

I pulled a face at him and stood up. 'Shall we go for a walk?'

Jack sprang to his feet, taking the hand I offered, our fingers interlocking as we began to walk.

'I suppose I learned the hard way. Once, when I was very young and impatient for life to begin, my Gran told my fortune. She was good at it, Jack – no, don't look like that! Sometimes she did see things . . . she did know what was going to happen.'

'So what did she see for you?' His eyes teased and challenged me.

'She said I had a long, hard road to travel, that I would have a child . . . she thought I might have more but that wasn't clear. She also said that I would make my own destiny.'

'I believe that much,' Jack said. 'You're a strong woman, Emma. You might not really know that yet. You tend to take too much notice of what other people think, worry too much about the feelings and intentions of others. One day you will decide to do things your way, and I imagine that is going to be quite something.'

'Is it so wrong to take account of other people's feelings?' I asked, gazing up at him.

'It can get you into a lot of trouble, Emma. I'm not saying you have to be unkind or greedy – but a leader stands by his own decisions. He takes responsibility for his own actions.'

'For good or ill?' I met Jack's eyes, trying to read his thoughts. 'I know that's what you do, Jack – but I am not sure I would ever be strong enough.'

He touched his fingers to my mouth. 'Maybe that's what your Gran meant when she said you had a long road to travel, Emma. Only when you are prepared to take what you want from life will you reach whatever it is you want.'

'At the moment all I want is you, Jack.' I reached up to kiss him on the mouth. 'Make love to me . . .'

'Willingly,' he murmured, his throat husky with desire. 'Never change in that way, Emma. You are very special as you are, and I want you more than I shall ever know how to tell you . . .'

Every day was filled with pleasure. Jack had such energy, such a capability for enjoying life, and he was generous enough to make sure that everyone around him shared in the magic he generated. My son was soon his adoring slave, quelled by a frown, uplifted by a smile. They romped through the lovely Sussex countryside, James on his *daddy's* shoulders, played ball games and built castles on the beach.

Hastings had a very stony beach, but there were quiet, unspoilt areas where few holidaymakers ever strayed. Some of the beaches had been shut off with barbed wire to guard against invasion by sea and were ringed with notices warning trespassers to keep out, but it was still possible to find safe havens and of course Jack knew where they were. He even had permission to visit some that were closed to the general public.

'Is there anything you can't manage to fix?' I asked him once. 'Does anyone ever get the better of you, Jack?'

'You did,' he said and he was serious as he looked at me. 'For a long time I thought you would never love me. *That* almost broke my heart, Emma. I don't know what I would do if I lost you. I can't lose you. I would do anything to keep you.'

'You won't lose me,' I promised recklessly. There was an odd expression in his eyes at that moment. I wasn't sure what it meant, but it sent a shiver down my spine. I sensed that Jack could be ruthless if he chose. 'Why should you? You know I love you. We are so right for each other. And James is a changed child in your company. I've never known him to be this content. He adores you, Jack.'

'And I adore you, Emma.' He kissed my fingers, sucking the tips, nipping the little one with his teeth. 'You are mine. I don't give up what belongs to me. You should remember that.'

'You *don't* own me, Jack. No man will ever do that – but I want to be with you. There's no need to look so murderous. There will never be another man who means this much to me, who gives me such happiness, such joy. I promise you I shan't fall into bed with someone else the minute your back is turned.'

Jack smiled oddly. 'I know that, Emma. I've never even considered it, though I know that side of things is important to you. It's your damned sense of duty that scares the hell out of me. I'm afraid you will never tear yourself away from your friends and family.' He pulled a wry face. 'I shall probably have to move my business to London after the war is over.'

'Would you do that for me?'

'If I had to,' he said, a glint of annoyance in his eyes. 'Does it give you a thrill to know you have that much power over me, Emma?'

'No.' I shook my head at him, my long hair falling over my face. I flicked it back so that he could see my expression. 'I'm not sure I do – but I shan't put it to the test, Jack. I want to come to America with you. I've often dreamed of going there . . . I'm greedy for all the things you promised . . . for the good life.'

'Let me take you there now, when I go back,' Jack said, and he seemed oddly nervous, unlike himself. 'I know I promised to wait until this is all over, but . . .'

I touched my lips to his. 'Don't, Jack. Please don't ask me to go now. You don't know how it tears me apart. I hate being asked to choose. I can't leave while things are so awful here. I'm sorry. I can't leave my friends just yet. When the war is over . . .'

'I know. I know!'

Jack rolled me beneath him in the dry grass. Our words were lost as we kissed and desire flared to a scorching heat between us. We had no need to argue, we were so perfectly in harmony when we touched, our bodies eager, needy, hungry for the joy we had found together.

And so we made love, again and again as the lovely days sped by and we lived for the moment, knowing that all too soon it would be over.

'I'm going to be around for a while,' Jack promised as he dropped me off at Sol and Margaret's house on our return to London. 'We'll manage a night together every now and then – but I'm going to be busy from here on in. I'll telephone when I can.'

'Things to do, people to see.' I smiled at him despite the ache in my heart. I wanted to scream my protests aloud. Why should Jack have to leave me when I needed him so? It wasn't fair, it wasn't right – but it *was* life. 'I understand. I'm not going to make demands you can't fulfil. Dream about me, Jack. I'll be dreaming of you.'

I kissed him and let him go without tears. Not so my demanding son. James screamed when Nanny took him off to the nursery. He sobbed bitter tears for his daddy, kicking and struggling against the arms that held him.

I understood his tantrums. Jack had lavished him with an easy affection, spoiling him and yet drawing both love and respect from a child who was now four years old and intelligent enough to understand what was happening.

He vaguely remembered Jack giving him his beloved pedal car. In my son's mind Jack was now very much his daddy, and he did not want him to go away again.

I did not think James could remember Richard. My first husband had hated him, doing his best to ignore his very existence because he was not his son but the child of Paul Greenslade. Jon had tried to be a father to the boy, but he had not been with him often enough to form a bond between them – and I had gone away with Jon twice, leaving my son in the care of others. I had an uneasy feeling that James had resented Jon because of that. I could not think that he would have clung to the man whose name he bore as he did to Jack.

Perhaps one day it would be possible to change James's name from Reece to Harvey. When the time came, I was sure Jack would want that. He would want to claim my son as his own, as he had claimed me.

After Jack had gone, I went up to the nursery. James was sitting on the floor. He had built a castle of bright blocks, but as he realized I was there he gave a scream of rage and knocked them flying.

'Want my daddy,' he said, his face red and tearful. 'Bad Mummy! Mummy go away. Want my daddy! Want my daddy!'

'Now then, Master James,' Nanny said in a scolding tone. 'Mummy has come to see you. You must not be a bad boy.'

'He isn't bad,' I said, bending to scoop him up into my arms. 'Mummy loves you, darling. Daddy has to go away, but he will come back just as soon as he can. I promise.'

James sobbed into my breast, his tears of heartbreak wounding me. I wondered if perhaps he had understood more as a baby than I'd imagined. Had he felt it when Jon went away? Had he been disturbed when I left March and came to live in London with people he did not know? I had thought him too young, but perhaps he had been more affected by the traumas which had changed our lives than I had realized. If so, it must be confusing for him. It was little wonder that Jack had charmed his baby heart, and that he was so distressed now he sensed things were changing once more.

I kissed his head, smoothing his soft hair until the weeping eased.

'Mummy goes away sometimes,' I whispered against his ear. 'She comes back again. Daddy will come back to us, darling. I promise. I promise faithfully.'

Perhaps I should not have given my word, but I wanted to comfort my son. I wanted to ease his pain, which was also mine.

We were lucky that summer, James and I. Despite his busy schedule, Jack made time to be with us as often as he could, and I knew it was because he loved us that he made the effort, often after he had been up for most of the night and was clearly in need of rest.

Jack never told me what it was that kept him so busy during those days and nights. I did not ask, because in a way I understood. He was an important man, not just as a general of the American Army but in other ways. I suspected that Jack was more wealthy than I would ever have dreamed of, and that a part of his importance to the British government was his ability to finance things that could have a huge bearing on the outcome of the war. I could not begin to guess at what went on behind those closed doors, nor did I wish to be told. All I cared about was the warm, loving, slightly wicked man who spent as many hours as he could with us.

He was there for Jane's party for the children of the women who kept the social club running. He and James took part in the father and son egg and spoon race, and of course they won first prize: it would have surprised me if they hadn't.

Jack could do no wrong. He seemed to bear a charmed existence and everything was brighter when he was there.

'You were always lucky with your men,' Sheila told me when I gave her a packet of sticky toffee for Lizzy and three more for Annie's children. 'But then, you're lucky in every way.'

'I work for my luck,' I said. 'But I *am* lucky to have Jack.'

'Todd has gone,' Sheila said, and for a moment I saw the sparkle of tears in her eyes. 'He told me he met you at the social club that night. He thought you were classy, Emma – especially when he saw you were General Harvey's girlfriend.'

Something about the way she said that grated, as if

she were insinuating that Jack was just using me to amuse himself over here, that he would go away after the hostilities ended and forget me.

'Jack has asked me to marry him,' I told her. 'We shall most likely go to America to live after the war.'

'Todd promised to come back for me,' she said. 'He was probably lying through his teeth, but I might get lucky for once.'

'I hope you do, Sheila,' I said, and hesitated. 'I've been meaning to talk to you about something . . . but perhaps today is not the best time. We'll have a chat when we're more private.'

'Oh, you needn't bother,' she replied. 'I shan't be going to your precious social club any more. I've found somewhere else . . . somewhere more exciting, where they don't have so many stupid rules.'

She turned away, calling to the children to follow her across the park greens. I watched her for a moment, feeling hurt that she was so resentful of me. I had always tried to be a friend to her, and it was not my fault that things had gone wrong in her life.

I was lucky, I knew that, but a part of my good fortune at least had come because I had worked for it. The London shop was doing well, and so was Gwen, and even Mrs Henty was still managing to make a reasonable profit – but I counted my true fortune as having so many people who cared for me.

Sheila was not lucky in that respect. I knew her mother never bothered to keep in touch, and she had not been back to March once to see her closest family.

All she had was her cousin Annie, and her daughter, Lizzy. Perhaps Todd would come back for her after the war as he'd promised . . . but I could not forget the way he had asked me to go with him when she was not at the club that night. If he really loved her . . . but that was not for me to judge.

I wondered if Sheila was finding it hard to manage. Sol paid her three pounds and five shillings a week, but she had to pay her cousin rent and food could be expensive these days. I had noticed that Lizzy and Annie's children were poorly dressed, and their clothes had not looked too clean. Perhaps I could find some clothes for the children. We had recently taken in a few items of children's clothing at the shop, and it was possible that some of the women's dresses could be cut down to fit Annie's girls, who were seven, ten and fourteen. I thought I might buy some new material and make two dresses for Lizzy myself.

It would be a peace offering, to try and make up a little for what Sheila had lost when her dreams of owning her own business had fallen into ashes.

I did not say anything about the clothes to Sheila when I saw her at work the following Monday. She seemed a bit subdued, her eyes apologetic even though she did not say she was sorry for having spoken so resentfully at the children's party.

I decided not to mention our disagreement either. Perhaps I had been at fault. I should not have listened to Pamela's complaints. Sheila was entitled to do as she pleased with her own life. Yet I could not help feeling anxious about her as I noticed the shadows under her eyes becoming darker as the days passed.

Sol was not pleased with her work. He complained to me that she was careless, and that she did not check the stock as she ought.

'We're short of a size thirty-eight hip in that blue dress with the short sleeves,' he told me with a frown. 'And there was ten shillings missing out of the petty cash last week . . . after she had been here alone. I left the tin in the desk when I went out. You were doing your fire duty, Emma, and I know the money was there when I left the showroom . . .'

'Have you asked her about it?'

He shook his head. 'What's the use? She would deny having taken it. I don't like thieves, Emma. Sheila is a size thirty-eight . . . and I know she has borrowed dresses before. I saw her putting one back once, and there was a stain under the arms. I had to mark it down as soiled goods.'

'Oh, Sol . . . why didn't you tell me? I could have spoken to her.'

'And have her turn sulky on you?' He frowned. 'It's not worth it, Emma. I'm thinking of letting her go.'

'Sol! You wouldn't?'

'I've had government people asking me about her hours,' he said. 'They don't think I need two girls in the showroom, especially as I've had her down as part time. I was willing to make excuses for her while she was doing her job properly, but now I feel we would be better off without her. Trade isn't as brisk as it was, and Fanny can come in from the workroom when you and I are both out.'

'What will you say to her?' I could see that he had made up his mind to let Sheila go, and it was his business. Although he treated me as a partner, I was only his employee in the showroom. I could not force him to change his mind. 'Are you going to accuse her of theft?'

'No.' His eyes did not quite meet mine and I wondered what he was hiding from me. 'I shall give her two weeks' money in the morning, and tell her I've been told I can't keep her. You needn't worry, Emma. She won't want for work. The government are crying out for women to do war work. She'll find a place in a factory easily enough.'

I nodded, but did not say anything. I felt upset for Sheila. I knew she would hate having to work in a factory again, and I expected her to be angry, not just with Sol but with me, too.

However, she seemed to accept her dismissal without fuss, almost as though she had been expecting it.

'I've had enough of this place anyway,' she told me when she came back from her interview with Sol. 'He's a mean old bugger. I don't know how you can live with him and his wife. I couldn't stick it.'

'Oh, don't say that,' I begged her. 'Don't be bitter, Sheila. I wish Sol could keep you, but it isn't possible.'

'Don't lie to me, Emma,' she said harshly. 'We both know why I've got the push. He hadn't got the guts to come out with it, because he suspects I know too much about him, but it was because of the money and the dress.'

'Sheila . . .' I stared at her in horror.

'I took them,' she said, lifting her chin defiantly. 'Lizzy was ill and I needed extra money to buy medicine for her – and I took the dress to wear when I saw Todd the last time. I meant to put it back, but it got stained all over the skirt and I knew I wouldn't get away with it, so I kept it. Annie washed it and it looks all right, but he would have known it had been washed.'

'Yes, he would,' I agreed. 'Why didn't you ask me for the money? You know I would have helped you, Sheila.'

'I don't like begging,' she said, a look of shame showing briefly in her eyes. 'He can afford it. You don't know the profits he makes on the sly, Emma. I wouldn't trust him if I were you. He probably cheats you as well as the government.'

'Sheila! Be careful what you say.'

'I'm not frightened of him,' she said, and her eyes gleamed with malice. 'He hasn't treated me fair. He's going to be very sorry one of these days, that's all I can say . . .'

'What do you mean?'

'You'll find out,' she said, gave me an odd look and headed for the door. There she stopped and turned to look at me once more. 'I might ask you for something one day. I'm only saying might . . .'

'We're still friends, Sheila. If you need my help, you only have to ask.'

'I'll send Annie to you if I do,' she said. 'Bye then, Emma. Thanks for everything – and watch Sol. I'm telling you, he isn't as sweet and wholesome as he appears.'

I did not reply, simply staring after her as she slammed the door behind her. Sol came out of his office, then walked up to me. I could see he was very annoyed.

'What was she saying to you, Emma?' He swore softly. 'She's a right little bitch, that one. A whore and a thief . . .'

I was shocked by his manner and the words he chose.

'Sol . . . that isn't very nice. I know she took the ten shillings, but Lizzy was ill and she needed the money for the doctor. And she only meant to borrow the dress but it got spoiled . . .'

'That's what she told you,' Sol said. 'You shouldn't believe everything she says, Emma.'

'I don't – but she has had a hard time, Sol. I would have replaced the money and paid for the dress if you had let me.'

'She takes advantage of you,' he said. 'She thinks you're a soft touch, but she knew I wouldn't stand for too much. I've known what's been going on for a while now, but I let it ride because she was your friend. Borrowing the dresses was one thing, I've turned a blind eye to that with other girls, but taking money is another. It wouldn't have stopped there.'

'No, I suppose not . . . but I can't help feeling sorry for her.'

'She's a bad lot and best gone.'

I nodded, then looked at him anxiously. 'She said she knew a lot about you, Sol. She said you would be sorry for not treating her fair one day. Can she cause trouble for you?'

'Not if she knows what's good for her,' he said, but I saw a flash of something in his eyes and I sensed he was keeping something from me. 'You leave her to me, Emma. I'll soon send her packing if she comes here again.'

I didn't answer him. I knew Sol got away with whatever he could. He found the government's restrictions frustrating, and didn't see why he shouldn't make money on the side if he could wangle it somehow. But I doubted there was anything very wrong with the showroom accounts, because he had started to leave them to me for checking, and they usually tallied within a little.

So what other little pies had Sol dipped his fingers in, and what did Sheila know that might cause trouble for him?

Jack took me to a party at his embassy that night. It was an official affair, part business, part social, but the people were friendly and I did not feel shut out of things as I had at the reception I'd attended with Sol.

Afterwards, when we were alone in his apartment, I told him that I was a little anxious for Sol.

'I don't know if he has been breaking the law,' I said. 'But Sheila seemed so certain she could cause trouble for him. Of course, he wouldn't tell me – but he might talk to you.'

'He would resent my interference,' Jack said. 'I don't meddle in another man's business, Emma – but I could talk to the girl if you like? If it's money she wants, I can probably sort her out. It's usually money in a case like this.'

'Would you do that?' I laid my head against his naked shoulder, nibbling at him teasingly. 'I don't like to ask, Jack, but I know Sol is hiding something from me – and I think he's worried, even though he wouldn't let me see it.'

'I'll see Sheila,' Jack promised. 'Get me her address and leave the rest to me.'

'It's so nice having a masterful man to look after you,' I said, leaning over to kiss his mouth. My hair brushed his chest. 'I must think of a way to say thank you nicely.'

'Witch,' Jack murmured throatily, and rolled me beneath him in the bed, his powerful body covering mine. 'I think you're worrying for nothing. Sol can take care of himself – but I'll check the girl out for you. Believe me, I'll know if she is bluffing . . . and now, my sweet, I believe you have a promise to keep . . .'

When I looked for Sheila's address in Sol's records I was surprised. She had told me her cousin lived in

Kensington, letting me think it was in one of the nicer districts, but in fact the address she had given was in a rather squalid area on the other side of Notting Hill High Street, a rookery of mean streets and slum houses. There had been talk often in the past years of clearing this area, but so far nothing had been done.

Sheila had led me to believe her cousin's house was a modern one with a garden for the children, a proper kitchen and full sanitation, but it was obvious that she had lied to me again.

I was not due to see Jack that evening, so I decided to see if I could talk to Sheila myself. The clothes I had been altering for Annie's children were ready, and I took them with me after work.

The house was even worse than I had dreamed, the windows filthy behind net curtains that were rotting into holes, and the paintwork peeling to the bare wood. When the door was opened by Annie, the stench of boiled vegetables and stale urine came out to me.

'Emma . . .' she said, looking awkward. We had met only twice before, when she came to the showroom to speak to Sheila, but she had looked quite smart then. Now she was dressed in a filthy skirt and blouse, her hair straggling and greasy on her shoulders. 'I'm sorry . . . I can't ask you in. I've got someone here . . .'

'I wanted to see Sheila.' I hesitated, then held the parcel out to Annie. 'These are a few clothes for the children. 'I made them myself. I hope you won't be offended, but I know how difficult it is to manage these days . . .'

'Lord bless you,' she said, smiling at me. 'I'm grateful for anything. I haven't got Sheila's pride – can't afford it. The girls will be so pleased. Thank you for taking the trouble, Emma.'

'I think they will fit,' I said, feeling relieved by her answer. 'Is Sheila in?'

'She doesn't live here any more,' Annie said, and frowned. 'We had a disagreement after she threw away that job you got her. I warned her what would happen if she kept borrowing dresses without permission, but she wouldn't listen. She thought she was being clever, taking things that didn't belong to her, but she didn't know when she was lucky, Emma, and that's the truth.'

'I would have helped her if she had come to me.'

'She knows that – but she doesn't like asking for anything. She's proud, and bitter – but there's no sense in dwelling on the past. Anyway, I didn't hold with what she was doing and I told her so. She went off in a huff and I haven't seen her since. I think she's living with some spiv . . . sells knocked-off goods down the market. He's a bad one and she knows it, but there's no talking to her.'

'Do you know where she is living now?' I asked. 'I would like to see her, to talk to her if I could. We parted badly, and I don't like that, Annie. We were always friends.'

Annie shook her head. 'No, I've no idea where she lives and I don't want to know. She has been nothing but trouble to me from the day she came. I may be poor, but I'm a decent woman, Emma – and I like things proper.'

'Yes, I'm sure you do, Annie.' I smiled at her. 'Well, I hope the children's things fit – and if you don't mind, I might bring you something else another day. Perhaps some tinned food . . .'

'You're very welcome to call,' she said. 'It's good of you to think of us, and I'm sorry I can't ask you in, but my neighbour is in the kitchen, and she's a rough sort. I wouldn't want you to be offended. If I hear anything about Sheila, I'll let you know.'

'I've been making some dresses for Lizzy,' I said. 'They are not quite finished yet, but I'll bring them round next time – just in case Sheila decides to come back.'

I was thoughtful as I walked home. It was obvious that Annie did not approve of Sheila's new lover. He was clearly a very unpleasant character. I could only hope that he would not let Sheila down too badly.

Chapter 11

Jack's time with us was coming to an end. He had spent more than three months in England, much longer than I think either of us had expected. I should have been grateful for what we'd had, indeed, I was grateful, but in a way it only made our parting all the harder. I had become accustomed to seeing him often, and his habit of surprising me with small gifts or trips to the theatre had spoiled me.

We spent his last weekend at the Cottage. It was early September now and the heat of the summer had given way to a more gentle warmth and days that sometimes began with a slight mist drifting over the low ground.

'I'm going to miss you so much when you go.'

We had been out to lunch at a small fish restaurant. Situated on a hill in Hastings, it had a magnificent view of the cliffs and the sea. Now we were driving slowly back through narrow lanes and heavily wooded scenery. The beauty all around me seemed almost to tear the heart from my body. Jack was a part of my life now and I could not bear the thought that soon he would not be here for me to touch or kiss, that I would no longer hear his voice calling to me or see his eyes light up when I turned to greet him.

'I shall miss you, my darling,' Jack said glancing at me. 'Don't worry, Emma. Things are beginning to go our way. This war can't go on for ever. In the end, Germany will crack – and when it's all over I shall come to claim you.'

'Yes, I know.'

For most of the summer the papers had carried encouraging reports of Allied advances into Sicily and Italy. German cities had been devastated by our bombs, Hamburg having been almost wiped off the map by a sustained attack. In the Ukraine, the Russians had made significant advances. I knew Jack was right when he said the tide was turning in our favour, but it didn't alter the fact that he was going away soon and my life would seem so empty without him.

We made the most of our last hours together. Jack's love-making was tender, passionate, deeply satisfying. As I lay in his arms afterwards, I knew that I had been truly blessed. Very few women were fortunate enough to meet their soulmate. Jack was mine. I would never know such perfect happiness with anyone else.

I shed no tears when Jack left. He had made no secret of the fact that he expected to see action, that he himself had been party to a grand design of offensives about to be launched by the Allies. No details were let slip, of course, but we understood each other so well that I did not need to be told. I had known instinctively that serious matters had kept Jack in London. As much as he loved me, he had not stayed for my sake.

So I kissed my lover goodbye once more and turned to my work for comfort as I always did, making sure that James had his fair share of my love and attention. He was sulky and restless for a while, but then he seemed to settle down and accept that his daddy would come back one day.

Sometimes he asked if we could go to the seaside again. I told him we would go soon, perhaps the next summer, and in the meantime I made him a puppet theatre with a set of characters to amuse him. We spent many happy hours with our plays, and I was so proud of the strong, sturdy, rather independent child who was my son.

James had so many toys that the older ones lay discarded at the bottom of a trunk. I gave a few of them to Annie's children when I visited her that autumn. I also took her tinned fruit and tea, both presents from Jack, and a fairly new dress of my own that I thought might fit her.

She was so pleased. She invited me into her house. Although it was in such poor condition, and there was nothing she could do about the smell – which I thought came from the drains – I could see she did her best to keep it clean inside.

'I can't be bothered with the windows,' she told me over a cup of tea. 'It's such a dirty area, Emma. If you wash the step in the morning it's filthy an hour later.'

'You should apply for one of the new prefabs when they're built,' I said. 'Sol was telling me about them. They are going to start building soon, to replace some of the houses that have been lost in the bombing. We've lost so many houses the government has to do something different. They are only temporary of course, but eventually they will be replaced with modern brick-built houses, and I think they're going to be rather nice.'

'I'd never get one,' Annie said and sighed wistfully. 'I used to think Hitler might do me a favour and blow this place up while we were out, but it didn't happen.'

'Oh, don't!' I said, feeling a chill at the nape of my neck. 'I know it isn't much of a place, Annie – but please don't tempt fate. I wouldn't want you and the children to be hurt, and when you wish for something you often get it, but in a different way to how you hoped.'

'You're a nice person, Emma,' Annie said, then frowned. 'I saw Sheila last week. She's left that spiv she was with. He beat her up a couple of times so she moved on. I think she's seeing some American airman now.'

'Is she all right?'

Annie shook her head. 'No, not really. I think she drinks too much. She had been drinking when I saw her. She's letting herself go, Emma. Her hair hadn't been washed and her shoes wanted mending. That isn't like Sheila, not how she used to be, always so smart and proud of her appearance.'

Annie's words made me fear for the girl who had been my friend. It was silly of me I suppose, but I couldn't help feeling a little responsible for Sheila.

Maybe if I hadn't let her rent the shop in the first place she wouldn't feel so bitter and resentful – and I'd found her the job with Sol. So in a way it was my fault she'd ended up like this.

'Do you know where she lives?' I asked Annie. 'If she's in trouble, I might be able to help her.'

'She wouldn't thank you for it,' Annie said. 'There's no talking to her these days. You'd best leave her to go her own way.'

I accepted that Annie was probably right. Sheila did resent my attempts to help her. She resented that I was making a success of my own life, in a personal way and in business.

And so I decided to take Annie's advice and leave Sheila to her own devices. What with the shop, my hours at the showroom, and the voluntary work I had taken on, I had plenty to look after in my own life, so much that the days and weeks seemed to just race away.

Now and then, a letter came from Jack and living seemed worthwhile. I believed that it was only a matter of time, perhaps months, before Jack would come back to me and then the war would be over and our life together could really begin

It was 1944 now. Restrictions on cloth were about to be lifted, causing much jubilation amongst the trade and the public. Now we would be much freer about how we designed our dresses. We could produce our popular pleated skirts again, and use all the buttons we liked. Men too could have turnups on their trousers, and the austerity suits would soon become just a memory. They had been so unpopular that many of them were unsold and were going to be given away to refugees in Europe.

Clothes rationing had saved the country millions of pounds, and tons of shipping. The reduction in output had cut down the need for staff in the trade, releasing thousands of older men and women for more essential war work, but the worst of the restrictions seemed to be over. Now people had started to talk with confidence of the way things would be once the war was finally won.

Sol was happier about our prospects.

'Once things get back to normal, we'll be able to expand again, Emma.' He gave me a thoughtful look. 'You'll have some money coming to you when the war is over. I was wondering whether you wanted to continue our partnership – or are you thinking of branching out on your own? You spoke of opening up a dress shop or two . . .'

'I'm not sure what I shall want to do,' I said. 'I might not be living in London, Sol, though that wouldn't necessarily prevent me from investing in a business with you. I could be a sort of silent partner, I suppose. Can we talk about it nearer the time?'

'Yes, of course.' He hesitated, then, 'You've not heard from Sheila recently?'

'I've heard of her,' I said. 'Her cousin Annie sees her from time to time. What's worrying you, Sol?'

'She took something of mine . . .'

I sensed the unease he was trying to hide. 'Something important?'

'An account book . . .' Sol saw my frown and shook his head. 'Nothing to do with the showroom. I wouldn't involve you in anything not quite . . . Just another little business I've had going on the sidelines . . . black market stuff. You know.' He looked uncomfortable. 'Not quite legal, of course, but nothing terrible.'

'Would you be in trouble if the book fell into the wrong hands?'

'Well, not really . . .' he hedged, then his eyes fell before mine. 'It was a very private book, Emma. I suppose I was stupid to write it all down. If the worst came to the worst, I might go to prison for a few months.'

'Oh, Sol . . .' I looked at him in dismay. 'I knew you cut a few corners here and there, but you must have done more than that to be in danger of going to prison. I'm . . . disappointed that you could have been so silly.'

'Feet of clay, Emma?' He pulled a wry face. 'Don't look at me that way, please? I know I've been a bit of a fool. I never meant to get so involved, but everything was so frustrating, and it seemed like fun at first. Just a few bits and pieces that got diverted from official channels – but somewhere along the line it grew. Rather too much for comfort if I'm honest.'

'Profiteering, it's called,' I said. 'I won't preach to you, Sol. I'm not above a little bit of black market trading in the circumstances, but not on a large scale. And if you were going to do it, why leave the book where Sheila could find it?'

'It was just a tiny black notebook. I carried it in my jacket pocket. I suppose it must have fallen out when I left it on the back of a chair in the office.'

'And you think Sheila has it?'

'I'm sure it was her.'

'She hasn't asked for money to return it?'

'She must be out to make trouble for me.' He frowned. 'When I let her go last year – I wasn't supposed to. There was a restriction at the time. Employers couldn't sack anyone, employees weren't supposed to leave unless they had good reason. I'd forgotten about it. When I was asked to explain, I said she had just stopped coming in. If they go after her, she may try to get back at me . . .'

'Oh, Sol . . .' I looked at him unhappily. 'Do you want me to see her, talk to her? I could offer her money for the book.'

'If you know where she is, I'll speak to her myself.'

'I don't know, but Annie may have some idea. I could try to find her – but you had best leave it to me, Sol. She is more likely to sell to me than you. I'm afraid she dislikes you rather a lot.'

He looked upset and ashamed. 'I didn't want to involve you in any of this, Emma. And I certainly don't want Margaret to know.'

'I'll help you if I can,' I promised. 'But you must stop this business, Sol. Think about what it would do to Margaret if you were sent to prison. It would break her heart.'

'Yes, I know. I've found it difficult to look her in the eyes recently. I've already called a halt, Emma. With any luck, business at the showroom will start to pick up this next year. I'll concentrate on that – and maybe you and I will open up a few shops together after the war.'

'We'll see,' I said. 'Meanwhile, I'll do my best to find out where Sheila is living.'

I wasn't so much shocked by what Sol had told me as upset, more for Margaret's sake than my own. She had been much more lively recently, happier, and she seemed better in health. It would be a cruel blow to her if Sol was arrested and tried for quite a serious crime. Of course I could not condone what he had been doing, but I'd suspected something was going on. Margaret had no idea and she would be very hurt. The discovery had not changed my feelings for Sol, but I wasn't sure what it might do to his wife. I believed she would feel the shame of his dishonesty very deeply.

Annie hadn't wanted to tell me where I could find Sheila, but I thought she might know more than she had let on. I would go and visit her again soon. Tell her that it was important I speak to her cousin . . .

When Annie reluctantly admitted the truth, I was so shocked that I hardly knew what to say to her.

'Are you sure?' I asked at last. I was really very disturbed and upset about what she had just disclosed.

'I've always known that Sheila liked men. She had a bit of a reputation when we both lived in March, but . . . prostitution . . . that's horrible, Annie. What about Lizzy?'

'That's what I wanted to know,' Annie said, obviously angry. 'I've already told her she ought to be ashamed of herself, and I think in her heart she is. She must be! Exposing that child to . . . goodness knows what. I'd have Lizzy back, but I can't afford to keep her. Sheila doesn't want her. I'm sure she neglects her. I'm not saying she doesn't try. It's hard enough for me – and I don't earn my living that way.'

Annie's husband was in the navy. Part of his pay came direct to her, but I knew she found it difficult to manage. Sheila's rent had been a big help to her. She had spoken once or twice of taking in another lodger, but she wouldn't entertain the idea of having a man, and it wasn't easy to find a woman who was prepared to come to a house like this.

'My Pete would go wild if he knew I'd had another man in the house,' she'd told me once. 'No, it has to be a woman or no one.'

'Would you take Sheila back?' I asked her now. 'If I could persuade her to come?'

She hesitated for a moment, then nodded. 'Blood is thicker than water as they say. I'll give it another go – but she'll have to give up that game. I don't mind her having boyfriends, but I won't have a prostitute under my roof.'

'I'll go and see her,' I said. 'Perhaps if I talk to her . . .'

'She hangs around this cafe,' Annie said, 'at least she does during the day. It's popular with British soldiers. At night she goes to one of three pubs, but you don't want to go there, Emma. They're pretty rough, and you can't go to the house where she's staying . . . it's where the girls do their trade and not at all nice. I'm sure you will find her at the cafe around midday.'

She gave me a piece of paper with the name and directions where to find the cafe written down. I put it away in my bag and stood up.

'I'll try the cafe tomorrow,' I said. 'Thank you for telling me, Annie.'

'I wasn't going to,' she admitted. 'Sheila won't thank me for it – but you've been good to us . . .'

'I shan't let her know you told me. I'll pretend I saw her by chance. I'm going to offer her the chance of working for me. Jane doesn't really want to work in the shop anymore. It was fun to her at first, but these days it's more of a business. The clothes are not particularly exciting, though we've kept up the quality as much as is possible. Margaret still goes in three afternoons a week, but she only does it for my sake. I thought Sheila might like to manage the place.'

'Lucky her!' Annie said, looking envious. 'I wish I had the chance of something like that. Maybe when my Beryl is a bit older . . .'

'Come to me when you're ready,' I said. 'If I can help, I will.'

'Thanks, I'll remember that.'

My visit with Annie had given me a lot to think about. I knew both Sol and my mother would think me foolish to give Sheila another chance, but Annie's revelations had shocked me. I hated the idea that my friend had been reduced to selling herself to men. I hadn't offered her the job at the time Sol sacked her, because it would have seemed to have gone against him, but things were different now.

I read Jack's letter, smiled and added it to the growing pile in my bedside cabinet drawer. It had taken six weeks to reach me, and I guessed that Jack was probably amongst the American forces that had recently stormed ashore at Los Negros in the Admiralty Islands. Their successful landing had come as a climax to several more Allied victories, and was seen as a beginning to a phase of island-hopping advances by the American forces.

Jack wrote of '*moving forward with our plans*' though nothing specific of course, and said that in his opinion it could not be more than a few months before it was all over.

I'll soon be back with you, darling Emma. Then we can begin to make our own plans for the future.

I was thoughtful as I went to bed that evening. Now that our future together looked as though it might really happen, I was starting to dream about the family we had discussed.

Neither Jack or I had taken any measures to hinder my having a child when we were together. I'd known I was taking a risk, but it hadn't seemed to matter when none of us knew what might happen from one day to the next.

I would have welcomed my lover's child, and I no longer cared that people might point the finger because Jack was not yet my husband. Everyone who loved me would have understood. Besides, it was a common enough occurrence in these uncertain days.

I was a little surprised that nothing had happened. I hadn't taken too much notice when I had not conceived Jon's child, perhaps because we had never really thought about children. Our marriage had been so painfully short. We'd had so little time together. I was more Jack's wife than I had ever been Jon's . . . and I had begun to think about a brother or sister for my son.

I believed it would be good for James. When he was conceived I had been very young and naive, not really ready to be a mother, but I had grown up and I knew that the instinct to have a larger family was strong in me. It seemed odd to me that I had fallen so easily the first time, but was apparently unable to do so now.

Perhaps I would visit a doctor. It might be best if I discovered any problems before Jack came home.

Sheila saw me the moment I entered the cafe. She was seated at a table, but stood up as I approached.

'If you've come to see me, we'll talk outside.'

'Don't you want to finish your drink?'

'It's only tea and it's cold. I've been here an hour already. They are getting ready to throw me out anyway.'

I couldn't help noticing how cheaply she was dressed, and the way her hair straggled. Her face looked pinched and I wondered if she was getting enough to eat.

'Let's go somewhere else,' I suggested. 'It's freezing out. I'll buy you a meal, Sheila. I'm ready to eat anyway.'

She seemed as if she wanted to refuse, then shrugged her shoulders. 'All right, if that's what you want.' Her eyes narrowed as she looked at me. 'I suppose you're after the book? Sol sent you to get it out of me, didn't he?'

'No. He did say you might have it, but he wanted to see you himself. He's not very pleased, Sheila, and he might have lost his temper. I thought it best if I came myself.'

'He doesn't frighten me,' she said, her face stiff with defiance. 'But you can have it if you want – for a price. He owes me. I was going to use it to have him locked up, but I don't care anymore. I need money. Ask him what it's worth to him.'

'How much do you want?'

She looked at me speculatively. 'Five hundred pounds. It ought to be worth that to him. If I gave it to the right people, he would be in a lot of trouble.'

From the way she spoke, I thought she was guessing. She probably didn't realize how important that notebook was, and I didn't believe she really knew what to do with it. I suspected she had taken it on the spur of the moment, and then put it away as a kind of insurance.

'I'll ask Sol if it's worth that much to him.'

'I'll bet his wife would pay quick enough. She wouldn't want her posh friends to know what her precious husband has been up to – and you wouldn't like it much either, Emma.'

'I wouldn't like my friends to be hurt,' I said. 'I know Sol hurt you, Sheila. I'm sorry about that. I shouldn't have let you go that day. It was awkward for me, but I should have spoken to you later. I was wondering whether you might like to manage my shop for me? You might consider living with Annie again . . .'

'She told you about me, didn't she?' Sheila's eyes flashed with anger. 'Don't lie. I know it was her. She's seen me at the cafe with men, and I know you've been visiting her because she told me.'

'Annie wouldn't do anything to harm you. She just wanted to help you to make a fresh start.'

'Well, I don't need her help,' Sheila said, her mouth hard with bitterness. 'Or yours. I've got plans of my own. Todd is coming back and he wants to marry me. He wrote me a letter. I'm going to live in married quarters at his base, and after the war he will take me back to America with him.'

'I'm so pleased for you!' I said. 'I really am, Sheila.'

'It's my chance of a better life,' she said, and there was a hint of desperation in her eyes. 'Todd cares about me. He said he didn't realize how much until he was away from me, but now he wants us to be together – and I love him, Emma. I've never felt like this about any other man. When Pamela gave me the letter – it had been at the club for weeks waiting for me – I knew it could change everything. I would be a good wife to him, Emma. I really would – but there's something I have to do before I can meet him.'

'What do you mean?' I was puzzled by her manner. She looked nervous and glanced over her shoulder as if expecting someone to be listening.

'I'm pregnant,' she said. 'I've no idea who the father is, and I don't care. I just want to get rid of it. That's why I need that money. It will pay for the operation and leave a few pounds over for some clothes. I need a perm and other things. I've got to look decent when I meet Todd next month.'

'Sheila . . .' I stared at her in horror. Surely she didn't mean she was planning to have an abortion? It was a terrible step to take. The only way of having it done was to visit some back-street clinic where the treatment she would receive would be both illegal and dangerous. 'You can't do that to your baby. You would be killing your own child . . .'

Her face was flushed with guilt. 'You don't under-stand. I have to, Emma. It's the only way. Todd wouldn't want me if he knew I'd been with other men while he was away. I can't have it anyway. I can't do my work once it starts to show – and you needn't look like that. I couldn't find a proper job. Sol didn't give me a reference or the proper release papers. If I'd gone for a government job I would have been in trouble for leaving my old job – and nobody else would take me on without a reference. It's as much his fault I'm doing this as my own.'

I could not dispute her words. Sol had treated her harshly. She had behaved badly, but so had he in his way. I blamed myself for having let it happen. It was too late for regrets. Now all I could do was to help her as much as I could.

'I'll get the money for you,' I said. 'Please give me the book, Sheila. I know you're angry and hurt, but there's no need to hurt others – is there? Margaret has never harmed you, has she?'

'No, I suppose not . . .' She looked slightly ashamed but was determined. 'Bring the money tomorrow and I'll give it to you.'

'What about Lizzy?' I asked. 'Will Todd accept her? Does he know you have a daughter?'

'Oh yes,' she said carelessly, so carelessly that I sensed she was lying. 'Lizzy will be fine. I'll make sure of that.'

I sensed something she was hiding from me, but I did not pursue it. Sheila would make her own arrangements for her daughter. Perhaps some of the five hundred pounds was meant for Annie. I was certain she would take the child if Sheila made it worth her while.

We had arrived at a Lyons Corner House. I turned to Sheila with a smile. 'Shall we see what they have on offer today?'

'I'm not hungry,' she said. 'I don't eat much these days. I'll go now, Emma. Bring the money tomorrow and I'll give you the book. I'll be at the cafe at ten o'clock . . .'

'But surely you could eat something?'

She shook her head, starting to walk away.

'Tomorrow at ten . . .'

'I'll be there.'

Sol looked at the notebook. He flicked through the pages, then gave a sigh of relief as he slipped it into his pocket.

'I should burn that if I were you.'

'I intend to.' He laughed harshly. 'How much did you have to pay her?'

'Five hundred pounds.'

'Good grief! You should have let me deal with the mercenary little bitch.'

'It was my money,' I said, and looked at him hard. 'I considered it worth every penny to save Margaret the pain of seeing you go to prison. Besides, Sheila is my friend.'

Sol had the grace to look ashamed. 'I'll pay you back, Emma. And you're right, Margaret's peace of mind is worth every penny. I'm sorry. I shouldn't have spoken to you like that. It's my own fault I was in trouble and I've no one to blame but myself.'

'Sheila needed the money,' I said and smiled at him, acknowledging his apology. 'I know you didn't like her much, Sol, but she was a friend to me years ago – and I don't forget my friends. That money is to help her get a new start in life. I don't want it back. You've done more than enough for me, and this was my chance to help you.'

'There's plenty of money coming your way soon enough,' Sol said gruffly. 'And made legally too, Emma, so don't pull a face. I know better than to offer you *black* money.'

'I'll believe you,' I said, twinkling at him.

'Thousands wouldn't, eh?' Sol chuckled. 'We make good partners you and me, Emma. I won't offer you your money back then, but you're getting a share of the profits from the showroom in future. Don't say no, because I've made up my mind. I think we might have folded these past months if it hadn't been for you. The customers kept coming despite all the troubles because they like you, and you've put in more than your fair share of work.'

'I wasn't going to say no,' I said and laughed. 'I can find a use for the money, Sol. I'm going to give Annie a little job at the shop. Just a few hours while her children are at school . . .'

'You'll never learn,' Sol scoffed. 'Business and friends don't mix, Emma.'

'Annie isn't like her cousin,' I said. 'You'll see. She

won't let me down. I'm going to visit her this weekend, take some things for the children.' I looked at him thoughtfully. 'Have you heard any more about those prefabs a friend of yours had the contract to build?'

'Thinking you'd like one for Annie?' Sol's brows arched mockingly as I nodded. 'She'll be way down the list. They're meant for bombed-out families and servicemen coming home.'

'I know. It's just that that house of hers is so awful.'

'Well, I'll see what I can do,' Sol promised, tapping the side of his nose. 'The first of them won't be on show until April, but after that they will be going up fast. Maybe I can swing it so Annie jumps up the list.'

'Don't tell me you're in that, too?' I was amused as he nodded. 'Well, this time I shan't grumble at you, Sol. I think the Prefabs are a wonderful idea. I shan't mention the possibility to Annie until it's settled, but I know she will be excited.'

'Sheila came to see me yesterday,' Annie said when she invited me in that weekend. 'She looked dreadful, Emma, really ill. You know about the abortion, don't you?'

'Yes, I know.' I frowned as Annie looked disapproving. 'It is horrible, but I couldn't tell her not to do it. She thinks it's all going to work out with Todd this time. I suppose it is a chance for her to make something of her life.'

'It's murder, that's what I told her,' Annie said. 'I've

told her I don't want to see her again. Not after what she's done.'

I was sorry Annie felt that way, but she was adamant.

'What is happening to Lizzy?' I asked. 'Did Sheila want you to take her?'

'I told her I couldn't, not unless she paid me regular money for her keep. I'm fond of the child, Emma, but I've three of my own to feed, and that's not easy. I shall manage a little better with the job you've promised me, but if I had Lizzy I couldn't do it. She's not four yet. Not old enough to go to school.'

'Do you think Todd knows about her?'

'No, I'm sure he doesn't. She never brought him here, it wasn't good enough for her.'

'What will she do with Lizzy then?'

'She said she didn't want me to have her anyway,' Annie replied with a shrug. 'Said she'd got plans for Lizzy – that she was going somewhere she would have a chance of a better life.'

'I wonder what she meant by that?'

'I don't know. She wouldn't tell me, but she looked sort of pleased with herself – as though she knew something I didn't.'

Annie couldn't tell me any more. I worried about it as I walked home that evening. Lizzy was such a beautiful little girl with dark brown hair that curled naturally and grey eyes. I would hate to think of her ending up in a home for orphans, even if it was a good one.

Perhaps Sheila might let me help her find someone

to help care for Lizzy? I decided to visit the cafe again, and see if I could talk to Sheila about her plans for her daughter.

I went several times over the next few days, but I didn't see Sheila there once. She seemed to have vanished, and I wondered if she had gone off with Todd. Perhaps we were worrying for nothing, perhaps she had taken Lizzy with her.

Chapter 12

I came out of the doctor's surgery one morning a week or so after my visit to Annie, feeling bewildered and stunned. His words had shocked me so deeply that at first I had struggled to take them in.

'Because of some injury to your womb when your son was born, it is unlikely that you will easily conceive another child. I'm not saying it is impossible, Mrs Reece, merely that it will take some time for your body to heal, though of course it may do so in time.'

'I'm not sure what you're saying . . .' I had stared at him in shock. 'Will I ever be able to give my husband a child?'

'Miracles do happen, Mrs Reece. You need not give up all hope just yet, but I must warn you there is a strong possibility that you will not conceive again.'

How I managed to answer him I would never know. I was close to tears, my chest painfully tight. Never to have Jack's child! It was so hurtful that I scarcely knew how to bear the pain. I had never considered the possibility that James's premature birth had damaged me inside. My doctor had not mentioned anything at the time, and we had all been too relieved that my son was healthy to think about what it had done to me. Now I felt devastated.

I had dreamed of the life I would have with Jack, of the children we would share. How would Jack feel about things? He loved me, but he also loved children. He might never reproach me, but he would feel it – just as Sol had.

Sol loved Margaret, but their marriage was incomplete because they were unable to have a child. I knew that her failure was a festering sore in Margaret's breast, a wound that would never heal.

Now, for the first time, I began to really understand how she felt.

I walked about for the rest of that day in a kind of daze. I was hurt, bewildered, angry. Richard Gillows had brought on my son's premature birth by his brutal attack on me. It was almost as if I could hear him laughing, as if he had taken his revenge on me from beyond the grave.

Margaret asked me what was wrong when I had tea with her later. I could not tell her the truth, because I knew it would hurt her almost as much as it was hurting me.

'I haven't been able to find Sheila,' I said to excuse my distress. 'I keep wondering what is going to happen to Lizzy. I told you Sheila was going to marry an American, didn't I?' Margaret nodded. 'Well, he doesn't know about her daughter. I'm afraid Sheila might put her in a home or something.'

'Surely she couldn't just abandon her own child?' Margaret looked upset by the idea. She was silent for a moment, thoughtful, then raised her gaze to meet mine. 'If Sheila doesn't want Lizzy . . . we could have her here, Emma.'

'Would you really let me bring the child here?'

'Yes, of course. You know I would, Emma.'

We smiled at each other.

'Then I'll go to the cafe again tomorrow . . .'

'What's wrong, Emma?' Pamela asked that evening. 'You've been staring at that slice of bread for the past five minutes.'

We were in the kitchens of the social club. I had kept my secret from Margaret, but suddenly I discovered that silent tears were running down my cheeks. Pamela came to me, putting her arm about my waist and looking at me in concern.

'Is it bad news, Emma?'

I nodded, fumbled for my handkerchief and blew my nose, telling myself not to be so silly.

'Not Jack. Nothing like that . . . it's just that I've been to see a specialist. A doctor . . . he says I may not be able to have more children because of something that went wrong when James was born. It seems there may be some scarring . . .'

'Oh, poor Emma,' Pamela said, her eyes meeting mine in sympathy and understanding. 'That's so upsetting. I know just how you feel. My Tom and me, well, we tried for five years before the war, but it just didn't happen. I thought about going to the doctor, but Tom said I had to be patient. If it was our destiny not to have children then we had to accept it . . .' She sighed. 'My sister says I'm lucky. She's got four and it has been a dreadful struggle for her. I wouldn't have minded just the one though.' She gave me a squeeze. 'At least you've got your James. You are very lucky, Emma.'

'Yes.' I swallowed hard. I knew what she was saying was true. I was lucky in so many ways. 'Yes, I've got James. I know I'm fortunate. I'm sorry you didn't get your baby, Pam, but perhaps you will when Tom comes home.'

'Yes, perhaps.' She smiled but I saw the echoes of my own sadness in her eyes. 'When Tom comes home . . .'

I made a determined effort to put my disappointment behind me. I had so much to be thankful for, and it would be wrong to give way to self pity. Besides, the doctor hadn't said I definitely couldn't have another baby, only that it was unlikely.

I began spreading margarine on the bread again; then I glanced at Pamela. She was perhaps ten years older than me, in her early thirties, but I liked working with her. She was a pleasant, friendly woman. Until now, our friendship had never gone beyond meeting at the social club, but there was no reason why it shouldn't.

'I'm going to take James to the park if it's fine tomorrow afternoon,' I said. 'Would you like to meet me and then come back to the house for tea?'

Pamela glanced up, staring at me in surprise. Her pale skin was slightly flushed but she looked pleased.

'I would enjoy that, Emma. It's very kind of you to ask me.'

'I should enjoy your company,' I said. 'And Margaret always loves to have visitors.'

I felt better somehow after that. Doctors weren't always right. Besides, James thought of Jack as his daddy so perhaps it wouldn't matter if I couldn't give Jack a son of his own.

'You should see what Gwen has done with your father's shop,' my mother said when she rang me the next morning. 'I can't believe it's the same place.'

'Is something wrong?'

'Oh no,' she said at once. 'Quite the opposite. It's really nice now, Emma. She's put the spirits behind the counter, and she's got a corner specially for the children, just where she can keep an eye on them – and she's just had some lovely cards in, for birthdays and anniversaries. Now she's started to sell cottons for sewing and embroidery.'

'We've never sold those before.'

'It's so nice to go in and have a chat,' Mum said. 'And I'm not the only one who thinks so. I was talking to Mary Edwards the other day – Mary Baker as was, you remember her?'

'Of course I remember Mary. She was always one of my best friends.'

'Mary asked after you when we met in the shop. She'd popped in to buy a card for someone. We had quite a long talk . . . she said she hadn't heard from you for ages.'

'I always send her a card at Christmas.'

'That's hardly enough, Emma. You should make time to see her when you come down next – When are you coming? It's months since you were here.'

'I've been saving my petrol ration. It isn't easy to get extra these days. I'll try to get down again soon, I promise.'

'I shouldn't grumble at you, Emma. I know how busy you are. It's a wonder to me that you have any time for yourself.'

'I will come soon,' I promised her. 'And if you see Mary, tell her I'll pop in while I'm there.'

'Good. Mary is a nice person, Emma. She's got two little girls as you know, and expects her third child this summer. You did know her husband was sent home wounded last winter? Well, he is a worry to her, and she was telling me how difficult it is to buy children's things in March. She's not much good at sewing. I told her to buy the material and I'll make the dresses. She was so pleased. She said she remembered how pretty the dresses I used to make you always looked.'

'You should start up a business, Mum.'

She laughed. 'Oh, I wouldn't want to do that. I'm not like you, Emma, always on the go, thinking of something new to fill your time. You must get your drive from your father. Besides, I don't want the work. I'm doing it for Mary because I like her. She brings the children to visit sometimes, and it's nice making little treats for them. I don't get much chance to do it for your son.'

I was thoughtful after my mother's phone call. If Mary found it difficult to buy children's clothes in the town, then others must have the same problem. I would have to talk to Madge about it. She might be interested in stocking a few dresses for young girls this summer.

'I have enjoyed myself,' Pamela said as we walked home from the park that afternoon, both of us holding on to one of James's hands to stop him from darting off somewhere. 'It was lovely, Emma.'

'I was glad you were there. James is so excitable, it takes all my time to watch him.'

My son had chased after the ducks at the edge of the pond, patted every stray dog that came within range, and almost fallen in the lake as he reached for his toy yacht, which had gone out a little too far. Nothing out of the usual. He spent so much time at home in the nursery or in our tiny garden, that when he came to the park he went wild. I couldn't blame him. He still remembered those carefree days of the previous summer when he had roamed the Sussex countryside with Jack.

I was pleased I'd asked Pamela to come to the park and not just to tea. Like most of my friends, she had fallen under my son's spell and was prepared to spoil him. The chocolate bars she'd bought for him must have taken her sweet rations for the week at least.

We were laughing as we went into the house

together. Mrs Rowan gave me a speaking look as she came out to the hall to greet us and take our coats.

'Mrs Gould is in the parlour,' she said in an odd tone. 'There is a person with her . . .'

'A visitor?' Something in the housekeeper's manner alerted me. 'Is something wrong, Mrs Rowan?'

'I'm sure it's not for me to say, Mrs Reece.' She sniffed in evident disapproval. 'Shall I take Master James up to the nursery for you?'

'Yes, please do.'

I was intrigued. Mrs Rowan quite clearly did not approve of our visitor. Who could it be?

I paused on the threshold of Margaret's sitting room. A young woman I had never seen before was perched on the edge of the sofa, and a small girl stood beside her. The child was crying, her face stained with tears.

'Lizzy . . .' My heart jerked with fright. Why was Sheila's child here? 'What's wrong? Where is Lizzy's mother?'

The young woman turned to stare at me. She was wearing rouge and lipstick, but did not look more than sixteen years old. I had a sudden intuition that she must be one of the prostitutes with whom Sheila had lived and worked for a while these past months.

'You must be Emma,' she said and stood up. She seemed ill at ease but defiant. 'I've been waiting for you. Sheila said I was to bring the child and this letter – and I was to see you got it yourself.'

'Where is Sheila?'

'She's gone. She went off with her bloke, said she

couldn't look after Lizzy no more and that I was to bring her here.'

I took the rather grubby envelope she offered and slit it open.

'*You still owe me, Emma.*' Sheila had written the letter in a bold, challenging hand.

You said you would help if I asked, so I'm sending Lizzy to you. It's up to you what you do with her. You can shove her in a home or keep her yourself. As far as I'm concerned, she's your responsibility now.

Enclosed with the letter was Lizzy's birth certificate and some margarine coupons.

Having read it twice to be certain I understood fully, I handed the letter to Margaret, then remembered my guest.

'Sit down, Pam,' I said, realizing she was still hovering, uncertain of what to do. 'We'll soon sort this out and then we'll have our tea.' I glanced at the young woman who had brought Lizzy to us. 'May we offer you something?'

She shook her head, her eyes sharp with suspicion. 'What are you going to do with the kid?'

'Lizzy has come to stay with us for a while,' I replied. I smiled at the little girl, who was still weeping. 'Are you hungry, darling?' She nodded and I knelt down on the carpet in front of her, taking her little hands in mine. 'Would you like a biscuit?' Her eyes widened in anticipation of such a treat. 'A nice one with chocolate on it?'

'Yes . . .'

'Yes please,' the young woman said. 'You know what your mother said before she went. Be good or the lady won't keep you.'

I saw the fear in Lizzy's eyes and was angry.

'I think you can safely leave Lizzy's welfare to us now,' I said, getting to my feet. 'I'll show you to the door, Miss . . . I'm sorry. I don't know your name.'

'You don't need to know it,' she muttered, glaring at me. 'All right, I'll go. I know when I'm not wanted.'

'It was kind of you to bring Lizzy,' I replied. I opened my handbag, which lay on the sideboard, took out a pound note and gave it to her. 'That's to say thank you for your trouble.'

She stared at the money as if she wanted to refuse, then almost snatched it from my hand. 'I can find my own way out, and don't worry. I shan't steal anything.'

I let her go without replying. She wore her resentment like chainmail. There was no point in trying to get through to her.

'Well . . .' Pamela said as the door closed behind her with a snap. 'What a rude young woman.'

'Yes, she was rather,' Margaret said and handed the letter back to me with a meaningful look. 'I should keep that somewhere safe, Emma. You may need it one day.'

'Yes, I had thought that,' I agreed. 'We'll talk later,

Margaret. I think we should all have tea now, don't you?'

'That is an excellent idea,' Margaret said. 'I'll ring at once.' She smiled as I sat on the settee and took Lizzy on to my lap. 'Isn't this nice? I've heard so much about you, Pamela. I'm glad you've come to visit us at last. So many visitors in one day. How lucky we are!'

When Mrs Rowan came in answer to the bell, I asked her to bring some orange juice and chocolate biscuits.

'Lizzy is going to have her tea with us today,' I said. 'In half an hour's time I shall bring her up to the nursery. Perhaps you would tell Nanny? I think James's last cot will do for Lizzy for a while. We'll see about a bed when she needs it.'

'I'm to take it the child will be staying then, madam?' She looked at Margaret for confirmation.

'Yes, isn't that wonderful news?' Margaret replied. 'Lizzy will be company for James. I think we are very lucky to have her come to visit us.'

Lizzy was sitting quietly on my knee. She seemed to be watching us with her large, soulful eyes. Although only four, a year younger than James, she was intelligent and I believed she understood she had been abandoned by her mother. Until I arrived, she had been frightened and upset, but now her tears had dried. She knew me well enough not to be apprehensive, perhaps because in the past I had always been the bearer of small gifts.

I was pleased that she had been washed, her hair neatly brushed, and was wearing a new dress. At least Sheila had made her presentable before sending her here. Her letter had appeared hostile at first reading, but I knew it was only Sheila's way. She had been certain I could not refuse to have the child, yet still too proud to ask. She had sent a friend to deliver Lizzy in a spirit of defiance, but she had known her child would be loved and cared for in this house.

From the gleam in Margaret's eyes, I knew she was preparing to spoil Lizzy just as she had James. Margaret would have welcomed any motherless child into her home, but there was no doubting that Sheila's daughter was a charmer. My mother had called her a little beauty, and she was right. Feeling the warmth of her thin body against me, I had to fight the urge to hug and kiss her.

Instinctively, I knew that I had to give Lizzy time to get to know us. She was bound to feel nervous at first, and perhaps a little shy. Hopefully, that apprehension would soon melt away.

I was not sure whether Sheila meant to come back for her daughter one day, but already I was beginning to hope she would go to America with Todd and forget all about us.

I had wanted a daughter so much, and believed I might never be able to have one. Now I had Lizzy. I smiled as I looked across the room into Margaret's eyes and knew that she was thinking the same thing.

Lizzy would be our child to love and care for. We

would share her, making the most of her *visit* – whether it was for days or years.

James was a little wary when I took Lizzy up to the nursery. He knew her, of course. They had played together at Jane's party, and met now and then when Sheila and I had had tea together. He listened as I explained that Lizzy's mother had gone away for a while.

'Lizzy has come to stay with us,' I told him. 'I want you to be a good boy, James. It will be nice for you to have a friend to play with. Perhaps you could show her your toys? She hasn't got any at the moment. You might find a few she can borrow.'

James was assessing the situation. I could see that he was not too certain he wanted another child in *his* nursery. He was not sure whether to be pleased or cross. In his heart, I believed he welcomed the arrival of a playmate, yet his instincts were to guard what belonged to him.

'You have such a lot of toys,' I said, bending to kiss the top of his head. 'Be a big boy and share a few of them, darling. Be nice to Lizzy, please?'

'Not car,' he said, a mutinous set to his mouth. 'Lizzy not go in car.'

'You show her how to build with your blocks,' I suggested. 'Tell her what she can play with, James. It is your nursery. You must be nice to Lizzy and look after her. She is your guest, and we should always be polite and nice to guests, shouldn't we?'

I knew that I was asking a lot of my son. He was a bright, intelligent boy, but still very young, and he had been accustomed to having his own way and being the centre of attention. He would find it difficult to adjust, and yet it would be good for him to learn to share. I had sometimes worried that he was being spoiled too much.

'Lizzy play with bricks,' he said, seeming to make up his mind. 'James show her, Mummy. Mummy go away now.'

'Go and play with James now,' I said, letting go of Lizzy's hand and giving her a little push towards him. 'Be a good girl, Lizzy. Nanny will look after you. You can ask her for the potty or a drink when you want one. I'll come and see you in the morning.'

She let go of my hand reluctantly, but as James began to talk to her, very much the master of his domain, I saw that she was fascinated, not just by the toys but also by him.

'May I have a word with you, Mrs Reece?'

'Yes, of course, Nanny. Come out to the landing with me. I think they will be all right on their own for a few minutes.'

She followed me outside, her manner a little affronted and clearly disapproving.

'Am I to understand that the child is to stay here permanently?'

'Lizzy will be living with us for the time being,' I replied. 'I am not yet sure whether it will be permanent.'

'I don't know that I can manage both, Mrs Reece. Master James is quite a handful, and the girl . . . well, we shall see how she turns out.' She sniffed her disapproval.

'If it is too much for you I shall have to think about getting help for you, Nanny. But Lizzy is usually a quiet child. And of course, James will be starting school next year. I could think about a nursery place sooner, but I had arranged for him to begin next spring. He will be coming up to six then and . . .'

'Oh no,' she said quickly. 'Don't send him to school yet, Mrs Reece. I didn't mean I couldn't cope. Just that I wasn't sure about the girl. How is she to be treated?'

'As if she were my daughter,' I replied. 'Lizzy is a lovely little girl, Nanny. I've always thought her good-tempered and obedient. Perhaps too quiet . . .'

A scream of outrage from the nursery seemed to contradict my words. As Nanny and I both rushed back to the room it was to see Lizzy and James struggling for possession of a rather battered old teddy bear. Nanny moved as though to intervene, but I laid my hand on her arm as Lizzy suddenly let go and turned her attention to the building blocks. James immediately dropped the bear and went over to his pedal car. Lizzy watched for a moment, then inched her way towards the teddy and picked it up, hugging it to her. James had seen her but was apparently unconcerned.

'It's probably best to let them settle things between themselves,' I said to Nanny. 'James just wants her to understand he is in charge, that this is his territory. I think he will rather enjoy having her here when he gets used to the idea.'

'We must hope so,' Nanny replied in a tone that showed she did not believe it for a moment. 'We must watch and hope for the best, madam.'

Yes,' I said and smiled at her. 'But I am sure they will get on very well, Nanny. There is no reason why they shouldn't, is there?'

She did not say another word, but her manner made it clear that she thought of Lizzy as an unwelcome intrusion into the nursery.

Sol did not take as kindly to Lizzy's arrival as Margaret had.

'You're a fool to let yourself be used, Emma,' he told me. 'Sheila will take advantage of you as often as you allow her to get away with it. You and Margaret will become fond of the child, then as like as not, Sheila will take her back.'

'Yes, I know it could happen,' I agreed. 'So does Margaret. We are not fools, Sol, but neither of us wants to put the girl in a home. Even if we could find one that would take her. You know how difficult things are still. They would probably send her abroad somewhere, Canada or Australia.'

'Well, you and Margaret will have the bother of her,' Sol said. 'I never interfere with Margaret in house-hold matters. If you're both content to have her here, so be it.'

He was obviously wary of the situation, but short of handing Lizzy over to a children's home, there wasn't much any of us could do, and he knew that neither Margaret or I would give her up.

My mother put her opinion even more bluntly.

'Sheila has been jealous of you for a long time, Emma. It was all right when she had the shop, but since then she's felt resentful that you've done so well for yourself.'

'Yes, I know,' I said. 'I've been aware of it for a while, Mum, but I've always liked her, and she has had a hard time. You can't deny that, can you?'

'So did you.' Mum grimaced. 'You helped her, gave her plenty of chances. Your father always did say she was a bad lot, and he was right. You mark my words. She'll let you get fond of the child, then she'll come and take her away from you. That will give her no end of pleasure!'

'Lizzy is Sheila's daughter. If she wants her back, she can have her. But for the moment, both Margaret and I are enjoying having her here. I'm going to give you her measurements and buy some material, so that you can make her a new dress – if you wouldn't mind?'

'Of course I don't,' Mum said. 'I've always thought Lizzy was a little love – but that doesn't mean to say that I like her mother. Or that I approve of you taking on Sheila's daughter.'

I wouldn't let my mother put Sheila down. I was already becoming fond of Lizzy and I hoped Sheila would leave her with us, but I had to be fair. If Sheila ever asked for her, I would have to let her go.

I had come down to visit my mother, bringing James with me but leaving Lizzy at home with Nanny and Margaret. I left my son playing happily with the cat in Mum's kitchen and walked into the town to spend some time with my friends.

I called at the butcher's shop first, and Mary invited me up for a cup of tea in the parlour. Her husband was sitting in a chair by the windows. He looked pale and tired, and I noticed he walked with a pronounced limp as he went out to leave us alone for a while.

'I heard Joe had been wounded,' I said. 'Is he getting over it, Mary?'

'He will never get over it completely,' Mary said and sighed. 'I suppose we're lucky he came home alive, Emma, but he went through so much. He won't talk about how bad it was, but I know it must have been awful.'

'Yes, it must have been. I'm so sorry, Mary. You must find things difficult.'

'It was terrible at first, but I'm getting used to the nightmares now.'

'Nightmares . . .' She nodded and I saw the worry in her eyes. 'I didn't realize it was so bad for you.'

'Well, at least I've got Joe home, and things are all right between us. He hasn't turned sour the way some men do. You lost Jon so soon. You were only married a few months.'

'Yes . . .' For some reason I didn't want to tell her

about Jack. 'Mum was telling me you were finding it difficult to buy children's things. I'm going to talk to Madge about stocking a few lines. What is it that you can't buy in town, Mary?'

Mary started talking about the price of children's clothes, and how difficult it was to buy a pretty dress that didn't cost the earth. When I left her to visit Madge Henty, I had a good idea of what was needed.

Madge was a little hesitant at first.

'I wouldn't know what to buy,' she said.

'Leave it to me, Madge. I think I know where I can get what we shall need. We'll try just a few things to start with, and see how we go on. If they don't sell we needn't have any more.'

'Well, you know best, Emma,' she said. 'You haven't gone far wrong yet. The shop earns twice as much as it did before we became partners, and that's during the war. Goodness knows what you will do given a proper chance. Send me what you like, and I'll put it out. I can't say fairer than that.'

We chatted for another half an hour, then I went along the street to Robinsons. Gwen had transformed the shop since my last visit. It had a light, bright, welcoming atmosphere and the shelves were bulging. She had crammed her stock into every inch of space and the business was clearly thriving. I had to wait while she served six customers before she had time to talk to me.

'I'm glad you've come, Emma,' Gwen said, smiling at me. 'Would you like to look at the accounts? We're nicely in the black at last. I've been putting every penny back into stock as we agreed, but now the cash is beginning to mount up again. I'll need to reorder regularly, of course, but I think I've gone as far as I can with the space we've got.'

'I shall have to get you a bigger shop,' I said and laughed. 'I knew you would do well, Gwen, but I never expected anything like this.'

Gwen smiled. 'I think we're more alike than either of us realized, Emma. I've taken to this shop keeping like the proverbial duck to water. I always thought I would like it, and I do.'

'I'm so glad, Gwen. You've made a success of the shop, and I'm going to give you a share of the profits. I want to – and you deserve it.'

Gwen looked pleased, more with the praise than any desire to share the profit. But it was only right that both she and my mother should benefit.

I told Gwen about the children's wear I was going to send Mrs Henty.

'Yes, I've often thought something like that was needed here. You might think about opening another shop after the war, Emma. I could keep an eye on it for you.'

'I'm not sure what I'm going to be doing by then,' I said. 'But it's a good idea, Gwen. I might be able to set it up for you and Mum before I go away. I should have some money to spare and it would be something you could both share.'

I was thoughtful as I walked back to my mother's

that evening. She was sitting in a rocking chair by the fire, James asleep on her lap. They both looked very contented and I knew a pang of regret.

Mum would miss James and me when we went to America. I wanted to go with Jack, longed for the day when he would come to claim me, but it would be hard to leave Mum and my friends.

She smiled at me.

'Put the kettle on, love. Bert will be back soon.'

'All right. Has James been good?'

'Good as gold. He always is with me.' She sighed deeply. 'I've been listening to the wireless. Things are going well in Burma. It looks as if the tide is turning everywhere. If the invasion of Europe goes ahead, this year may see the end of the war.'

'I do hope so, Mum.'

'So do I, love. There's been too much killing, too many lives lost. I'll be glad when the men start to come home – though some of them will never be the same again. You have only to look at Joe Edwards. He's a shadow of the man he was, Emma.'

I nodded. 'Yes, I know. He looks so pale and Mary says he has nightmares.'

'I'm not surprised. Who wouldn't after what he's been through? I feel sorry for her, though. I think it's going to be hard for her – still I suppose there are men in a worse state than Joe.'

I nodded and turned away. I tried not to worry about Jack or what might be happening to him, but sometimes it was impossible. There were moments during the long nights when I felt close to despair, when the doubts plagued me and I believed I would never know true happiness again.

'Please come back, Jack. Come back soon. I need you so much my darling. I need you so much . . .'

The words were only in my mind, but I said them over and over again.

Chapter 13

I read in the newspaper that General Dwight D. Eisenhower had turned Britain into one huge armed camp. The plans for the Allied invasion of *Fortress Europe* was under way and all coastal areas were closed to visitors. Also, all overseas travel by foreign diplomats in London had been curtailed for the moment. It was evident by the extent and number of troop movements up and down the country that something big was on the cards.

I suppose I expected that Jack would be involved somewhere, and it was a welcome event but not really a surprise when he walked in as Margaret and I were having tea one Sunday afternoon towards the end of April.

'Oh, Jack!' I sprang to my feet, my heart pounding madly. 'I'm so very pleased to see you. Why didn't you let us know you were coming? Or did you write? I haven't had a letter for weeks.'

'My letters must have gone astray,' Jack said. He kissed me. 'It's all a bit hectic, Emma. I can't stay long now – but I wanted to see you. I have to talk to you.'

'What's wrong?' My mouth was suddenly dry. His manner was so odd. I had never known him to be this reserved. 'What have I done, Jack? You're angry . . .'

'Can we be alone?' He glanced at Margaret apologetically. 'Forgive me if I seem rude, but I haven't much time, and there's something important I must say to Emma.'

'Of course.' She smiled at him. 'I understand.'

'We'll go to the study.'

I led the way. My stomach was churning. Something awful had happened. Jack was angry, even nervous – but why?

In the study, I turned to face him. 'What is it, Jack? Please tell me. I know something has happened.'

'It is very possible that Jon is alive.'

His words were so unexpected that I could not immediately take them in. For several seconds, I stared at Jack in stunned disbelief. After all this time! Was it possible? I had given up all expectation of such news long ago.

'Jon alive . . .' I took a deep breath. 'How? Where is he?'

'In France. In a small hostel run by nuns somewhere in the Loire Valley.' Jack frowned as I went white and sat down on a chair as my legs seemed to give way. 'I'm sorry. I should have broken the news more gently, but there was no easy way to say it. Are you feeling faint?'

'A bit . . .' I sighed, my hands trembling. 'It's such a shock, Jack. After all these years . . . no word at all and now this. Are you sure it is Jon?'

'Pretty sure.' He looked at me oddly. 'I heard about the possibility last year . . .'

'You knew – when you were here last summer?' He nodded, eyes intent on my face, seeming to ask for understanding. I was shocked, upset. 'But you didn't tell me. You knew Jon might still be alive and yet you never mentioned it once. Why, Jack?'

'Because we were happy that summer. I didn't want to spoil things for either of us. Besides, there was nothing we could have done then. Jon is ill, Emma. He almost died at that time. He had been with the French resistance . . .'

'With . . . then why didn't anyone know?'

'It seems he was . . .' Jack hesitated, clearly reluctant to tell me the details. 'After the crash he was taken prisoner and tortured. When he was being transferred to another prison, the convoy was attacked by French resistance fighters. Jon escaped during the shooting, but when the French got to him he was more dead than alive. He knew he was British, but had forgotten everything else. He recovered his health but not his memory, and worked with the men who had saved his life for almost two years, then he was badly injured in a sabotage attack that went wrong. Since then he has been with the nuns.'

'Oh, my poor Jon,' I whispered, feeling sick and faint again. 'He was suffering so much pain and all this time we thought he was dead. We had given him up . . .'

I had given him up. I had taken a lover and planned a future that did not include him.

'Perhaps it might have been better for him if he had died.'

'What do you mean?' I looked at Jack fearfully. 'You must tell me the truth.'

'I would rather you had never needed to know,' Jack said. 'But if the invasion goes well . . . Jon may be coming home to England, to a hospital here. I understand he will need treatment. I wanted to tell you before anyone else could.'

'I don't understand . . .'

Jack looked grim. 'Apparently, a few days ago Flight Lieutenant Jonathan Reece remembered who he was and asked for a message to be sent to you. You will receive official confirmation that your husband is alive soon, and he will be one of the first to be repatriated when the fighting is over.'

'How do you know all this?' I asked, but of course he would know. Jack had access to British intelligence reports.

'It is my job to know,' he said. 'Besides, you asked me to find him. I never go back on a promise, Emma. I always meant to tell you one day. I believed he might never recover his memory, and of course I couldn't be absolutely sure it was him.'

'But you are now?'

He nodded. 'Quite sure.'

'You say he is ill?' The news was so distressing. My mouth felt dry and I could hardly breathe. 'You said he needs hospital treatment. What is wrong with him, Jack?'

'He was badly burned in the sabotage attack, apparently the bomb went off too soon and he got caught by the blast. One hand is useless, and the left side of his face is scarred . . . and he has a chest infection which makes him cough a lot. I understand that they thought he might die of an infection last winter, but somehow he pulled through. He must be a very tough customer, Emma.'

There was a grudging respect in Jack's words.

'I never realized he was that determined to hang on to life,' I said. 'I thought he might let go . . . and perhaps he did in a way. Perhaps losing his memory was Jon's way of coping with all he went through.'

'I have to go,' Jack said, glancing at his watch. 'I'm not sure that I shall see you again for some weeks . . .'

'Oh, Jack . . .' I felt the pain strike deep inside me. I knew what that meant. He would be going to France with the invasion force, whenever that happened. 'What are we going to do? I'm Jon's wife . . . I can't desert him . . .'

Jack took two strides towards me, catching me up in his arms. For a moment he stared into my face, and his expression was so grim that I was almost afraid of this man – a man I scarcely knew.

'You belong to me, Emma. You know that in your heart. You know you never loved Jon, not really – oh, as a friend, yes I don't doubt your feelings for him were warm and tender – but you were never in love with him.'

'No, I was never in love with him.' I could not lie to Jack. He meant too much to me, was too much a part of me. 'I've never felt this way about anyone else and I never will, Jack.'

'You are not to worry about this,' he told me fiercely.

'If Jon is sent back before I can come to you, he will be in hospital. I very much doubt if he will ever come out. He couldn't come home to you, Emma. He is too ill. He will probably always be an invalid, and I understand the scarring is pretty horrendous. You will have to get a divorce or an annulment or something. I'll see to it when I come back.'

'Jack, no . . . you don't understand. I came to you because I believed Jon was dead. I can't desert him . . . especially now. He will need help and love. I owe him that much at least.'

'You owe him nothing,' Jack said, and his eyes glittered with anger. 'Listen to me, Emma. I'm not going to let you throw away your life. I won't stand by and see you chained to a wreck of a man. We've so much to live for, my darling. I know this hurts you. I know it has been a shock, but by the time I come back, you will have thought it over. You will know how impossible it would be.

'Oh, Jack . . .'

I clung to him as I kissed him, my whole body yearning for his. Perhaps he was right, I could not know. At this moment I wanted only to be with him, for things to be as they had been last summer. My dreams had been so sweet and I did not want to let go of them – and yet it would be so cruel to simply abandon Jon to the life of an institutionalized invalid.

How could I simply walk away with Jack and leave my husband?

'I can't leave him for you,' I whispered. 'I love you, Jack – but I have to stay with Jon. I have to . . .'

'I love you, Emma,' Jack said, and his voice throbbed with passion. 'I'm never going to give you up. Make up your mind to it, Emma, because when I come back I'm not going to take no for an answer.'

His kiss seemed to drain the very life from me. When he walked out of the room, I felt myself sag and I almost fell, managing to stagger to the sofa where I collapsed in a heap.

Jon was alive. My gentle, loving husband, who had given me so much and loved me so tenderly, was alive, but very ill. How he must have suffered. I was wracked with guilt as I imagined his pain, his hours of fear and distress, as he tried in vain to remember even his own name.

How could I leave a man like that to waste away in a home for men who could no longer be a part of society? How could I desert him when he needed me so much? His first thought when he remembered who he was, was to ask that I be informed.

Jon needed me, and I was beginning to see that I would not be able to turn from that need.

'Jon's mother will have to be told, of course,' Margaret said. 'Or perhaps you should wait for confirmation that he has actually been sent home? Rather than raise false hopes . . .'

'I thought I might go over and see her and Pops tomorrow. I think I ought to warn them that there is a possibility Jon may be coming home.'

'Yes, I suppose that might be kinder.' Margaret

looked at me anxiously. 'What will *you* do now, Emma?'

'I'm not sure.' The pain inside me was so intense that I could scarcely breathe let alone think clearly. 'Jack believes Jon will need to be in hospital for the rest of his life, but I'm not sure. He would hate that. If there's any chance at all of his coming out . . .'

'Are you thinking of bringing him home here?'

'Would you mind? I should need to get someone in to help care for him, of course.'

'Of course I wouldn't mind, Emma. I was afraid you might think it necessary to have a house of your own, and I should miss you and the children so very much.'

'I would rather stay here if I may. It won't be easy, looking after an invalid and the children . . . and I don't want to give up my work.'

'Are you sure this is what you really want to do? There are some very pleasant nursing homes where Jon could be cared for properly. You could visit him now and then . . .'

'I couldn't leave him in a hospital, not if he is able to come out, Margaret. You know what sort of a life he would have shut away . . . it doesn't bear thinking about.'

'What about Jack? I thought you might marry him after the war?'

'It was our intention . . .' My throat tightened. 'I'm Jon's wife, Margaret. How can I leave him now?'

'I don't know, my dear.' She looked at me sadly. 'It

would be very difficult for you. But perhaps you need to be strong. I'm sure you believe the right thing would be to have Jon home, but it might not be – for you or him.'

'How can it not be the right thing for him?'

'It depends how bad the scarring is, Emma. It might be that if his injuries are too awful, he would not be able to bear life in the outside world. I believe you should wait before making your decision. Remember that what you do now will affect the rest of your life.'

Margaret's wise words calmed me a little. I knew that I was going to have to make the most difficult choice of my life. Either I abandoned the man I had married – or I gave up the man I loved.

How could I bear to make such a choice?

I went to the social club that evening, because I was too restless to stay at home. I had expected to see Pam, but she wasn't there. Another woman I hardly knew called Ellen had come in her place.

'Where is Pam?' I asked. 'Is she ill? I've never known her to miss her turn before.'

'Haven't you heard?' Ellen looked stricken. 'Pamela is a friend of yours. I thought you must know – her husband was killed at sea a few days ago. She heard about it yesterday.'

'Pam's husband . . . Tom has been killed?'

She nodded. 'I know. It's awful. And just when it looks as if the war is nearly over.'

I couldn't answer her. I was devastated by the news,

reaching for the back of a chair as the room seemed to spin for a few seconds.

'Are you all right, Emma?'

'Yes . . .' I lifted my head as the faintness cleared. 'It was just the shock.'

I'd had two shocks in one day and this last had left me feeling disorientated. But my own problems suddenly seemed to have shrunk beside Pam's. Tom was all she had, apart from a sister she hardly ever saw, who was too busy to visit her often.

'Could you manage here alone this evening?' I asked. 'I'm sorry, but I feel I ought to go round to Pam's. She will be on her own, and I know what she must be going through.'

'Yes, of course I'll manage. It's only a few sandwiches. You get off, Emma. It's good to have a friend with you at times like these.'

I picked up my coat and bag and rushed out of the kitchen. As I went through the community room, I thought I heard someone call my name but I was so upset that I didn't bother to look round.

It was only when I was sitting in the taxi taking me to Pam's house that I realized the officer had used my first name. I vaguely recalled that he had been wearing an air force uniform, but I couldn't think who he could be. No one who came to the club really knew me well enough to call me Emma.

I forgot the small mystery as I paid the taxi driver and rang Pam's front door bell. It was a moment or two before sounds from inside indicated that someone was coming. When Pam opened the door, she looked terrible. Her hair couldn't have been brushed all day, and her eyes had a terrible, blank staring expression.

'Emma . . .' She started to cry as she saw me, the tears slipping helplessly down her cheeks. 'Oh, Emma, I'm so alone . . .'

I stepped into the hall and put my arms around her. She was shaking, as if she had been chilled right through.

'It's all right, Pam,' I said, holding her until the fit of sobbing began to ease. 'I'm here now, and I'm going to stay for a while. Come into the kitchen. I'll make you a cup of tea.'

She stiffened, seeming to resist the move to the kitchen, then turned and led the way. It was cold. She hadn't lit the old-fashioned range, and the remains of a meal were left on the table, a telegram lying amongst the debris. She must have been about to eat when the news came, and by the look of things she hadn't eaten since.

I went to fill the kettle and light the gas stove. Then I saw the bottle of pills and a glass of water on a wooden draining board next to the stone sink. All the pills had been tipped out, as though she had intended to swallow every last one. I looked at the label and then at Pam in dismay as I realized what she had been about to do.

'What are these?'

'The doctor gave them to me to help me sleep. I thought if I took them all, then put my head in the gas oven . . .'

'You were going to take them all, then turn the gas on? Oh, Pam . . . my dear . . .'

She sat down on a chair, her body slumped in defeat. 'What's the use of going on, Emma? Tom is dead . . . I shall never have a child. I might as well be dead. I'm no use to anyone.'

'Of course you are!'

I felt chilled. Pam's house had a terrible, empty atmosphere and was depressingly dark. If I hadn't arrived when I did . . . she would have taken those pills, and to make quite certain would have gassed herself. If I'd left it until the morning, I would have been too late. I knew that I couldn't leave her here alone. Not tonight. Not until she felt able to face things again.

'Who needs me?' she asked.

'I need you,' I said, improvising swiftly. 'Nanny is finding it too much for her to cope with both James and Lizzy. I want you to move in with us, Pam. As a matter of fact, I may be needing your help in other ways very soon.'

'What do you mean, Emma?'

'My husband may be coming home. We all thought Jon was dead, but we were wrong. It isn't certain yet what will happen – but he is very ill, Pam. I am not sure whether he will be able to leave hospital, but if he does he will need constant attention. I'm going to need someone like you – and I would rather it *was* you. A kind, generous person I know I can trust.'

'Do you mean it?' She was staring at me, and I could see the colour begin to return to her cheeks. 'Live with you . . . be a part of your family?'

How lonely she must have been all the time Tom

was away! And I had never realized it, never thought about why Pam was always ready to come into the club at a moment's notice. I felt ashamed that it had taken me so long to make friends with her.

'Would you come?' I asked, kneeling down on the floor in front of her and taking her hand. 'I'm going to need a good friend, Pam. Margaret is wonderful, but she couldn't help me to nurse Jon. I know you would be good to him when I couldn't be there – and James likes you. Please say you will. Please let me take you home with me now, this evening. I don't want you to stay here alone.'

'What will Mrs Gould say?'

'Margaret likes you. Let's go and pack a few things, Pam. You can come back and sort the house out when you're feeling better.'

She hesitated for a moment, then smiled. 'I've wanted to be your friend for a long time,' she said. 'Tom's gone, Emma. Nothing will bring him back – but Jon is alive. Between us, we might be able to keep him that way.'

She stood up, and I could see a new determination about her as she led the way upstairs. For the moment she was blocking out the grief and despair that had almost driven her to take her own life. They would come back, of course, but now that she was no longer so alone, she would be able to bear them.

'Another of your lame ducks?' Sol was amused when he discovered he now had a permanent resident in the

second-best guest room. 'We have one more room to
spare – any likely candidates?'

'Oh, Sol!' I cried, knowing that he was merely
teasing me. 'Pam isn't a lame duck. She's usually a
very cheerful, capable woman. She will help look after
the children – and Jon if we bring him home.'

'Yes, you will need someone to help look after him,'
Sol agreed. 'You won't want to be tied to the house.
I think you've done a good deed for yourself as well
as Pam.'

I already knew that Sol was pleased at the idea of
my bringing Jon home. The two men had always got
on well together – and it would mean I would not be
leaving London to go and live in America. Sol could
not hide his satisfaction, despite knowing that I was
having to make a choice that caused me pain. He did
not want me to be unhappy, yet he did not want to
lose me either.

My mother had surprised me by telling me straight
out that I was doing the right thing. I had expected
her to say I was a fool, that I should think of my own
happiness, but instead she told me it was my duty to
take care of my injured husband.

'Jon has done his bit for us all,' she declared roundly.
'You owe him the chance to live a reasonably normal
life. Besides, you are his wife. He has the right to
expect your loyalty.'

'Yes, I know. I do care for Jon . . .'

'But you're in love with Jack?' She didn't wait
for my answer. 'I know you're giving up a lot, Emma,

but I don't think you have much choice. I don't think you would be happy if you went away with Jack . . . not knowing that you had condemned your husband to life in an institution. You're not made that way, love.'

In my heart, I knew Mum was right. I knew that I did not have a choice. I could not simply abandon Jon to his fate. That didn't stop me hurting. It didn't stop me weeping bitter tears into my pillow, or pacing the floor during the long lonely nights. It didn't stop me wanting Jack, wanting to be in his arms.

I had made up my mind that I would bring Jon home if it was possible . . . but would I be strong enough to resist Jack when he came back to claim me as he inevitably would?

Mrs Reece began to cry as soon as I told her that there was a chance Jon might be coming home.

'You mustn't hope for too much,' I said as she started up out of her chair, clearly excited. I hated to destroy her feeling of joy, but she had to know it all. 'If he does come home he is going to be an invalid, perhaps for the rest of his life – and I have been told he is badly scarred.'

'Who told you about him?' Mrs Reece stared at me, her eyes a little wild as she sank back in her chair. 'How do you know he is still alive and in France?'

'A friend of mine has been informed by British Intelligence. Jon has been cared for by nuns for some time now. After the crash, he didn't know who he was.

He had no idea of his own name until recently – that's
why no one informed us that he was alive before this.
My friend said that he had been working with the
French resistance until he was wounded so badly some
months ago.'

'Your friend . . .' Her eyes narrowed suspiciously.
'I suppose you mean that wealthy American. I've heard
about you and him, Emma. You and your fancy man
have been the talk of the social club more than once.
I've scarce known where to put my face at times for
the shame of it!'

Her voice was sharp with spite and bitterness. I
knew she was close to hating me in that moment.

'Dorothy!' Pops warned her. 'Please don't talk to
Emma like that. She believed that Jon was dead . . .
we all did.' He reached for my hand, his own trembling.
'Just how bad is he, my dear?'

'Very unwell,' I said. 'I wasn't even sure whether I
ought to tell you yet, Pops. Even if he comes home
to this country he may never be well enough to leave
hospital . . .'

'And that will suit you, won't it?' Mrs Reece said,
a cold, scornful note in her voice. 'Then you can go
swanning off to America with your fancy man and
forget my poor boy.'

'That isn't my intention,' I said, controlling my urge
to snap back at her. 'I'm sorry you think I have behaved
badly, Mrs Reece. I did wait for quite a long time, but
I couldn't face the thought of living alone for the rest
of my life . . .'

'Are you thinking of having him home, Emma?' Pops asked. 'Where will you take him?'

'He will come here, of course,' Mrs Reece jumped in before I could answer. 'This is his home. He should be here with his family.'

'I have already made arrangements at home,' I replied, keeping my voice level. 'I have someone, a very nice woman, who will help me to care for Jon. I couldn't manage him alone, naturally, and it would disrupt your household, Mrs Reece. Besides, I think Jon would prefer to come home to me, and I have no intention of living here. It just wouldn't work. I'm sorry, but my mind is made up on that.'

'You've never liked me,' she replied and began to cry. She dabbed at her cheeks with her handkerchief. 'You kept Jon away from us before he was shot down, and now you're trying to deny us the chance to see him. Our own son . . .'

'That isn't true. If he can travel, I shall bring Jon to see you – and if he is unable to move far, you can visit him.'

'You couldn't look after him, Dorothy,' Pops said. 'I'm enough trouble to you as it is.' He patted my hand, smiling at me in his own sweet way. 'You're a good girl to consider having Jon back, Emma. I dare say there's a good many who would be only too pleased to let someone else take the burden.'

'Jon is my husband,' I said. 'I do love him. I always have. I could not just walk away when he needs me.'

Mrs Reece gave me a disbelieving stare, but Pops

leaned forward and kissed me. 'Knowing you, I would not expect you to do anything else,' he said. 'Thank you, my dear.'

Tears stung my eyes. The determination to stand by Jon had grown over the past few days.

All I had to do now was to wait for the official confirmation that he was back in an English hospital, and that could not happen until after the invasion of Europe, which I, like everyone else in the country, knew must happen very soon.

Jane carried two suitcases of clothes into the shop one morning in late May. 'I thought you might as well have these,' she said. 'I don't want anything for them, Emma. I shall be going home very soon, and I'm sick to death of everything I brought with me.'

'Oh, Jane,' I cried. 'I shall miss you when you leave!'

'I shall miss you, Emma, but we'll be seeing each other when you come out to America with Jack. I'm going to invite you to stay often.'

'I'm not sure I shall be coming, Jane.'

She stared at me in dismay. 'You haven't fallen out with Jack? I can't believe it! You two are so right for each other.'

'We haven't fallen out. Jon is alive. Jack told me himself. He's very ill. I don't think I can just walk away from that.'

'Oh, Emma,' she was shocked and upset. 'How awful for you. Whatever will you do? You can't simply give up everything you had with Jack! It doesn't make sense.'

'I don't see what else I can do.' I stopped her as she would have protested. 'No, Jane. Jon is my husband. He has never done anything to harm me, in fact he always helped me, always stood by me. How can I do less for him? He needs me. Put yourself in my position. You wouldn't desert Robert if he needed you – would you?'

'But you're in love with Jack. Don't deny it, Emma. I know it's true.'

'I'm not going to deny it. Being with Jack has given me more happiness than I've ever known in my life.'

'Then how can you think of giving him up? Quite apart from the fact that it will devastate him, you are going to be utterly miserable. Is it worth ruining your own and Jack's life for a mistaken sense of duty?'

I could not answer her. Jane was asking all the questions I asked myself over and over again in the night. I was being torn in two by conflicting loyalties. All I knew for certain was that I would never be truly happy with Jack if I deserted my husband when he needed me.

'So when do you think you will go back home?' I asked. 'You and Robert must come to dinner before you leave. I know Margaret would like to see you again.'

'It depends on the way things go in France,' Jane said. 'We're going to be very busy for a while, Emma. Can I give you an answer another day – when I know more about Robert's schedule?'

'Yes, of course.'

I had the feeling that she was angry with me. Quite obviously, Jane did not agree with my decision to give up Jack. She was puzzled and hurt by what she saw as my rejection of not only Jack but the life he had offered me – and by implication, her. Had I gone to America as we'd planned, we would have continued to be good friends, but now it was unlikely we would meet again after she left London.

'Well, I must dash,' she said, then gave me a hard, reproachful look. 'I think you are a fool, Emma. I'm sorry, but I do. You're throwing away so much for some self-sacrificing ideal that means nothing, and I believe you will regret it.'

I stared after her as she left the shop, knowing that I might well have lost Jane's friendship for good.

Chapter 14

D-Day had finally arrived and the Allied troops stormed ashore in Normandy. Mr Churchill had broadcast to the nation, telling us that things were going as well or better than had been forecast. We had suffered fewer losses at sea than expected, and though there would be many losses in the battles to come the future now looked much brighter.

Every day Margaret and I listened to the wireless for news of the invasion; it might be going well, but now we had something else to trouble us. Hitler had threatened a new secret weapon, and it had come in the form of the *buzz bomb* or *doodle-bug*, a deadly menace that became dangerous once the odd-sounding engine stopped or the flame of orange it emitted ceased. It took about fifteen seconds for the bomb to explode once the engine ran out of fuel, and the attacks could happen at any time of day or night. Crowded shopping streets had felt its full force, and it was very frightening. Yet we accepted it as we had the blitz before it, and carried on with our lives as best we could.

'It's nearly over,' Annie said to me when I went into the shop one afternoon towards the end of June. 'The way the invasion is going, the Germans will soon be defeated. Don't you think so, Emma?'

'It certainly seems to be going our way, at least in France.'

'They will be coming home soon,' Annie said, her eyes reflecting a mixture of wistfulness and hope. 'Our men. Brothers, fathers, uncles, husbands – it's wonderful, isn't it? I'm so excited, Emma. I can't wait for Pete to come home.'

'When he does you will have some good news for him.' I smiled at her. 'Sol has managed to get you a prefab. You can have the keys next month.'

'Oh, Emma . . .' She looked at me excitedly. 'You're so good to me! I would have had to wait ages if it hadn't been for you.'

'I'm glad Sol could help,' I said. 'He's the one you should thank – and he says he will take your eldest girl on as a trainee machinist when she leaves school this summer. You said Ruth was interested in learning the trade, and we shall be needing new staff in the workshop and the showroom. We're going to expand now that cloth isn't rationed. You'll still need coupons to buy clothes, of course, but that's bound to end sooner or later.'

'What will you do about the shop?' she asked. 'People won't be so keen on second-hand stuff then – at least not good stuff at your prices. They'll want new if they can afford it, and those that can't buy off the market anyway.'

'Yes, I know. This was just something to fill the gap when things were so difficult, Annie; I never expected it to carry on for ever. I've been thinking about the future. Now that Jane no longer has an interest in the shop, Margaret and I have decided to make changes. We both think there is a going to be a continuing demand for material by women who want to make their own clothes. We're having some paper patterns made up for us, and we're going to start selling them and a range of sewing cottons, and from next month we shall have a certain amount of new material to offer.'

'Will you keep the second-hand stuff? Only if you wanted to clear it out, I know someone who runs a stall on the market in Petticoat Lane. He would give you a few pounds for it.'

'We'll get the new material in and see how things go first. Once we're up and running, I might have ready-made dresses here too. This shop is going to be the first of several, Annie. I want to take things slowly at the start, see what sells best before I invest too much.'

'You won't be going to America then?'

'No,' I said, controlling the swift surge of pain her words aroused. 'At the moment, I can't see that happening.'

I was still hurting as I left the shop. An official letter confirming that Jon was alive but badly injured had arrived just a few days earlier. I would be sent further details when they were available.

My eyes were stinging with unshed tears as I began to walk towards the Portobello Road. Such mixed emotions were raging inside me. I was glad Jon was alive, of course I was glad about that, but distressed and concerned about his injuries. Would he be well enough to come home within days or weeks – or would he be confined to hospital for a much longer period?

My mind was set on having him home if it was possible, and if not then I would visit him as often as I could. I had made my decision but the pain of making that choice was still raw. Yes, I cared for my husband – but giving Jack up was like tearing out my own heart.

I knew that I would always love him, always miss him, but there was no choice. I could never desert Jon.

As I went into the showroom, I noticed a man in the uniform of an RAF officer talking to Sol. He turned as I entered, and my breath caught as I saw his face and knew him. It was Paul Greenslade.

'Emma . . .' He came towards me, smiling in the way that had once had the power to make my knees go weak. He was still as darkly handsome as ever, but I had long outgrown my infatuation for this man. 'I was sure it was you I saw at that club some weeks ago. I made inquiries and traced you here. Your friend has just been telling me about Jon. I'm so very sorry. It must be a worry for you.'

'Paul . . .' I stared at him, a trickle of ice wending its way down my spine. The last time I'd seen James's father, we had not parted on friendly terms. 'What are you doing here? Why have you come?'

'I just wanted to see you.' He frowned, sensing my hostility. 'Are you still angry with me? I know I said things I ought not to have said when we last met. I apologize for my behaviour then – and previously. I would like to be friends, Emma, perhaps to see James. I know I don't deserve anything, but . . .'

'No, I don't think you do deserve any consideration from me, Paul.' I was gripped by a sudden fear I could not explain. 'You can't see James. It would upset and confuse him. He hardly remembers Jon. He might think you were him, because of the uniform.'

'You *are* angry,' Paul said. 'Please don't be, Emma. I haven't come to try and harm you or the boy. Believe me, I wouldn't do that. I'm not a monster. I've regretted the way I treated you many times. Please try to forgive me.'

'I don't quite believe you, Paul. I'm sorry, but I really don't think you should see James. At least, not until he is older and can understand. It would upset him too much.'

'As you wish.' He gave in more easily than I had expected. 'I came home to fight for my country, but I shall be going back to America after the war ends.' He hesitated, then, 'I married an American girl, Emma. We have a daughter. She's not quite three years old. When I last saw her she was just a baby.'

'I see . . .' Some of my alarm receded. 'I'm glad you have a family, Paul. I'm sorry to be so stubborn, but I just don't think it's a good idea for you to see James. I could send you some photographs if you like?'

'Would you? I should like that.' He took a card from

his pocket. 'This is my address. I shall be there for a few more weeks at least.'

'I'll send them before that – but James is mine, Paul. You gave up all right to him long ago.'

'Yes, I know that.' He smiled oddly. 'I was a fool – but there's no use crying over spilt milk, is there?'

'None at all.' I offered my hand. Paul hesitated, then gripped it for a moment. 'Goodbye and good luck, Paul.'

'Oh, I wouldn't say it's goodbye, Emma. I dare say we shall meet again one day.'

I watched as Paul walked from the showroom. Something about his last words chilled me. But surely there was no need to be anxious? There was no way he could take James. My son did not even bear his name.

Sol came up to me. He looked at my face, then frowned.

'What's wrong, Emma? Did he upset you? He said he was a friend of yours.'

'That was James's father. He asked if he could see him. I refused. It's silly, but I was frightened. Just for a moment I had the most awful feeling that he was going to try . . .' I looked at Sol anxiously. 'He couldn't take James from me – could he?'

'No, of course not. Don't worry, Emma. We wouldn't let him if he tried. If you had been living alone in poor conditions, he might have had a case for applying for custody – but as it is, he doesn't stand a chance. Believe me, there's no need for you to worry.'

'No, of course not. It was just a foolish idea that

he might try to get James.' I laughed as the fear passed.
'I was being silly.'

'It is never foolish to be on your guard, Emma.
Children have been snatched in such cases before this,
but it isn't going to happen to James. I promise you.
Besides, it was probably just a whim on his part. Maybe
he saw you by chance and decided to trace you out
of a sentimental urge to relive his past.'

'He has a wife and daughter in America.'

'There you are then,' Sol said. 'Why should he want
your son when he has his own family?'

'I don't suppose he does, not really. His wife is hardly
likely to want a child of a former girlfriend is she?'

'So you can stop worrying,' Sol said. 'Come and look
at this new dress, Emma. It's a bit like one we used to
make, but we've come up with some new features . . .'

I went with Sol to inspect the new dress, which had
a gored skirt, lots of fancy stitching, a wide belt that
cinched into the waist, and elbow length sleeves. My
nerves had stopped jangling, but I couldn't help
wishing that Paul had not seen me at the social club.

I would feel safer when I was sure he had gone
back to America, and I decided I would not tempt
fate by sending Paul pictures of my son.

When I got home that evening, the house was in an
uproar. I could hear the voices raised in dispute the
moment I entered the house. I went into the parlour,
stopping in surprise as I saw Nanny and Pam standing
awkwardly in front of a very angry Margaret.

'What is going on?' I asked. They had all gone silent as I entered, the faces of both Nanny and Pam looking rather anxious and a little guilty. 'Why are you angry, Margaret?'

'I'm so sorry, Emma,' Margaret said. 'There has been an unfortunate accident . . .'

'Has something happened to James?' My heart stood still as I had visions of my son somehow being snatched in the park.

'Not James,' Margaret said. 'Mrs Rowan is with him now. It's poor little Lizzy. She had a tumble down the nursery stairs.'

'She fell down the stairs . . . but surely . . .' I looked at Nanny and then Pam. 'Why was she on the stairs?'

They both started to speak at once, their voices sharp with accusation.

'It's not my fault, Mrs Reece. I only turned my back for a moment and she was off . . .' Nanny rushed into excuses.

'Mrs Rowan called me for my lunch,' Pam said. 'I'd hardly got down to the parlour when I heard Lizzy scream – I ran back, and there she was lying at the foot of those wretched stairs, her poor little arm twisted under her.'

'Is she badly hurt?' I asked, feeling alarmed and distressed.

'Her arm is fractured,' Margaret said. I took her to the hospital myself, Emma. They are keeping her in overnight, to make sure she has suffered no other injuries, but she was very frightened and in some pain

I'm afraid. However, they gave her a drink with something in it to make her sleep after her arm was set, and she was quite peaceful when I left her.'

'Poor little child,' I said, and looked at Nanny. 'How did it happen? Didn't you notice that she wasn't in the nursery?'

'Master James and the girl were quarrelling over toys again,' Nanny said, a look of resentment in her eyes. 'I gave Lizzy a smack and put her in her cot, but she must have climbed out of it after I went to prepare lunch for her and Master James. The next thing I heard was screaming – and then Pamela came rushing up and started to accuse me of having let the child fall. It's that frayed carpet, Mrs Reece. She caught her foot in it. I've mentioned it to you before – dangerous that carpet is. It's a wonder that one of us hasn't tripped on it before now.'

'Yes, I know it is dangerous,' Margaret said, looking upset. 'I'll ask Sol to take it up immediately. We might not be able to get a decent carpet at the moment, but we can probably buy some cord or something. Anyway, the carpet comes up this evening as soon as Sol gets home, even if we have to have bare boards.'

'I can do it,' I said. 'Pam will give me a hand – won't you?'

'Yes, of course,' she said. 'I'm sorry, Emma. I feel terrible. They were playing quite happily together when I left. I didn't dream anything like this would happen.'

'No, of course you didn't,' I said. 'And nor did Nanny when she put Lizzy in her cot. However, I don't think it was a good idea to leave them entirely alone, Nanny. Perhaps in future one of you could always be with them, at least while they are still at this initial stage of settling in.'

She pursed her lips in disapproval. 'It's that Lizzy, madam. We never had any trouble until she came.'

'Oh, she isn't really any trouble at all . . .' Pam seemed as if she wanted to add more, then changed her mind. 'They are both rather high-spirited children, both determined to have their own way – there's bound to be quarrels sometimes. Especially when Lizzy tries to get into the pedal car. James protects that very fiercely. He usually doesn't bother about the other things, and of course Lizzy has several toys of her own now. But she does try to take the car every now and then . . .'

'She does it deliberately, because she knows Master James won't have it,' Nanny said. 'It would be just the same if you got her her own car. She likes to make him cross. She is a born troublemaker.'

'I can't let you blame it all on Lizzy,' Pam said, her cheeks red. 'It isn't true, Nanny. James has a temper on him, and he has been used to having too much of his own way. You have rather spoiled him . . .'

'I think I know how to conduct my own nursery.'

Nanny looked so enraged that I had to intervene, although I half agreed with Pam. Nanny had let James have too much of his own way, and it wasn't good for him.

'No one is blaming you, Nanny,' I said. 'We all

know what children are – and I think it's half a dozen of one and six of the other. The fault is mine for not insisting that the stair carpet was changed a long time ago. We've had it repaired twice, but it was beginning to fray again. I'm sure you are right, Nanny. I expect Lizzy caught her foot in it and fell . . .'

There was something in her eyes at that moment, an expression that was partly satisfaction and partly guilt. I sensed she was frightened. What was she hiding from me?

'I'll go up and see James now,' I said. 'I shall talk to him, tell him what has been happening, and explain that he must try not to quarrel with Lizzy so much.'

I was thoughtful as I went upstairs. Had Lizzy fallen – or had someone given her a push? Nanny might have discovered her at the top of the stairs, startled her by shouting at her, or even made a grab for her – and in avoiding her, Lizzy had missed her step and fallen.

It was a possibility. Something had caused that expression in Nanny's eyes. She had been relieved that I had accepted the excuse of Lizzy catching her foot in the carpet – which meant that she might feel herself at fault in some way.

I was certain that whatever had happened had been an accident, and Nanny had given good service for several years. I did not want to accuse her of anything. Perhaps Lizzy would tell me what had happened when she came home, though she could not often be persuaded to talk to the grown-ups: the only one she would ever talk to was James, and then it was usually in whispers.

When I went into the nursery, I saw James sitting in a corner staring at the bricks in front of him. He turned as I entered and I saw his cheeks were wet with tears.

'James not a bad boy,' he said, rubbing his fist in his eyes. 'James not push Lizzy down stairs.'

'No, of course not,' I said, looking at Mrs Rowan. 'Who suggested that to him?'

'Not me, madam. Mrs Gould asked me to come up while she spoke to Pam and Nanny about the incident. I have no idea what happened – but I do know Master James is very upset over something. He has been sitting there crying for ages.'

I knelt down by my son's side. 'No one is blaming you, James,' I said. 'Did you see Lizzy fall? Were you fighting with her?'

'Lizzy go in car. James hit her,' he said, his eyes falling before mine. 'Nanny get cross and smack Lizzy. She take her away, then Lizzy scream . . . Nanny says James is a wicked boy . . . she says James make Lizzy fall but James not a bad boy, Mummy.'

'No, of course you're not, my darling.' I held him in my arms, stroking his hair as I soothed him. 'But did you see anything, darling? Can you tell Mummy what happened?'

'Nanny take Lizzy away,' he said, nuzzling his face against my neck. 'Lizzy scream. Nanny bad. Nanny hurt Lizzy. I don't like Nanny. Don't want Nanny. Mummy send Nanny away . . . bad, bad, Nanny.'

'Nanny didn't push Lizzy,' I said, kissing his head. 'She fell, darling. It was an accident.'

'Bad Nanny,' James repeated. 'Mummy send Nanny away. Pam stay. Nanny go away . . .'

'We'll see, my darling,' I said. 'Stop crying now. No one blames you. Lizzy isn't badly hurt. She has hurt her arm, but she will come home soon. You will have to be good to her, James. You must look after her and see she doesn't hurt her poor arm again. Will you do that for me?'

'Let Lizzy go in car,' James said, gazing up at me, his eyes misted with tears. 'Mummy send bad Nanny away and James be good.'

He was so insistent that Nanny should go that I started to wonder. I knew she had begun to find it tiring to look after James even before Pam came. It was just possible that she had taken her temper out on the children. I did not think that she had deliberately pushed Lizzy down the stairs, but it might be that it was her fault the child had fallen.

'I'll talk to Nanny,' I promised. 'I'll see what she says, but I'm sure it was just an accident, darling. Nanny wouldn't hurt Lizzy, not on purpose.'

Nanny looked stricken when I interviewed her in the study later that evening.

'I don't know how you could think it, Mrs Reece,' she said, looking upset and angry. 'After all these years. I've never harmed a child in my care, and I resent . . .'

'I'm not accusing you of anything,' I said. 'I just wondered if there was something you wanted to tell me?'

She seemed to hesitate for a moment. I thought she was going to tell me something, then she set her mouth stubbornly.

'I've told you all I know, Mrs Reece. If you don't believe me, then perhaps I should leave?'

'There's no need for that, Nanny,' I said. 'We shall consider the incident closed, but please make sure that nothing like this happens again. I understand that you have smacked the child several times. I would prefer it if you did not do so in future.'

'Who has been telling tales about me?' She looked indignant. 'I've merely disciplined the child, Mrs Reece. Lizzy is a very naughty little girl. I have to smack her sometimes or she would never obey me.'

'I would prefer if it you did not,' I said. 'Let's see how things go, Nanny. If you really feel that you can't manage the children . . .'

'I'll do my best,' she said, and her anger had turned to distress. 'I don't want to leave, Mrs Reece.'

'Nor do I wish it,' I replied. 'A little smack does no harm once in a while, but I do not want Lizzy to be punished unnecessarily. Not to the extent where she might try to run away and perhaps fall again.'

Nanny's eyes fell before mine, and I thought perhaps my guess had been right. 'No, Mrs Reece. I'll try to manage without smacking her.'

'Or James,' I said. 'At least, only a gentle tap if he

is very naughty – but I prefer that he should respect you without smacking, Nanny. He is old enough to understand if you talk to him properly.'

'Yes, madam.' Her eyes shied away from mine.

'Very well. Please go and rest now, Nanny. I am sure this must have been a very tiring day for you.'

She went without a word. I sat on in the study, wondering whether I had done right. James had obviously turned against her. I was not certain why. I would just have to wait and watch . . .

'I've always thought there might be something like that going on,' Mum said when I telephoned her later that evening. 'I should sack her if I were you, Emma. James has told me once or twice that Nanny smacks him hard. He screamed once when he knocked something over at mine, as if he thought I was going to hurt him. Of course I didn't. I've never believed in that kind of discipline.'

'Nor do I,' I said. 'I've given Nanny another chance, Mum – but I'm going to be keeping an eye on her.'

'Well, I'm coming up for a visit next week,' she said. 'I was thinking about it anyway, and now I've made up my mind. If that woman has been hitting them, I'll soon have it out of her.'

'You know you're always welcome, Mum, but I think Nanny has had her warning. I'm sure nothing like that will happen again.'

'You would be better off with a younger girl,' Mum said. 'But we won't argue about it, Emma. Have you

heard any more about Jon yet? Have they told you
when he's likely to be coming home?'

'No, not yet, but I don't suppose it will be long.
Once the Allies take over France . . .'

'Yes, well, that's another reason for getting someone
in to replace Nanny,' my mother said. 'You'll need
Pam to help with Jon when he's home, and Nanny will
never cope with two children alone. She's too old,
Emma.'

I was thoughtful as I replaced the receiver. If James
was really that frightened of being smacked by Nanny,
perhaps it would be best if I let her go.

Mum settled it when she came up the following week.
Lizzy, back from the hospital and inclined at first to
be quieter than usual, was screaming her head off.
When Mum rushed in, she discovered Nanny shaking
James hard, and turned on the woman in a fury.

'I soon told her what I thought of her, Emma,' Mum
said. 'Pam had already confided in me that she has been
concerned about Nanny's behaviour ever since she came
to the house, but didn't want to cause trouble for you
– and Lizzy says Nanny pushed her down the stairs.'

'Lizzy told you?' I stared at her. 'Lizzy hardly ever
says anything, Mum. Are you sure it wasn't James
who told you?'

'Lizzy pointed at her when she was hitting James
and said, "Push Lizzy down stairs." She said it quite
clearly, Emma. I know she doesn't often say much,
but she was positive. I asked her if she meant Nanny,

and she nodded her head. And James thinks that's what happened, though he will only say that he doesn't want Nanny near him. That's why she was hitting him apparently, because every time she tries to touch him he kicks out at her. He refuses to be touched by the woman, just keeps saying she is bad over and over again. Pam has to do everything for him, because he won't let Nanny.'

'What did Nanny say?'

'She denied it, of course. She maintains that she was in the nursery kitchen getting their lunch, but I'm sure she's lying. I think she may have done it accidentally, but I'm sure she was there when it happened.'

'Then I shall have to ask her to leave,' I said. 'And I suppose I'd better do it at once.'

Nanny was wearing her coat and hat when I went up to her room. She was sitting on the edge of her bed, and I could see she had been crying. Her bags were packed, and I sensed that she had known I was going to dismiss her.

'I'm sorry this has happened, Nanny,' I said. 'You've been such a help to me these past years.'

'It's been getting too much for me,' she said, not looking me in the eyes. 'I think I shall retire, Mrs Reece. My niece has been asking me to go and live with her. She has four children under nine and can do with some help. She'll be glad of me in the house . . .'

'Good. I'm glad you have somewhere to go, Nanny. And I'm giving you three months' wages to help until you get settled.'

'Thank you, madam.' She got to her feet, picking up her bags, one in each hand. 'I'll arrange for the rest of my things to be sent on, Mrs Reece.'

'Yes, of course. Just let me know where you are, and I'll see to it.'

'I'm sorry to be leaving,' she said, hesitated, then, 'Watch them, Mrs Reece. You've not seen the last of the trouble between those two, believe me.'

'I know they can both be naughty.'

She shook her head. 'They're a law unto themselves, that's all I can say. They fight each other, but there's no parting them. Lizzy would lie through her teeth for James, and he would do the same for her. You'll have to sort them out one day, mark my words.'

'I expect they will grow out of it,' I replied. 'They are just children, Nanny.'

She gave me a darkling look. 'Imps of Satan the pair of them,' she muttered. 'I was nowhere near Lizzy when she fell, Mrs Reece. I know Mrs Fitch thinks I was bullying her or that I made a grab at her and caused her to fall – but that's not the truth. I don't know for certain, but I think she and Master James were out there on the landing, fighting as usual.'

'I very much doubt that,' I replied, feeling angry that she was trying to blame my son. 'James told me you had accused him of it, and I must tell you that I think that despicable. Lizzy has already told us who made her fall, though I was inclined to believe that it was an accident – but now I am not so sure. Had you been doing your duty properly, Nanny, it would never have happened.'

'I knew it would be me who got the blame, that's why I didn't want to say anything at the start,' she said. 'But I've seen James hit her – and a lot harder than I ever did. You just watch that boy of yours, Mrs Reece. He has a nasty little temper on him when he likes.'

'Please leave,' I said. I was furious. 'If my son had been the cause of her accident, I hardly think Lizzy would have blamed you. She would have told us it was James.'

'That's what you think,' Nanny said, a note of bitterness in her voice. 'There's not a penny piece to choose between the two. You mark my words, Mrs Reece. You'll have cause to wish you'd not brought that girl to this house. James was manageable before she came.'

I walked away and left her, refusing to listen to her spite. James could be sulky and difficult, but I was now beginning to think that Nanny might be to blame for that. If she had been hitting him all this time . . . I was angry that I had not realized what was going on.

I loved James very much, and the thought that my beloved child had been subjected to the spite of a frustrated woman was very hurtful. I would make very certain that the next nurse I employed was a kind woman, who would be good to both Lizzy and James.

'I know of someone who might be able to help you,' Annie said when I saw her a few days later. 'She was a Sister in a hospital, but she hurt her back lifting heavy patients and had to retire. She has been looking for a job, and she said she would like to look after children. Her name is Sarah Miller, and she comes into the shop now and then to buy something for herself or her sister. She bought a dress yesterday, and she's coming back for another this afternoon. Shall I ask her to call on you?'

'Yes, please do,' I said. 'An ex nursing Sister is exactly what I need. She might be willing to help with Jon as well as the children. Ask her to come tomorrow morning at ten o'clock if she will, Annie.'

I felt better after I left the shop. Pam had told me not to worry about replacing Nanny as she could look after the children easily.

'They are as good as gold together now,' she told me. 'I think James may have been frightened of Nanny. He hasn't had one temper tantrum since she's been gone, and he lets Lizzy play with anything she likes.'

'Even his precious car?'

'Well, he isn't too happy about her using it, but he has let her have it a few times recently. If she gets her own way she soon tires of it and goes to play with something else.'

It seemed that I had been right to dismiss Nanny. Her remarks when leaving had been spiteful, and I was inclined to think she had spoken out of temper. I certainly didn't believe that James had pushed Lizzy down the stairs.

I was pleasantly surprised when Sarah Miller came to the house the next morning. She was an attractive woman with dark hair and eyes, and softly spoken. I took her up to the nursery to let her see the children, and within minutes she had them both crawling all over her, pulling her long hair and patting her face.

'Do you think you would enjoy working here?' I asked when we left the children with Pam. 'I've been told by their last Nanny that they are a handful, and Pam will be helping me to look after my husband when he comes home from hospital.'

'Has he been badly wounded, Mrs Reece?' Sarah looked at me sympathetically. I explained what kind of wounds Jon had sustained and she nodded. 'He will need some nursing then,' she said. 'I would be willing to help with that, of course, though I can't do much lifting I'm afraid.'

'I don't think he will need lifting,' I said. 'I believe it's more a case of simple care.' I smiled at her. 'So – do you think you would like to come to us, Sarah?'

'Oh, yes,' she said. 'I think I should like that very much, Mrs Reece.'

'When can you start?'

'I'll move in this evening if that's all right?'

'I think it would be just right,' I said. 'I'm so glad Annie told me about you, Sarah. I shall look forward to having you here.'

'She's not bad-looking,' Sol said to me after he had seen Sarah for the first time. 'An improvement on the last one anyway . . .'

'Oh, Sol!' I pulled a face at him. 'I don't care what

she looks like. All I want is for her to look after the children properly.'

'She will do that,' he said. 'Seems a nice woman. And she will be useful to have around when you bring Jon home.'

'Yes . . .' I looked at him thoughtfully. 'I wonder when that will be? They know where he is; why don't they send him back?'

'I suppose it's a case of making sure it's safe. If he could travel rough they would have had him back long ago, Emma.'

'Yes, I suppose so,' I said and sighed. 'I just wish I could hear something, Sol. It's the waiting I find so difficult.'

'It can't be long now,' he said, patting my hand. 'They've taken Normandy, Emma, and they are pushing on. It can't be all that long before they are in Paris, and then it will be all over for the Germans in France. You'll see. It won't be long now before the whole of France is free . . .'

Chapter 15

'What does the letter say?' Margaret looked at me anxiously across the breakfast table as I read the single sheet over and over again. 'Is it the news you've been waiting for, Emma?'

The summer had almost gone. Each month we had read of Allied successes in France, and finally in September the welcome news that the German troops were retreating all over Europe. All through those months I had waited for an official letter or some word from Jack. Nothing had come from Jack, not one letter in all these weeks, but at long last I had news of my husband.

'Jon is in an English hospital,' I said, glancing up. 'He has been there for a week while they assessed him. Not in central London as we'd hoped. He has been taken to a small military hospital in Hampshire. Apparently, they think he needs the peace of the countryside for a while. I can visit if I make an appointment first.'

'That makes it more difficult for you,' Margaret objected and frowned. 'Perhaps we could have him moved nearer so that you can visit more often?'

'I shall drive down this weekend. If the doctors will release him, I shall bring Jon back with me.'

'Do you think that's wise? Wouldn't it be better to

let Jon get used to the idea first? He has been away from you for a long time. He will need to adjust – and so will you. If he needs to be in the country . . .' She shrugged. 'Perhaps that's best for now, my dear?'

'I don't know.' Now that the waiting was finally over, I felt choked with emotion. 'I'm not sure about anything, Margaret. I just know I can't desert Jon.'

'Visit him this weekend,' Margaret suggested gently. 'Telephone the hospital and let them know you're coming. I'm sure they've asked you to do that so that Jon will expect you. You must realize that he has been through a terrible time, Emma. You can't understand how he feels until you've seen and spoken to him.'

'You're so wise, and so good to me,' I said, and kissed her cheek. 'Thank you for being my friend, Margaret. I don't know what I would have done without you recently.'

She smiled and touched my hand. 'I'm so fond of you, dearest Emma. Do you want anyone to come to the hospital with you, or would you prefer to go alone?'

'This is something I have to do for myself,' I said. 'I have to face this, Margaret. I want to bring Jon home, but I'm not sure if I'm strong enough to cope with all that entails.'

'That is something I have never doubted,' she said. 'I'm not certain this is the wisest thing for you or Jon – but I know that once you have set your mind to something you will do it.'

I smiled at her and put the letter back into its enve-lope, but my heart was heavy. I had faced up to life more than once, fought it and won, but I had never felt so afraid as I did now.

I telephoned the hospital that morning and made an appointment.

'You are aware that your husband has facial burns, Mrs Reece?' the Sister asked.

'Yes, I have been told.'

'Sometimes people find it too much for them. If you think you might not be able to bear the shock, it might be best if you waited for a while. We may be able to help your husband in time.'

I felt a little irritated by her manner. She was trying to stop me visiting Jon, but I was determined not to be put off.

'I'm coming down on Sunday. I need to see Jon, to talk to him. I think he needs to see me. He needs to know that I want him to come home as soon as possible.'

'Doctor Richards will speak to you about that on Sunday, Mrs Reece. It would be best if you did not say too much about that to Jon for the moment. Let him know you want him home, by all means, but don't make it all important.'

The Sister's tone was not encouraging. She had been quite severe in her warning. Obviously, she did not want her patient upset.

I felt like weeping but knew I must not give way to my emotions. Now or in the future.

Jane came to the house that evening. She looked oddly subdued as Mrs Rowan showed her into the sitting room.

'I've come to tell you we're leaving this weekend,' she said, 'and to apologize for the way I've behaved. Robert thinks you're wonderful to contemplate bringing your husband home. He told me what Jon's injuries are likely to be . . .' She drew a shaky breath. 'I think you're very brave, Emma. I couldn't do what you're doing, but I sort of understand.'

'I'm glad you came,' I said and smiled at her. 'It would have upset me if our friendship had ended for good.'

'I would be an idiot to do that,' she said, and I saw the sheen of tears in her eyes. 'I'm going to miss you, Emma – I *have* missed you since I was so awful to you. Rob made me come. He knew I was miserable. He said I should grovel if I have to, because friends like you don't come along that often.'

'You don't have to grovel,' I said. 'Sit down and have a drink. You can give me your address in America, Jane. We'll both write as often as we can – and perhaps one day we can visit each other.'

'Yes, I'd like that,' she said. She gave a strangled laugh and we hugged each other. 'Forgive me?'

'Of course. Don't desert me, Jane. I need you.'

'Poor darling, Emma,' she said. 'The odd thing is, I need you just as much.'

I was apprehensive as I parked my car and walked towards the front entrance at the hospital. It seemed a decent enough place, with pleasant gardens. I supposed if one had to be in hospital for a long time, this was probably as good a place as any.

Sister Jones had told me to ask for her before I attempted to see my husband. I did so, and was shown into her office at once. She had obviously been waiting for me.

'Come in, Mrs Reece,' she invited. 'Do please sit down.'

Her gaze went over me. I had dressed simply in a pale blue dress with a pleated skirt and elbow length sleeves. She nodded, a grudging approval in her eyes.

'You've dressed very sensibly, Mrs Reece. Sometimes it upsets the men if their wives look too smart. That dress is just right.'

I ignored her comments on my appearance. 'How is Jon today? Does he know I'm coming?'

'As well as can be expected – and yes, he does know. He has mixed emotions about that, Mrs Reece. Naturally he wants to see you, but he is also frightened because of the way he is now.'

'You said the doctors may be able to help. Does that mean Jon will have to stay here for a long time?'

'He will need to have several operations. Doctor Richards will explain what that entails after you have seen your husband – if you are still concerned.'

'What do you mean?'

'You are an intelligent woman, Mrs Reece. I don't have to tell you that many difficulties lie ahead. Jon is in almost constant pain. He has one hand that is never going to be of much use to him, and his chest is weak. He may never work again, or be able to do very much at all.'

'He doesn't need to,' I said. 'I have my own business. I earn sufficient money to take care of Jon. I already have a retired hospital Sister on my staff, and good friends. I can take care of my husband, Sister. All I want to know is when I can have him home.'

'The answer to that is not yet. It will be several months at least. If you are prepared to visit often, it will help Jon recover. He's going to need all his strength and *yours* if he is to survive.'

'Thank you for being frank with me, Sister.'

'You may feel I have been unnecessarily cruel,' she said. 'But my concern is for Jon at the moment. He is my patient. You have a choice, Mrs Reece. He doesn't.'

'I understand that.' I raised my eyes to hers. 'Do you think I could see him now?'

'Yes, of course.' She smiled as if I had passed some test, and stood up. 'Please follow me. Jon shares a room with two other patients, both of whom have similar injuries. We think it best the men shouldn't be alone – but they have both been taken elsewhere for treatment this afternoon. I shall let you go in by yourself, Mrs Reece. I don't often do that, but in your case I am willing to trust you.'

I realized she was paying me a compliment, but did not smile. I had answered her questions calmly enough, but my heart was beating wildly. Whatever happened in the next few minutes, I must not show disgust or horror. Jon would know if I felt revulsion, and it would destroy him. I had prepared myself for the mutilations

he had suffered through several months, and I believed
I could cope. I was praying for the strength to accept
whatever I must.

'Here we are then,' Sister Jones said, stopping
outside a door. 'Go in, Mrs Reece – and good luck.'

I paused, took a deep breath and went in.

Somehow Jon must have sensed I was near. He was
standing by the window, his back to me as he gazed
out at the garden, and I could see the tension in every
line of his body.

'Hello, Jon,' I said softly.

'It's peaceful here,' he said, without looking round.
'But the abbey in France was really beautiful. I wanted
to stay there for ever, but then I remembered . . .'

He turned to face me and for one terrible moment
I could scarcely breathe. The left side of Jon's face
was puckered and scarred, his eyelid bare of lashes,
and his left hand was twisted, the fingers turned
inwards like claws. I thought it was a wonder he had
survived such injuries, then I lifted my gaze to look
into his eyes and I saw he was Jon – the man I had
loved. Still loved as the dearest of friends.

'Can you bear it, Emma? They say they can make
me look a bit better if I'm prepared to go through the
operations.'

'Jon my dearest . . .' I moved towards him as the
love and pity swelled inside me, and I could hardly
see his face for my tears. But they were not tears of
despair or horror, and he knew it. 'All I want to know
is when I can take you home.'

I went to put my arms around him. He was painfully thin, and as I laid my head against his shoulder, I could hear his harsh breathing, and I knew he was still very ill.

'Oh, Emma,' Jon whispered as his arms closed about me. 'All the time my memory was lost I knew there was someone waiting for me. I didn't know her name or anything about her, but sometimes I could see her face. I knew she loved me, wanted me to come home. Just having that belief to cling on to helped me to keep going.'

I gazed up at him. Half of his face was just as it always had been. Perhaps with skill and care they could somehow make the scars less ugly, and if not – I could bear it.

It wouldn't be easy for him. I knew that at once. Not everyone would be able to accept Jon's face as it was now, or as it would be when the surgeons had done what they could for him, because I knew he would always be disfigured. They might make the scars less obvious, but they would always be there.

'You're going to come home, dearest,' I said, my throat tight with emotion. 'It won't be for a while – perhaps months or years even – but it will happen. I promise you.'

'I love you, Emma,' he said in a muffled voice against my hair, and I felt him tremble. 'I love you so much . . .'

*

'You look exhausted,' Margaret said, her gaze going over me anxiously when we met the next morning. 'Was it very bad, Emma?'

'The drive was tiring,' I replied. 'I think I ought to stay overnight next time – but the rest of it wasn't bad at all. No, really, I mean it. I had been afraid that Jon might have changed, might have become a stranger, but he's just the same.'

'Just the same, Emma?'

'The scars are bad,' I admitted. 'His hair has gone grey at the temples; he looks so much older, and he is very ill, Margaret – but he's still the man I married. I'm not sure how to explain. It seemed to me as we talked that the man who had lived through all those terrible things was someone else. Jon was detached from all that, as if he had somehow used his loss of memory to protect his inner self. Now he has allowed that self to come back.' I wrinkled my forehead. 'Does that make any kind of sense to you?'

She was thoughtful for a few moments, then she nodded. 'Yes, I can see what you mean. You believe Jon was too sensitive to face what happened to him after he escaped the crash, so his mind somehow blocked out everything he held dear rather than defile the memories of happier times.'

'Yes, something like that. Now he has recovered his memory, and is trying to come to terms with his injuries. I think he will block out what happened in France as much as he can.'

'You mean he doesn't want to face reality?'

'I'm not really sure what I mean,' I admitted. 'He spoke several times of the abbey and the kindness of the nuns. They allowed him to potter in their garden once he was well enough to leave his bed. He was happy there. If he had not remembered who he was, I think he would have been content to spend his life there.'

'And now?' Margaret asked. 'What does Jon want now?'

'I don't know. We spoke of his coming home, but that can't be for months, perhaps more than a year. His doctor told me that he will need a series of operations. He said that I must be prepared to wait for a long time. Jon has other problems besides the scars. His lungs were damaged, as were other parts of his body. He needs a lot of specialized treatment.'

'It's going to be hard for you, Emma.'

'But much harder for Jon. He has already been through so much, and the operations will be difficult and painful. He could not be expected to go through all that alone.'

'No, of course not.' Margaret looked upset. 'It's so sad, my dear – for you both.'

I knew what she was thinking. I was still only twenty-five years old. Young enough to want so much of life, and I would be tied to a husband who would always be an invalid – a man who would probably never be able to be a proper husband to me again.

Doctor Richards had told me of Jon's other wounds, things I would never speak of to anyone else. Not

Margaret or even my mother. I was not even sure that Jon realized the extent of his own injuries as yet.

'It will be a miracle if he lives more than a few years,' his doctor had told me. 'He has got this far on sheer stubbornness, Mrs Reece. He may believe his impotence is due to his present weakness, but there is internal damage. Whoever patched him up after he was wounded took the metal shards out of his flesh but he was badly torn in his groin and the surgery was just not good enough.'

'You mean he may never be able to make love to me?'

'Your husband will never give you a child – as for the rest . . .' He frowned, looking slightly awkward. 'There are ways of achieving physical pleasure without a sustained erection.'

'Yes, of course.' I met his eyes unflinchingly. 'Does Jon know?'

'We have not thought it necessary to tell him. The body sometimes mends itself. Besides, he has enough to cope with for the moment, don't you agree?'

'More than enough.'

I believed that Jon would feel his inability to make love deeply. It was his memory of our precious time together that was giving him the courage to go through with the painful operations he was facing in the coming months.

I knew he was doing it for my sake. Would he put himself through all that pain if he knew the truth?

The terrible thing was, that it made no difference either way. I loved Jon, but I was not in love with him.

Even if he had never suffered those burns, I could never have felt the pleasure I had known with Jack in my husband's arms.

I felt guilty and ashamed of what I had let happen, and yet I could not regret one moment I had spent with Jack.

A note was delivered by special messenger the next morning. It was from Jane and written on the day of her departure for America.

> *Dearest Emma. I have heard from Jack. He's quite well and expects to be in London by next month at the latest. I thought you should know. I haven't time for more now. Love, Jane.*

I stared at the letter for ages. Why had Jane thought it necessary to warn me? Unless she had sensed that Jack was very angry, which I already knew. The absence of a single letter to me spoke clearly of his anger at my refusal to leave my husband. He had warned me once that he did not give up what belonged to him – and he did think of me as his own.

I believed that our meeting would be stormy. Jack had held back from me all this time. He was angry. He would be even more so when he discovered he could not change my mind.

In the past, Jack had always been so good to me, but I knew that he had a temper when roused. I was not looking forward to facing his anger, but nothing he could do or say would persuade me to leave my husband and go away with him.

'General Harvey is here,' Mrs Rowan said, looking uncomfortable. It was a week later and early evening. 'He asked to see you, Mrs Reece. Shall I show him in?'

I glanced at Margaret as she started to gather her things. 'No, don't go. There's no reason why you should leave.'

'I think I must,' she said. 'Jack will want to speak to you in private, Emma. You owe him that much, my dear.'

'Yes, of course.'

I had panicked for a moment, but I knew she was right. As she left the room I rose to my feet, my heart racing wildly.

Jack was in the hall. I heard him speak to Margaret, and the sound of his voice made goose bumps all over my body. My throat felt as if it were closing. The moment I had dreaded for so long was here. I was terrified, close to tears.

'Emma . . .' Jack smiled at me and my heart caught. 'You look lovely as always. I'm sorry to barge in like this. I should have let you know I was back, but I was angry with you – and afraid you would refuse to see me if you knew I was coming tonight.'

'I knew you were angry. You didn't write . . .'

I was trembling, and I felt the colour draining from my face as the coldness settled inside me.

'There wasn't much to say.' His gaze narrowed. For

a moment I saw the anger, then it was banished, controlled. This man was not the Jack Harvey who had pursued me for months, laughing at my refusals, determined to win me. 'You haven't changed your mind I suppose? You are still determined to bring Jon home?'

'When he is able to leave hospital,' I said. 'That won't be for months, of course. He needs several operations.'

'Yes, I know. I've seen him, and I've spoken to his doctors.'

'You've seen Jon? Why?' I stared at him, my heart jerking. 'Why did you go there, Jack?'

'Don't worry.' Jack's eyes glittered. 'He doesn't know about us. I don't use those tactics, Emma, not against a man who can't fight back. I want you to leave him, you know that – but I won't force you. Either you come of your own free will or you don't.'

I had been expecting anger, persuasion – but I was unprepared for this calm reasoning. He was forcing me to choose – him or Jon, giving me no chance for excuses. I had to be brave enough to make that choice, and from somewhere inside me I found the strength.

'I can't abandon him, Jack. I am his only hope of having some sort of a life outside hospital.'

'Yes, I suppose you are – but what about us, Emma? You're not in love with Jon. You never were – were you?'

'No, I never was. I married him because he loved me so much, and I cared for him in a way – as a dear friend. I didn't realize it then, though I should have done.'

'Do you think Jon knows that?' I shook my head and Jack took a step towards me. 'How will he feel when you turn from his loving? I don't mean the scars, Emma. You could accept those. You are strong enough – but can you forget this? Can you live without it?'

Before I knew what he meant to do, Jack swept me into his arms. His embrace crushed the breath from my body, and his kiss sent my senses swirling. Against my will, I responded, melting into him, surrendering myself to the heat of desire and the pleasure of his lips on mine.

While he kissed me, I could think of nothing else but my need of him. I wanted him, wanted him to make love to me, hungered for the touch of his hands. I wanted to feel him lying by my side, the burn of his hard, firm flesh against mine, the excitement and satisfaction only he could give me.

Then at last he let me go. As I gazed up into his eyes, I saw a kind of pleading there and I knew his need was as great as mine.

'I do love you, Jack,' I whispered. 'I want you so much . . .'

'Come away with me, Emma. Jon will never live in the real world again. It would be cruel to expect it. Why can't you accept that? Why can't you see that it's wrong for him and wrong for you? You are forcing him to go through so much pain, unnecessary pain. Let him go, let him find a dark hole to crawl in and lose himself. It would be so much kinder. You are throwing away all that we had, all that we could have together in the future – and for all the wrong reasons.'

'Jack I can't . . .' I cried. I was hurting so badly. He was tearing me apart. 'I just can't.'

'That's your final decision?' His eyes burned into me. 'I'm asking, Emma, but I won't beg.'

I nodded miserably and he turned away. He was leaving and I couldn't bear it! I loved him, wanted him – needed him. I reached out and caught his coat sleeve.

'Jack, couldn't we . . . be together? Just once more? While you're in London . . .' I knew it was wrong even as I spoke the words, but I was desperate. 'You might come back to London sometimes. We could see each other . . .'

'You would be willing to grant me a few favours? Is that what you're offering, Emma? You want to be my mistress . . .'

'No – it isn't like that. I just thought . . .' Of course I hadn't thought at all. I'd spoken impulsively, out of need and a desperate longing.

'What is it like then?' Jack's face had gone hard. 'You want both of us, is that it? You can't give up your precious duty, but you don't want Jon, not in your heart. You want me.' His eyes flashed with fury. 'I was willing to admire you for what you were doing, Emma. I was hurt that you were prepared to give up what we had, and I meant to take you from him if I could – but now . . .' He paused and the

look in his eyes made me feel faint. 'I'm not sure I
know you. You are a selfish little bitch, Emma. You
want to play Florence Nightingale in public, make
everyone think how wonderfully selfless you are –
but behind the scenes you're willing to carry on an
affair with me. You want to keep me on your string
. . . prolong the agony. But you won't give up your
foolish ideals for me. You don't care that you've
broken my heart . . .'

'Oh, Jack, please don't,' I begged. I held back the
tears. His cruel words were tearing me to shreds but
I deserved them. How I deserved them! What I had
suggested was despicable and it shamed me. 'I didn't
mean to hurt you . . .'

'Do you really care? Do you care for anyone but
yourself? You like to play the good friend, but deep
down you do it for your own satisfaction. I don't think
you know what love really is . . .'

I lashed out at him, striking him across the face. He
made no attempt to stop me or to hit me back, but the
expression in his eyes hurt more than any blow.

'You have no right to say such things to me, Jack,'
I cried shrilly. 'I have loved you – you know that . . .'

'Mummy . . .' We both heard the child's voice and
turned as one to see James standing in the doorway
in his night-clothes. 'Daddy . . . why are you shouting
at Daddy?'

I felt a coldness deep inside me as I saw the accusation in my son's eyes. How had he come to hear us?
Our voices could not have carried to the nursery, and

he seldom came down at night – should not have been allowed out of the nursery alone.

'Hi there, son.' Jack took a couple of steps towards the door and James rushed at him. He was swept up into Jack's arms, tossed into the air. His gleeful cries made my heart ache. 'What are you doing up, young man? You should have been asleep ages ago.'

'Saw you from the window,' James said, giggling with excitement. 'I wanted to see you, Daddy. Are you back now?'

Jack's eyes met mine across the room. I knew what he was telling me. It was not just our lives I had blighted by my stubborn refusal to give Jon up. When Jack went away for good, it would hurt my son. He loved Jack and he was going to be badly hurt when he began to realize he wouldn't be seeing Jack again.

'Jack has to go home,' I said. 'He will be away for a long time.'

'No!' James burst into noisy tears and clung to Jack, winding his arms about his neck. 'Stay with James. Daddy not go away again. Bad Mummy! Mummy not send Daddy away . . .'

'Hang on,' Jack said, holding the boy away from him so that he could look at his face. He frowned as he saw how desperate James was. Until this moment he had had no true idea of how much the boy adored him. 'No more tears, son. Daddy will come back and see you one day. I promise. But you mustn't cry. I don't want you to cry like this. Big boys don't cry. Understand?'

James stared at him. He was torn between making a scene and obeying the man he adored. 'Promise? You promise you will come back?'

James was growing up fast. Sometimes he reverted to his baby talk, but more often now he was beginning to put whole sentences together.

'That's a promise between you and me, James,' Jack said. 'When I come, it will be just to see you. Don't blame your mummy for my going away. I have to go and defeat that nasty Mr Hitler. There's more work for Daddy. Do you understand me?'

James nodded. I wasn't sure whether he understood about the war or not, though he must have heard it mentioned many times, but he understood the note of authority in Jack's voice.

'You will come back? To see me?'

'One day,' Jack promised. 'Until then, you've got to be a real man and look after Mummy for me.'

'Jack . . .'

'Mrs Reece. I'm so sorry,' Sarah apologized as she came in at that moment. 'I went to check on him and realized he must have slipped down here. He is getting so adventurous. There's no keeping him in the nursery these days.'

'James ought to go to school,' Jack said as his nurse scooped him up and carried him off to the sound of loud protests. 'I know he's young, but he's too active to be kept as a baby any longer – and he shouldn't be just with adults. He needs the company of other children.'

I bristled angrily. I had been grateful for what he'd said to James about his going away not being my fault – but James was my son. I would do as I thought best for him.

'He isn't alone,' I said. 'I have a little girl visiting while her mother is away. They are company for each other.'

Jack's eyes narrowed. 'If I'd been here, I would have sent him to a nursery school before this,' he said. 'That child needs to be stimulated; he needs a challenge and a firm hand. Otherwise he will make trouble for himself. But that's your own business, Emma. I shan't interfere, even though the boy means a lot to me.'

'I do love you, Jack,' I said, as his eyes seemed to burn into me. 'Whatever you think . . . I always shall.'

'You don't love me enough,' he replied and I heard the bitterness in his voice. 'If you did, you would have moved heaven and earth to be with me. I was willing to do it for you.'

I had no answer for him. He stared at me for a few minutes longer, then he turned and walked from the room without another word. I let him go. There was nothing left to say . . .

Chapter 16

I wept that night, deep, bitter tears that drained me of all feeling and emotion. I knew that Jack would not come to me again. He had asked, but he would not beg. I had sent him away, hurt him, disgusted him with my suggestions of a clandestine love affair. It was over. My dreams of being his wife, all gone.

His bitter words of rejection had struck me to the heart, but perhaps I had deserved them. I had spoken out of my need, but it was wrong. If I could not give Jack the whole-hearted love he wanted, I should not have offered anything else. He had rejected me, because deep down he was an honourable man.

He might sail near to the wind in matters of business, but in every other way he was a decent man. I could not have loved him so much if he had not been. I should never have offered to be his mistress – because that was exactly what I *had* offered.

Such bitter words had been spoken! And like the speeding bullet that strikes its victim to the heart, those words, once unleashed, could not be recalled.

I knew I would never forget the look in Jack's eyes as he spurned my offer. I would carry his scorn to my grave.

There were moments during that night when I almost

wished I could die. I was so close to despair that I could not see how it was possible to carry on.

I had been given such a precious gift in Jack's love, a gift I had thrown away. Perhaps I had not truly realized how I had been favoured by the gods until now, when it was too late.

It was so very hard to bear my loneliness, but I knew that I would. I had made my choice and I would stand by it come what may.

'Jon doesn't want to see anyone else just yet.' I was aware of Mrs Reece's indignation even as I spoke. 'He asked me to visit and explain. He is sorry, but it would be too much for him at the moment.'

'You are just saying that to stop me seeing him,' she cried, her voice sharp with accusation. 'How dare you suggest that it would be too much for him? I'm his mother. I have as much right to see Jon as you!'

'Emma knows best, Dorothy,' Pops said, looking at me anxiously. 'How is he really, my dear? Please tell us the truth.'

'The scarring isn't so very bad,' I said. 'Not once you get over the initial shock.' I had been to visit Jon three weekends in a row and hardly noticed anymore. 'But his chest is weak, and sometimes he finds it difficult to breathe. We walk round the garden together, but we have to stop often for him to rest.'

Mrs Reece was crying bitterly. I could understand how she felt and was sorry for her distress.

'I'm sorry,' I said. 'I did ask Jon if I could take you

down next weekend, but he said no. He doesn't want you to see his face until the doctors have improved his appearance. Sister won't let you see him if you go. She is a dragon where her patients are concerned. I'm not allowed to visit this weekend, because he's having the first of his operations. There's some tightness at the corner of his eye, which they are going to relieve. I shall not be able to visit until the following Saturday.'

'It's so unfair,' she wept, dabbing at her eyes with her handkerchief. 'I don't understand. Why did it have to happen to Jon? He never harmed anyone in his life.'

I looked at Pops but didn't say anything. Jon had done many things during his time with the French resistance. He was fighting his memories, but I knew he sometimes had nightmares.

That weekend I decided to take James to visit my mother. I could not manage to find enough petrol to drive down, so I took my son on the train. The novelty excited him, and he hardly kept still the whole journey. He had been sulky with me ever since he'd witnessed my quarrel with Jack, refusing to hug or kiss me, and looking at me with reproachful eyes whenever I tried to talk to him. However, the train journey brought him out of his moods, and after a few hours with my mother he seemed more like himself.

After James was in bed that evening, we sat talking by the fire. Mum with her sewing and me with some knitting.

'So what are your plans for the future, Emma?'

'I'm making a cardigan for Lizzy. It's just pearl and plain. I can't do fancy stitches the way you do.'

'You know that's not what I meant.' She frowned at me. 'I'm talking about you, Emma. Your life. Are you going to open another shop here in March? Gwen was asking, and so was Mary. There's an empty shop to rent almost next door to Madge Henty. You could sell children's clothes there, and Gwen could keep an eye on the place for you. I don't mind serving a couple of mornings a week myself.'

'Perhaps.' I sighed. 'I'm not sure, Mum. Somehow I can't think straight at the moment. There doesn't seem much point to anything.'

'You're pining for Jack.' Mum gave me a straight look, reminding me of my beloved Gran. As she got older, the likeness had begun to show more. 'I never thought I would ever have to say this to you, Emma – pull yourself together, my girl! Stop feeling sorry for yourself. So you've lost the man you wanted. That's sad, but so have thousands of others. You've got a lot to be thankful for. If you'll take my advice, you will go and have a look at that shop tomorrow. Keep busy. It has worked for you before, and will again.'

I knew she was right. For the past few weeks I'd been living in a haze of pain, going through the motions, coming to life only when I visited Jon. The only way I could cope with the agony of losing Jack had been to block everything out, but it was over.

I had to think about the future, to plan for the time when I could bring Jon home.

I took my mother's advice and went to see the shop in the High Street. It was a decent size and had been a book shop. I knew at once that it was ideal for what we planned, and my spirits lifted as I began to think about the refurbishment. We could keep some of the shelving, but we would need cabinets and a glass counter.

It was on offer for sale or rent. At first I thought I would have to rent it, but Sol asked me how much I would need to buy the property.

'Six hundred pounds,' I told him. 'I do have the money, Sol – but it would take most of my capital. I shan't have enough for the stock.'

'Yes, you will,' he said. 'You're quite a rich young woman, Emma.'

'What do you mean? I stared at him in surprise.

'You've several thousand pounds coming to you. Most of your money was invested abroad at the start of the war. I'm not sure exactly how much you will get when those investments are realized, but there will be a healthy profit. You might get as much as three times what you put in. In the meantime, I'm willing to advance you a thousand or two.'

'A thousand pounds is more than enough,' I said. 'If you can really spare it, Sol. I'll ask my lawyers to buy the property and start looking for suitable stock.'

'That's the way, Emma,' Sol said and smiled at me.

'You've been a bit down recently – but you'll feel better once you've got a new project on the go.'

'Yes, perhaps I shall.'

I did not believe that I would ever rid myself of the dull ache in my heart, but in time it might be easier to accept. For the moment all I could do was work – and visit Jon.

Margaret had a heavy cold. She had been coughing for almost a week, and did not look at all well. It was November and the weather was unpleasant, damp, murky nights and days when the fog hardly cleared.

'I should feel better if we could have some frost,' she said to me that morning, and then coughed several times. For a moment she seemed to fight for breath and I was alarmed. 'This dank weather doesn't suit me at all.'

'Do you think you should have the doctor?'

I felt anxious about her. She looked slightly feverish. I had planned to spend the weekend with Jon, but now I was in two minds whether to go or not.

'Should I stay with you this weekend? I can visit Jon next week, when you're feeling better.'

'You mustn't disappoint him. He looks forward to your visits so much,' she said and smiled at me. 'There are plenty of people in this house, Emma. I shan't be alone.'

'No, of course not.'

Margaret hated anyone to make a fuss over her health. I knew she would be well cared for, and it was just a cold – yet I was uneasy as I set out that weekend. Margaret had been considered delicate for years, but this time I couldn't help feeling that she might be really unwell.

'Mrs Reece . . .' Sister called to me as I passed her office that Saturday afternoon. 'May I speak to you for a moment please?'

'Yes, of course.' I followed her into her office. 'Is something wrong? Jon isn't worse?'

'No, as a matter of fact he seems better than he has for a while. His last operation was successful, as you know. I wanted to ask . . . His mother telephoned me this morning. She asked if she could visit soon. Do you think she could cope with her son's appearance?'

'She is not an easy person to understand or deal with,' I said. 'But I may be prejudiced. She does not care for me much – but I believe she sincerely loves Jon. You must ask him if he would like to see her. I would think it might be best if she waits a little longer, but perhaps I am wrong.'

'No, Mrs Reece. I think I agree with you. I have asked her to wait for a little longer. She was quite upset about it, so I thought I would speak to you. I don't want to be unfair to her, but Jon must come first.'

'Yes, of course. I'll visit her again – tell her that his scars are still rather startling until you get used to them.'

We talked for a few minutes, then I walked along

the hall to Jon's room. He smiled as he saw me. His operation had eased some of the tightness around his eye, but there was still a long way to go.

'Would you like to go for a drive in the car?' I asked after I had kissed him. 'Sister says I can take you to the village today. There's a nice little teashop. We could have tea there – if you felt up to it?'

'My first step back to the outside world?' Jon arched his brows, a mocking smile on his lips. 'I know about the teashop, Emma. The staff and customers are used to us now – they don't stare or faint at the sight of us. Yes, why not? I'm beginning to feel less of a freak.'

'Jon darling!' I shook my head at him. 'Don't say that – don't think it. You should bear your scars with pride.'

'Should I, Emma?' His eyes held an oddly bleak expression. 'I was trying to blow up a convoy of German soldiers – just men like me, flesh and blood and bone. Instead, I blew myself up. Where is the pride in that?'

'It was war, Jon. People do what they have to do to survive. Besides, it is over now. You can forget about it, my darling – think about the good things. Think about coming home . . .'

'Coming home?' He looked at me thoughtfully. 'Where is home, Emma? To you it's where you live now, but I'm not sure I could live there . . . not anymore.'

I felt a stirring of unease but smothered it. 'You don't have to, Jon. We could buy a house in the country if you would rather. I can go up to town whenever I want to. We could choose somewhere near my mother if you like or perhaps somewhere prettier.'

'I was thinking more of France,' Jon said, then shook his head. 'No, I mustn't be selfish Emma. I know how much you love London, and your friends. We'll decide together when the time comes.'

'Yes, of course,' I said. 'Now let's go for our ride.'

Jon was in a cheerful mood as we drove back to the hospital. Our visit to the teashop had gone well, perhaps because the villagers were accustomed to seeing men with terrible scars, but it had been a pleasant outing, and I was pleased that Jon seemed to be beginning to think about a future outside the sterile world he lived in now.

He still had many months of treatment ahead, of course, but the day would come when he would leave here. I was growing more certain of that as the weeks passed.

What would I do if he repeated his wish to live in France? I knew it was the peace of the Abbey he was remembering – a time when he had not needed to face a painful reality – but I supposed there must be a peaceful village where we could find a home.

It would be a wrench for me, but I would go with Jon if it was what he truly needed. After all, I could sell dresses in France as easily as England. Jon spoke the language fluently. He could teach it to me.

I had been willing to go to America with Jack. I would go to France if Jon asked it of me.

I parked the car and stopped to lock it, letting Jon go ahead of me into the hospital. When I heard a woman's shrieks coming from the main entrance hall, I did not take much notice immediately. But when I followed Jon inside, I stopped in dismay, my heart sinking. Jon's mother was pulling at his arm and weeping noisily. She appeared to be having hysterics, and was clearly distressed.

As I went up to them, Sister came out of her office and dragged her away. Jon strode off at once. He did not turn his head as I called to him, asking him to wait. I started to go after him, but as I reached Mrs Reece, she grabbed at my arm, her voice rising shrilly.

'You lied to me,' she said, her voice wild with accusation. 'You told me the scars were not so terrible . . . you let me come here thinking my poor boy looked almost normal . . . my poor, poor boy . . . how could you do that to me?'

'Pull yourself together,' Sister said sharply and gave her a none-too-gentle shake. 'Be quiet, you foolish woman. Do you want the whole hospital to hear you? I will not have my patients upset by your foolishness, do you hear me?'

Mrs Reece looked at her, so shocked that someone had dared to speak to her in such a way that she was silenced.

I pulled away from her grasp, not bothering to answer her accusations, and ran after Jon. He was standing by the window in his room, his back to me.

I could see the tension in him. He did not turn round, though he knew I was there.

'Am I such a monster, Emma?'

'Of course you're not, Jon.' I went to him and put my arms about him, laying my head against his back. 'Your mother was just shocked, Jon, because she loves you.'

'This is so unfair on you . . .' Jon pulled away, then turned to face me. 'It would have been better for you if I had died in that crash . . . better if I had never remembered who I was.'

'No! Don't you dare say that to me,' I said. 'I know you are going through terrible pain, and that it must be awful for you to be so scarred – but it makes no difference to the way I feel about you, Jon. I still love you. As much as I always did.'

'Do you, Emma?' He stared at me for a moment, then nodded. 'Yes, of course you must. You have given up so much for me . . .'

'What do you mean?' My heart wrenched with fear. What had Mrs Reece said to him before I got there?

'You give up your time for my sake,' Jon said, 'and the chance of a normal life. I can't take you dancing or do any of the things I know you love. I may not always show it, but I do appreciate all you're doing, Emma.'

'Oh, Jon,' I said, my heart aching as I saw the way his shoulders sagged and felt the hurt and humiliation his mother had inflicted. 'Please don't let her hurt you.

It was my fault. I've become used to the scars. I hardly see them. I should have warned your mother . . .'

He smiled oddly. 'You really don't see them, do you?'

'No . . . they don't bother me. It's just you, Jon. My kind, generous husband and my friend.'

'I never was particularly good-looking,' he said, and I saw the tension begin to ease out of him.

'You had other qualities.' I smiled and reached up to touch the unmarked side of his face. 'We were happy together, Jon. We shall be happy again.'

'Yes, perhaps.' He frowned, then a shudder ran through him. 'As long as I never have to go and live with my mother. I would rather stay here for the rest of my life.'

'I can promise you that,' I said, giving him a roguish look. 'I'll live anywhere you want, Jon – Siberia or the moon if you like – but not with Dorothy.'

'Thank God for that!' The tension was finally gone as he laughed at my teasing. 'Poor Mother. It's not her fault. She never did have much tact, did she?'

'She isn't important, Jon – and nor is anyone else who reacts in the same way. If they haven't got the wit to see beneath those scars to the man you really are, then they are not worth bothering with.'

'As long as I have you,' Jon said. 'I can bear it. Without you, I think I should just curl up and die.'

'You foolish man!' I said, giving him a speaking look. 'I could shake you. You do have me – and if I ever die on you, there's Pops and other people who

care for you. Plenty of people who couldn't care less
if you do have a few scars, as long as you go on being
the lovely, decent man you are.'

Jon smiled. 'Never stop scolding me, Emma. It's
good for me.'

'The sooner you are out of here the better,' I said.
'It's frustrating and depressing for you. But we have
to be patient, Jon. The operations will help . . .'

'Yes,' he agreed. 'They might make it possible for
my mother to look at me without screaming.'

'It was just the shock, Jon,' I said. 'When she calms
down she will be so sorry to have upset you.'

He looked disbelieving, but I knew it was true.
Dorothy could not help being the way she was, and I
knew she would regret her behaviour today – at least
as far as Jon was concerned.

She hated me, of course. I knew it, but there was
nothing I could do to change things. She would never
forgive me for refusing to live with her – or for what
she thought of as betraying my marriage vows.

I just hoped she would not decide to tell Jon about
it one day, because if she did, she would destroy him.

As soon as I walked into the house on Sunday afternoon, I was aware that something was wrong. It had
an odd, hushed atmosphere that disturbed me.

Mrs Rowan came out into the hall, and her eyes
were red from weeping. 'Oh, Mrs Reece,' she said.
'I'm so glad you're back. It happened so suddenly. We
none of us knew what to do . . .'

'What do you mean?' I asked, the icy feeling at my nape making me shiver. 'What has happened?'

'It's the mistress,' she said and caught her breath on a sob. 'The morning you left, she came over queer. We sent for the doctor. He was here within a few minutes. He sent her straight to bed. She was very ill, Mrs Reece.'

'Why did no one telephone for me?' My heart caught with fear. 'I would have come back at once.'

'She wouldn't have it, Mrs Reece. She said we were not to tell you until you came back . . .'

'I'll go up to her now . . .' I started forward, but something in her eyes held me.

'You don't understand,' Mrs Rowan said. 'It's too late. She died not twenty minutes ago. The master was with her. He's sitting with her now. He asked me to tell you.'

'Margaret died . . . twenty minutes . . .'

I was stunned. It was impossible to believe. The pain of loss was so sharp that I gasped. I loved her so much. She had been such a good friend to me, and now she was gone – and I had not been with her at the end.

Why wasn't I here?

It was a question I would ask myself over and over again.

I left Mrs Rowan in the hall and walked slowly upstairs. Outside Margaret's room, I paused, then knocked and went in. Sol was sitting by the bed, his head in his hands. He looked up as I entered, the expression in his eyes one of utter devastation.

'She's gone,' he said, sounding bewildered and lost. 'She's gone, Emma.'

'Oh, my dear,' I said and went to his side. 'I'm so sorry. So very sorry. I know how much you loved her.'

'I didn't show it enough,' he said. 'Not recently. I've been too frustrated, wrapped up in other things . . .'

'But she knew. She always knew.'

'Did she, Emma?' His eyes implored me for comfort. 'Did she know how precious she was to me?'

'Of course – and she loved you, Sol. She always loved you.'

'And you. She spoke of you just before . . .' He choked on his grief. 'She wanted you to have her things . . .'

I shook my head as the tears I had been holding back spilled over. 'Please, don't . . . not now. I can't bear it.'

I gazed down at the face of the woman I had loved almost as a mother. She was peaceful and looked young, much younger than when I had last seen her. I bent to kiss her forehead.

'You will miss her,' Sol said. 'We shall both miss her.'

'Yes.' I stood beside him, my hand on his shoulder. 'We shall both miss her very much.'

His large hand closed over mine, holding on as the tremors shook him.

'I'm glad you're here, Emma. I don't think I could have gone on alone.'

'I'll always be your friend, Sol.'

He glanced up at me. 'We wanted children, Margaret and me. She couldn't have them. I tried to make up for it, but I never could. You gave her so much happiness. You brought your son to this house, and you gave her a reason to live. She was so much brighter these past few years. She might have died years ago, but she struggled on because she had you and the boy.'

'It wasn't just me, Sol. She had you, too.'

'I let her down,' he said. 'She would have been so ashamed if I'd gone to prison. As I might have done if it hadn't been for you.'

'I did very little . . .'

'You did what was needed. No one can do more.'

'You and Margaret . . . you both mean a lot to me.'

'We'll go on together,' Sol said. 'I'll never let you down, Emma. I give you my word. I'll be straight with you. You won't have to worry about any little tricks. That's all over. I promise.'

'Sol . . .' I paused, knowing I couldn't tell him that I might have to go and live in France. Not now, not at this moment. Besides, it was not certain yet. I would face that when I came to it. 'I'll leave you with her for a while. We'll talk later.'

Alone in my room, I found I could not cry. Tears would not have helped at that moment.

I sat down on the edge of the bed and opened the

top drawer of the little cabinet beside me, taking out the bundle of letters I had tied with blue ribbon. Jack's letters. For a moment I cradled them in my hands as if they were made of delicate porcelain; then I replaced them in the drawer and closed it.

From somewhere came the memory of my beloved Gran. It was almost as if she were very close to me. I could hear her voice in my ear, scolding me as she was wont to do, very gently.

'There's no use in weeping over things as can't be changed, lass.'

I raised my head, almost expecting to see her face.

'Why must I always lose those I love most?' I cried aloud. 'What have I done that was so wicked? Why must I be punished?'

'You'll have a long, hard road to travel, Emma. But you'll make what you will of your life.'

'It hurts, Gran,' I said. 'It hurts so much.'

'Keep your chin up, lass. You've a way to travel yet.'

Of course I was only remembering the things she had so often said to me in the past. Gran hadn't really come to me, and yet somehow I was comforted. I knew that what she had told me all those years before was still as true now as it had been then.

Life was never easy for anyone. It certainly hadn't been for her, but she had never given in. I'd never heard her complain about her troubles, and she'd certainly had her share. She hadn't buckled under, she had simply got on with life, taking the knocks and making her own happiness.

I raised my head as a new determination hardened in me. I wasn't going to waste the rest of my life in regret for what I had lost.

I had no idea where the future would lead me, or what it might hold, but I knew that I was strong enough to face it.

I would open the dress shops I had dreamed of owning – whether here or in France. It hardly mattered. Nothing would stop me.

I had lost Jack, and now Margaret had gone, too, but I had other friends. I had my mother, James and Lizzy. And Jon loved me. Fate had dealt me terrible blows, but I had also been given much that was good.

For most of my life so far I had done as I was told, or given way to the wishes of others. Not in recent years because I was forced, but because I had a strong sense of duty. In the future I would think more carefully before I obeyed my instincts.

The pain of loss was still with me, but I had thrust it into a tiny corner of my heart. It would always be there, but I could cope – as I always had.

From now on I would not look back. I would not allow myself to dwell on the past. I was going to make a success of my life. Somehow, I would win for myself all the things Jack had promised me.

It would not be the same. Nothing could ever be as it was that summer Jack stayed in England for nearly three months. I would never be as happy as I had been when I lay in his arms, but I would reach out and take what I wanted from life.

As my determination grew, I started to feel excitement. This was not the end. This was yet another beginning. And this time, I would do things my way . . .

Enjoyed *Emma's War*?

The saga continues in

Emma's Duty

Read on for an exclusive extract

Coming soon from Ebury Press

EBURY
PRESS

Chapter 1

I heard the clatter of noisy feet down the stairs and went out into the hall to investigate just as James and Lizzy arrived, their nurse following close behind. It was a glorious summer day, sunlight filtering through the stained glass of the front door, sending a shower of rainbow colours across the pale carpet.

'I'm sorry, Mrs Reece,' Sarah Miller apologized, the sparkle of laughter in her eyes. 'They're excited because of the school concert. I hope they didn't disturb you?'

'I haven't really started to work yet,' I said, kissing and hugging both my son and Lizzy with equal warmth. It didn't matter to me that Lizzy was the daughter of my friend Sheila. During the years she had lived with us, she had become as dear to me as my own child. 'But I must start in a moment. Sol and I have a lot to get through this morning.'

'You are coming to the concert this afternoon?' James demanded, a hint of mutiny in his expressive, dark chocolate eyes as he struggled free of my embrace. Although charming and very loveable, my son had a forceful personality and was fond of his own way. 'You promised, Mum. I've told everyone you're definitely coming this time.'

'I promise faithfully,' I said. 'I'll be there at half-past two.'

'James is singing all on his own,' Lizzy said, her large, soulful eyes solemn and awed. James was Lizzy's hero, and I believed she loved him more than anyone else in the world. 'Don't you think he's ever so brave, Emmie?'

'Yes, darling. Very brave and very clever.'

I looked at my son with pride. He was eight years old now, a sturdy, healthy boy with the promise of startlingly good looks when he was older. His slightly curling hair was more black than brown, and his cheeks tinged with rose, but there was a stubborn jut to his chin.

I believed he would break hearts one day – and that was hardly surprising, His father had been both charming and handsome when we first met. I had thought him very like one of the film stars I had admired so much in those days. I had been very young and immature then.

James did not look particularly like Paul Greenslade, but sometimes there was an expression or a frown that reminded me of my first lover.

James was an active, energetic child. However, his school had discovered a talent none of us had ever dreamed he possessed. He had the most beautiful, clear soprano voice, the kind of pure sound that brought tears to the eyes. He looked so innocent when he sang in the school choir – like a beautiful angel – which was very misleading!

My son was more devil than angel!

Both he had Lizzy were forever into some kind of mischief, and I wasn't sure who was the instigator of their naughty escapades. The two were forever whispering into each other's ears and giggling at their own secrets, which the grown-ups were seldom allowed to share. James appeared to be the leader, but Lizzy was never far behind.

Although in no way related, they looked as though they might be brother and sister, for Lizzy's colouring was much like my son's, though her hair had developed rich highlights as she grew older. She was, however, a beautiful child, her smiles full of a naughty but wistful charm that almost always gained her her own way with less effort than my son exerted for the same reason.

She too would break hearts when she was older!

'Off you go, you two,' I said, giving them a little push towards the door. 'I'm sure it's all going to be lovely. After the concert, we'll go out to tea.'

I smiled as the children and Sarah left the house together. Sarah was genuinely fond of them both. They tried her patience sorely, but she was an attractive, helpful, good-humoured woman, well able to manage them, and I never needed to worry when she was with them.

She was much kinder than their previous nanny. I had had to dismiss her after an incident which had caused Lizzy to fall down the nursery stairs and break her arm. Fortunately, no lasting damage had been done, but I had always felt guilty that I had been too busy to notice that Nanny was ill-treating Lizzy.

I returned to the front parlour after the children and Sarah had gone. It was an elegant, spacious room decorated in shades of green and gold, but the hangings had faded over the years and some of the upholstery needed re-covering. I had been reluctant to do anything, because it had been Margaret's favourite room, and even though she had been dead for nearly three years now I did not want to make changes. I knew Sol felt the same way about his late wife's parlour. We had both loved her very much, and we still missed her: changing her room would seem almost a betrayal of her memory.

Sol was poring over the papers and some sketches of Dior's New Look we'd had specially brought over from Paris; it was an exciting design that was already creating waves in the press. After the Utility fashions we had all been forced to wear during the war, which were so plain and skimpy, the softer, fuller look seemed like a miracle.

Even after some of the clothing restrictions had been lifted in 1944 the Utility label had still clung on. The quality was reliable, and anything not covered by the label usually needed extra coupons, so that not everyone could afford the luxury of choosing such items.

We had hoped that when the war finally ended, we would see the abolition of rationing, but in some instances it seemed almost worse now than during the war. Many people were becoming very angry with the government for not getting the country back on an even keel before this. In Paris some of the fashion houses had continued to function right through the war, and the French designers had clearly decided that the women of Europe had had enough of austerity fashions, and in America, where a certain amount of rationing was still in force, things were much better than here.

'Children get off all right?' Sol asked, glancing up as I sat opposite him. 'It's James's concert this afternoon, isn't it? I should have liked to come, but I shan't have the time.'

'That's a pity,' I said. 'It would have been nice if you could have come too, Sol.'

Sol and I were partners in the wholesale clothing business we ran from the Portobello Road, but we were also close friends. He and his wife had taken me into their home and their hearts when I first came to London, and despite all that had happened during the war years, and Margaret's death, I was still living in his home.

'What do you think of this New Look then?' Sol asked. 'Everyone seems to be going mad over it – but what is your honest opinion?'

'I like it,' I said, picking up a sheaf of papers. 'Let me study it for a while.'

The new fashion was certainly very different and very attractive. Dior was just one of the French designers making news at the moment, but his New Look was grabbing the headlines.

Fashion was changing quickly this year. I rather

liked the designs of Claire McCardell, who had created what was known as the American Look during the war and was now as much admired as some of the Paris designers. She had been the first to use denim for dresses, a fashion which I thought rather exciting, but which hadn't as yet really caught on here.

My friend Jane Melcher had sent me some of Claire McCardell's designs – those she presented for Townley, the New York ready-to-wear manufacturer – as a personal gift, after she returned to America at the end of 1944.

Jane and I kept in touch regularly, and I got most of my information on the American ready-to-wear market from my friend. Her letters, together with pictures from magazines, and a few samples, had given me a lot of ideas we could use in the showroom. Our own range was now much more substantial than it had been even before the war.

This had helped me a great deal in setting up my small chain of retail dress shops, because the profits I was able to make on direct purchases from our own workshop were quite substantial. I was becoming a woman of some property. As well as the three separate businesses in my home town of March, I had three small shops in London now – which I had bought outright – and recently I had begun to make plans to expand by taking on a concession in a large department store.

'I suppose we shall have to try and copy it,' Sol said as I was silent for longer than he thought necessary. 'Are you going to stock it in your shops, Emma?'

'Not this expensive version,' I said. 'But something more affordable I expect. Annie said she had a woman in the other day asking when we would have it in.'

'Annie . . . she's Sheila's cousin, isn't she? You put her in charge of one of the shops recently, didn't you?'

'Yes. Now that her children are so much older, she can work more hours, and I know I can trust her. That shop does better than the other two.'

Sol nodded. He had helped with the finance of the London shops initially, though when my share of the money he had invested abroad before the war came through, I was able to repay him. I had received a cheque for thirty-five thousand dollars, more money than I had ever expected to earn in my life.

And that was due to Jack, of course. *Jack . . . oh, Jack, my darling. Where are you today? Are you thinking of me? I think of you every day, every night of my life.*

I was still in love with Jack Harvey – the wealthy American who had been my lover for a short time during the war – though it was years since I had seen or spoken to him.

I had kept his letters and gifts, and I still took them out of the bedside cabinet where they were stored sometimes, but I had grown accustomed to the sense of loss I'd felt when I'd sent Jack away, and it no longer hurt in quite the same way. I missed him, but

I could think of him now without pain, or at least only a very little.

Jack had sent the money my investment had earned direct to Sol, because we had quarrelled bitterly when I refused to abandon my invalid husband and go to America with him. Such terrible, cruel things had been said, things that I regretted, but that was all behind me now. I had thrown myself into my work – and into helping my husband begin a new life.

'You look very thoughtful, Emma?' Sol looked at me over the top of his gold-rimmed reading glasses. 'Still thinking about your answer – or are you miles away?'

'I was just thinking of Jon . . . wondering how he was getting on. He sounded a bit down when he rang last night . . .'

'You worry too much, my dear.'

He was right, of course, but I couldn't help it.

Jon had been severely injured during the war, and from the first moment I'd heard that he had been found alive, but badly wounded, I had been determined to bring him home as soon as he was able to leave hospital.

Although Jon had spent several periods of a few weeks at a time with me in London during the last two years, he was back in hospital again at the moment for a further operation. His recovery had taken much longer than anyone had ever expected, because Jon had been very ill on two separate occasions, and the long process of restoring some sort of normality to his

poor, burned face had had to be postponed to give him
time to rebuild his strength. However, his stay in the
hospital should be short this time, and then he would
be home for good, all the months of pain he had
endured behind him.

So far Jon had seemed content to spend the time he
was allowed out of hospital at Sol's house in London.
He had once spoken to me of a wish to go and live
in France, but had not mentioned the idea again. I had
not pushed the idea. It suited me to live in town,
because of my partnership with Sol – something that
had gone from strength to strength since Margaret's
death.

The death of Sol's wife, who had been my dearest
friend, had brought Sol and I even closer together.
It would have been hard to define our relationship
to a stranger. We could have been father and
daughter, but there was something different about
the bond that held us – we were more like twins,
though we had no blood ties and were far apart in
age and appearance. We suited each other, our ideas
about work and fashion complemented each other's,
and we thought alike in many ways. Both of us
liked to work for work's sake. We enjoyed success,
shared the same jokes, the same triumphs and
disappointments.

After the war, we had decided that we would expand
our workshops. We now had two more besides the one
Sol had owned before I came to work for him, and
they took all Sol's time and energy. I had offered him

a partnership in the shops, but he had thought about it and then declined.

'I'll leave that part of it to you, Emma,' he had told me. 'It's best if I stick to this end, but I want you to be a part of the expansion of the workshops. I need you, your energy and drive. You've got more ideas than me for what's needed these days.'

It was the perfect combination of our talents. Sol had so much experience in the trade, but I had youth and enthusiasm – and a hunger for success.

I was better off than I had ever been in my life. Money was no longer a problem, but I wanted more than that. I was searching for something, though I could not explain even to myself what I wanted. To the outsider, I would appear to have everything: a husband who loved me, children to love and care for, and a comfortable life. Yet there was a need in me, a restlessness . . . perhaps simply a wish to find my own way in life, not to rely too much emotionally on others, because I did not wish to be hurt again.

Sol was looking at me, an anxious expression in his eyes.

I knew I was fortunate in having Sol as my friend. Without his help and encouragement I would never have come this far.

Solomon Gould was a well-respected name in the clothing trade, and he could cost a new dress in his head within seconds. I could do it, but I needed a pencil and paper, and Sol could usually beat me both in terms of speed and price. He knew every way there was of saving an inch of material. He'd had enough practice during the war, when we were only allowed a certain amount of cloth for each garment.

Things were much better now, and our businesses were flourishing. The only real problem we'd had recently was finding the time to get round all we had to do. Which was why my son was so anxious about his school concert. I had let him down the last time.

I was determined to be there *this* afternoon, but first Sol and I had to plan our strategy for the New Look.

'Don't you worry about me,' I said and smiled. 'I'm just dreaming and I do have an answer for you. I was just thinking about the way things were – but I'm ready now.'

'Fire away then, Emma! What's the verdict?'

'It's romantic,' I said to Sol as I flicked through the photographs and sketches, applying my mind to my work at last. 'Really feminine. Look at those soft shoulders, the narrow waists and lovely full skirts – way below the calf. I would love to be able to reproduce it exactly, but we shall have to modify it, of course.' I looked at him. 'How soon do you think we could get our version into production?'

'Within a few hours if we dare. The government isn't going to like it, Emma. I know they eased the restrictions on our use of cloth, but they won't be pleased if all the manufacturers bring this style in.'

'If we don't, everyone else will. The government will have to give way this time. Women have had enough of being told what they can or can't wear. Besides, I think we can reproduce the look and still stay within the limits. A costume like the one I've picked out would cost about fourteen coupons and sell at a price our competitors would find hard to match.'

We had started to manufacture costumes this last year, though the showroom was still best known for its dresses.

'What I was thinking . . .' I made a quick sketch of a dress I had in mind. 'If we did a nipped-in waist with a skirt that reaches to mid-calf . . . it would be sort of midway between the short skirts everyone is so fed up with, and the new length. I believe a cotton version would sell retail for about three pounds nineteen shillings, and probably require six clothing coupons.'

Sol did a rapid calculation in his head. 'Seven coupons, and we could sell a rayon version for thirty-five shillings in the showroom.'

We looked at each other and smiled. There was always a spirit of competition between us on price. Whatever I suggested, Sol would find a way of under-cutting me.

'Emma . . .' I glanced up as Pam came to the door of the sitting room. She looked at me apologetically. 'I'm sorry to trouble you – but these flowers arrived for you. I thought you might like to see them before I put them in water.'

Pam was one of my closest friends these days. She

was some years older than me, a quiet, pleasant woman who had come to live with us after her husband was killed during the war. I relied on her for so much. She lived as a part of the family, and did anything that needed doing, usually without being asked. I knew she helped Mrs Rowan with the house quite a lot, saving the housekeeper all kinds of small tasks, and she was always there to lend a hand with the children or act as an unofficial secretary for me.

She was carrying a large and very beautiful bouquet of lilies and roses. They had clearly come from an expensive store and were slightly ostentatious.

'There's a card here,' she said, offering the flowers for me to smell their perfume.

'Thank you.' I took the card and looked at the message. The flowers were to thank me for my help in selecting an order, which had apparently been successful, and had come from one of the regular customers at the showroom. He owned a large department store in London, and was a wealthy man. He had been showing a lot of interest in me recently, though he was well aware that I was married. 'Put them in water if you will, Pam. I'll write a thank you note to Philip later.'

'Don't put him off, Emma,' Sol said with a grin as Pam carried the flowers away with her. 'Philip Matthews is one of our best customers. His order gives us a lot of prestige in the trade. We don't want to lose him.'

'I don't know why he keeps sending flowers,' I said

and sighed. 'That's the third time this year. He must know I'm married. I've spoken to him about Jon many times.'

'You're far too attractive,' Sol said, a hint of amusement in his voice. He had aged a little since Margaret's death, but although almost fifty now was still very attractive himself, with smoky grey eyes and wiry hair that had gone a kind of rusty colour with grey streaks at the temples. It made him look worldly, a man of experience who turned heads wherever he went. 'You can't blame a man like Matthews for trying in the circumstances. You don't look or sound married, Emma.'

I said nothing, but in my heart I acknowledged the truth of what Sol was saying. My marriage had been in name only for a long time. Jon and I had slept in the same bed on a few occasions, but there had been nothing but kisses and a loving embrace between us. As far as I knew, Jon still believed that his inability to be a proper husband to me was temporary and would change once we were living together as man and wife.

I knew it was unlikely. His doctor had made it clear to me from the start that the severe injuries Jon had received in the sabotage attack, which had gone wrong, had damaged him. There was always the chance that his body might mend itself, but it was only a chance.

In a way we had both been damaged, for during the war I had been concerned that I had not conceived my lover's child and visited a specialist. I had been told it was not impossible that I would have another baby one day, but because of some internal scarring after the premature birth of my son, it was unlikely.

That had caused me some grief, because at the time I had believed Jon was dead, and I had been planning to marry Jack Harvey at the end of the war. It was, however, something I had learned to live with and made little difference to me these days. Jon could never give me a child, and there was no one else in my life now.

It was not for want of offers. Philip Matthews was not the only man who had shown an interest in me these past few years. Most of the customers at the showroom, where I still worked from time to time, knew that my husband was an invalid. I had been asked out to dinner or the theatre on many occasions, and some men, like Philip, took every excuse to send me flowers or small gifts.

I had refused them all with a smile and a small joke. It was not that I disliked Philip. He was a good-looking man with fair hair and soft blue eyes, and his manner was always gentle. Had I been a widow, I suppose I might have been tempted to accept some of the invitations I received, though there was only one man I would ever truly want.

'What do you think of this costume?' Sol asked. 'It's not so very different from one we already make – except for the length of the skirt.'

'The jacket has longer cuffs, which give it that extra style,' I said. 'But you are right. It is almost the same.'

We exchanged smiles. Of all my friends, Sol was the one I always went to when I was in trouble. He knew my secrets, my hopes and fears – even those I tried to keep private. There was nothing about my past that was not an open book to him.

Sol knew there had been four men in my life: Paul Greenslade, who was my son's father; Richard Gillows, my first husband; Jack Harvey and Jon – but Jack was the one who had given me the greatest happiness.

Sometimes, when I was alone at night, and my body ached for his touch, I almost regretted my decision not to go with him to America – but then when I saw Jon again, the tenderness I felt for him came flooding back, and I knew I could never have been happy if I had deserted him when he needed me so desperately.

Jon was a dear friend. I had known him long before I met Jack. He had been there when I needed him, when I was tied to a man I could never love and utterly miserable. He had given me money and hope, hope that I would one day escape to a better life. I would always be grateful to him for his gentleness and kindness, and in my own way I loved him very much.

I shuffled my papers and sighed, wondering why I could not settle to my work.

'Something wrong, Emma?' Sol asked, sensing my restless mood.

I shook my head, unable to explain why I was haunted by thoughts of the past that morning.

Jon's face looked much better now than it had when I first saw him in the hospital. He had been injured while working with the resistance movement in France during the war. He would always bear the scars of his wounds, of course, but his mother was able to look at him now without going into hysterics – which she had on that terrible afternoon she first saw the burns.

I was fetching him home at the weekend, and if all went well he would not have to go back to the hospital that had been home to him for so many months. He would be free at last to live a normal life, or as normal as was possible for Jon.

He was conscious of the scars, of course, even though they were so much better than they had been at the start, but he was aware that people still stared when they saw him in the street. It was something he had accepted for my sake, because he loved me and he wanted to try living the way we had before he was injured. We had been to the theatre once during his visits home, and to the pictures, but I knew he preferred to stay home and listen to the wireless in the evenings.

He was always happiest with a book, sitting quietly in his own room – or walking in the countryside. Sometimes, I took him away for the weekend, and that was when he felt most relaxed, away from people and noise. I knew that eventually I might have to consider buying a house in the country.

It would present no problems as far as money was concerned. Jon had a small income of his own, which would have supported us had we needed it, but I was earning many times what he received. I supposed that now my businesses were running so smoothly I need not work myself, but without my work I would have had too much time to think.

'You're far away, Emma,' Sol said, recalling me to the task in hand when I had been silent for some minutes. 'Still thinking about Jon? About fetching him home?'

'Yes.' I smiled at him. He could usually read my thoughts. 'I was thinking things might have to change soon, Sol. I may have to buy a house in the country.'

He nodded, his expression serious. 'Make sure it has a good mainline station near by, Emma. You'll want somewhere not too far away so that you can pop up to town when you like.'

'Yes.' I had known Sol would understand me. 'I wouldn't want to be too far away . . .'

I had been turning the pages of my newspaper idly. Suddenly, a face from the past was staring up at me. I read the accompanying article aloud.

'*Mrs Sheila Jansen, wife of the popular American jazz singer Todd Jansen, was having tea at the Ritz yesterday. She is in the country to visit old friends and make arrangements for her husband's concert tour next month . . .*'

Sol looked at me as I finished reading. He knew what was in my mind. 'You're afraid she might try to take Lizzy from us?' I nodded, staring at him in apprehension. He reached forward and patted my hand. 'Don't worry about it, Emma. If she had wanted the girl, she would have been in contact with us before this.'

'I hope you're right, Sol. James and Lizzy are inseparable. I don't know what they would do if they were parted.'

'I can't see Sheila wanting to take her.' Sol frowned as he saw the distress I was feeling. 'Her husband doesn't know she had a child, does he?'

'He didn't know,' I said, swallowing hard. My throat was dry and I was really upset. 'But supposing she comes here? Supposing she does want her daughter back?'

'Then we'll fight her,' Sol said. 'You still have the letter she sent when she gave Lizzy to you?'

'Yes . . . but I can't do that, Sol. I love Lizzy, but she *is* Sheila's daughter. She gave her up because she had a chance of a new life with Todd. You can see that things have gone well for her – she looks marvellous. She's wearing the New Look, and not a copy either. She must have bought that in Paris. Jane told me that Todd was doing well, but I hadn't realized he was as successful as all that – though I know he's a good singer.'

'All the more reason for her to hang on to what she's got with him,' Sol said. 'If she comes, it will probably be just to see Lizzy. Believe me, Emma. That woman is as selfish as they come. There is no way she would risk her comfortable lifestyle for Lizzy's sake.'

Sol had never liked Sheila, and perhaps he had good reason. We had always been friends, though she had been jealous of my success for a while after her own attempt at shop keeping had failed at the start of the war. By the way she looked in the photograph, she had no need to be jealous of me now. Todd was obviously giving her everything she had ever hoped for.

All I could do was pray that she didn't want Lizzy back!

Chapter 2

'You made it in time then?' Sarah Miller whispered as I took the seat next to her in the school assembly hall a few minutes after the concert had begun. 'I'm so glad.'

'Me too. I wouldn't have missed this for the world.'

'Doesn't he look wonderful?' Sarah whispered as James came to the front of the stage.

'Yes. Wonderful.'

I was so proud of my son.

My eyes filled with tears as I listened to James singing the beautiful hymn. Where had his talent come from? No one in my father's family that I knew of had a singing voice, nor my mother's. So perhaps he had inherited it from Paul?

Thinking of Paul renewed my fears about Sheila's intentions. There had been a time towards the end of the war when I had feared that Paul would try to take James from me, though my fears had proved groundless. It would have been difficult for him, because James's name had been changed to Reece when I agreed to marry Jon. My husband had been a lawyer before the war, and changing James's name was one of the first of many things he had done to protect us.

Neither of us had wanted James to bear the name

of my first husband, because Richard Gillows had been a self-confessed murderer. Nor had we wanted James to have his true father's name.

I was not certain what James thought of Jon. When he first visited us after the war, on a rare break from the hospital, I had introduced him as my husband, explaining privately to James that he had been away fighting for a long time.

James had protested that he wanted his *daddy* back, but I had told him that was impossible. Jack Harvey had returned to America and we had to stay here. Whether or not James had vaguely remembered Jon from before the war was impossible to say. Just how much could a child of a year or so remember?

He had never spoken of Jon as his daddy, but to my relief James had accepted my husband when he came to the house. He had not screamed or made a fuss when he saw Jon's face, merely taking the mutilations in his stride. He had never been affectionate towards Jon, but treated him with the same kind of politeness he would show a stranger.

His school had taught him that. As a small child he had often screamed and kicked up a fuss to gain his own way, and I was not sure he had ever forgiven me for sending Jack away. He never spoke of that night in late 1944, when he'd crept down from his nursery to hear us quarrelling, but I knew he had not forgotten the man he had called Daddy.

James had long outgrown the pedal car Jack had once bought him as a Christmas gift, but he refused to be parted from it. I sometimes wondered if he remembered the promise Jack had made him to return just for his sake one day.

I thought the enforced parting from the man he adored might be one of the main reasons behind his attitude towards me at times. James loved me as I loved him, but there were moments when I felt that perhaps he did not quite trust me.

I tried hard to show him that I loved him more than anyone, but I was not always able to give him as much of my time as he needed. Lizzy never seemed to resent it when I had to work, though of course as much as I loved her she was not my own child. She remembered another life – a life that had been much less pleasant – and she was always grateful for whatever I gave her.

But I was allowing my mind to drift from my son's performance. Sarah and I both clapped enthusiastically as James finished his song and went back to stand with the other performers.

'He was so nervous,' Sarah whispered. 'But he pretended not to be.'

I wiped the tears from my eyes as the applause for James's singing reverberated round the hall. He looked such a little angel. No one would believe that this was the same child who had recently put a frog in Mrs Rowan's bed!

She had made such a fuss! I had had to punish both Lizzy – who insisted she was the culprit until James owned up – and my son, by cancelling a trip to the pictures for them both. It had been a Laurel and Hardy film, which they had both been looking forward to seeing. I had regretted having to discipline them but it had had to be done. However, I was going to give them a special treat this afternoon, and perhaps we could go to the cinema another day, during their summer holidays.

The concert was to celebrate the end of term, and most of the children who could sing were performing.

Sarah touched my arm. 'It's Lizzy's turn now. She looks so pretty – but very nervous.'

A woman behind made a shushing noise and Sarah pulled a face, subsiding into silence.

Lizzy was singing in the chorus. Her voice was not remarkable, but she made up in enthusiasm for what she lacked in tunefulness. I had chosen this particular school because it accepted both girls and boys, but the time was coming when they would have to go to separate schools. I did not look forward to the day I had to part them.

What was I going to do if Sheila wanted her daughter back?

Sol and my mother had both warned me that this might happen one day. I had dismissed their fears at the time, but now I was beginning to worry. Lizzy had become so dear to me that I would miss her terribly – but not as much as my son. He would be devastated, and so would Lizzy.

The concert was over now. I got up and moved to join the other parents who were claiming their children. Mr Smithson, the children's head teacher, came up to me, his face wreathed in smiles.

'You must be very proud of James, Mrs Reece?'

'Yes, I am. Very proud.'

'I am so glad you could come this time. You missed the last concert, and that was such a shame.'

'Unfortunately, I was working.'

He nodded, but I caught the disapproval in his eyes. Obviously he did not approve of mothers who worked, not now that it was no longer our patriotic duty, though it had been very different during the war of course. Jon's mother held much the same opinion. Dorothy was always hinting that she thought I ought to give up work now and devote myself full-time to looking after my husband and the children, but that was something I was not prepared to do, despite my devotion to them.

Lizzy and James ran towards me.

'Did you see me, Mum?'

'Emmie – wasn't James good?'

'Yes, darlings. I saw you both and you were both wonderful.'

'Lizzy was scared but I wasn't,' James boasted.

'Can we have ice cream, Emmie?

'Yes, I should think so, darling.'

I nodded to Mr Smithson and took the children by the hand. Their chattering was relentless throughout the car journey, and tea, which we had at Lyons, because they preferred it to a hotel, where they felt they had to be quiet.

We had rolls of vanilla ice cream, little cream cakes, tea for Sarah and me, and fizzy orangeade for the children. It was a happy occasion, and I indulged their liveliness, even though I noticed one or two matrons giving me a rather jaundiced look.

Well-brought-up children were not supposed to be quite as noisy as my two, but I didn't see why they shouldn't enjoy themselves. Perhaps they were spoiled, but I loved them both so much that I did not like to curb their natural excitement – though I stopped James when he started flicking the paper from his ice cream across the table at Lizzy.

'That's enough of that, darling,' I said. 'It's time we went home now.'

They protested that they wanted to go to the park, but I did not give in. The wind was cool that afternoon, and Lizzy was prone to chills if we were not careful. Besides, I had some work to do. I had given up the afternoon to attend the concert, but I would have to make up for it by working on my figures that evening.

'Mum . . . can we go to the seaside this summer?' James asked as I opened the car door for them to pile in. 'Pam said her sister would have us for a week – but I would like to stay in a hotel this time, or somewhere different. Like the place we went with Jack that year . . .'

My heart stood still. He had not mentioned Jack for so long that I had almost believed he had forgotten him. Yet in my heart I knew he would never do that – any more than I could.

'We might go to a hotel somewhere,' I replied,

carefully keeping my voice level. 'But we can't go there, darling. Not to the Cottage. It belongs to Jack.'

'He would lend it to us if you asked,' James said, pulling a face. That hint of mutiny was in his eyes again. He would never truly forgive me for sending Jack away. 'I know he would. If you wrote to him in America and asked.'

'I don't know his address,' I said. 'Besides, there are lots of other nice places we could stay.'

'But I liked it there . . .'

'Well, we'll see,' I said, hoping to change the subject. 'I'm not sure Jack still lets people stay there. He might have sold it . . .'

It was unlikely that Jack had sold the Cottage. It was a lovely old house that had been in his family for generations. I did not know if he ever visited it these days – or if he even came to England.

I had heard nothing from him since the night we had quarrelled.

I was still thinking about Jack, and the few days we had spent at his cottage in Sussex, as I parked the car, then ushered the children into the house.

Mrs Rowan came out into the hall, her face wearing its disapproving look.

'You have a visitor, madam. I asked her to wait in the parlour.'

'Thank you, Mrs Rowan. Did she leave her name?'

'Mrs Jansen,' the housekeeper said. 'I think she's American.'

My heart caught with fright as I told the children

to go with the housekeeper. Sheila had come, just as I had expected after reading that newspaper article that morning.

I went into the sitting room. Sheila was standing by the window, looking out at the street. I knew she must have seen us come in. She turned to me and smiled, and I saw she was wearing a very smart costume, similar to the one she had been wearing in her photograph. Her shoes were made of the finest leather, and her hat was both smart and attractive. Her hair looked lighter, as though she had had it rinsed to an ash blonde, but it had been done professionally and did not look cheap or tarty. She was wearing a large diamond ring as well as her wedding ring, and looked very comfortable with her new status.

'Hello, Emma,' she said. 'Are you pleased to see me?'

'That depends on why you've come,' I replied. 'Lizzy is very happy here with us, Sheila. I wouldn't be very happy if you wanted to take her away from us.'

Sheila laughed. She looked attractive and well, much more like the girl who had come into my father's shop in March to buy her favourite toffee pieces than she had when I'd last seen her, but with a confidence she had never had in those days.

'Good grief, no,' she said. 'Todd has no idea Lizzy exists. I just wanted to make sure she was OK, that's all. I couldn't possibly have her with me. Todd doesn't want children; it would interfere with his career. We travel all the time, Emma. We shall be here for several weeks while Todd is on stage in London, and down in Bournemouth. He's starring in a seaside show.' Her eyes met mine. 'You did know he's a famous singer these days, didn't you?'

'Yes, I had heard it from Jane Melcher, but I didn't realize how successful he was until I saw your photograph in the paper this morning.' I was relaxed now, my fears receding. 'Have you got time to see Lizzy? She and James have been singing in their school concert. I took them to tea afterwards. If I'd known you were coming, I would have come straight home.'

'I didn't mind waiting,' Sheila said. 'I've got nothing much to do for a few days. Todd is still in Paris. He will be here next Tuesday. I came on ahead to make sure of hotel bookings and things . . .' She hesitated, then, 'I wondered if I could take Lizzy away for a couple of days, Emma. You and James could come too if you like?'

'They don't finish school until Friday, and I have to fetch Jon home from hospital on Sunday . . .' I saw the flicker of disappointment in her eyes and made a swift decision. 'I could send a note to their school, I suppose. We could go tomorrow morning, and come back on Saturday afternoon if you like? It would only be two days . . .'

'Bless you,' Sheila said. 'I wouldn't blame you if you thought I was a rotten mother and refused to let me near Lizzy . . . but I have missed her.'

'I understand, Sheila. It was your chance and you took it. Besides, I've loved having Lizzy with us. She's like a daughter to me – though of course I know she isn't mine'

'You haven't had any more children?'

'No, I haven't.' I kept my smile in place. It wasn't so very hard, even though there was a secret hurt deep inside me. 'Not yet. Things have been difficult with Jon in hospital on and off . . .'

'It must have been a shock for you when you heard he was still alive,' Sheila said, then blushed as my brows rose. 'I met Jane Melcher at a charity concert in New York once. She told me about Jon, and the sacrifice you'd made.'

'It wasn't a sacrifice, Sheila. I love Jon. He is a wonderful man.'

Sheila nodded. 'Well, Jane seemed to think you were some kind of saint.' She shrugged her shoulders. 'Have you seen my cousin Annie recently? I went back to her old house, but someone said she'd moved ages ago.'

'Yes, I know. She and her family live in a prefab. Her eldest daughter works for me, and the younger ones are going to start when they leave school. Annie manages one of the shops for me now. She could only do a few hours to begin with, but now works a full day.'

'Can you give me her address?'

'Yes, of course. I'm sure she would like to see you.'

'I'm not too sure about that. The last time I saw her she said she was finished with me for good – but perhaps she will think differently now. Anyway, you and me can talk to our hearts' content this next two days.' Sheila grinned at me. 'Where shall we go?'

'We can't go too far,' I said, 'or we'll spend all our time travelling. I'll think about it, Sheila, perhaps ring a few hotels, see where we can get booked in at short notice.'

'And you'll talk to Lizzy,' Sheila said, looking a bit awkward. 'Explain that it's just a little holiday . . .'

'Yes, I'll tell her,' I said. 'Don't worry, Sheila. You haven't seen Lizzy and James together yet. They are close friends and it would have upset them both had you wanted to take her away.'

'I knew she would be all right with you,' Sheila said, her awkwardness vanishing. 'I told you to put her in a home if you didn't want her, but I knew you wouldn't.'

'No,' I said. 'I would never do that . . .'

'So all's well that ends well,' Sheila said. 'I can give you money towards her keep now, Emma.'

'Perhaps you can send her some pocket money,' I replied. 'I'll leave that to you and Lizzy . . .'

'You're a glutton for punishment,' Sol exclaimed when I told him I was taking two days off for a short holiday with Sheila and the children. He frowned at me. 'She'll let you down again, Emma. You would be a fool to trust her.'

'No, I don't think she will do anything to harm me or Lizzy,' I replied. 'Sheila had a bad time during the war, that's all. She sent Lizzy to me when she went off with Todd because we were friends, and that shows she trusted me to look after her. I think she will be straight with me now.'

Sol shook his head, clearly unconvinced.

My mother was even more forthright when I telephoned her with my news.

'Have you lost your wits, Emma? That woman used you before, and she will do so again. You should have more sense!'

'What Sheila did hasn't harmed me. I've loved having Lizzy live with us. And the rest of it is water under the bridge, Mum. Anyway, how are you – and Bert?'

My mother's second husband was the best thing that had ever happened to her. After enduring years of unhappiness tied to my father, she had married her first love just before the start of the war. Unfortunately, Bert Fitch had been having bronchial trouble for the last few winters, which had left his chest a bit weak, and I knew Mum worried about his health.

'He's a little better this morning,' she said. 'But he's not the man he was a few years back, Emma. He gets terrible tightness in his chest, and the coughing pulls him down sometimes.'

'I was going to ask if you wanted to come when I take the children on their proper holiday next month. You and Bert – or you on your own – but you won't feel like leaving him?'

'We'll see,' she said. 'I wouldn't mind a holiday, and it would do Bert good to be by the sea for a few days. Where were you thinking of going?'

'I thought I might take a house – somewhere in Cornwall.'

'I see . . .' She sounded interested, Sheila forgotten. 'A house in Cornwall . . . that would be lovely. All together as a family. I'll definitely give it some thought, Emma.'

I was smiling as we hung up. Mum had been feeling a little down recently. Her own health had never been really good, but she'd been so much better since she married Bert. She came to stay with me in London sometimes, and I took James down to stay with her in my home town of March. There wasn't much going on in the small Cambridgeshire market town, but I liked visiting my friends, and there were the three shops to consider.

My father's sister looked after them for me on a day to day basis. She had discovered a talent for shop keeping after her own mother died, and I never bothered to do more than check on our stock levels so that I knew what to send Madge Henty, my partner in the dress shop, and for the children's wear shop, which was just next door. Gwen ran that, and the newsagent and tobacconist shop that had been my father's, like clockwork.

I would have asked Gwen if she would like to come with us to Cornwall, but I knew she would be too busy. Besides, she preferred to live her own life, and I knew she had made a lot of friends in March. She had her own little car now, and Mum had hinted that she might be courting. She had already told me that she was going to close the shop for ten days in July while she had a holiday in Yarmouth.

It was a long time since I'd taken the children anywhere other than to my mother's or to stay in Hunstanton at Pam's sister's boarding house. They were excited at the prospect of going away for two days, though Lizzy had pulled a face when I told her her mother was coming with us.

'Don't want her to come,' she said, a look of apprehension in her eyes. 'I want to stay with you and James. Don't let her take me away, Emmie. I don't want to leave you.'

'She won't take you away,' James said fiercely, but with an anxious look in my direction. 'We shan't let her – shall we, Mum?'

'Lizzy's mother doesn't want to take her away,' I reassured them with a smile. 'She has just come on a short visit, and she wants to have a little time with Lizzy. We'll all be together. I'm not sending you on your own, Lizzy.'

Lizzy came to me, clinging to the full skirt of my dress. 'I love you, Emmie, and James. I never want to leave you.'

'Not even when I punish you by not letting you go to the pictures?'

She gazed up at me, her eyes wide and earnest. 'Not even then. I like living here with you and James.'

'Then I expect you will stay with us,' I said. 'But you might change your mind when you see your own mother again, Lizzy.'

She shook her head, a look of determination on her face.

'Lizzy can't go away. I want her here.'

James had that mutinous expression in his eyes, and a hint of accusation hung about him, as though he were blaming me for something. It did not seem to matter how often I showed my love for James, there was always that little bit of uncertainty in his mind.

It was my fault, I knew that. I had allowed him to learn to love Jack Harvey and he would always blame me for sending his *daddy* away. Looking back I saw how hard that must have been for him. And of course I was not always around when he needed me.

'I want her here, too,' I said, 'but Sheila is Lizzy's mother. She has a right to see her sometimes, darling. Lizzy isn't your sister; she is your friend. You must accept that, even though she lives with us, she might have to leave one day.'

James didn't answer, but his mouth had set in a hard line. I knew there would be trouble if Sheila did try to part them.

However, I need not have worried. I had booked into a small but prestigious hotel in Southend-on-Sea, and we took the children down on the train. Sheila bought them sweets, colouring books, crayons and a box of puzzles for the journey, which kept them amused. By the time we arrived Lizzy's hostility towards her mother had faded.

We spent the next two days spoiling them both. We took them on the pier, letting them play with the penny slot machines as much as they liked, bought them fish and chips wrapped in newspaper to eat on the beach, ice creams and sticks of peppermint rock.

James went on the donkeys, but Lizzy thought they were smelly creatures and would only watch from a safe distance.

During the day, our time was devoted to the children. The weather was kind to us, the sun warm enough to make it pleasant to sit in a sheltered spot on the beach or pier. We took the children shopping on Friday morning. Sheila bought Lizzy some pretty shoes and a new dress, and I bought James a new engine for his train set, which was so magnificent that it took up half the floor of the playroom at home.

When they were safely in bed on the Friday evening, Sheila and I sat in the hotel lounge and talked. The years seemed to roll back as we laughed about the time we had gone to the church social, me with Richard Gillows and Sheila with the man who was to become her first husband.

'That all seems part of another world, like something out of the dark ages,' Sheila said. 'My life is so much better these days, Emma – and it's all due to you.'

'Why? I should have thought it was for an entirely different reason.'

'Oh, yes, it's because of Todd, too,' she agreed, catching the teasing smile in my eyes. 'I really care

about him, Emma – and he loves me. He's so jealous.
I daren't look at another man . . .'

'I shouldn't have thought you'd want to?'

'No, of course I don't – but you know what I mean.'
She looked a bit like the cat who had found the cream.
'I'm so lucky now – and I might never have met Todd
if you hadn't made me help out at the social club
during the war.'

'According to Pam, you didn't do much helping,' I
said, and laughed. 'But I do know what you mean,
Sheila. It's funny how things work out, isn't it? You've
helped me, and I've helped you – that's what friends
are for.'

'Yes, I suppose I did help you a bit when you were
having a bad time with Richard,' she said. 'But I
know I owe you, Emma. If there's ever anything
I can do . . .'

'I'll know where to come,' I replied. 'All I want is
for you to let Lizzy stay with us, at least until the
children are older. James would be so upset if you
took her away.'

'I told you, Todd doesn't know about her,' Sheila
said. 'I couldn't have her with me if I wanted but . . .'
She looked at me oddly, slightly apprehensive, as if
unsure of my reaction. 'I wouldn't mind doing this
again one day. And I would like to send her things
now and then . . . if you don't mind?'

'No, I don't mind,' I said. 'I think it would be . . .'

The words died on my lips as I glanced across the
room. Three men had just entered, and one of them

was someone I knew well. The sight of him made my
heart beat wildly. He was every bit as darkly handsome
as he'd always been, though he looked older, a sprinkling of silver at his temples, but all the power, all the
magnetism was still there.

'What's wrong?' Sheila asked, looking at me in
concern. 'You've gone as white as a sheet.' She
turned to look over her shoulder, then nodded as
she saw the reason for my shocked expression. 'The
man in the grey striped suit – that's Jack Harvey,
isn't it?'

'Yes . . .' I felt breathless. 'Yes, that's Jack . . .'

The protests were drumming in my brain. What was
Jack doing here, in this hotel? Why couldn't he have
chosen somewhere else? How could Fate be so cruel
as to let him walk in here just when I'd chosen to
come for a couple of days?

I prayed he wouldn't see me. I hoped desperately
he would leave again without glancing towards the
settee near the window where I was sitting, but my
prayers were in vain.

Jack was looking straight at me. He was frowning,
his expression cold as ice. I thought he seemed angry,
unforgiving. He stared at me for some seconds, our
eyes meeting briefly before mine dropped, then he
turned and spoke to one of his companions.

I watched from beneath lowered lashes as the three
men walked out of the room together. Jack did not
look at me again as he left. For a moment I felt as if
I had been struck across the face.

'Well, that was a bit rude of him,' Sheila remarked. 'He might have come across to say hello.'

'We had an argument before he left to go back to America,' I said, feeling sick and shaken. 'It was after the invasion of Europe, but before the war was really finished. He said then that there was nothing left to say – obviously he didn't want to speak to me.'

'He might have nodded or something,' Sheila said, looking concerned. 'Are you all right? He has upset you, hasn't he?'

'Yes . . .' I took a deep breath to stop myself shaking. 'It was just the shock of seeing him like that. I had no idea he was in the country. I haven't heard from him – or of him – for years.'

Sheila hesitated, then, 'So you didn't know he was married?'

'Married?' My heart twisted with pain. There was no reason why Jack should not have married, of course, but it was a shock and I hadn't expected the news to hurt so much. 'No, I hadn't heard.' I swallowed hard, my throat dry. 'When . . . how long?'

'About three months ago,' Sheila said. 'Before we left America on our European tour. In April, I think. I'm sorry, Emma. If Jane Melcher didn't tell you, I probably shouldn't have . . . I didn't mean to hurt you. It wasn't done out of spite, believe me.'

'No, of course not,' I said. My head was beginning to clear a little. 'I would rather know . . . I would rather know . . .'

That wasn't quite the truth. Alone in my hotel room

that night, I found myself unable to sleep, and tossed restlessly on my pillows as the thoughts tumbled in my mind.

Jack was here in England. I had no real need to wonder what had brought him to Southend. Knowing Jack, it would be business. He was a wealthy, powerful man and had always been caught up in some deal or other even during the war.

I switched on the bedside lamp, reaching for the library book I had brought with me. It was Scott Fitzgerald's *The Beautiful And The Damned*, which I had wanted to read for a long time, but I was too disturbed to settle to it. Sheila's news had shocked and distressed me, and the words blurred on the page.

Jack married . . . What was she like, his wife? Was she pretty? She would be, I knew that. Much prettier than me. Did he love her? Were they as good together in bed as Jack and I had been?

The stupid, petty jealousies were like needles in my flesh. I wanted to scream or cry, but there was no sense in giving way to my feelings.

I had thought I was over the pain of losing Jack, but it was back, cutting me to the bone. I was still in love with him, as much as ever, and very aware of what I had thrown away.

This was madness. I must not let myself think this way!

'You made your bed, lass, now you must lie on it.'

I seemed to hear my beloved Gran speaking to me down the years. She had been a very wise lady, and I knew she would scold me for letting myself look back with regret.

'*No regrets, Emma. Look to the future.*'

I had made my choice. I had chosen Jon and sent Jack away. I knew I would do the same if I was forced to make that choice all over again . . . so why did I feel like weeping?

I prayed that I would not bump into Jack any more. We were leaving Southend on the Saturday afternoon, and the children wanted to go on the pier again before we caught our train. With any luck I would not be forced to see Jack again. I could push the memory of him back to a corner of my mind, where it could not hurt me – at least, not as much as it was hurting now.

'Mum, when can we do this again?' James demanded as we walked back to the hotel, loaded down with our parcels. Sheila had enjoyed spending money on both children, and I had not tried to stop her, so they had lots of good things to take home. 'It was fun. I want to stay in a hotel again one day soon.'

'I was thinking I might take a house in Cornwall for a few weeks next month,' I replied. 'Grandma and Bert could come with us – and Sarah. It would be more fun like that . . . don't you think so?'

James did not reply. I thought he was considering my question, but when I glanced down at him I saw he was staring at a man who was walking along the street towards us.

'Daddy . . .' he yelled and started to run. 'Daddy . . .'

My son had grown out of calling me Mummy since just after he started school, but Jack was still his *daddy*. That hurt somehow. My heart caught as I wondered how Jack would react. I watched as he suddenly became aware of the young boy charging eagerly towards him. For a moment he hesitated, then he started to grin and took swift steps to meet James, catching him up and swinging him off the ground.

'Hello, son,' he said, his manner natural, welcoming. 'Well, this is a surprise. I was coming to see you in London next week. I've got a present for you.'

Sheila looked at me as I paused uncertainly.

'Go on,' she hissed. 'Now's your chance. Make him crawl, Emma. Tell him to get the hell out of your life.'

'I can't,' I said. 'James adores him.'

I walked towards Jack, my heart jerking, Lizzy still clinging apprehensively to my hand. 'Hello, Jack,' I said as I reached him. 'I'm sorry about this . . .'

'Why?' His brows rose, and I could see him looking at Lizzy. He seemed angry, but was trying to conceal it, probably for James's sake. 'Because of last night I suppose. Well, I won't deny it was a shock. I was with colleagues and thought it best not to intrude. I was going to call next week . . . to see James as I promised I would next time I was in London.' He ruffled James's hair, something that would have made my son squirm if I had done it, but which he seemed to enjoy coming from Jack. It was quite clear that whatever place Jon had in his life – Jack was his father. I doubted that he had thought about the meaning of the word. Jack was the *daddy* he recognized and loved.

I met Jack's intense gaze. 'You haven't been back to London since the war?'

He shook his head. 'No, I've had other things to keep me busy.'

'Yes, so I believe.' I raised my head, hoping no sign of my inner turmoil showed as I looked into his eyes. 'I understand congratulations are in order?'

'You mean because I'm married?' I nodded and Jack's expression became even colder, if that was possible.

'Emmie . . .' Lizzy tugged at my hand. 'Can I have an ice cream please? Just one more before we go home?'

'I'll take her,' Sheila offered. 'You'll find us in the cafe over the road, Emma.' She held out her hand. 'You coming, James?'

He shook his head. His expression was tortured. It was obvious he wanted that ice cream, but he wanted to stay with Jack more.

'No, I want to be with Jack,' he said. He had remembered he was grown up now, his expression slightly apprehensive as he looked at his *daddy*. 'Are you really going to come and see me next week, sir?'

'Yes, I really am,' Jack said. 'I promise. I'll take you out somewhere – if your mother says it's OK?' I nodded, and Jack gave him a little push towards Sheila and Lizzy. 'Go with your friend,' he said. 'I want to talk to your mother now for a few minutes.'

James was silent, still hesitant; then he nodded and

ran off to join Sheila and Lizzy. For a moment Jack
and I stood absolutely still, just staring at each other.

'I'm sorry,' Jack said. 'I was rude last night, Emma.
I should have come over and said hello.'

'You were surprised to see me,' I said. I was desperately trying to stay calm. 'It was a shock for me, too,
seeing you walk in like that. We only brought the
children down for a couple of days. Sheila has been
in America since the war. She came over to visit Lizzy,
who lives with me, and book the hotels for her
husband's tour. Todd Jansen, the jazz singer.'

Jack nodded, his expression thoughtful. 'Yes, I sort
of recognized her. We met once at a charity concert
in New York. I vaguely remember she was a friend of
yours once . . .'

'We are friends,' I replied. 'We don't see each other
often, but we're still friends . . .'

'Am I still your friend, Emma?'

My throat was tight with emotion. 'Do you want
to be?'

'It might be easier . . . for the boy's sake.' Jack's
eyes were intent on my face. 'I would like to see
something of him while I'm here – and keep in touch
in the future.' He frowned. 'I thought he might have
forgotten me by now. 'It was my intention to bring
him a present and then go quietly away again if he
had forgotten about me . . .'

'James has never forgotten you . . .'

My heart was aching. I had not forgotten Jack either,
but I would not let him see that if I could help it.

'In that case, you won't mind if I call to see James?'

'No, I don't see any reason why you shouldn't.' I hesitated, then raised my gaze to meet his. 'I am fetching Jon home from hospital tomorrow. He doesn't know about . . .'

'About us being lovers?' There was a faint smile in Jack's eyes. 'No, I didn't imagine he would. I'll be careful, Emma. All your husband needs to know is that I'm James's friend. I'll tell *him* I prefer to be called Jack now he's grown up.'

'Yes, that might be best . . . more tactful. James does call Jon Father occasionally . . . though only out of politeness. He clearly still thinks of you as his daddy.' I took a deep breath. 'Well, I ought to be going . . . we have to catch the train at two-thirty this afternoon.'

'I shall see you next week then,' Jack said. His gaze narrowed. 'Thank you for being so reasonable, Emma.'

'Why should I be anything else?' I asked. 'I did what I had to do, Jack. I never meant to hurt you.'

'No,' he said, and there was an odd expression in his eyes now. 'I believe you did what you thought was right . . . and perhaps you were. Who knows about these things?'

'You wouldn't have met your wife if I had left Jon . . .'

'No . . .' Jack smiled, a mocking, challenging look that made me flinch as if he had struck me. 'I wouldn't, would I, Emma?'

'I wish you every happiness, Jack.'

'Thank you, Emma. Believe me, I am as happy as I deserve to be.'

I nodded, and turned away to cross the road.

'Are you happy, Emma?'

His question held me. For a moment I paused on the edge of the pavement, glancing back at him. 'I'm as happy as I expected to be,' I said, then I ran across the street and did not look back.

Also by Rosie Clarke:

EMMA

All she has is her reputation . . .

When Emma Robinson discovers she is carrying Paul
Greenslade's child, there are harsh consequences after
he disappears rather than marry a common shop-girl.

Forced by her tyrannical father to marry Richard
Gillows, Emma learns quickly that a jealous husband
is a violent one. How can Emma escape the ties that
bind her, to build a life for herself and her child?

EBURY
PRESS

Coming soon from Rosie Clarke:

EMMA'S DUTY

The war is over, but Emma's battles continue at home . . .

Emma Reece is slowly adjusting to her husband's return from the war, even though his appalling injuries mean their marriage is in name only.

But then tragedy strikes, and Emma finds she cannot turn to Jack Harvey, her long-standing friend and one-time lover – for while he still loves her, he is now a married man . . .

EBURY
PRESS

Also by Rosie Clarke:

THE DOWNSTAIRS MAID

She is a servant girl . . .

When her father becomes ill, Emily Carter finds
herself sent into service at Priorsfield Manor in order
to provide the family with an income.

He will be the Lord of the Manor . . .

Emily strikes up an unlikely friendship with the
daughters of the house, as well as Nicolas, son
of the Earl. But as the threat of war comes ever
closer, she becomes even more aware of the vast
differences between upstairs and downstairs, servant
and master . . .

If you like *Downton Abbey* you'll love this!

EBURY
PRESS

Rosie Clarke was born in Swindon. Her family moved to Cambridgeshire when she was nine, but she left at the age of fifteen to work as a hairdresser in her father's business. She was married at eighteen and ran her own hairdressing business for some years.

Rosie loves to write and has penned over one hundred novels under different pseudonyms. She writes about the beauty of nature and sometimes puts a little into her books, though they are mostly about love and romance.

Also by Rosie Clarke:

The Downstairs Maid
Emma

'Heartfelt . . . A wonderful example of Spangles Lit'
Daily Mail

'. . . . . g novel
about growing up, love, sex, mothers and everything'
Kate Eberlen, author of *Miss You*

'You're in for a treat with this one'
Red

'A bittersweet delight. Perfectly captures the awkwardness
and longing of those who don't quite fit in'
Sarra Manning, author of *After
the Last Dance* and *House of Secrets*

'An enchanting, heartfelt and nostalgic read'
Prima

'Funny, poignant and absolutely brilliant'
Rachael Lucas, author of
Wildflower Bay

'Tender and with a wince-inducing evocation of adolescence,
you'll fall for the awkward Dido as surely as she falls for
the boy next door'
Sunday Mirror

'A must-read'
Independent

'Nostalgic, funny and charming'
Stella magazine

The Queen of Bloody Everything

A former broadcast journalist, Downing Street political adviser and government speechwriter, Joanna Nadin is the author of more than sixty books for children and teenagers, including the *Flying Fergus* series with Sir Chris Hoy, the bestselling *Rachel Riley* diaries, also set in Saffron Walden and based on the author's teenage years, and the Carnegie Medal-nominated *Joe All Alone*, currently being adapted for television. She has a PhD in young adult literature, and lectures in creative writing at Bath Spa University. This is her first adult novel.

Also by the author for young adults and older teens

Wonderland
Undertow
Eden